FACES
OF FEAR

FACES
OF FEAR

A NOVEL

JOHN
SAUL

BALLANTINE BOOKS / NEW YORK

Copyright © 2008 by John Saul

Published in the United States by Ballantine Books, an imprint of The Random House Publishing Group, a division of Random House, Inc., New York.

BALLANTINE and colophon are registered trademarks of Random House, Inc.

Library of Congress Cataloging-in-Publication Data

Saul, John.
Faces of fear : a novel / John Saul.
p. cm.
ISBN 978-0-345-48705-6 (acid-free paper)
1. Plastic surgeons—Fiction. 2. Stepfathers—Fiction. 3. Stepdaughters—Fiction.
4. Face—Surgery—Fiction. I. Title.

PS3569.A787F33 2008
813'.54—dc22
2008016616

Printed in the United States of America on acid-free paper

www.ballantinebooks.com

1 2 3 4 5 6 7 8 9

First Edition

Book design by Susan Turner

For Helen and Frena
and Burt and Lynn

FACES
OF FEAR

He had to look.

He had to look at it all, and be objective, and make the final decision.

He let the damp towel fall away from his waist and drop to the floor in a sodden heap around his feet, steeling himself as not only his face but his entire body was revealed in the full-length mirror in his bedroom.

He stared at his image quietly, suppressing the instinctive urge to turn away, forcing himself to view it with utter detachment, as if it were nothing more than some hideous sculpture an inept student had produced, and which he must now find a way to turn into a work of art.

Not that it was all bad: he had kept himself lean and strong, and a fit body had at least given him good legs.

The torso would eventually take care of itself.

But the face. The face was the key to everything.

The key to his future.

The key to his happiness.

He took a deep breath and focused his entire attention on what he had come to think of as nothing more than a canvas upon which the original artist had put nothing more than a rough sketch, but that he would turn into a masterpiece. It was simply a matter of analyzing each feature and making the decisions that would not only put them all in perfect balance, but please the viewer as much as the artist himself.

He began.

The jawline was too square, too prominent, and the chin was marred by a deep cleft. Bone would have to be shaved in order to achieve a softer look.

The ears were far too large.

The brow line too prominent, leaving the eyes too deeply set.

The cheekbones were not prominent enough.

And the nose. Though not yet thirty, it was the nose of an old man, a nose that would grow into a bulbous purple-veined monstrosity if it were left alone.

But it would not be left alone; none of it would be left alone. He already knew exactly the nose he wanted.

And not only the nose. He also knew the ears, the brows, and even the lids that would give the eyes the perfect almond shape he craved.

Though anyone else would think it was an impossible job, he knew better. It was simply a matter of removing a millimeter or two here, adding a millimeter or two there, until the framework was right. Then it would all go together.

Beauty was all about proportion.

He knew what he wanted; he'd done his research. And, after all, it was only the face that would require anything even faintly experimental, and he himself had rehearsed the new procedures he had devised to the point where, in all fairness, they couldn't truly be called experimental at all.

They were perfect.

He himself had perfected them.

He stood back now, finally willing to appraise his full body in the mirror. And now—now that he was looking at it truly objectively— he realized that the raw material was actually excellent.

The skeleton was proportionally perfect.

The soft, supple skin was nearly hairless.

The makeover would be simple, and he would finally be what he was always meant to be.

He gazed deep into the mirror, and in his mind the masculine lines of his body morphed smoothly into the softly curving lines of a shapely woman.

The reflection in the mirror became indistinguishable from the vision of his dreams: a beautiful, perfect woman, desirable, fashionable, successful.

All he needed was patience.

But it had been so long, and how much patience could be expected from anyone, let alone from him? How much longer must he wait before his body and face would be a perfect reflection of the woman he had always been?

Soon, he told himself. Soon. But if he didn't keep a firm rein on himself—if he lost control and couldn't wait just a little longer—he'd never realize his vision. Patience. That was the key. Work slowly, work carefully, work methodically. Keep the goal in sight.

And make no mistakes.

He tamped down the emotions roiling within him and went back to the clinical evaluation of what he saw in the mirror.

The breasts would be easy, as would the work on his genitals. Those techniques had been perfected more than half a century ago. But the rest of it . . .

He rehearsed it all once more in his mind, reanalyzing his image piece by piece, feature by feature, the tips of his fingers twitching as if they held the scalpels themselves. He went through it all a third time, and then a fourth, and as he took it all apart in his mind and put it all together again, the truth slowly sank in.

He was ready.

Finally ready.

Exquisite.

He picked up the telephone from his nightstand and punched in a speed-dial number. "It's time," he said to the person who answered. "It's finally time."

Part One

CHANGES

1

ALISON SHAW FELT GOOD. REALLY GOOD. SHE MADE THE FINAL TURN around the smooth cinder track with long, easy strides. She'd done six full laps, but with the cool breeze coming in from the beach four blocks away, there wasn't even a hint of the choking exhaust that usually drifted directly from the Santa Monica Freeway onto the playing fields. She felt she could do at least three more laps when she heard the coach's whistle. End of period; end of day; end of week. A shower, and she could go home. She slowed her pace so Cindy Kearns could catch up with her.

"There's a party at the beach tonight," Cindy said, catching her breath and wiping more perspiration from her forehead than was on Alison's entire body. "Jeff Simmons is going to be there." Cindy was pretty sure Alison had a crush on Jeff, but if she did, she wasn't showing it. In fact, she was shrugging like she couldn't care less.

"Can't," Alison said. "My mom has to go to some fancy banquet for one of her clients tonight and I'm fixing dinner for my dad."

"How domestic of you," Cindy said. "What about after dinner?

It won't even get dark until after eight, and it could go until midnight."

Alison rolled her eyes. "And Jeff Simmons will bring a keg of beer, and everybody will get drunk, and the cops will come, and then we'll all have to call our folks to come get us. Gee, it sounds like so much fun, how can I resist?"

Cindy decided to ignore her sarcasm. "So if you don't want him, can I have Jeff Simmons?"

Alison glared at her best friend in not-quite-mock exasperation. Ever since she'd turned fifteen last month, all Cindy seemed to think about was boys—as if some kind of switch had been turned on. "I barely even know Jeff," she said. "And I'm sure he's no more interested in me than any of the other boys are, which means not at all, which is fine with me. Besides, even if I wanted to go, my dad's bringing home a movie. So add Jeff to your list of conquests, and call me with all the details tomorrow."

Once again Cindy ignored Alison's tone, and pushed through the double doors into the girls' locker room, which was even warmer than the air outside, and muggy from the showers that were already going full blast. Cindy quickly stripped off her sweaty gym clothes and dropped them in a dank pile on the floor.

Alison had just shed her shorts when Coach DiBenedetti walked through the locker room, a bra dangling from her fingers. "Lost and found," she announced. "Who left a bra under the bench?"

Paula Steen, one of a half-dozen seniors in the class, snickered. "Well, we know it's not Alison Shaw's," she called out, eliciting exactly the laugh she was looking for from her friends.

Seeing Cindy open her mouth to take a shot at Paula, Alison spoke first. "Is it a training bra?" she called out to the coach, loud enough for everyone to hear. " 'Cause if it isn't, Paula's right—can't possibly be mine." When even Paula's friends giggled, she decided to push it a little further. "I'm still looking for the pretraining model!"

The coach smiled at Alison. "You're just a late bloomer," she said. "And the last blossoms are often the best of the season."

In the silence that followed, it seemed to Alison that everyone was staring at her.

"You've got a model's body," Cindy Kearns put in a second before the silence would have gotten awkward. "In fact," she said, turning to stare straight at Paula Steen, "you've got exactly the body Paula's always wanted."

"But she doesn't have the face I have, does she?" Paula shot back, tucking her own gym clothes into her backpack.

"I'll see you in my office, Paula," the coach said, sternly.

"It's okay," Alison said, suddenly wishing she'd just kept her mouth shut. "Really."

"It's not okay," Marti DiBenedetti said. "My office, Paula."

Paula glowered at Alison. If she was already in trouble, she figured, she might as well get the absolutely last word. "The longer you stay a little girl, the less competition for the rest of us," Paula sneered as she hefted her backpack and followed the coach to her office. "Only gay boys like bodies like yours!"

"Just ignore her," Cindy said as Paula disappeared around a corner.

"Ignore what?" Alison countered, forcing a tone far lighter than she was feeling. She undressed quickly, still smarting from Paula's ridicule, and self-consciously wrapped herself in the skimpy gym towel. "I don't know what's so great about big boobs anyway. I'll either get them or I won't—it's not like I have anything to do with it." She followed Cindy to the cavernous shower room, which was empty except for Gina Tucci, who was leisurely washing her hair at the farthest showerhead.

And who was Paula Steen's best friend.

Alison hung her towel on a hook, braced herself for whatever Gina might say, and stepped under a showerhead. She rinsed off quickly, then wrapped the towel around herself again before returning to her locker. Gina was still washing her hair. Maybe everyone wasn't staring at her after all.

She was almost dressed when Cindy came back from the shower.

Alison tucked her blouse into her jeans and buckled her belt, then sat on the bench brushing her hair while Cindy dressed and rummaged in her backpack. Then, using the mirror she'd affixed to the inside of her locker door, Cindy erased smudges of mascara around her eyes and carefully applied dark pink lipstick.

"Want to get a Coke?" Alison asked her.

"Can't. My mom's picking me up."

"What about tomorrow?"

"Call me," Cindy said, picking up her backpack. "I'll give you the full report on tonight."

Then Cindy was gone and Alison was alone in the locker room. She stuffed her dirty gym clothes into a plastic bag and shoved them into her backpack, then caught glimpse of herself in one of the mirrors on the locker room wall. Rising to her feet and carrying her backpack with her, she moved closer to the mirror and took a look at herself.

And what she saw wasn't bad. In fact, she looked fine. She didn't need a lot of makeup, and she didn't need pounds of hips, and breasts, either. And she sure didn't need to compete for one of those idiot boys who Paula—and even Cindy—seemed to think were so hot. So what was she worried about? Paula and all the other girls like her could have all the boobs and all the boys, if that was what they wanted.

She looked just fine, and felt good.

And she knew she'd keep telling herself that until the sting of Paula's comments wore off and she once again truly felt as good as she had half an hour ago, when she'd come off the track.

MARGOT DUNN SAT at her vanity table, her hand trembling as she gazed at the diamond earrings that lay on her palm. She could hear her husband cursing in his dressing room as he fumbled with the bow tie to his tux, but his voice sounded oddly muffled, as if coming from much farther away than the few yards that lay between them. But even if she'd heard him clearly, there was no way she could help him. Not the way she always had before. The gulf between herself and Conrad Dunn—between herself and everyone else in the world—had grown too wide.

The hairdresser had come, done his job perfectly, and gone; her makeup man had come and done his best. And she had actually been able to slip into the gray silk Valentino that Conrad had chosen for her to wear to the banquet tonight.

The Dunn Foundation banquet.

The single event where everyone she knew was certain to be present, and certain to be opening their checkbooks, if not their hearts, for her husband's charity.

The event at which she herself had always been the crown jewel.

Yet when it came time to actually put on the glittering diamond earrings and pronounce herself ready to go, she couldn't do it. She couldn't find the energy, just as she couldn't find the energy to help Conrad with his tie.

Right now she didn't even have the energy to cry.

But she had to find the energy, had to dig deep within herself and find the resources to get her through the evening. Taking a deep breath, she twisted her head to the right and lifted her eyes from the earrings to her reflection in the mirror. For a brief moment, when all she could see was the left side of her face, she felt her spirits rise ever so slightly, and seized the moment to attach one of the jewels in her hand to her left ear.

But even as her fingers worked to slip the post through the tiny hole in her earlobe, she caught a glimpse of the puckered sag of her right eye, and almost against her own volition found herself turning her head to expose the other side of her face to her gaze. Where once she had beheld on the right side of her face only the perfect reflection of the left, now three thick jagged scars sliced from the lower edge of her jaw up through the plane of her cheek, their upper extremity pulling her lower eyelid down so a red semicircle always glowed beneath the deep blue of her iris.

Her eye, formerly so beautiful, was now as hideous as the rest of that side of her face.

Red, white, and blue. Like some fucking Fourth of July bunting, hanging from her ruined face.

Ramón, her makeup specialist, had done his best, but no amount of makeup could cover those shining purple gouges, and no mascara could mask the bloodred semicircle that underscored her eye.

Her face—the face that Conrad Dunn himself had worked so hard to make perfect—looked utterly incongruous with the elegant simplicity of the dress and the perfectly coiffed hair.

She closed her eyes and willed herself the strength to finish dressing, to accompany her husband to this fund-raiser, to eat, to drink, to smile and greet his clients, friends, and donors. To pretend to be oblivious to the fact that while the left side of her face still looked like it belonged on the cover of *Vogue,* the right side of that same face now made people turn away, trying to hide not only their revulsion at how she looked, but their pity as well.

Nothing could hide the damage their yacht's propeller had done to her face last summer.

It all seemed so impossible. It had been such a perfect day. They'd been on the foredeck, and she was enjoying the single drink she allowed herself on Saturdays and Sundays, and all she'd done was stand up to get a better view of Catalina. And the boat hit a wave, and pitched, and she felt herself lose her balance, and the next thing she knew, she was in the hospital with her entire face bandaged.

And after that, nothing had been the same again, and now, tonight, she could no longer pretend that it was.

She just couldn't do it.

Feeling Conrad's warm hands on her shoulders, she opened her eyes and saw his reflection in the mirror, concern in his eyes. "We have to go," he said softly, as if feeling every agony she was going through.

"I can't."

His grip tightened, as though merely by touching her he could transfer his own strength and character into her. "Of course you can," he urged, his voice gentle. "You must. I need you with me. You look wonderful, you know—that dress is perfect." His lips curled up into a playful smile and he lifted a single brow in a comical leer. "Shows just the right amount of your exquisite cleavage."

Margot turned from the mirror to look up into his soft eyes. "Conrad, stop lying. You can't be seen with me looking like this. Not tonight. Your father would turn over in his grave."

"My father loved you, Margot, and he would want you to be there, adding at least a little class to what has always been nothing more than our family begging for money with the unspoken threat of not keeping the women looking as young and beautiful as they like if they don't cough up enough money so our real work can go on. My father would have wanted you there, and I do want you there. You belong with me."

"But—"

"But nothing. I'm going to fix your face. You know that. I made you perfect once, and I can do it again. You know I can, and you know I will."

Margot turned back to the mirror and dabbed at the moisture that continually leaked out of the sagging lid of her ruined right eye. "I am the worst possible advertisement for a plastic surgeon," she said.

"Think of yourself as the 'before' model," Conrad said, keeping his voice as light as he could. "Next year, you'll be the 'after' model, and knock them all dead. Think what they'll cough up when they see what I can do! Now just put on your other earring, my darling, and let's go." He gave her shoulders another reassuring squeeze, and Margot, knowing that his will that she accompany him was stronger than her will to stay at home and hide, found the strength to add the other diamond to her right ear.

Conrad took her hand and drew her lightly from the vanity stool. He turned her to face him, and she flinched as he touched the terrible scars that had destroyed her once flawless face.

"You will always be beautiful to me," he said, and kissed her gently on the forehead. "Now come on, let's head for the banquet and make the grandest entrance anyone's ever seen."

Margot closed her eyes and nodded. She had a job to do tonight. She was Conrad Dunn's wife, and she would not fail him. She took a deep, determined breath, and let her husband lead her from her room.

Somehow, she would get through the evening.

2

As far as Risa Shaw—and practically everyone else in Los Angeles—was concerned, any excuse to go to the Hotel Bel-Air was a good one, and as she gave her Lexus to the valet and she and Alexis Montrose crossed the small stone bridge onto the perfectly groomed hotel grounds, she decided that the air in Stone Canyon smelled sweeter than it did anywhere else.

Discreet signs bearing the Dunn Foundation logo directed them past the gracefully floating swans and through a courtyard with a bubbling fountain to the Garden Room, where members of the Dunn Foundation staff waited, offering each guest a small card bearing their table number, and directing them toward the bar if they wanted more than the champagne the waitstaff was deftly carrying through the throng that had already gathered. For half an hour Risa followed Lexie though the crowd, then found her seat at a table only three away from the one at which Conrad Dunn and his wife were sitting.

An hour later, as the staff cleared the empty plates with quiet efficiency, Corinne Dunn introduced the mother of the last recipient of her brother's expertise and her family's generosity. As Rosa Alvarez spoke, so softly that everyone in the room had to strain to catch her words, images flashed on the huge screen behind her.

First came photographs of the tiny baby that had been born to her only ten years ago. José was born with a cleft palate so severe that he couldn't nurse from his mother's breast; he was fed through a tube until he was two years old. For years after his birth, his life had been lived in the shelter of his home and his mother's love, the rest of the children in his village unwilling even to look at him, let alone play with him. But then, by the grace of the Dunn Foundation and "St. Conrad," as Rosa called Conrad Dunn, her son's defect had been repaired, until all that remained was a tiny scar from his nose to his lip.

Now, even that small mark was quickly fading away.

As the photos on the screen dissolved from the baby's twisted face to that of a beautiful, smiling, brown-eyed ten-year-old, Risa saw that she wasn't the only one who took out her checkbook to divert or mask the tears glistening in eyes at every table. Then José Alvarez himself appeared, his face illuminated by both a spotlight and an enormous smile. Running to his mother, he threw his arms around her.

"It is a miracle," Rosa said, gathering her son to her. "Thank you. Thank you all for making this possible."

As Corinne Dunn rose to lead the applause for her and then led Rosa toward the garden where the party would continue, Conrad Dunn and his wife rose to follow his sister and their guest of honor. Responding to that cue, the crowd quickly began drifting from the Garden Room into the garden itself, and Risa quickly wrote out her check, adding an extra thousand dollars to the sum she'd initially decided to contribute.

Lexie Montrose, leaning over her shoulder to peer at the check, whistled softly. "Wow! Really? That much?"

"If ever there was a good cause," Risa said, "this is it. Let's go find the Dunns—I want to give this to Conrad personally."

The two women followed the flow of people until they spotted Conrad, standing next to an extravagant dessert buffet. Rosa Alvarez

was at his side, and they were surrounded by his guests. Risa and Lexie
joined what had become a simple reception line, as tuxedoed waiters
circulated with trays filled with yet more champagne glasses. The garden glowed with subtle lighting that made it seem as if the huge old
oak trees were illuminating the evening.

Conrad Dunn managed to greet each guest by name, find a few
words for every one of them, accept their checks with an appreciation
that was heartfelt but not cloying, and keep the line moving as if by
some kind of social magic. He also managed to keep shaking hands
while simultaneously passing the checks to Margot, who seemed intent
on staying in the deep shadows behind her husband as she discreetly
slipped each check into a silk wallet. Even in the soft and flattering
light, Risa could see not only how unhappy Margot Dunn was about
being on display, but also the scars that no doubt were the cause of her
unhappiness.

"Risa?"

The soft voice came from behind her, and Risa turned to see
Danielle DeLorian. "Danielle! How nice to see you!" Risa kissed the
air just far enough from Danielle's cheek so the gesture wouldn't dis-
turb the perfect makeup that was not only Danielle's hallmark, but her
trademark as well.

A year ago, even Risa had begun using DeLorian cosmetics, despite
their outrageous price. "What the hell?" Lexie had told her. "So it
costs a million to look like a million—the way you're selling these
days, you can afford it."

Drawing back from Danielle's cheek, Risa introduced her former
client to her best friend.

"Risa navigated me through an absolute nightmare of a deal a couple of years ago," Danielle told Lexie in a soft southern drawl that belied her sharp intelligence. "I'll be forever grateful."

"I'm so glad it worked out for you," Risa said, then turned to see
that the line had moved and Conrad Dunn, a bemused expression on
his face, was waiting for her.

Flushing, she quickly moved forward. "Conrad!" she said, handing him her check as she leaned in to kiss him on the cheek. "Thank you so much for including me in this. I'm just—" She hesitated, searching for the right word, then shook her head helplessly. "I'm just overwhelmed. What you're doing is wonderful, and I'm so happy to be able to help."

"And I'm just as happy to have you here. You know we built the new clinic on that piece of land you helped us buy."

"Actually, I did know that," Risa replied. "I'm just glad I was able to help." She turned toward Lexie. "Do you know my friend Alexis Montrose?"

Conrad turned his warm gaze on Lexie. "Thank you for coming." He smoothly eased them toward Margot to keep the line moving, and Risa extended her hand, which Margot seemed hesitant to accept. Even when she finally did, she still hung back so her face was deep in shadow.

Clearly, Margot Dunn wished she were elsewhere, and was eager for the evening to be over. Risa couldn't blame her. As far as she knew, this was the first time Margot had been out in public since the accident a year ago, which had received far more publicity than Risa thought it deserved. Still, she, along with everyone else, was finding it hard not to stare at Margot's scars, and as she and Lexie moved away from her toward the dessert table, Risa heard one woman whisper to another, loud enough to be heard by everyone within twenty feet, "Did you *see* those horrible gouges in Margot's face?"

"There's Mitchell Hawthorne," Lexie said, dropping half the chocolate truffle she'd been nibbling onto the table. "You should meet him. He's in the industry." She took Risa's elbow and began steering her through the crowd. "Absolutely tons of money," she whispered, bringing her lips close to Risa's ear, "and living in a terrible piece of crap out in the Valley."

Risa winced at Lexie's habitual crude directness. "Always happy to meet a potential new client," she said, following her friend to a tall, silver-haired man holding a glass of champagne and speaking with two other men, one of whom had a familiar face.

Like the two women who had brushed by Risa a few moments ago, the men were talking about Margot's scars. "Frankly, I don't see how she can show herself in public," the silver-haired man said as Lexie reached out and took his arm to draw him around.

"Mitchell," she said, greeting him with a warm hug. "I want you to meet Risa Shaw. When you decide it's time to buy something decent to live in, she's the one to call."

Risa took Mitchell Hawthorne's extended hand, but before she could say a word, one of his friends cut in.

"Christ, Lexie," the familiar face—who turned out to be a minor TV actor—said. "What was Conrad Dunn thinking, letting Margot show that gargoyle of a face tonight? Who'd want to contribute after seeing her? If I were him, I'd lock her up where no one could ever see her again."

Risa glanced nervously around, hoping Margot Dunn was nowhere in the area, but as she scanned the crowd she realized that it wouldn't matter where Margot was; everywhere she looked, she could see people whispering to each other, then looking guiltily toward the Dunns, obviously hoping they weren't overheard. After forcing herself to chat a moment longer with the three men—and pocketing three business cards—Risa aimed Lexie toward the ladies' room. There, at least, she might not have to overhear any more talk about their hostess.

As they passed the bar, they saw Corinne Dunn standing alone, sipping a martini. "You make a terrific emcee," Risa said, pausing to introduce herself and Lexie.

Corinne smiled warmly. "I can't tell you how gratifying it is to see all these children go on to lead normal lives," she said. "You'd be amazed at how many of them stay in touch with us for years afterward."

"It's a wonderful thing the foundation does," Risa said, then followed Lexie into the ladies' room, where her friend bared her teeth in front of the mirror to make sure not a fleck of anything was marring their whiteness.

"Boy," Lexie said as she fished in her bag for her lipstick. "This is the place to schmooze the rich and famous, isn't it?"

"It's an admirable charity," Risa observed archly, even though she knew at least half the people in attendance were there for exactly the reason Lexie had just stated. "But I'm worried about Margot. She doesn't look well."

"I wonder why her husband hasn't fixed those appalling scars yet?" Lexie said. "Everybody—and I mean *everybody*—is talking about it."

"I'm sure he will," Risa replied in a tone that clearly told Lexie she didn't want to talk about it anymore.

As usual, Lexie ignored her tone. "I mean, how long has it been? A year? Don't you think he would have done something by now if he could have?"

"I don't know," Risa said, freshening her own lipstick. "And I don't think we need to talk—"

"She's probably just going to have to learn to live with it," Lexie broke in, carefully adjusting her studiously casual hairdo. "How awful would that be?"

"Very, very awful," Risa replied. "And she certainly seemed depressed. I feel so bad for her."

Lexie's brow rose sardonically. "Well, she better get undepressed or she's likely to lose that gorgeous husband of hers. Every woman in this place would kill to take him over."

Risa gave her a sidelong glance in the mirror. "Including you, Mrs. Happily Married?"

"I could be Mrs. Happily Unmarried in a heartbeat if Conrad Dunn came on the market!"

A toilet flushed, and a moment later Margot Dunn emerged from one of the stalls. Risa's cheeks burned as she quickly replayed in her mind everything she and Lexie had said while standing in front of the mirrors, and wished she could drop through the floor.

Not even acknowledging their presence, Margot walked directly to the sink, calmly washed her hands, then dried them and left the room.

Risa slumped against the wall, her stomach churning, her face still burning with embarrassment.

Lexie, though, only shrugged. "So what if she heard us?" she asked, reading Risa's mind. "It's not like any of it was news to her."

Risa said nothing, but made a mental note to call Margot in the morning and apologize.

If, that is, Margot Dunn would even take her call.

CAROLINE FISHER BALEFULLY EYED her last customer of the evening, who was still sitting at the round table in the corner, still sipping his decaf, and still reading the paper. He'd been there for at least an hour and seemed in no hurry to leave, even when she'd made a fairly unsubtle show of locking both doors and turning off the OPEN sign in the window.

Now, at seven minutes past her ten o'clock closing, Rick was cleaning the espresso machines while she finished straightening the displays of coffees, mugs, and other caffeine-related accoutrements the shop sold, then began to put the chairs up on the tables.

"Oh," the man said, finally folding his paper. "I didn't realize it was so late."

Caroline gave him a smile she hoped looked warm. "You can just leave your mug there," she said. "I'll take care of it."

"Thanks," he said, tucking his paper under his arm as he waited for her to unlock the door to let him out into the warm Encino evening.

"Some people have no place to go," Ricky said as he gave the countertops a final desultory wipe-down.

"Well, I *do,*" Caroline said, "and I don't want to be late."

"Yeah, me, too. I think I'm finished here."

Caroline nodded, looking at the clock and deciding that whatever else needed to be done could wait until tomorrow. "We're good. I'll leave a note for the morning crew to sweep up."

"See you tomorrow."

Caroline locked the door behind Ricky, then swept her gaze around the small coffee shop she'd managed for the last year. It looked good. If Corporate sent a shopper in for a cup of coffee in the morning, he—or she—would have nothing to complain about, especially with her numbers not only far better than those from a year ago, but going steadily up every single week. She might be only a single store manager now, but within two more years she intended to be running at least the whole district, if not the region itself.

For now, though, the long day was over. She turned out all the main lights, leaving only the two small fluorescents glowing behind the counter, and went into the tiny room that barely met the legal standards for an "employees' lounge" to begin the process of getting the smell of coffee off herself and freshening up for her date. Terry—if that was even his real name—was probably already at Weasel's, waiting for her. According to the clock on the wall, they were to meet in five minutes. She'd be late, which wasn't good, and not like her at all. Besides, the later it got, the more crowded Weasel's would be, which would just make it that much harder to find him. When they were chatting online last night, he said he'd be wearing a white button-down pinstripe shirt and jeans. Blond, blue-eyed, six feet tall, waiting for her at the bar.

She hoped he looked at least *something* like the photo he'd put up with his profile.

She taped a note to Sheila's locker asking her to sweep up before opening tomorrow morning, then took a pink cotton sweater and jeans out of her locker, along with her makeup kit, and headed for the unisex restroom. She'd have to hurry: being a few minutes late would be all right, but if she was too late, Terry just might stop waiting and start looking around at whoever else was cruising the bar.

Caroline peeled off her white top and black slacks, and then, wearing only bra and panties, dampened a paper towel to wipe away the smudges under her eyes before freshening up her makeup. At the last minute she added a little dark eye shadow for some extra evening drama.

She was just pulling her favorite pink sweater over her head when she thought she heard one of the bathroom stalls open.

Who could still be here? Keisha? Impossible—her shift had ended an hour ago. Or had she been in the bathroom all this time?

Could Keisha be sick?

Caroline struggled with the sweater for a moment, trying to figure out what she could do if Keisha really was ill. If the girl couldn't drive, then she would have to take her home, and that meant—

Before she could finish the thought, a rubber-gloved hand grabbed her hard around the mouth and jerked her head back. She barely saw the glittering flash of the blade before it sliced across her throat and she began to choke.

It took a moment—a half second or two that seemed an eternity— before she realized she was breathing in blood instead of air.

Her own blood.

But there was no pain—no pain at all! How was that possible? How could she be sinking down to the floor, feeling her own blood gushing from her throat, choking on the very fluid that gave her life, and not feel anything?

The light in the restroom began to throb in strange synchroniza- tion with her own heartbeat, and a terrible melancholy settled over Caroline as her life drained away onto the bathroom floor. Mutely— numbly—she watched as her assailant sliced through her sweater and her skin and laid open her abdomen.

And still she felt nothing.

She watched as a detached observer as her intestines were torn out and flung aside, as greedy hands reached deep inside her as if searching for some specific thing.

The blade glimmered once more in the now fast fading light of the restroom, and the awful spurting of Caroline Fisher's blood slowed to nothing more than a dribble.

Her last thought was of Terry. Blond, blue-eyed Terry, waiting at the bar.

Waiting for her.

Waiting for eternity . . .

3

RISA SHAW REACHED OVER AND SPOONED TWO DOLLOPS OF YOGURT from the container in front of Alison into her own bowl, added some cereal, and topped her breakfast off with a large handful of blueberries, earning herself a quizzical look from her daughter.

"Mom! You don't even *like* blueberries."

But even with Alison's words ringing in her ears, Risa could barely focus on the food in front of her. Rather, her entire consciousness had been filled with only two things since she'd awakened this morning: the fact that Michael had not only not come home for dinner last night, but still hadn't been home when she finally fell asleep sometime after midnight; and Lexie Montrose's words from the banquet the night before.

I could be Mrs. Happily Unmarried in a heartbeat if Conrad Dunn came on the market!

Had some ambitious young talent thought the same about Michael Shaw? The thought had begun to haunt her as soon as she got home and found not only that Michael's side of the garage was empty, but that he hadn't even called to say he'd be late until Alison already had dinner on the table and waiting for him. Indeed, it had still been on the table when she herself had come home, and instead of being worried that he'd been hurt in an accident or something, as she would have in the first years of their marriage, she found herself instead recalling Lexie's sleazy comment.

Was it possible that Michael had spent the evening with another woman?

Of course it was possible—in this day and age, in fact, it was even probable.

Still, the thought was both infuriating and terrifying.

"Well, maybe I'll just have to learn to like blueberries," Risa said, gazing at her bowl morosely. "Maybe I'll have to learn to like a lot of things I hate." She poured a glass of juice for Alison and another for herself, pushing Alison's across the breakfast bar.

"Aren't you going to pour one for Dad?" Alison asked as Risa set the pitcher down, leaving the third glass conspicuously empty.

"If he wants it, he can pour it himself," Risa said, and regretted her sharp tone when she saw Alison recoil. "Oh, I'm sorry, honey," she went on, too quickly. "I guess I'm just a little cranky this morning. Plus I have an early appointment. I have to be at the marina in half an hour." She gulped down her orange juice, decided to ignore the blueberries, then wondered if that could be symbolic of something, and blew on her coffee in hopes of cooling it fast enough to drink at least half a cup before she had to leave. "Are you coming home right after school today?"

"Track practice," Alison said. "I'll be home by six. Why?"

"Just trying to keep up with you," Risa said, forcing a smile.

"Keep up with *me*?" Alison shot back. "Give me a break, Mom— I'm the one who has to keep up with *you*."

The smile her daughter's words brought to her lips faded when she heard her husband's footsteps on the stairs, and she tried to renew it. The last thing she needed this morning was a confrontation with

Michael, especially in front of Alison. Yet even as she told herself to let it go at least until she and Michael were alone, she felt the bitter anger rising in the back of her throat. Then Michael came around the corner—fresh from the shower, wearing an open-collared shirt and sport coat over chinos, and looking far younger than his forty-two years—and she knew she wasn't going to be able to hold her temper in check.

"Good morning, ladies," he said, as if he didn't have a care in the world. He reached for the orange juice.

"Morning, Dad—" Alison began, but abruptly cut herself short when her mother reached out and clutched her father's wrist, keeping him from the pitcher.

"What time did *you* roll in last night?" she demanded, a hard edge of anger in her voice.

"Late," Michael said.

A little too smoothly? Risa wondered.

"I worked until after midnight," he explained, "then went out for a nightcap."

Risa stared at him until he lifted his gaze to meet hers.

He was lying—she could see it in his eyes. "Alison stayed home to make you dinner, and you didn't even bother to call until it was already on the table."

"Oh, cupcake, I'm sorry," he said, and walked around the bar to kiss the top of his daughter's head. "Sometimes the newsroom just doesn't care that I have a real life."

"She was home *alone* until I got back from the banquet about ten," Risa said.

"Mom, I'm fifteen!" Alison protested. "It was no big deal."

"That's not the point!" Risa snapped.

"I'm sorry, babe," Michael said. "What can I say? You know the news doesn't stop for my convenience."

"But apparently your daughter can be ignored."

Michael sighed heavily. "Maybe we should have this conversation another time."

"Fine," Risa said. "How about tonight? Or won't you be home tonight, either?"

Alison's eyes glistened as she looked up at her parents. "Come on, you guys. Don't fight."

"We're not fighting, honey," Michael said, his eyes pleading with his wife to let it go, at least until they were alone. "I was inconsiderate, and your mom has a right to be mad."

Risa took a deep breath, checked her watch, and decided she had neither the time, the energy, nor the stomach for whatever might happen if they kept talking right now. Without responding to Michael, she poured a fresh cup of coffee into a traveling mug, though she was certain her stomach was already far too upset for her to drink it. "I've got to run." She looked directly at her husband. "You'll be home tonight?"

Michael nodded. "As usual."

" 'Bye, Mom."

" 'Bye, honey." Risa grabbed her briefcase and hurried through the house to the garage.

A *wife always knows,* her mother had told her.

And Risa knew.

Michael was having an affair.

MARGOT DUNN SAT quietly in the tiny glass chapel overlooking the Pacific where she and Conrad had been married a dozen years ago. The joy of that day—when her own beauty exceeded even that of the setting she had chosen for her wedding—was only a faint memory now, but the serenity of the Wayfarer's Chapel imbued her spirit as much today as it always had. Through all the years since she'd married Conrad, this small church had been her refuge, the single place where everything else in her world could be shut out, and today, with the bright sun of the clear morning pouring through the great glass panels and filtering through the branches of the redwoods outside, Margot knew she was at last going to be all right.

For the first time since the accident, her soul was truly at peace.

Uttering a final silent prayer, Margot rose from the pew and left the chapel, threading her way though the crowd around the front door, paying no attention to the glances and whispers of the people who recognized her.

She found her Lexus parked in the lot, drove it down the hill to the Pacific Coast Highway and turned right. After less than a mile she turned off the highway and made her way through a maze of small cul-de-sacs until she pulled up in front of a tiny park she'd discovered a few years ago when she came to look at one of the houses across the street.

She hadn't particularly liked the house, but had fallen instantly in love with the park. She'd come back the very next day, bringing Ruffles with her, and the dog had liked it as much as she did. The best thing about it—aside from the view and the thunder from the surf that constantly crashed at the base of the cliff—was that it was almost always deserted. Now, already anticipating an hour of running loose on the lawn, the little white terrier was peering eagerly out the passenger window of the Lexus, as if struggling to get his tiny nose through the glass itself to suck in the tangy salt air beyond the confines of the car.

Margot braked to a stop, turned off the engine, and let her hands drop to her lap as her head fell back onto the headrest.

Peace.

She took a deep breath and then gazed out over the cliffs to the glistening ocean spread out in front of her. A haze lay over the sea this morning, hiding the distant form of Catalina. The horizon had all but vanished, the sea and sky blending so perfectly that there was barely a hint of where they met.

Nothing but blue for as far as she could see.

Ruffles whined to be let out of the car, but Margot only reached across to give his flank an affectionate rub. "Hush," she whispered.

Sensing something, the little dog instantly quieted.

Again Margot gazed out at the sea, quieting her mind, concentrating on her breathing, using the yoga she had learned years before.

Then she pulled down the visor, flipped open the lighted mirror, and faced her reflected image.

The scars, uncovered by makeup today, were far worse than she had made herself believe. With neither the magic of Danielle DeLorian's line of cosmetics nor the subdued lighting with which she had surrounded herself for the last year, the scars looked even worse to her now than on the day the bandages were removed. Clearly reflected in the mirror, fully exposed by the glare of morning light, Margot Dunn gazed silently at what other people saw whenever they looked at her: the hideous purple gouges that had ruined her face forever.

The peace she had found in the chapel and the serenity of the vast sea were abruptly shattered by the voices she'd overheard at last night's banquet.

How could she live, looking like that?

Why hasn't her husband fixed those dreadful scars?

If he could, he would have, wouldn't he?

I'd never show my face in public if I looked like that.

Margot turned her eyes from the hideous vision in the mirror and gazed at the beautiful ocean before her, sparkling in the sun.

Beautiful. Beautiful and eternal: the sea would be forever enchanting.

How could she live, looking like that?

How, indeed?

She reached into the backseat and took one of the fashion magazines from the stack she'd put in the car just before she left the house. She gazed at the cover: the magazine was *Elle,* and that issue had been one of her best covers ever. She'd worn leather and fur for the shoot, and the camera had caught the seductive little wink she offered as she showed off not only her perfect face, but her flawless legs as well.

Perfect no more, she thought as she looked again to the mirror in the visor.

She snapped it closed, and flipped the magazine over so she could no longer see the image on its cover. But in the backseat there were at least a dozen others, each bearing testament to what she had been. She hadn't brought them to look at—they were there as nothing more than evidence, so people would understand.

So Conrad would understand.

The ocean stretched before her, shimmering in the sun.

I'd never show my face in public if I looked like that.

The remark resounded in her memory so clearly that Margot actually jumped, startled, as if the woman who had uttered it last night were right here in the car with her.

Consciously settling her rattled nerves, she fished in her purse for her cell phone. Just as her fingers closed around it, it began to ring.

Conrad's name and phone number glowed on the small screen.

After a moment's hesitation, she answered. "Conrad?"

"Margot, where are you?"

"Palos Verdes."

"P-V? What are you doing way out there?"

"Just . . . taking a day," she said.

The pause before Conrad spoke again was a little too long, and when he finally did speak, she could hear the worry in his voice.

"Are you okay?"

Margot considered the question, and found the one answer that would not only ease his worry but was absolutely true as well: "I'm fine."

Another hesitation, but not nearly as long. "Should I worry about you?"

Margot felt her lips curl into a wry smile. There was nothing for anybody to worry about. Not anymore. Not ever again. "Not at all, darling."

"Okay, then. I'll be home at the usual time."

"Okay."

"I love you," he said.

"Love you, too," she said, then clicked off the phone before the emotion in her chest made it to her voice. "I love you so very, very much," she whispered, holding the phone to her cheek, pressing it against the scars.

What had that woman in the restroom said? Something about snapping Conrad up if he ever came back on the market?

She dabbed a tissue at the moisture leaking from her damaged right eye, then opened her phone again and pressed the MEMO button.

"I'm so sorry, Conrad," she said, her voice soft. "I can't go on this way and I can't subject you to my misery for the rest of your life. Please give Ruffles to Danielle—she's never had anyone to love her. And you take good care of yourself. Never forget that I love you."

Checking off items on a well-rehearsed mental list, Margot phoned the police to report an abandoned, locked Lexus parked at Vanderlip Park with a dog inside. She rolled down the window far enough so Ruffles would have plenty of cool ocean air but not enough so he could wriggle out. She set her cell phone on the dashboard, then got out of the car, pressed the button on the key that would lock the doors, and dropped the keys back into the car, through the slightly opened window, to the floor behind the driver's seat.

The ocean breeze lifted strands of her hair as she looked out to sea, walked to the bench overlooking the sea, and sat down on it.

A hundred or so feet below, the surf pounded at the base of the cliff, spray shooting high into the air as the waves exploded against the rocks of the shoreline.

A few hundred yards offshore, a sailboat was cruising southward, its foredeck crowded with people.

Beautiful people.

The world belonged to the beautiful people, and nobody understood that better than she did.

She rose to her feet and stepped to the edge of the precipice. She gazed down upon the rocks thrusting up from the ocean floor.

The rocks that would be her salvation.

If Conrad couldn't, or wouldn't, fix her face, the rocks would.

She stood a little straighter, closed her eyes, and raised her arms in embrace of her final act.

Then she took a deep breath and dove, headfirst—face-first—into oblivion.

MICHAEL SHAW SCANNED the news release about a group of disabled veterans opening a new restaurant for no more than three seconds before scrawling *BR* on the top with a red felt pen. The story would be perfect for Barry Rivers's first week on the job—if he was the kind of reporter who wrote off human-interest stuff as fluff beneath their reportorial standards, better to find out about it right now. Dropping the release into his out-box, he picked up the next one from the stack that just seemed to keep on growing, no matter how often he attacked it.

"Michael!"

Tina Wong's voice startled him as much as her sharp rap on the door. How was it possible that a woman who could produce perfectly modulated tones on the air always sounded like fingernails scratching on a chalkboard in real life? And why could she never—not once in the five years she'd worked for him—wait for even an acknowledgment of her presence before wading into his office, let alone an actual invitation? But here she was, already changing the video input on one of his monitors and stuffing a DVD into the player on his credenza.

"The Starbucks manager who was murdered in Encino?" she began. "The kid who opened the store and found the body shot some footage with his cell phone before the cops got there." The screen that normally monitored CNN went blank, and a moment later, shaky, poorly lit images came on the screen: a bathroom mirror, a sink, some stall doors.

Then a woman's body.

She lay sprawled on the floor, her clothes torn away, her torso ripped open from the groin almost to her throat.

The organs that should have been inside her body were now

strewn across the floor around her, black blood pooling on the tiles of the floor and seeping into the grouted cracks between them.

Flies had already found the corpse, and seemed to be creeping everywhere.

The carnage was so complete that there was no way of telling what color the woman's clothes might have been. The camera slowly panned the grisly scene. Whoever took the footage had even knelt down and shot under the wall of one of the stalls. For a moment Michael didn't understand the point of the shot, but a second later saw it. There was an almost shapeless mass of bloody tissue lying near the base of the toilet, which he realized had once been the woman's heart. Then the camera moved in on the young woman's face. Impossibly, it was utterly unblemished, and unmarked by even a single spatter of blood.

"Jesus," Michael Shaw whispered.

"The kid wants ten grand for the footage," Tina Wong said, her voice betraying no emotion in response to the carnage on the television screen.

"Tina, I can't authorize—"

"Of course you can," she cut in. "And you not only can, you *have* to. If we don't buy this, he'll only sell it down the street. And we have"—she glanced her watch—"exactly seven minutes left to make up our minds."

Michael stretched his neck, buying a few seconds.

Did he want Risa to see this?

Worse, did he want Alison to see this?

No way.

"If it bleeds, it leads," Tina said, reading Michael's hesitation and punching the remote control to show the twenty-second clip again. "Who taught me that, Michael?"

He sighed heavily, knowing the decision was already made, but still wishing he could turn his back on the carnage that riveted his eyes to the screen. "I know, I know." He'd taught that phrase himself, not only to Tina, but to every young reporter who came to work for Channel 3.

"Well, this bleeds," Tina said, setting the remote down on his desk. "This bleeds more than anything since Nicole Simpson, and I want it to lead the noon news. In fact, I want to break into regular programming with it in"—she checked her watch again—"ten minutes."

"We're not interrupting programming for a murder in Encino," he said.

"Noon news, then?" Tina countered, and Michael understood too late that her asking him to break into the schedule had been no more than a bargaining ploy.

He leaned back in his chair and looked at her. Tina Wong had already come to the attention of every other station in Los Angeles, as well as the network headquarters in New York, and he'd been told more than once, and in no uncertain terms, to keep her happy. But in the long run he knew there was no way of keeping her happy. She would eventually make a career move, and everyone wanted it to be up the line to national, and not to a competing network.

She was valuable because she knew her stuff, worked eighteen hours a day, and both looked and sounded great on camera. Plus, she had instincts; she knew what made a story and how to present it. And, perhaps most important, she never missed an opportunity to ask the hard questions and keep at them until she got answers.

Yet he still hesitated. Was this the kind of carnage people really needed to see on their lunch break?

"Think of the ratings," Tina said, again reading his mind.

She was right, of course; this would be the footage all the big guns would want to buy from them after their noon broadcast. He'd parlay that ten grand into fifty before the day was out. Bottom line: business was business, whether he wanted Alison to see something like this or not.

"Okay," he said.

Tina Wong put the form, already filled out, on his desk in front of him.

Michael scribbled his signature with the red Sharpie he still held in his hand.

Bloodred, he thought.

Tina snatched the paper off the desk as if he might yet change his mind. "Thanks," she tossed back over her shoulder as she disappeared out the door.

Michael picked up the remote and started the footage one more time, once again unable to turn away from the horror unfolding on the screen. He tried to imagine what kind of nightmares the poor kid who found that mess would have for the rest of his life, but already knew what they would be.

Endless replays of the horror he was watching.

A shiver ran through him as he played the clip yet again.

This was no murder of passion by a jealous lover, and this was no random robbery.

This was something only a monster could have done.

A monster who was on the loose right now somewhere in the vastness of Los Angeles.

Jesus God.

Tina was right. The public had a right to know. This was a big story.

The phone rang. For a moment Michael thought of letting it ring through to voice mail while he watched the footage one more time, but instead he picked up the receiver. "Hello?"

"Hey, sexy."

Michael smiled and relaxed back into his chair. "Hi, yourself."

"I'm thinking we should have a drink after work tonight."

He glanced over at the frozen last frame of carnage on the television screen. "I think I'm going to need more than a drink."

"In that case, how about my place at six-thirty?"

"See you then," Michael said, and replaced the receiver, making a mental note to call Risa and tell her he'd be home late.

4

CONRAD DUNN FINISHED DICTATING THE DAY'S SURGICAL NOTES, then checked his watch. Two-thirty: plenty of time for the afternoon rounds before heading home.

He paged Twyla to let her know he was on his way, then took the stairs down to the second floor of Le Chateau. As usual, the nurse was already waiting for him in front of the Rose Suite, apparently having once more anticipated his page. As he approached, she attempted a dance step the choreographer she'd been named after would have been ashamed of, and handed him Patricia Rothstein's chart.

The kind of routine facelift that kept the place going, but in which he had little interest. Still, Patricia Rothstein had as much right to his full attention as anyone else, so he scanned the chart quickly to make sure nothing negative had happened since he'd seen her early this morning, knocked twice on the door, then opened it and walked in. Patricia Rothstein gazed up at him in obvious misery. Bruised eyes and a shock of dark hair were the only things visible amid the bandages that swathed her head.

"How are you doing today?" Conrad asked, resting a reassuring hand on the woman's shoulder.

Patricia's daughter sat in a chair next to her mother's bed, holding a cup of water with a drinking straw, but the dinner tray was untouched, which didn't surprise him.

"No appetite?" he asked.

"Not kosher," the woman mumbled through swollen lips. "Not Atkins."

Conrad turned to Twyla, who stood just behind him with a clipboard. "Make a note for the kitchen," he said. "Kosher and lean." Then he turned back to his patient. "I'm sorry about the confusion. I'll have a fresh meal brought up right away. How's your pain level, on a scale of one to ten?"

"Twenty," the woman said.

Conrad flipped through the pages on her chart. "Well, we can certainly fix that. And tomorrow we'll get those bandages off your face."

The woman grunted, and he smiled at the daughter, who smiled back.

Next door in the Magnolia Suite, Conrad found Imee Abeya looking far tinier than the average thirteen-year-old in the big hospital bed. The lower half of her face was lost behind massive white bandages, but her mother—not much larger than Imee—smiled and stood as Conrad entered, taking the doctor's hand in both of hers and bowing.

Conrad gently disentangled his hand from Mrs. Abeya's. "How's our patient this afternoon?"

"She good," Imelda Abeya said in her recently acquired and still very uncertain English. "Very good."

"That's what we want to hear." He turned to the girl. "Imee, I'm going to take your bandages off now and we'll see how everything looks, all right?"

The girl nodded, her eyes showing both excitement and fear.

Conrad wheeled over a stool, and as Twyla opened a sterile tray of instruments, he pulled on a pair of surgical gloves. Picking a pair of scissors from the tray, he carefully cut the bandages and gently unwound them. The gauze was stained with a little seepage, but the girl's bleeding had completely stopped, which was unusual for a cleft palette reconstruction.

He gave Mrs. Abeya an encouraging smile and a thumbs-up before proceeding.

The woman only kept chewing nervously on a knuckle.

Very slowly, Conrad unwrapped the gauze, and bared the repaired face of the young Filipina. Imee's lips were still bruised and swollen, and a dark scab covered the stitch line from her nose to her lip, but the wound was healing very well. He peered inside the girl's mouth with a small mirror and even smaller flashlight, then smiled at Imee.

Imee tried to return the smile, wincing when her lips moved.

"Easy," Conrad cautioned, then turned to Imelda Abeya. "Much better."

"Ah! *Sí!*" The woman wiped a tear from her cheek.

"She's beautiful," he said, eyeing Imee appraisingly.

"Beautiful," the girl whispered.

"*Sí,*" the mother said.

"I'm going to rebandage this," Conrad said quietly to Twyla, then went on speaking as he worked. "Keep her on liquids and pain meds for the rest of the night. Tomorrow I'll have her start on a liquid diet, and she can go home the next day, so Sandra can go ahead and get their plane tickets. Make an appointment for her follow-up with Dr. Sabayán in Manila. Fax him and have him bill the foundation. Arrange for the translator to come tomorrow to explain all the post-op instructions to Mrs. Abeya, and make certain she understands that she must send us good, clear photos in three months."

As Twyla finished with her notes there was a soft knock on the door and the office manager stepped into the room. "Dr. Dunn?" she said softly.

"I'm with a patient, Sandra," Conrad said.

The woman bit her lip but didn't move. "You're needed in your office right away."

Conrad Dunn frowned darkly. "I'm with a patient," he repeated.

"I can finish bandaging," Twyla offered.

"I'll do it," Conrad said. Sandra knew as well as the rest of the staff that he was never to be interrupted when he was with a patient. What was she thinking? "Whatever is in my office can wait five minutes." Refusing to be hurried by even so much as a second, he carefully finished the bandaging, then smiled at the young girl and checked her IV drip. Only after a few last words with Imelda Abeya did he finally leave the room and head for his office on the third floor.

Sandra was waiting outside his door, her face pale, her expression strained. "I'm so sorry," she whispered as she held the door open for him to go in.

A man stood looking out the window at the view that swept down from Le Chateau over the hills above Westwood then on to encompass most of the greater Los Angeles basin. The morning haze had cleared, the outline of Catalina Island was barely visible on the horizon.

"May I help you?" Conrad asked.

The man turned around, and it wasn't simply the grim expression on his face that told Conrad Dunn what had happened.

Rather, it was the sight of Ruffles in the man's arms.

"Lieutenant Dickson, Dr. Dunn," the man said. "LAPD."

Conrad felt the blood drain from his face. He knew. Oh God, he knew.

He sank to the edge of the sofa.

The lieutenant set Ruffles on the floor, and the little white dog ran to Conrad and jumped up into his lap, whimpering and licking at his face.

"I'm sorry, Dr. Dunn," the policeman said, "but we found your wife's body on the beach below Vanderlip Park in Palos Verdes." He hesitated, but when Conrad only looked mutely at him, finally spoke again. "She'd called in a report that a locked Lexus with a white dog had been abandoned there. She . . . " His voice trailed off as he drew a cell phone from his pocket.

Margot's cell phone—the one studded with diamonds—that he'd bought her only last month.

"She left a message on this for you," Lieutenant Dickson said.

"Margot," Conrad whispered as a cold numbness began to spread through his body.

"I'm so sorry," the lieutenant murmured, and set the phone down on the corner of the desk.

Starting to tremble, Conrad pressed the little dog to his chest as if to transfer the warmth from its body to his own, barely aware of the voices around him as Sandra spoke with the policeman.

"Margot," he whispered again, grief burning inside him.

Grief, and something else.

"Why did you do it?" he whispered. But of course he already knew why.

Now the guilt began to burn hotter than the grief. He should never have made her go to the banquet last night. She'd told him she wasn't up to it, but he'd insisted. And it had been too much.

It was all his fault. If only he'd begun the repair work on her face . . .

He looked up and saw her, stunning in a red Versace gown on the cover of *Vanity Fair*. He'd had the cover blown up, framed, and hung on his office wall. "How can I go on?" he whispered. "How can I possibly go on without you?"

But the calm beauty on the cover offered him no answers.

ALISON HEARD the garage door rattle open and checked the time. Eleven-thirty, which meant her mother thought she was asleep instead of talking with Cindy on her cell phone about going to a party Friday night. If her dad had seen her light on and told her mother, she could lose the phone for a week. On the other hand, so far her father had either never noticed her light on late or, if he had, hadn't told her mother. And that thought led to another idea.

"My dad's home," she said, "gotta go. But when he comes in to say good-night, I'll ask him about Friday night. That way I can tell my mother that Dad already said yes when I talk to her in the morning."

"Okay," Cindy said.

"I'll call you back."

"Tell me tomorrow," Cindy said. "I'm going to bed."

"Okay." Alison clicked off her cell phone, moved from her bed to her desk—might as well at least *look* like she'd been studying—and waited.

And waited.

As the minutes ticked by and she still didn't hear her father coming up the stairs, she went to the door, opened it, and listened.

Though she couldn't quite make out the words, she heard her mother's voice coming from the kitchen in that low, you-better-understand-what-I'm-saying voice her mother used when she'd done something wrong.

Maybe she'd wait and ask her dad about Friday night in the morning, at breakfast.

But before she closed the door to her room, she heard her mother's voice rise abruptly and a single word resound clearly up the stairwell: *"Lying!"*

She froze.

Lying? Who was lying? What was going on?

She crept to the head of the stairs, where she could hear both of them clearly, then hesitated, wanting to find out what was going on but also to go back to her room, close the door, and pretend nothing was happening.

Knowing she should go back to her room, she sat down instead.

Sat, and listened.

"I CALLED the station, Michael," Risa said, trying hard to control the anger that had been simmering inside her for the last two hours. She didn't want to shout at him, and she certainly didn't want to cry—whatever was going on wouldn't be solved by either of those reactions. "They said you left the office at six." Michael sank onto one of the stools at the breakfast bar, his eyes not quite meeting hers. "So please don't tell me you were at work until eleven. I'm not stupid."

"Of course you're not—"

"And I can smell liquor on your breath, so you've been drinking."

Michael nodded. "I had a couple of drinks," he agreed. "But I'm not drunk—nowhere near."

"So who were you with?" Risa sat on the stool next to him. Before he could reply, she went on. "And please don't tell me it was 'a business associate.' If it was, you'd have said so in the message you left."

Michael looked at his hands. "It's not what you think," he finally said, still failing to meet her eyes.

Risa took a deep breath, forcing herself to keep her voice calm, to betray none of the anger that was rapidly coming to a boil. Of course it was what she thought it was; what else could it possibly be? "For God's sake, Michael," she said when she could trust her voice not to tremble. "We've been married for almost twenty years. We've been best friends—partners!" She took another breath, which escaped in a sigh of defeat only a second or two later. "My mother told me that a woman always knows when her husband is having an affair, and it turns out she was right. I know you're having an affair—I can feel it."

She saw Michael's body tense, but still he said nothing.

She laid a hand on his arm, and at least he didn't pull it away. "Michael, I know our sex life hasn't been everything it could be. And I'm more than willing to take at least some of the responsibility for that." A sob caught in her chest, and she paused before continuing. "For God's sake, Michael, don't just sit there saying nothing at all! At least tell me who she is!"

He finally turned to face her, unconsciously straightening on the stool, and when their eyes at last met for the first time since Michael had come into the house from the garage a few minutes ago, Risa felt a cold terror begin to spread through her body. Her husband betrayed no anger at all, or defensiveness, or anything other than two simple emotions.

Love and sorrow.

Whatever had happened, she knew with absolute certainty that it wasn't just an affair.

"There isn't another woman, Risa," he said softly, taking her hands in his own.

Risa gazed at him in puzzlement. If there wasn't another woman—

The truth came to her just as he spoke the words:

"It's a man."

As she tried to come to grips with what her husband—the man she'd lived with and loved for almost two decades and thought she knew as well as she knew herself—had just told her, the other shoe dropped.

"And we're not having an affair," he went on, his voice quiet but clear. "We've fallen in love."

Tears sprang to Risa's eyes and overflowed her lids. But even as her tears flowed, she realized she had absolutely nothing to say. Of all the things she had imagined over the last couple of weeks, this—*this*—had never even entered her mind.

"I never wanted to hurt you," Michael said, and put one hand on her cheek. His words and his voice were gentle, and his hand felt warm.

She jerked away. The last thing she needed was his affection or—worse—his pity. Not now. The pain of betrayal seared through her guts, and suddenly she could barely breathe.

"I wish it were different," she heard him saying, and now his voice sounded as if it was coming from far away, from a place she already understood she could never go. "I've wished that for years now."

"Years?" she demanded, snatching at the single thing she could grab onto to save herself. Her voice took on a hysterical edge. "You've known for years?"

Michael bit his lips, nodding silently.

"You've been carrying on with another . . . a *man* for years?"

He looked at her as if she'd slapped him. "Of course not!" He tried to take her hands again, but she pulled them away from him. "I still love you, Risa," he said. "I've always loved you, and I always will. Just not . . . " His voice trailed off. "Oh, God, Risa. I'm so sorry."

Sorry. *Sorry!* What the hell did that mean? And yet she could see in his eyes, in his expression and body language, that he was, indeed, sorry.

And all it did was make her feel helpless, more helpless than she'd ever felt before. "What's his name?" she finally asked while she tried to assimilate his words, tried to look back and find clues to this inconceivable news, this unexpected body blow from which she wasn't sure she could ever recover.

"Scott," Michael said. "Scott Lawrence."

"How long?"

"A couple of months. One month, three weeks, and two days, actually."

"Which is almost a week longer than it took you to propose to me," Risa said, making no effort to keep the edge out of her voice anymore. "At least I know you waited to tell me until you were absolutely sure." Finally the sorrow in her husband's eyes was replaced by pain, and she almost detachedly noticed that his pain somewhat assuaged her anger. And knowing that, she realized how much she wanted to inflict the pain and anger within her on him. But if she gave in to it— gave in to her own desires as readily as Michael had obviously given in to his—the fight wouldn't be contained, and it wouldn't hurt only Michael.

Alison was in the house, and if she woke up and heard them fighting and understood what it was about—

"You'd better go," she said, her voice quiet as her eyes instinctively flicked toward the ceiling and Alison's bedroom on the floor above.

Reading her upward glance, Michael nodded. "I'm so sorry," he whispered.

"Me, too," Risa said, her voice cracking. She got off the stool and went into the den, leaving him alone.

A moment later she heard the door from the kitchen to the garage open, and a second later the garage door began grinding upward. As she heard him start his car, then pull out of the garage, close the garage door, and finally drive away from the house they'd shared so long, she pulled a pillow to her stomach, held it close, and began to cry.

All the plans they had for the future began streaming through her mind: seeing Alison off to college, being empty-nesters, and traveling the world. Alison's college graduation, and her marriage, and the birth of their first grandchild. All the future Christmases and Thanksgivings with the family around the table. Growing old together.

She and Michael.

And all of it was gone. All her dreams, everything she had counted on, shattered in a single ten-minute conversation.

As her tears flowed, she thought she could actually hear her heart breaking.

A warm hand rested on her shoulder, and Risa opened her arms to let Alison slip into them, then gently rocked both of them together.

"It'll be all right, Mom," Alison said, and though Risa knew she was trying to be reassuring, her words were belied by the catch in her voice, her red face, and her swollen, streaming eyes.

Risa smoothed Alison's hair away from her warm forehead and brought her back close again.

"I know," she sighed. "It's just that right now, it doesn't feel like it's going to be all right. It doesn't feel like it's ever going to be all right again."

SCOTT LAWRENCE PUNCHED the pillow under his head, rolled over, then gave up trying to go to sleep and clicked the bedroom television on to the news on Channel 3, which he hadn't watched until he met Michael Shaw a little less than three months ago. Now he usually went to sleep with the newscast Michael produced, since he couldn't go to sleep with Michael himself.

Tonight the entire newscast was centered around the murder in Encino, and though every channel was playing it, Michael's network had by far the most graphic—and the most compelling—pictures.

Scott shivered, wondering what the carnage the killer had left meant. Maybe a former boyfriend had killed the woman, but from what he could see in the shaky cell-phone footage Channel 3 played again and again, it looked like the man had to be some kind of nutcase.

Which meant this might only be the first of what was going to be a series of killings, which was exactly the theory that the reporter— a pretty but shrill woman named Tina Wong—was not only promoting, but actually seemed to be hoping for. Freaking ghoul, he thought as he clicked over to Comedy Central.

Just as the channel changed, the doorbell rang.

A chill ran through Scott. Who in the world would be ringing his bell after midnight?

Should he open the door?

He looked again at the television, and thoughts of a homicidal maniac going through the neighborhood with a hunting knife in his hand, ringing doorbells and waiting to see who would be foolish enough to open their door, ran through his mind. "Stop it!" he said out loud, turning the TV off and silently cursing Tina Wong for so successfully spooking him. Nobody was going to come all the way up to the Hollywood Hills to slaughter him.

As the bell rang again, he pulled on his robe, went down the hall and through the living room, then turned on the porch light and peered through the peephole.

Michael Shaw stood on his doorstep.

Scott threw the dead bolt and opened the door, a surge of happiness welling up in him that he didn't try to hide as he grinned at Michael. But as he saw the look on Michael's ashen face, his grin faded. "What is it?" he asked. "What's wrong?"

"I told Risa," Michael said, his voice catching. "She threw me out."

"Oh, Christ," Scott said, pulling the door wide. "You okay?" Michael seemed about to lose his balance, and Scott reached out and took his arm, drawing him in and closing the door behind him. "Stupid thing to say—of course you're not okay. Sit down and I'll get you a drink."

Michael collapsed on the sofa, and Scott poured each of them two fingers of scotch, handed one of the glasses to Michael, then sat down next to him.

Michael drained half his glass, then finally managed a weak smile. "Thanks. You have no idea how much I needed that."

"Actually, I probably do," Scott said. "I went through the same thing fifteen years ago. So, what happened?"

"I hurt her so badly," Michael said, choking as a sob rose in his throat. "And I never meant to—I never wanted to hurt anyone at all."

Scott gave Michael's shoulder a reassuring squeeze. "She was going to find out sooner or later," he said. "Better to get it over with now than drag it out."

Michael nodded. "I guess." He took a deep, ragged breath. "Can I stay here tonight? Tomorrow I'll move into a hotel until I can find a place."

"First you have to tell me why you didn't call before you came over," Scott countered.

Michael turned to look directly at him, hesitated, then blurted, "Because I was afraid you might tell me not to come."

Scott's brows arched. "So at least I know you're not quite as smart as I thought you were, which is good. Puts us on more of an equal footing. And of course tomorrow you can do whatever you like," he went on, "but it sort of seems like moving into a hotel is going to cost you a lot of money you might not be able to afford, at least if Risa turns as mean as my ex did."

"So I can stay until I find a place?" Michael asked, sounding to Scott like a little boy who'd just found a puppy under the Christmas tree.

"Why not just move all your stuff in here?" he said, doing his best not to sound as anxious as he was suddenly feeling. But when Michael turned to face him, the look in the other man's eyes and the tone of his voice told Scott all he needed to know.

"You really mean that?" Michael asked. "I mean, the way I hope you mean it?"

"I would have meant it the day we met if I'd had the guts to say it, but I was sure if I did, it would only scare you off. So, yes—I really mean it now. We're going to end up together anyway." The words seemed to hang in the air for a moment, and then something in Michael's eyes changed.

The love Scott had been certain he saw there only a moment ago had shifted into a look of uncertainty. "Oh, God," he whispered, the happiness draining out of him. "I'm an idiot. What am I pushing you for? Just forget what I said. Do whatever feels right to you. If you don't want to live here, that's fine. We'll find you somewhere else—"

Michael shook his head. "It's not that. It's Alison—" He fell silent. How could he tell Scott what he was thinking as he imagined Risa telling Alison that her father was gay and now living with another man? Would he lose Alison, too? He couldn't! Suddenly he wanted things to be the way they'd been only a few hours ago, when he'd had a family. He *liked* having a daughter, and he liked having a wife. Alison had been the center of his world since the day she was born, and Risa his best friend for more than twenty years.

Except, he realized, that wasn't quite true. If she'd truly been his best friend, wouldn't he have told her the truth about himself years ago? And if she was truly his wife, why hadn't they acted like more than roommates for more than half of those twenty years?

Now he looked at Scott, at the face of a man whom he loved more than he could ever have imagined loving another human being even three months ago. A man who was not Alison, but who had become every bit as important to him as his daughter.

And he knew he couldn't go back to being Risa's husband. He'd gone way past that a long time ago, and there was no turning back, even if he wanted to.

Scott let the silence hold. He knew exactly what Michael was going through, and it was a process Michael had to go through himself. Though he was already certain that, in the long run, Alison would love her father just as much as she ever had, he also knew how hard that idea might be for Michael to accept right now. Scott knew that all he could do was let Michael know that whatever he was going through, he was not alone. "I love you," he finally whispered.

Michael's tortured eyes fixed on him. "It seems like I hurt everyone who loves me."

Scott smiled. "I'm willing to take that risk." He reached over and took Michael's hand. "I know you won't believe me right now, but everything really is going to turn out all right. Risa's not going to kill you, and Alison's not going to hate you, and you and I are going to be just fine."

Michael closed his eyes and felt Scott's warmth next to him. Was it possible? Could he finally live with no more lies, and no more wondering if everyone knew about him? But as he felt Scott's arms slip around him, he suddenly knew as much as he could know, at least right now, that he was with the person he wanted to be with, needed to be with.

"Come on," Scott said, pulling Michael to his feet. "Let's go to bed."

An hour later, with Scott's arms still wrapped around him, Michael fell into the deepest sleep he'd had in years.

He was home.

5

CONRAD DUNN STARED DOWN INTO THE SMASHED FACE OF HIS WIFE, and all the love he'd ever felt for her dissolved into a cold, dark fury.

On purpose. Margot had done this on purpose.

Diving head first onto the rocks below the bluff in Palos Verdes was one thing, but diving *face first* was entirely another.

What Margo had done wasn't simply a matter of killing herself. No, she had taken it much, much further, deliberately destroying the best work he'd ever done.

Sabotage. After all he'd done to make her so beautiful—to turn her face into a work of art—her dying act was to destroy not only herself, but his work—his *brilliant* work—as well.

The last of his grief and his guilt evaporated as he gazed down at the pulpy mess Margot had made of his greatest, most perfect creation, and he had to grip the edges of the stainless-steel table to maintain his balance.

Danielle DeLorian, already wearing a rubber apron, took the dress he'd brought from Margot's closet from his hand before he dropped it, hung it carefully on a hanger the mortuary had provided for that purpose, then stood next to Conrad as he fixated on the ruin that had been his wife.

"She did this on purpose," Conrad breathed, his voice trembling.

"You don't know that," Danielle countered.

"I know," Conrad assured her, his eyes boring deeply into hers. "Believe me, I know."

"Well," Danielle said, looking up at the clock, more to break the lock Conrad held on her gaze than because she needed to know the time, "we have a lot of work to do if you're still going to insist on an open casket."

"Oh, we're having an open casket all right," he said, his voice grim. "I told her I would make her beautiful again, and by God I intend to do it right now."

The act of putting on an apron and a pair of rubber gloves gave Conrad a moment to reject his rage and put both his brain and his emotions into professional mode. This was a reconstruction job, nothing more. He'd been doing those all his life, and as he looked down at the wreckage that lay on the table, he knew exactly what needed to be done to repair it.

All of it.

He gripped the chin and moved the head back and forth.

The head, not *her* head.

"Fortunately, most of the damage was done to the right side," he said. Much of the scarred skin was missing, along with the underlying tissue. Bones had shattered, and what skin was left had blackened at the edges.

The eyeball was missing.

He turned the head and probed with practiced fingers. "On the left, it's mostly abrasions and contusions." His fingers probed further. "There's an orbital fracture here, but that's relatively simple."

"Perhaps there's a way to orient her in the coffin so her good side—" Danielle began as she tested the iron in preparation for curling Margot's newly washed hair into gentle waves.

"When I'm finished," Conrad cut in, "there won't be a good side. There will be two perfect sides."

He set to work, first filling Margot's mouth with cotton, so her cheeks wouldn't appear so sunken, then doing the same with the empty eye socket. The lids would be closed anyway, so there was no need to replace the eyeball itself. Next he trimmed off the black, curling edges of skin with a pair of surgical scissors and began cutting away the mess of crushed flesh and shattered bone beneath. When the last of the debris had been cleared away, he picked up a jar of putty from the tray of instruments and began to sculpt one half of Margot's face.

"Be careful not to tug," he warned Danielle as he smoothed putty around the cotton-stuffed eye socket.

She nodded silently and continued working as efficiently and expertly as Conrad himself, laying the flowing waves of hair around Margot's head so they would neither be soiled by his work nor be in his way. Only when the face was finished would she finally lay the hair over Margot's shoulders.

Two hours later the reconstruction was finished. Conrad stood back, regarding his work with the detachment of the complete professional. The face looked smooth and blank, like a freshly fired ceramic doll's head.

Danielle opened her cosmetics case and laid everything out on a tray. "Go get a cup of coffee or something, Conrad," she said, looking up at the big clock on the wall. "Or lie down for a while. You're exhausted."

"Not until she's perfect," he replied.

With an expertise in her own field that was equal to Conrad's in his, Danielle began applying makeup to the colorless putty from which he had rebuilt Margot's face, and as Conrad watched, his wife slowly began to emerge from the blank, expressionless facade he had created.

He could no longer pretend that this was just another head, just another face.

This was Margot, the love of his life, dead and lying on a slab.

"Conrad?"

He tore his eyes away from his beautiful wife and looked up at Danielle. Perspiration dotted her forehead.

"Are you all right?"

"Yes," he said, his eyes drifting back to Margot's face.

"We need to dress her."

Conrad stripped the plastic off Margot's favorite dress, a burgundy Versace. He had also brought black lace Oscar de la Renta lingerie; Margot would be as perfectly dressed in death as she had always been in life.

As Danielle carefully peeled away the sheet that covered Margot's body, Alston Bedwell, the funeral director, pushed the mahogany coffin through a set of big doors and into the cool preparation room where they had been working.

Conrad pulled the sheet back up to cover his wife's nakedness as Bedwell wheeled the coffin next to the table where she lay. The funeral director stopped short when he caught sight of the classic beauty of Margot Dunn, lying in graceful repose as if ready for a photo shoot.

"Oh, my," he said. "You've done an extraordinary job. She looks . . ." He paused, searching for the right word, but only one would do. "She looks alive," he finished.

Conrad's gaze shifted from Margot to Bedwell. "For me, she'll always be alive," he said softly.

The funeral director stepped forward and laid a professionally gentle hand on the grieving man's shoulder. "We need to take her upstairs now."

"Conrad?" Danielle said.

Reluctantly, Conrad drew the sheet back, and the three of them began to dress Margot Dunn.

Twenty minutes later they were finished and Margot looked utterly flawless.

Danielle flicked her blush brush over Margot's décolletage one last time and smiled gently at Conrad. "She's ready to meet her guests."

Conrad's heart ached as he gazed at the face of the woman he had vowed to love until death. But it wasn't long enough—he would love her far beyond something so fleeting as death. "You see?" he whispered to her. "I've made you perfect again. You should have trusted me. You should have waited for me."

But she hadn't waited, and now he had to figure out what to do with the rest of his life.

RISA SHAW PULLED a simple black crepe dress from the back of her closet and carefully examined it for spots or other flaws. "I guess I should have sent this to the cleaner's after the party at the Wilmingtons'," she muttered ruefully, more to herself than to Alison, who idly sprawled on her mother's bed.

"It looks okay from here," Alison said.

Risa picked a bit of lint from the hem and turned it around. "Well, it's going to have to do." She held it up and looked at herself in the full-length mirror. "It'll pass," she decided, rehung the dress on the hanger, and started rummaging through her lingerie drawer. "What are you doing this afternoon?"

Alison hesitated. "Dad's picking me up," she said. "We're just gonna hang out."

Risa froze as cold fury rose inside her, but she bit back the angry words that came to her lips. Though the wound Michael had inflicted on her still oozed bitter anger, she had decided that no matter how she felt, she wouldn't let her anger or her pain drive a wedge between Alison and her father. What had happened was between them, and Alison had no part in it at all.

She found the bra and panties she was looking for but kept rummaging anyway, buying time while deciding how to respond to her daughter. Alison had a perfect right to spend time with her father. She wasn't about to deny that, and she certainly wasn't going to be jealous about it. *Be casual,* she told herself. *Don't say anything you'll wish you hadn't.* "Going to a movie?" she finally ventured, struggling to sound as if nothing was wrong.

"I'm not sure. . ." Alison said in a tone that told Risa she *was* sure, and whatever they were doing, they wouldn't be going to a movie.

Risa turned and looked straight at her daughter. "You're going to his place?"

The stricken look on Alison's face gave it away so quickly it was almost comical. Alison had never been able to lie, and obviously still couldn't. "I didn't want you to feel bad," she said, her voice quavering and her eyes glistening with tears. "Dad—well, Dad wants me to meet Scott."

Scott. So there it was. Every instinct in Risa wanted to scream at her daughter, to demand that she refuse to be a party to Michael's betrayal of her. But even as the words rose in Risa's throat, she pushed them away, reminding herself once more what she already knew to be true: that Michael hadn't betrayed her at all. Falling in love with another woman would have been a betrayal. But it hadn't been another woman. It was something Michael had been struggling with for years, and she knew, in her heart, that it was something he could in the end do nothing about. Indeed, if he'd told her he was gay before they'd married, they would still have been friends.

Good friends.

And she'd believed him when he said he hadn't known he was gay all those years ago.

She'd seen the genuine torment in his eyes when he told her the other night what had been going on. It wasn't torment for having been caught, but at the pain the truth was causing her.

The pain she was still feeling.

Now, as she saw the pain her daughter was suffering just at the thought of hurting one parent by seeing the other, Risa decided that she and Michael had borne enough pain for all of them, and that whatever happened, she wasn't going to put any of hers onto Alison. Not onto Alison, and not onto Michael either. "Of course he wants you to meet Scott," she said. "He wants to share his life with you, and he always will." A tiny tear dropped off Alison's lower lid and landed on her cheek. Risa sat on the edge of the bed and wiped it away. "He loves you, honey. Nothing will ever change that. Nothing."

Alison nodded and brushed tears from her eyes with both hands. "So you won't be mad at me?"

Risa thought quickly, wondering how many hurdles she could make it over in one day. The one she'd just jumped had seemed far too high a few moments ago, but she'd made it. And felt exhausted.

She slipped her arm around Alison's shoulders. "Honey, I'm going to ask you for a huge favor."

Alison tensed. "What kind of favor?"

"I'm wondering if it would be too much to ask you to let me meet Scott first. That way, I'll at least know who you're spending time with."

Alison frowned. "You don't trust Dad?"

"Of course I trust him," Risa hurriedly assured her. "But you have two parents for a reason, because parents balance each other out. Would it be a terrible thing for you to go with me this afternoon and meet Scott another time?"

Alison shifted away from her mother. "I never even met Margot Dunn. Why would I want to go to her funeral?"

"Well, she was an international supermodel, and there will probably be lots of famous people there."

Alison looked more interested, but not much. "Like who?"

"How would I know?" Risa countered, frantically searching for the name of someone, anyone, who would not only interest Alison, but be likely to show up at the funeral. "Probably some movie stars," she finally ventured, hoping it might be enough.

"Really?"

Risa shrugged casually, then stood up and went back to her lingerie drawer. Pulling out the underwear she'd already chosen, she laid it out on the bed.

"Yeah, but a *funeral*?" Alison said, still obviously unconvinced.

Risa decided to lay her cards on the table and trust her daughter. "I have to go because Conrad Dunn is a client and a friend, and he needs all the support he can get right now. And I gotta tell you, hon, right now I could use some support, too." As Alison wavered, she played her last card: "Please? For me?"

Her daughter hesitated, then uttered the words that told Risa she'd given in: "What am I supposed to wear?"

"You have that black skirt you wore when you sang in the Christmas chorale. Just wear that with a simple white blouse."

Alison shrugged. "Okay. I'll call Dad and tell him I'll meet Scott sometime next week." She eyed Risa, waiting for an answer. "Okay?" she pressed. "Next week?"

"Next week," Risa promised. "We'll make it happen, okay? Now jump in the shower. Lexie will be here to pick us up in an hour."

"I have to call Dad first."

"I'll call him," Risa said. "I'll explain everything. He'll understand."

"Okay," Alison said, but made no move to get up.

Risa waited.

"Are you and Dad going to fight?" Alison finally asked. "Are you going to hate Scott no matter what he's like?" Another tear rolled out of the corner of her eye, trailing toward her ear.

"No, honey." Risa said. "We are not going to fight. Your father doesn't want to fight, and neither do I."

"But it seems so weird, Dad living somewhere else, and with a guy." Alison took a deep, quivering breath.

"I know, sweetheart, but it will be all right. Trust me. It's going to be hard for a while, for all of us, but we'll get through it. And we'll get through it without fighting, okay? I can't say I'm happy about all this, but I know there's nothing I can do to change the way people are. Your father is who he is, and I'll just have to get used to it. I'll do my best not to get angry, but if I ever do—and I probably will—you'll just have to forgive me, okay?"

Alison nodded. "Life is weird," she finally said.

"Indeed it is," Risa agreed. She hugged her daughter and silently vowed to keep the peace with Michael and Scott.

No matter what.

THE DOORBELL RANG just as Scott poured himself and Michael a second cup of coffee, the remains of a Belgian waffle feast still on the dining room table. As the bell rang again, Scott sighed in resignation. "There goes our lazy Saturday morning."

"Not necessarily," Michael replied. "Maybe it's just the postman. Isn't he the one who always rings twice?"

Abandoning the coffee, Scott headed for the front door. "Mine never rings at all—he just leaves things on the porch and hopes for the best."

He opened the door to find Tina Wong hovering impatiently, her finger poised to press the bell a third time. She spotted Michael sitting at the table in the dining room, and ignoring Scott, walked right in, brushing past him as if he didn't exist. "You turned your phone off," she said accusingly.

"It's Saturday," Michael said. "And good morning to you, too."

Scott shot a questioning look at Michael. "Shall I offer her a cup of coffee?"

Tina didn't wait for Michael to respond, and either didn't catch his sarcastic tone or chose to ignore it. "Black, with one sugar." She turned to eye Scott as if he were a recalcitrant waiter. "Not Splenda, or Equal, or any of that crap. Sugar." Then she set her briefcase on the dining room table, snapped open the locks, and sat down next to Michael. "I've got a lot of stuff on the Caroline Fisher murder."

Michael shrugged a helpless apology to Scott as Tina pulled a folder from her briefcase and opened it. She spread the contents out on the table as Scott disappeared into the kitchen.

"Not only was she mutilated," she said, "but the killer stole parts of her." She spread out five eight-by-ten photos.

Michael was still looking at the pictures a minute later when Scott reappeared and set a mug of coffee in front of Tina. "Jesus," Scott breathed as his eyes fell on the images, "isn't it a little early in the morning for that kind of stuff?" He touched Michael's shoulder. "How about I leave you two to your business? I'll be out by the pool."

"The killer not only mutilated with apparent glee," Tina said as soon as Scott was out of earshot, "but took the breasts, vagina, and—get this—glands."

Scott quickened his step, disappeared into the kitchen, and closed the door behind him.

"Glands?" Michael repeated hollowly.

"Glands. Both adrenals and the thymus."

Michael sat back. "Okay, I'll grant you that's pretty weird. But how does it merit interrupting my Saturday?"

"Because," Tina said, riveting him with her trademark piercing stare, "this is not the first time that glands have been taken from a murder victim." She handed him two faxed autopsy reports. "San Diego, and San Jose, one week apart, fifteen years ago. And now again, Caroline Fisher in Encino."

"Fifteen *years,* Tina?" Michael said, handing her back the pages without so much as a glance. "That's a long time. It doesn't mean anything."

"Wrong!" Tina declared, pushing the papers back at him. "We've got a serial killer here, Michael. Right now we're ahead of the other stations, and I don't even think the cops have put it together yet. But they will." She leaned toward him, a posture he'd seen her use during many an effective interview. "Before they figure it out, I want to run a special that will blow the roof off our ratings."

Michael shook his head. "Two murders fifteen years ago is no longer news," he said.

But Tina wasn't about to be put off that easily. "I'm telling you, Michael—there's a monster out there. And right now I'm the only one who knows this isn't his first kill. The murderer, me, and now you—we're the only ones who know."

"Then shouldn't you be taking this to the police?"

"Oh, I will," she said. "I'll go to the police with the tape of my special precisely one hour before we air it."

Michael leaned back in his chair and gazed at Tina speculatively. "Are those other two murders still unsolved?"

"Yes!" Tina leaned even farther forward, sensing impending victory.

"Do you have crime scene photos?"

Tina nodded.

"Is the M.O. the same?"

Tina hesitated. "I don't know yet. I'll have to go to San Diego and San Jose to find all that out. That's why I need a budget."

Michael sighed, sagging like a tire losing its air. "Sorry. The whole thing's way too weak. I can't authorize a budget for something that goes back fifteen years without any kind of connection at all."

"Women murdered *for their glands,* Michael," Tina said, leaning in again. "This is going to be big. This isn't just going to be news—this is going to be a book and a movie, and the whole ball of wax. And I want it."

"You can want it all you want, Tina," Michael said, unimpressed by her theatrics. "Maybe there is a book, and a movie, and a ball of wax—whatever that is—but at least for now, it's not a news special. Not in a newsroom I'm running."

"You're going to regret it. I'm telling you."

He smiled thinly. "I've regretted decisions before, and I'm sure I will again. But for the moment, I don't think this will be one of them."

"What will it take to convince you?" Tina put her files back into her briefcase.

"One more body," Michael said. "More recent than fifteen years ago, and the same M.O. If you can give me one more body, and prove that the M.O. on all four is the same, I'll get you a budget and you can have your special."

"One more body." She nodded. "If it's out there, I'll find it." She stood up and grabbed her briefcase, her coffee still untouched.

He followed her to the door and opened it.

"I'll find it, Michael."

"I have no doubt," he said, then watched her walk across the porch and down to her car, parked next to a fire hydrant in front of the house.

He knew that if there was another body out there, Tina would find it, even if she had to make it herself.

He closed the door and went to find Scott.

They had a leisurely Saturday morning to resume.

6

ALISON HAD NO IDEA HOW MANY TIMES SHE MUST HAVE PASSED THE old mission-style church at the corner of Bedford and Santa Monica Boulevard, but as her mother searched for a parking spot, she found herself looking at it as if for the first time. Gazing up at the twin towers that flanked the main sanctuary, and the three crosses that surmounted the entire structure, she wished she weren't coming here for a funeral. The whole idea of someone's body lying in a coffin for everyone to stare at made her skin crawl, and for a moment she wished she'd found a way to beg off. But when she saw two familiar faces in the crowd moving up the steps and through the doors—two faces she'd seen just last week in a movie—her misgivings vanished.

By the time they got inside the church itself, it was almost overflowing, not only with people, but with more flowers than Alison would have thought the place could hold. Perfect arrangements filled tier after tier behind the altar, and were banked around the casket as well, and whoever had arranged them had managed to combine the rainbow of colors into gentle waves that seemed to cradle the coffin and the beautiful woman who lay inside it, her head resting on a satin pillow that raised her face high enough to be clearly visible even from the back of the church.

Even though they were half an hour early for the service, the only space they could find was on a pew way in the back. As she waited for the service to begin, Alison scanned the congregation, searching for more familiar faces. And just as her mother had promised, they were everywhere, some of them so close that she could have reached out and touched them.

Finally the service began, and as the music swelled, Alison tried to prepare herself for a long, dull hour or two. But it didn't happen. Instead, two people talked about Margot Dunn for no more than ten minutes each, the priest recited a mass for the dead, and then a woman who looked vaguely familiar sang, "You Are So Beautiful." When the priest finished the final prayer, a classical guitarist began to play softly, and everyone stood up. But instead of leaving the church, Alison followed her mother and Lexie Montrose down the aisle to file past the coffin in which Margot Dunn lay, her beauty on display for the last time.

"I heard that Danielle DeLorian herself did Margot's makeup," Lexie whispered to Alison as they slowly made their way toward the front of the church. Alison stared at Lexie. How was that possible? The head of DeLorian cosmetics herself? Doing a dead person's makeup? Alison shuddered, just imagining someone putting makeup on a corpse. Yet when she finally reached the casket and got a clear view of Margot Dunn's face, she could barely believe what she was seeing. The woman looked as if she had merely fallen asleep on her white satin pillow while reading or watching television in bed.

Everything about Margot Dunn's face was flawless, and appeared so lifelike that for a moment Alison couldn't believe she was dead at all. She found herself looking for a flutter of eyelashes, for the rise and fall of the woman's chest as she took a breath.

But there was nothing. No movement at all.

Yet the face was perfect. There was no mark, no scar, not even any discoloration—no evidence that she had fallen onto the rocks last week, or that a propeller had gouged chunks of flesh from her right cheek a year ago. It was as if they were about to bury someone who was still alive, and Alison stood rooted to the spot until she felt a tug from her mother to move along.

For the five minutes it took to walk the four blocks to the reception at the Beverly Hilton Hotel, she couldn't get the vision of Margot Dunn's body out of her head, and was certain that from now on her face would haunt her dreams. Even now, in broad daylight, she could imagine the woman waking up in her coffin, desperate, gasping for air, screaming for help and clawing at the satin lining of her coffin with her perfectly manicured fingernails. Alison shivered yet again, and once more wished she hadn't agreed to come along.

Following the crowd moving through the hotel, they made their way to the International Terrace, where servers wearing white shirts and black bow ties strolled by with trays of hors d'oeuvres and glasses of champagne, as if it were a wedding instead of a funeral.

At least a dozen poster-sized photographs of Margot stood on easels that dotted the perimeter of the ballroom. Wherever Alison looked, the image of the woman in the coffin gazed back at her, and it occurred to her that Margot Dunn had looked as perfect in her coffin as she did in all these pictures. She tried to pay attention as her mother introduced her to people, but her eyes kept straying toward the photographs, particularly one near the bar. Finally, she went over to get a closer look. It was a larger-than-life black-and-white photograph of Margot looking directly at the camera, chin on her hands.

But she wasn't just looking directly into the camera. Margot was also looking directly into her eyes.

Alison stood as if transfixed, gazing at the clear eyes, perfect skin, exquisite features, and thick, luxurious hair. How was it possible that someone could ever have been this beautiful? Or that anyone this beautiful could have been so unhappy over *anything* that she killed herself?

She was still staring at the photograph when she sensed someone standing beside her. "Magnificent, wasn't she?" Lexie Montrose said.

An unexpected sadness flowed through Alison. "Why would she kill herself?"

Lexie squeezed her shoulder. "She was afraid she was never going to look like that again, sweetheart. When she first got here, Margot couldn't even get an agent. Then she met Conrad, and the rest was— shall we say—the stuff of plastic-surgery legend."

Alison finally tore her eyes away from the photograph. "Where's Mom?"

"Waiting in the reception line to meet Conrad and his sister. C'mon."

With one more glance at the photograph, Alison followed Lexie back to the other side of the terrace, where the crowd had gathered, and wished she didn't have to stay to meet Conrad Dunn or anyone else.

All she wanted to do was go home.

RISA HAD a moment of déjà vu when she approached Conrad Dunn, who stood with his sister Corinne, quietly receiving the murmured condolences of his guests. Was it possible that it hadn't even been a week since she had stood in line to greet him in a different hotel at the Dunn Foundation banquet with his wife at his side instead of his sister?

"Risa!" A wan Conrad took her hand warmly and kissed her cheek. "So good of you to come."

"I'm so terribly sorry about Margot," Risa said.

He nodded. "Thank you."

"You remember Lexie Montrose, don't you?"

"Of course." Conrad nodded to Lexie, then his eyes shifted to Alison. "And who is this?"

"My daughter, Alison. Alison, this is Conrad Dunn."

Conrad took Alison's hand. "I'm very pleased to meet you."

"It—It's nice to meet you, too," Alison stammered, instantly certain she'd said the wrong thing, but having no idea what the right thing might have been. She felt herself blushing, then breaking into a cold sweat of embarrassment.

"Is your husband here?" Conrad asked Risa.

Now it was Risa who blushed. "I'm afraid not," she began. "We're—well, we—"

"They're separated," Lexie Montrose said softly when it became clear that Risa was just going to go on stumbling.

"Oh," Conrad said, his voice shifting from the impersonal tone of social platitudes to something much warmer. "I'm so sorry. I hope it won't be permanent."

Risa bit her lip. What was she supposed to say? But again—and to her own further mortification—Lexie jumped in again.

"It will be," Lexie said. "Some things can't be fixed."

Risa felt her embarrassment deepen, but this time it was Conrad Dunn himself who stepped in to rescue her.

"Then we're all in mourning today," he said softly, and turned to Alison. "I'm so sorry—it has to be hard for you." His gaze shifted back to Risa and he put a hand on her shoulder. "If there's anything I can do, please call."

"I'll be fine, Conrad," Risa said. "And today we're here for you."

Conrad smiled at her, and then his tired eyes moved on to the next guest in line.

"YOU CERTAINLY SHARED a lot of personal information that wasn't necessarily yours to share," Risa said as the three of them walked the few blocks back to her car.

"Hey," Lexie said, dismissing her words with a wave of her black-gloved hand. "He's single now, and so are you, and in Beverly Hills there is no such thing as a decent interval."

"As I recall," Risa said coolly, "last week *you* were the one who talked about getting divorced the minute Conrad was 'back on the market,' as you so graciously put it."

"And I could be," Lexie said, refusing to rise to Risa's bait. "But he doesn't have eyes for me." She paused to let the meaning of her words strike home. "I think you should call him, just like he said."

"Are you kidding?" Alison demanded. "He's creepy—the whole thing was creepy. What they did to his wife's face—I mean, it was like they were trying to make her look like she was still alive! And all those photographs! She was beautiful, but it was all fake, like you said, Lexie. She didn't look like that at all until she met him!"

"Oh, sweetie," Risa said. "He's not creepy. He's just a plastic surgeon, and fixing faces is what they do. And Conrad is not only a very good plastic surgeon, but a very good man as well."

"Maybe so, but you still don't need to call him," Alison replied.

"Okay," Risa said, giving her daughter's shoulder a squeeze. At this point, she knew there wasn't a man anywhere that Alison wouldn't resent, but if Lexie was right, she wouldn't have to call Conrad Dunn. If Conrad wanted to get in touch with her, he already knew her number.

If Lexie was right.

But of course she couldn't be, given that Conrad Dunn wasn't even over the shock of his wife's death yet, and wouldn't be for many weeks to come. Still, just the thought of hearing his voice on the other end of the telephone gave her more pleasure than she'd felt since the night Michael had moved out.

Perhaps, after all, there would be life after her divorce was final.

Part Two

NEW
BEGINNINGS

7

One Year Later

ALISON SHAW PUT HER LUNCH TRAY DOWN ON THE TABLE IN HER usual place—a place that hadn't changed by even a single chair since last year—but glared at Cindy Kearns before sitting down. "I don't even know why I'm sitting here," she said, picking up a fork and jabbing angrily at the limp lettuce that was supposed to be a "garden-fresh salad."

"You mad at me?" Cindy asked, a tiny forkful of macaroni and cheese pausing halfway to her mouth.

"That was a private message," Alison said coldly. "It was personal, and now the whole school knows."

"Knows what?" Anton Hoyer asked around a mouthful of his hamburger.

Alison threw a "don't you dare" look at Cindy.

Cindy blithely ignored the look. "Alison's mom is marrying Dr. Conrad Dunn," she said.

"Who?" Anton asked, looking blankly from Cindy to Alison. "Am I supposed to know who that is?"

Cindy rolled her eyes. "He's only like the most famous plastic surgeon in the world," she declared. "Don't you know anything?"

Anton ignored her tone. "So her mom's marrying a doc. So what?"

"So she's moving to Bel Air and she's transferring to Wilson Academy."

Anton's eyes widened. "Wilson? That's a great school. You can go anywhere from there. Harvard, Yale—you can practically pick it!"

"That's not the point," Alison said. "I like it *here*."

"UCLA is, like, four miles from my house," Lisa Hess, the fourth of their lunch table regulars, chimed in. "And most of Bel Air's even closer. Your new stepdad will probably buy you a car for your sixteenth birthday and you can come visit us. It's no big deal."

Cindy sipped a Diet Coke through a straw. "A car," she sighed. "In what, two months?"

"Plus which," Lisa went on, leaning across the table and dropping her voice so no one but her three friends would hear, "you can get as much plastic surgery as you want—for free!"

Alison could barely believe her ears. She was being dragged out of school in their sophomore year, moved out of Santa Monica, and getting stuck with a stepfather she didn't even like, and all they could talk about was colleges, cars, and plastic surgery? "I don't *want* any plastic surgery," she snapped back at Lisa, "and I don't care where I go to college, and I don't like Conrad Dunn."

A momentary silence dropped over the table at Alison's outburst. Then Anton grinned mischievously. "You'll all please note for the record that she didn't say anything at all about the car."

"And I don't want a car," Alison added, but felt a blush giving her away.

"See?" Anton said. "She's turning the same color red her new Porsche will probably be."

In spite of herself, Alison giggled. "I hate red," she said. "If I get one, I want white. And not a Posrche. Maybe one of those little Lexuses."

"Well, at least we know she can be bought," Lisa said. "And stop worrying about the guy your mom's marrying. Nobody likes their stepparents at first. Give the guy a chance—he didn't do anything wrong."

Alison shook her head. "It's not that. There's just something about him."

"Oh, come on," Cindy said. "I've had two stepdads, and at first I really hated the newest one. But he turned out to be pretty cool—in some ways he's even better than my real dad."

"*Nobody's* better than my dad!" Alison snapped.

Cindy pulled back in exaggerated alarm. "Jeez! Nobody said anything about your dad."

"And it's not going to be all that bad," Lisa put in, realizing just how upset Alison was. "You can have a big sixteenth birthday party and introduce us to all those Wilson Academy guys. And you can take us all for a ride in your new car."

"After you introduce *me* to all those hot Wilson Academy *girls,*" Anton countered.

Alison shook her head. "But I like our house in Santa Monica, and I like going to school here, and I don't want to move." She sighed heavily. "I just don't want things to change."

"No," Cindy said, her voice turning dead serious. "What you really want is for your parents to get back together, but that's not going to happen."

Alison knew Cindy was right, but she also knew she wasn't ready to accept that fact.

"Your dad's happy," Cindy continued. "And even if he weren't, he wouldn't be going back to your mom. He'd find another guy. So don't you think your mom should be happy, too? In two years you'll be going to college somewhere. What's she supposed to do? Just sit around by herself, having passed up true love with the most famous plastic surgeon in the western world just because you didn't want to move five miles? Grow up, girl—it's not like it's the end of the world.

It's not even like you're going to Kansas or something. It's Bel Air, for God's sake! If you want to stay here so bad, I'll tell you what—we'll just swap places, and you can live in my room and walk to school and I'll move to Bel Air and go to Wilson and drive the car over to see you every single weekend. How's that?"

The way Cindy put it made Alison feel like a complete idiot. "I'm being a real jerk, aren't I?" she asked, half hoping nobody would answer, but knowing that Cindy, at least, would. But instead it was Lisa who spoke.

"Only about half a jerk, and so what? If it was Cindy, she wouldn't want to move, either. As for me, I'm looking on the bright side—maybe you can get me a discount on some new boobs." She pulled her sweater tight and looked dolefully down at her flat chest. "And God knows Anton here could use a nose job."

"And Mr. Dryer could use a chin," Anton whispered as their history teacher walked by.

"And Mrs. Hoffman!" Cindy put in. The principal's baggy eyes, double chin, and sagging jowls were legendary enough that behind her back everybody called her the shar-pei. Even Alison started giggling.

"See what good you could do in the world?" Anton asked.

"Oh, all right," Alison said to Cindy. "Maybe I have been a jerk. But you still shouldn't have blabbed."

"I'm sorry," Cindy said. "I didn't think it was such a big deal, since everybody was going to know sooner or later."

The bell rang and everybody grabbed their lunch trays, shoved them onto the racks, and headed to their next class.

Everybody except Alison.

She sat for a moment longer, considering everything that had been said.

Her parents really were not getting back together.

Bel Air really was only a short drive away.

Her mother did deserve to be as happy as her father was with Scott.

And while it was still true that she didn't like Conrad Dunn anywhere near as much as she liked Scott Lawrence, so what? Lisa was right: in two years she'd be off at college anyway.

So maybe, after all, it was no big deal.

And one thing was for certain: nobody liked a crybaby or a whiner, and she wasn't about to turn into one.

Alison took a deep breath and decided that, all things considered, she was pretty lucky.

Things could be a lot worse.

RISA SHAW TURNED slowly in front of the three full-length mirrors, admiring the fit of the pale yellow silk suit from every possible angle.

"That is perfect," Lexie Montrose declared, echoing Risa's own unspoken verdict on the outfit. "Buy it."

Yet Risa still cocked her head and looked again. Even though the suit was, indeed, perfect for her going-away outfit after the wedding reception, its price tag still gave her pause. "I don't know."

"Of course you do," Lexie urged. "Buy it and let's go have lunch."

The saleswoman smiled at her as she rehung Risa's rejected dresses. "You look beautiful."

"And looking beautiful is getting to be very expensive," Risa said. "Given that this is the second time around for both of us, I think we should be a little more conservative."

"It's a suit!" Lexie said. "What's more conservative than that? You'll wear it a thousand times."

"I was talking about a more conservative *budget*," Risa said. "The wedding dress costs as much as Alison's first year of college tuition will." She took another turn in front of the mirror. "Still, I love it."

"Then buy it," Lexie decreed. "It's not like you're broke—you're a Realtor, for God's sake! One commission and you'll pay for the whole wedding ten times over. Except that Conrad's paying, remember?"

Risa sighed, knowing that arguing with Lexie was useless, especially when both of them knew Lexie was right. Besides, the suit needed no alterations at all, which Risa decided was a sure sign she was meant to have it. She nodded at the saleswoman. "Okay, I'll take it. Can I pick it up on our way back from lunch?"

Lexie jumped up from where she'd been sitting. "Perfect timing," she said, glancing at her watch. "I made reservations for us at The Grill."

RISA PICKED at her small salad, the only entrée she could allow herself if she wasn't going to gain any weight between now and the wedding. "I'm going to have to do an hour on the treadmill just for this," she said, glowering at Lexie's lean body, into which a dozen escargots were fast disappearing. "I can't afford to gain even an ounce and still fit into that slinky wedding dress."

"It's worth it," Lexie said, blithely downing another snail dripping with garlic and butter. "The dress is a stunner and you look fabulous in it. Makes me want to get married again."

Risa set down her fork and sipped her iced tea. "What I really want," she said slowly, "is to know for certain that I'm doing the right thing. It's barely been a year since Michael moved out and Margot died. What if Conrad and I are really only on the rebound? What if this is all a terrible mistake?"

"Don't be silly," Lexie said, airily waving her fork and splattering butter on the tablecloth. "You're way past the puppy love stage. You know what's real and what's not. Michael's happy with Scott, and you and Conrad have found each other. You should be counting your blessings instead of wondering what may or may not go wrong in the future."

"It's not just me," Risa sighed. "It's Alison, too. Saying she's not happy about the marriage is an understatement."

"Alison will come around," Lexie assured her. "You'll see. Conrad will make a fabulous stepfather."

"Maybe so, but even after almost a year, she still doesn't like him. What if she never warms up to him?"

Lexie finally put her fork down and leaned forward, both her voice and her expression turning serious. "Take it from one whose been there a few times, Risa. Kids can take a long time to get over a divorce. Alison might be refusing to meet Conrad halfway just because she thinks it would be disloyal to Michael, or because she thinks if you don't marry Conrad, you and Michael will get back together again. But she'll come around. Besides," she added pointedly, "Alison will be off to college in two years, making her own life. Are you willing to give Conrad up for two years with your daughter, and then a lot more all by yourself?"

Risa frowned, still unconvinced.

"Okay, then try this," Lexie went on, leaning back and picking up her fork to stab the last escargot. "Ask Michael to talk to her. You two are still on good terms, right?"

Finally Risa smiled. " 'Good terms' doesn't quite do it justice. Who'd have thought he'd turn out to be my best friend? Best *male* friend," she quickly added as Lexie started to put a hugely hurt look on her face.

"Thank you," Lexie said. "I'd have hated having to sling a snail at you right here in public."

"But you'd have done it," Risa archly observed. "Anyway, it's weird how once I realized that Michael's leaving truly didn't have any-thing more to do with me than the fact that I'm a woman, I stopped being mad at him. And it's impossible *not* to like Scott—if he was straight, I might have fallen for him myself." She paused. "If I hadn't been married to Michael, of course."

"All right, all right, I get it," Lexie interrupted. Not being on speaking terms with any of her own ex-husbands, she wasn't about to listen to Risa extolling the virtues of the man she'd divorced less than a year ago. "So Michael's a saint, and Scott's a regular Mother Teresa. Between the two of them, they ought to be able to set Alison straight, you should pardon the pun. And for God's sake, eat something. After the wedding, Conrad can give you back the perfect figure with a little liposuction." She raised an envious eyebrow. "You've got it made, girl."

Risa finally smiled. Her head had been clogged with wedding plans since the night Conrad proposed over dinner at Spago, presenting her with an emerald-cut diamond, and since then the only problem had been Alison's dark disapproval of what she'd decided to do. But maybe Lexie was right—maybe she should have Michael talk to her. At least it was worth a shot.

"So what's in your bouquet?" Lexie asked, determinedly changing the subject from Alison back to the wedding plans.

"Don't know," Risa said, her smile spreading into a grin. "Henrik is going to surprise me."

"You trust a wedding planner to make that decision on his own?"

"I do," Risa said. "He found the designer and dressmaker for me, and you should see what she's sketched for Alison. And every time I think up something to worry about, Henrik has already taken care of it."

"Okay, that's it," Lexie said, wiping the last of the butter from her lips. "I'm divorcing Dick and getting married again just so I can use Henrik."

Risa laughed out loud, looked longingly at her tiny, unfinished salad, then covered it with her napkin and smiled at her best friend.

Lexie, she decided, was right.

Thanks to Henrik, everything was going to be perfect, and in the end even Alison would come around.

CONRAD DUNN GAZED at the marks he had drawn on Lucinda Rose Larson's face. Lucinda Rose lay anesthetized on the operating table, draped with green sterile sheets, awaiting her annual tune-up. Today he was performing liposuction under her chin and along her jawline, a simple procedure, as well as taking a few tiny tucks on her eyelids. He'd drawn the dotted lines on her face earlier, when she was standing up, and now he tugged on the crepey skin around her eyes to gauge its elasticity. Although only fifty-seven, Lucinda Rose had inherited thin northern European skin, and too many sun-worshipping years on the Spanish Riviera had wrinkled her far beyond her years. An annual tune-up kept her at least comfortably fashionable among her peers, and Conrad was good enough that even though everyone always asked their friends who had done their work, no one ever thought Lucinda Rose had had anything done at all.

"Kate?" he asked, the rest of the question unnecessary.

"Vitals are stable," the anesthesiologist replied. "She's ready to go."

"Music, please."

Judy, who had been his scrub nurse long enough to know exactly what he wanted, turned on the MP3 player, and light strains of Stravinsky flowed through the room. Conrad felt himself relax into a mood of serene, utterly self-assured competency.

This was his world, his theater, and nobody anywhere was a better performer. In this room, Conrad Dunn truly was king of the world. "Scalpel," he said, uttering the command, initiating the procedure that in the end would add a little more beauty to a far-too-ugly world.

Just the sound of the word sent a tingle of excitement through his body, but the hand he held out was rock steady.

Judy deftly and firmly placed a scalpel in his palm, and after a quick glance at the big clock on the wall, Conrad made the first cut along the black line above Lucinda Rose's right eye.

"How are the wedding plans coming along?" Kate asked when she saw that Conrad had settled into his groove.

"Good," he replied. "Risa had the final fitting on her dress today, in fact."

"You're a lucky man. She'll make a beautiful bride."

With tweezers, Conrad lifted a tiny strip of skin from Lucinda

Rose's eyelid and placed it on a square of gauze. "Not as beautiful as Margot."

Startled, Kate and Judy glanced at each other.

"Don't tell me you're already planning to remodel her," Kate said. "Can't you at least wait until you've married her?"

Conrad chuckled. "Risa is just fine the way she is. She's happy with her looks, and so am I. I have no surgical plans for Risa at all." He matched the two sides of Lucinda Rose's eyelid incision and began sewing them together with nearly invisible stitches. "I was just talking in the abstract. Even you have to admit that Risa doesn't quite have either Margot's perfect symmetry or her beauty."

"Margot didn't, either, when you first met her," Kate retorted. "But it's nice to know that even you have finally figured out that looks aren't everything."

"Still, they pay our bills," Conrad reminded her. "And very handsomely, too."

"I'm not arguing that point," Kate said, scanning the monitors on the wall above Lucinda Rose's head. "But look at Risa's daughter. Alison's a plain girl, but after talking with her for even a couple of minutes, you see what a lovely girl she is on the inside, and she becomes beautiful on the outside as well."

Conrad tied off the last suture and blotted away the few drops of blood that leaked out. Satisfied, he repositioned himself to begin work on Lucinda Rose's left eyelid. "It isn't all about personality with Alison," he said, receiving a clean scalpel from Judy. "She's got a lot more than that. She has the bone structure." He looked up at Kate. "The next time you see her, take a good look at her facial bones. The cheekbones, the jawline, even her chin." He rested his hand on Lucinda Rose's chest for a moment, visualizing Alison in his mind's eye. He had studied her face for over a year now, and could picture it from every angle. He could even see the muscles under the skin and the bones beneath the muscle.

He knew the anatomy of Alison's face as well as he'd known Margot's.

Kate again peered over her mask at Judy, who waited with a gauze square. Judy gazed back at Kate with one raised eyebrow.

"Vitals stable," Kate reported, hoping to shake Conrad out of the reverie that had fallen over him.

"Yes," Conrad said. He began the second incision. "Classic bone structure. She's a plastic surgeon's dream." His fingers tightened on the scalpel just a little too tightly and the blade slipped through a centimeter more skin than he had planned.

Judy gasped.

Conrad glared at her. "It's nothing," he said as he finished the incision, then placed the small slice of skin onto Judy's waiting square of gauze. "I can fix anything." He took the sharp needle and began the fine stitch work, then looked up at Kate and smiled, although he knew she could not see his smile behind his surgical mask. "I could even make Alison Shaw beautiful."

8

SLUTTY.

That was the only word Kimberly Elmont could think of to describe the pictures Tiffany Barton had taken of her only this morning. But the poses had seemed like such a good idea when Tiffany was setting them up. Oh, well . . .

She scrolled slowly through the rest of the photos she had uploaded from her camera and tried to decide which ones to post on her new MySpace page, since the ones Tiff had taken obviously wouldn't do. A couple of the best ones were from last Christmas, but they seemed too cutesy, and while she was interested in meeting some new people online, she didn't want to give the wrong impression.

Not too cutesy, but not too slutty, either.

Then she spotted one that seemed to strike a pretty good balance. It was from this morning, but Tiffany had taken it before she started posing her. Kimberly blew the image up and looked at it carefully. It was a profile shot. Hair tucked behind her ear, she was looking down at a book, pencil in hand. It had a nice, sort of contemplative look to it, and she named it "Thinking" and uploaded it to MySpace. Then she chose another that Tiffany had taken, of her leaning against a tree. It was the least slutty of all the shots Tiffany had set up, but it showed her whole body, and anybody cruising MySpace could see she wasn't an elephant or anything. She cropped out most of the background, saved it as "Tree hugging," and uploaded it.

A soft tap on her door made Kimberly jump, but then her mother's voice settled her down again.

"Honey?" The door opened. "Dinner's almost ready," Janice Elmont said, coming over to stand behind her daughter. "What are you doing?" She peered over Kimberly's shoulder at her computer monitor.

"Just uploading some photos to my MySpace page."

Janice laid her hands on Kimberly's shoulders. "Do you really think that's a good idea? You don't know what kind of people are out there looking for a pretty fifteen-year-old girl like you."

Kimberly shrugged her mother's hands away. "Come on, Mom. I know what I'm doing—I'm not stupid."

"Of course you're not, honey, but anybody can be fooled. I just don't think you should be doing this."

"Everybody on the *planet* is on MySpace, Mom," Kimberly said. "At least everybody I know. Besides, I never chat with anybody I don't know."

Janice shook her head. "Have you seen that television show where those men show up to have sex with girls even younger than you?"

Kimberly rolled her eyes. "We've all seen that show. I'm smarter than that. Trust me a little bit, will you?"

Janice hesitated, but then leaned over and kissed her daughter on the top of the head. "Okay, I'll trust you to set up the page. But I'll also trust you to consult me before doing anything that you think may be even the slightest bit questionable. Okay?"

Kimberly nodded.

"Deal?" Janice said, wanting to hear her daughter agree out loud. "Kimberly?"

"Deal, Mom."

"Okay, sweetheart. Dinner in twenty minutes. You can come set the table."

"Okay. I'll be down in a few minutes."

Kimberly turned back to her computer as soon as her mother had left. Someone had already seen the photos she'd posted and left her a message. His name was Dean, and in the thumbnail photo, his face was mostly in shadow. Very mysterious.

She opened the mail.

HEY. SEE YOU'RE IN THE VALLEY. WHAT SCHOOL DO YOU GO TO? I'M IN BURBANK.

Burbank! Sally Ann, Kimberly's sister's best friend, used to date a guy from Burbank. He was very cool, with his own car.

She clicked on Dean's name and his MySpace page opened up. He went to Burbank High. She was hoping for more photos of him, but he had only posted the one. His page looked a lot like hers: under construction, with very little information on it yet.

The little green flashing icon said that he was online right now.

Kimberly felt her heart beat faster. Should she talk to him? Right after she'd told her mother she would only talk to people she knew? But what was the harm? This was just another kid.

A kid from Burbank.

But what if it wasn't a kid?

She'd know—of course she'd know. She'd know just by the way he wrote his messages. Adults could never sound like kids—they were way too old even to know what kids were thinking about, let alone how they talked to each other.

She clicked Instant Message on Dean's page and typed: HEY, DEAN. IT'S KIMBERLY. I GO TO DAILY HIGH IN GLENDALE.

His message came back only a few seconds later.

KIMBERLY! HEY, GLENDALE ISN'T SO FAR AWAY. WHAT KIND OF MUSIC DO YOU LIKE?

Kimberly adjusted her chair and thought for a few moments before responding. She had to be cool. What was the coolest music she could mention?

Within moments their messages were flying back and forth as quickly as if they were talking to each other on the telephone. Dean was funny and nice, and it wasn't long before all thoughts of dinner and setting the table were far, far away.

❖   ❖   ❖

The soft sound of the computer's beep reached the listening ears first, then echoed through the room, quickly dying away. But even before the sound deserted the ears, the legs and feet swiveled the chair around so the eyes could see the monitor.

SEARCH COMPLETED
FIVE MATCHES FOUND

The heart beat faster.

A single finger clicked on the mouse, and a window opened on the screen. Five small photographs appeared.

Five women, all young.

The arm moved; the finger clicked twice on each of the first four pictures. One by one each was expanded to fill the screen.

One by one the eyes scrutinized the pictures.

One by one, the mind rejected them and the finger on the mouse reduced them to their original tiny size.

Perhaps the parameters were incorrect.

Then the finger clicked the mouse twice more and the last photograph expanded.

The skin tingled with excitement.

This last one looked exactly right. The photograph showed the face in profile.

Young. Fresh. And with a perfectly shaped ear.

The heart beat faster.

The finger tapped again, enlarging the photograph further, for an even closer examination and detailed, professional analysis.

Yes! This was the one.

The finger tapped faster, enlarging the photograph again and again until the ear filled the entire screen.

A fingertip reached out and gently traced the shell-like contours of the girl's pale pink ear.

Even the girl's lobe—the most variable part of the ear—was a perfect match.

Perfect . . . all of it perfect.

The tongue licked the parched lips.

The fingers went back to work on the mouse.

The photograph was reduced to its normal size. A few more twitches on the mouse, and its source became clear.

The program had located the photograph on a MySpace page.

Perfect.

The finger tapped on the mouse once more, and the arm moved slightly so the mouse highlighted a single word on the screen.

SAVE

The first piece of the puzzle had been found, but there was still more to be done—much more.

Now the fingers abandoned the mouse to fly over the keyboard.

A new set of instructions was entered into the search program.

Centimeters, millimeters, geometric ratios, color scale.

The fingers moved back to the mouse.

The arm moved the mouse itself so the arrow on the screen hovered over a button at the bottom of the screen:

EXECUTE SEARCH

The finger clicked one last time, sending the program's spider out to crawl the World Wide Web, searching inexorably for a perfect match to the precise parameters requested.

It would take time, but when the spider had found its prey, it would beep an alert.

For now, though, there were other things to do.

Preparations to be made.

9

ALISON SHAW SAT VERY STILL AND TRIED TO BE PATIENT AS SCOTT
stroked shadow onto her eyelids. He had turned her away from the
mirror while he worked on her makeup, but not being able to see herself hadn't kept her from taking in every detail of the suite she was in
at the Hotel Bel-Air. The bellman had told her it was the Princess
Grace suite, where Grace Kelly herself had stayed whenever she was in
Los Angeles after she moved to Monaco. It had two bedrooms flanking a large living room with a fireplace that was itself flanked by two
pairs of French doors that opened onto a large walled garden with a
fountain.

They were at the end of the hotel closest to Sunset Boulevard. She
couldn't remember how many courtyards they'd walked through yesterday afternoon before they finally came to the door to this suite. She
and her mother had stayed here last night, and tonight her father and
Scott would occupy the master bedroom, since her mother and Conrad
Dunn were flying to Paris right after the reception. Now, as Scott
worked on her face, Alison tried to commit every detail of the suite to
memory so she could tell her friends about it on Monday morning.

But how long was her makeup going to take? And what on earth was Scott doing to her? With every new pencil, brush, or pot of color he used, her fears increased. All she ever used was maybe a stroke of blush on her cheeks and a little lip gloss, and even that only occasionally—most of the time she didn't bother with anything at all. But Scott had started at least an hour ago with all kinds of things she sort of knew about but had never tried before.

Exfoliating, moisturizing, applying a foundation . . .

And even though he'd kept up a running commentary about what he was doing, all she could think was that she would end up looking like some kind of gargoyle.

And for her mother's wedding, for God's sake!

As if reading her mind, her father, who was lounging in a chair watching Scott work, winked at her. "Stop worrying about what he's doing and just be glad you don't have to pay him. Last time he worked on Sandra Bullock, he got five hundred an hour, plus expenses."

"Which were at least twice my fees," Scott said through the handle of the brush he was clenching between his teeth.

Alison tried to focus her eyes on him and failed. "Really?"

"Actually, she was easy," Scott went on, taking the brush out of his mouth and eyeing her carefully. "You'd be surprised how many hours I've spent right here in this suite, turning some very strange-looking women into the beauties you see in the magazines." He stood back to gauge the overall effect of his work. "I even worked on Clint Eastwood."

"*He* wears makeup?" Alison gasped.

"For a movie!" Scott retorted. "All that blood and all those scars and wounds don't come naturally, you know. And just in case you're still worrying, I'm doing my best not to put any scars on you."

"Relax, honey," Michael said. "Scott's been doing this for a lot of years."

"More years than I'll admit in public," Scott said. "Now close your eyes."

Alison took a deep breath, praying she wouldn't look like she was wearing stage makeup. "Just . . . just don't overdo it," she said as he touched her eyelashes with the brush.

"Overdo it?" Scott said, standing back to appraise her one last time. "This is Hollywood, honey. Nobody holds back on anything." He rummaged through the suitcase that served as his makeup kit and came up with an eyebrow pencil. "Besides, my job is to make people look how they want to look, and I always know what they want a lot better than they do. More to the point, I also know how to do it so it doesn't look like anyone's wearing anything at all." He sharpened the pencil and stroked it lightly across her eyebrows. "You need to have your brows arched, Alison. Not much—just a little. I'll do it another time. We can't have pluck marks today."

"I like my eyebrows," she protested.

"Everybody likes caterpillars," Scott said, "but they like butterflies better. And wait until you meet the kids at Wilson Academy. You'll want to know every trick I can teach you." He brushed her eyebrows to blend the strokes. "If they're anything like their mothers—and you can bet they are—half of those girls have already had work done by your new stepfather, and the other half are planning some." He looked her square in the eyes. "All you have to do is keep in mind that those girls are as phony on the inside as they are on the outside, and you'll be fine."

"I don't even worry that much how I—" Alison began, when her father interrupted.

"Why would you worry?" he asked. "You look spectacular."

"Ready?" Scott asked.

Alison nodded, though she wasn't quite sure she was.

Scott turned the chair so she faced the mirror. For a strange, surreal instant she thought there was a mistake, that she was looking at someone else. But a moment later she realized that the young woman in the mirror looked familiar.

Familiar, but different.

Not at all like the person she had always before seen in her own reflection. This girl looked like a mature young woman—exactly the kind of young career woman she had always admired but was sure she could never emulate. "Oh. My. God," she breathed, coming to a full stop after each word. "Is that really me?"

"It sure is, sweetheart," Michael said. "And what a beautiful young lady you are."

Alison gazed at her reflection in utter silence for almost a full minute, coming to realize that Scott was right: what she was seeing was exactly how she'd always wanted to look. But no matter how hard she tried, she couldn't see the makeup.

It was, just as he'd promised, utterly invisible.

"I—I—" she began, her voice choking as she tried to find words to express what she was feeling. "I never thought—" She fell silent again as Scott snatched a Kleenex from the box on the vanity table and caught the tear about to overflow her right eye.

"Don't you dare start crying," he told her. "If I have to do repairs, I'm going to charge you, and believe me, even Michael can't afford my reconstruction fees!"

By the sheer force of her own will, Alison forced the tears back, then grinned at him. "Why don't both of you change your minds and come to the wedding? You've been invited. Please? For me?"

Michael shook his head. "This is your mother's day. The last thing she needs is to have to explain to everyone why her ex and his boyfriend are here. And starting tomorrow, we'll get to have you for a whole week while your mother and Conrad are partying in Paris."

There was a soft knock on the door to the suite's living room. "Just a moment!" Scott called, and turned Alison around to inspect her one last time. He feathered on just a little more color with a lipstick brush, then pulled the cape from around her shoulders.

Her father took her hand and helped her to her feet, and then Scott circled her, checking the drape of the floor-length, silk lavender sheath dress that had seemed too old for her when she put it on an hour and a half ago but exactly right now that Scott had worked his magic.

"Stand over here," he said, positioning her in front of the bedroom's set of French doors, so the light played softly over her hair and face. "Okay," he called toward the door. "Come see your maid of honor!"

The door opened and Risa stepped inside, her breath catching when she saw Alison.

Alison smiled at her mother, who was more beautiful than she'd ever seen her, in a gray strapless wedding gown with a mermaid silhouette and a spray of tiny flowers in her hair. "Mom, you look fabulous," she breathed.

"Not compared to you," Risa replied, her voice trembling. "This is the only wedding in history where the maid of honor is going to outshine the bride."

"No crying!" Scott ordered. "Control yourselves—both of you."

Risa stepped over to Scott and kissed him lightly on the cheek. "I'm not going to cry, and neither is Alison. But I am certainly going to thank you for everything." Keeping one arm around Scott, she pulled Michael close with the other and kissed him, too. Then she glanced at Alison. "There's a bottle of champagne in the living room. Why don't you bring it in, and we'll have a little toast." As Alison left the room, Risa squeezed the arms of the two men flanking her. "Sure you won't change your minds?" she asked. "I should think you'd both *want* to give me away, considering the way I acted a year ago." Alison reappeared at the door and stopped uncertainly, but Risa dropped Michael's arm and motioned her in. "It's all right—I was just trying to get them to change their minds."

"They won't," Alison said. "I already tried."

When they all had glasses in their hands, Risa raised hers high. "To us," she said. "First, to Scott, not for just finding Henrik and doing everything he could to make this day perfect, but for taking such good care of Michael, too. And to Michael, for still being my best friend." She turned to Alison. "And most of all, to you, sweetheart, for putting up with your father and me while we sorted things out." They all took a sip, then Risa stepped over next to Alison and raised her glass once more, this time to Michael and Scott. "May Conrad and I be half as happy as you two."

"Now I really *do* want to give you away," Scott grumbled, though the slight tremble in his voice belied the sarcastic tone he'd aimed for. "Aren't we all just the image of the perfect American family?" Giving Risa and Alison each a careful peck on the cheek, he ushered them to the front door. "Now get out of here, both of you—you don't want to be late for your own wedding."

Risa followed Alison through the courtyard and gardens of the hotel, reveling not only in the perfect spring afternoon, but in everything else as well.

She was getting married.

She was going down to the edge of the swan lake, to be married to Dr. Conrad Dunn.

And it all felt right.

ALISON WATCHED Conrad kiss her mother after the judge pronounced them husband and wife, barely able to believe it had all happened. Even as she stood behind her mother under the bower next to the swan lake, the afternoon sun warming the air to a perfect temperature, the air itself perfumed by the profusion of flowers that filled the hotel grounds, it was still almost impossible to believe it was all real. And yet it was—the next words she heard brought the reality home with enough force that she almost cried.

Almost, but not quite.

"It is now my great pleasure to present Dr. and Mrs. Conrad Dunn," Judge Rousseau said, and everybody who had been sitting in the white satin-covered folding chairs rose and began to applaud.

Alison handed her mother's bouquet back to her and prepared to take the best man's arm, to follow the bride and groom out from under the bower and down the aisle toward the lawn on which the reception would be held. But before she knew what was happening, Conrad smiled at her, put his arm around her, and drew her up so she and her mother were both beside him.

Not even close to what they had done at the rehearsal, and as Conrad's hand tightened around her waist, Alison resisted an urge to pull away from him.

This was her mother's wedding day, and she would do whatever it took to not let anything spoil it. Her mother loved Conrad, and she would learn to like him. Or at least she would find a way to tolerate him for a couple of years until she went to college. But even as she forced herself not to pull away, her skin crawled at his touch. *Stop it,* she told herself. *Mom loves him, and he loves her, so just deal with it.*

Still, relief flowed through her as she moved next to her mother in the receiving line while Conrad stayed on the other side with his best man, someone named Alex Fox, who hadn't even bothered to show up for the rehearsal yesterday. For the next twenty minutes she stood almost mute as her mother met one after another of Conrad's friends, colleagues, associates, and clients, and then introduced them to her.

Her mother, she knew, would remember every one of their names from now on. She herself couldn't remember a name the second after she'd heard it, and the twenty minutes in the receiving line seemed to go on for hours.

When the last of the well-wishers had finally filed by, Alison heard her mother tell Conrad she was going to the ladies' room to repair her makeup, and she felt a new wave of relief at the prospect of getting away from the mass of people, even if only for a couple of minutes.

"Don't be long, Mrs. Dunn," Conrad said, kissing the tips of his wife's fingers. "And while you're gone, I'll introduce Alison to some of her new classmates."

Alison's relief ebbed as quickly as it had flowed over her a moment ago as Conrad took her arm to steer her through the throng of people on the lawn, some of them already picking at the tables laden with food, but far more of them edging toward the bar. They passed the head table, adorned with an exquisite centerpiece of white orchids so perfectly arranged that they wouldn't interfere with anyone's sightlines even when the table was full. Alex Fox was already sitting there, two drinks in front of him, and for a moment Alison had a horrible feeling that Conrad was about to abandon her to the nearly empty table. Instead, though, he steered her over to a table where five kids about her own age were chattering together, at least a dozen empty champagne glasses in front of them.

"Hey, guys," Conrad said. The group at the table fell silent, a couple of them glancing guiltily at the empty glasses, but Conrad paid no attention to them. "This is Alison Shaw. She'll be joining you at Wilson after spring break."

Alison flushed as one of the girls eyed her appraisingly. "Love your dress," the girl finally said.

Unsure if she meant it or was being sarcastic, Alison decided she didn't care. At least it was an opportunity to escape from Conrad, and she seized it in an instant.

"Thanks," she said, dropping into one of the empty chairs at the table, but not relaxing until Conrad headed back to the head table to join his best man.

"I'm Tasha," a deeply tanned girl with thick brown hair said. She nodded toward the small blonde sitting next to her, the one who had commented on Alison's dress. "This is Dawn, and these guys"—Tasha swept the three boys with a look of mock scorn—"think they're far hotter than they are. We only put up with them because so far nothing better's come along."

"Plus," one of the boys put in, "almost all our parents have been married to each other at one point or another, which means dating each other would be incestuous." He leered at Dawn. "Not that I'm always opposed to incest. Just as long as we don't have any two-headed babies." He grinned at Alison. "I'm Trip, and these two are Cooper and Budge."

"Budge?" Alison echoed without thinking, then wished she could take it back when she saw the boy, who was shorter than the other two boys and looked a lot younger, blush.

"His real name's even worse," the lanky boy, Cooper, said. "That's why we call him Budge. Back when we were all in first grade, we thought it was cool. So now he's stuck with it. Right, Budgie-poo?" he added, grinning maliciously at the shorter boy, who responded by punching Cooper in the arm, hard enough to make it hurt. "All right, all right," Cooper cried. "Budge! I'll never call you Budgie-poo again!"

"Right," Budge replied. "And you'll also invite me to wherever you're going for spring break. And you'll go liberate some more champagne for us."

"That's what we were talking about when Dr. Dunn brought you over," Dawn said as Cooper got up and headed for a waiter who was just leaving the bar with a tray full of champagne.

"So where are you all going?" Alison asked.

"Dawn and I are going to France," Tasha said. "Dawn's dad isn't using their jet, so we get it all to ourselves."

"Maybe I should go with you instead of Cooper," Budge said. "Or not," he added when Tasha rolled her eyes.

"I'm going skiing," Trip said.

"Yeah?" Budge asked. "Where?"

"St. Moritz," Trip replied as Cooper returned bearing the tray he'd "liberated" from the waiter. "With the fam."

"Can I come?" Budge asked.

Everybody ignored him.

"*St. Moritz!*" Cooper said. "I'm only going to Key West."

"Okay, so I guess I don't want to go with *you*," Budge said. "My dad has a house in Aspen, so that's where we're going. I hate it, but it's better than Key West."

"What about you, Alison?" Tasha asked.

"Nowhere," Alison said. "I'm staying with my dad for the week, and then when Conrad and my mom get back from their honeymoon, we'll be moving."

"And *then*," Tasha said, "you'll get all the liposuction, implants, nips, and tucks you want for free."

Alison stared at her. "Why would I want any of that?"

Now it was Tasha who stared, her eyes remaining on Alison's chest long enough that Alison felt her cheeks burning.

"About one hour at Wilson and you'll know exactly why you'll want it," Dawn said.

"Come on," Trip put in. "If Alison thinks she's just fine the way she is, let it alone." The thank-you that was about to emerge from Alison's lips died in her throat as Trip went on. "Just because we think she could use some major renovation, so what? I mean, who are we to say?"

Alison stared at her fingernails, blushing again, feeling her eyes filling with tears. *Ignore them,* she told herself. *Just get up and walk away.*

Then she remembered her mother, greeting everyone in the receiving line, smiling graciously even at people Alison was sure she didn't like. But what should she say? What *could* she say? Then, just as the silence was starting to get totally unbearable, the orchestra started up.

"C'mon, Dawn," Trip said. "Let's dance."

Dawn and Trip, and Cooper and Tasha, got up and headed for the dance floor, and Budge followed them, leaving Alison sitting by herself.

She wanted to run to her mother, but what good would that do? Her mother was busy on the other side of the lawn with her Conrad Dunn, talking to another couple who Alison knew she'd met but whose names she'd forgotten.

She gazed around the garden, at all the beautiful people who seemed to know each other and fit perfectly together.

So perfectly that she was already sure there wasn't going to be any room for her at all.

Not here, and not at Wilson Academy, or anywhere else in her new life.

What was she going to do?

10

KIMBERLY ELMONT PICKED AT HER SALAD, WONDERING HOW IT WAS that Jennifer Livingston could eat a double Whopper with fries, drink a Coke, and then eat a Cinnabon roll for dessert and never gain an ounce. Even though it had been that way since kindergarten, when they became best friends, Kimberly still couldn't quite deal with it, since she herself had to diet constantly just to fit into her jeans. "And speaking of jeans," she said out loud, "there's a sale at Macy's."

"Who was speaking of jeans?" Jennifer said, dipping a french fry into a blob of ketchup, then slipping it into her mouth as delicately as if it was a toast point covered with caviar.

"We weren't. But I was thinking about them—I need a new pair."

Jennifer shrugged indifferently. "Okay. Macy's is good."

Kimberly pushed her salad away, knowing she couldn't eat another bite and then try on clothes, and pulled out her cell phone to check for new text messages.

One new message was waiting.

CAN YOU COME TO THE RAVE TONIGHT? BRING A FRIEND. –DEAN

If she were at home, she would have stood up and yelled, "Yes!" but here in the mall she merely folded up her phone, put it in her purse, and smiled at Jennifer.

Jennifer wadded up the paper leftovers of her meal and took a long drink of her Coke before noticing Kimberly's grin, which had taken on the sort of frozen quality that she knew meant Kim was bursting to tell her something. "What?" she asked.

Kimberly glanced first in one direction, then the other, and when she spoke, her voice had dropped to a conspiratorial tone. "Want to go to a rave tonight?"

"A rave?" her friend echoed. "Really?" Though Jennifer had the face and body of a model, she hardly ever went out, and never went on dates—all the guys she knew were too intimidated by her looks to ask her out. But at a rave, she knew there would be all kinds of guys— probably older guys—and maybe they wouldn't be so shy. "Where? With who?" Not that it mattered, really, since Kimberly's mom would never let her go. But maybe this time Kim wasn't planning to tell her mom.

"A guy named Dean just invited me, and he told me to bring a friend."

Jen frowned. "Who's Dean?"

"A guy I met on MySpace. We've been chatting for a couple of nights."

Jennifer eyed her. "A guy you met on MySpace? Are you nuts?"

"He's a nice guy, and I know a lot about him. He's seventeen, and goes to Burbank High, and likes all the same things we do. He's cool, Jen. And he'll have cool friends."

Jennifer's brows arched skeptically. "Have you talked to him on the phone?"

"Not yet," Kimberly replied, unable to keep from sounding defensive.

"Then you don't have any idea who he really is, do you? He could be some forty-year-old perv."

"But he didn't ask me to come alone," Kimberly countered. "If he was some kind of pervert, he'd want to meet me alone, right? But he didn't—he asked me to bring a friend along. So I'm asking you."

Jennifer gave her a withering look. "And when you tell him you're actually *bring*ing a friend, he'll back out."

Kimberly met Jen's gaze straight on. "I bet you're wrong."

"Or else he just won't show up," Jennifer went on, "and then he'll call you later and ask you to meet him by yourself."

"Want to bet?" Kimberly said. "I bet you he shows up and he comes with a really cool guy. Besides, what else were you going to do tonight? Paint your nails?"

Jennifer shook her head. "It's just not a good idea," she insisted.

Kimberly looked around the crowded food court, then leaned across the table so no one else would hear her pleading. "C'mon, Jen. It's a *rave*! Have you ever been to a rave?"

"No. And neither have you."

Kim sat back triumphantly in her chair. "Then it's settled."

"It's not settled at all."

"What can happen with hundreds of kids around?" Kimberly argued. "Even if we don't meet up with Dean and his friend, we'll have fun. I bet we even see people we know."

Jennifer thought for a moment while she pushed the last of the french fries aside and pulled a little piece from her cinnamon roll. "All right," she sighed, knowing that once Kimberly made up her mind about something, she never gave up. Besides, Kimberly was right— there would be hundreds of people there, and they wouldn't be alone. "Tell him you actually are bringing a friend, and if he doesn't back out, I'll go."

"Super!" Kimberly opened her phone and hit REPLY, then entered her text message: SOUNDS FUN. WHERE? WHEN? WE'LL BOTH BE THERE. She hit SEND and closed her phone. "What'll we wear?"

Jennifer stuffed another piece of the cinnamon roll into her mouth and wiped her hands on her napkin. "Something new," she decided, then gathered the remains of their meal onto her tray. "C'mon. Let's see what's on sale at Macy's."

Twenty minutes later, when Jennifer had disappeared into the fitting room with an armload of things while Kimberly was still hunting through the sale racks, the cell phone in Kim's purse buzzed insistently.

She fished it out.

One new text message.

She opened it.

11PM KESWICK AND TOBIAS VAN NUYS. CU THERE!

She knew the light industrial area of Van Nuys—her dad's company had a warehouse out there.

And a lot of kids at their school went to parties in those warehouses almost every weekend.

Good thing Jennifer had a car.

Kimberly tapped out a quick confirmation, then headed to the fitting room to tell Jennifer the good news.

Now the hunt was really on to find something perfect to wear.

Sexy, but not too sexy.

Margot!

Risa could still hear Conrad's voice reverberating in her head as he cried out his dead wife's name in the middle of their lovemaking.

Actually, not exactly in the middle—more like toward the end, at the precisely worst moment, making the wave of ecstasy that had been building within her suddenly collapse away to nothing.

So much for their first night in Paris.

And Conrad didn't even seem to know he'd done anything.

Risa gazed at her reflection in the big bathroom mirror, her mascara smudged from the tears she'd barely been able to control until she was alone. The peach peignoir Lexie had bought her for their wedding night flowed over the curves of her body, but she no longer felt sexy in it. In fact, she wanted to rip it off and throw it away, ridding herself of even this reminder of the mistake she'd made.

Why had she ever thought it would be a good idea to marry Conrad while he was still grieving for Margot?

Margot.

That single word, uttered with a passion that would haunt her memory for the rest of her life.

Maybe if he'd said it next year, or next month, or even next week, she'd have been able to laugh it off. But he'd said it *tonight,* the first night of their honeymoon.

The most important night of their marriage.

And he'd said it after one of the most magical evenings she had ever experienced—dinner at La Tour d'Argent, with a view of the Seine and Notre Dame, followed by a slow walk through a perfect Parisian night back to the Hotel de Crillon, where they'd sipped champagne and danced on the terrace of the suite that had been Leonard Bernstein's favorite.

It had all seemed like a fairy tale.

And then that word.

That one word that had ruined everything.

Risa slowly massaged Danielle DeLorian's new moisturizing cream into her face while she listened to her new husband breathing rhythmically in the bedroom.

Maybe she should pack up and leave—leave the room, leave the hotel, leave Paris.

Now *that* would be melodramatic! Straight out of the kind of romance novel she hated, even though she'd never actually read one.

And too impulsive, too.

Sighing, she pulled two tissues from the holder and began removing the makeup from her face, and as her real face emerged, so did her sense of fairness.

How long would it be before she herself slipped and called Conrad "Michael"?

She sank down onto the velvet bench in front of the vanity and fantasized about telling Lexie why she had left Conrad after only two days of marriage.

It sounded ridiculous, she abruptly realized after using every word she could think of to make herself sound terminally wounded.

So he'd had a slip of the tongue. So what? If she couldn't overlook this one small thing, then she didn't deserve to be married to a man as wonderful as Conrad Dunn. And he certainly didn't deserve to be stuck with someone as thin-skinned as she obviously was.

"Get a grip, Risa," she whispered grimly to the mirror. "Get over yourself."

She finished removing her makeup, dropped the tissues into the gilt wastebasket, then clicked off the bathroom light, walked across the darkened room, and slipped back into bed.

"Honey?" Conrad said sleepily, pulling her close. "Where've you been? You're cold."

His warmth seeping into her, she snuggled into him. What happened earlier had been no more than a slip of the tongue, and one of the more common ones at that. Not only would she never mention it to anyone, she wouldn't even think about it again. She was married to a man she loved, and one who loved her, and she was in Paris on her honeymoon, and she wasn't about to let a single word ruin everything for her.

A moment later Conrad was snoring softly, and a few minutes after that she, too, drifted into a peaceful sleep.

11

Kimberly Elmont flushed the toilet and pushed her way out of the grimy stall into the crowded warehouse restroom. She wet her hands, but there was no soap, and the only paper towels in sight were overflowing the trash bin and littering the floor, so she shook her hands as dry as she could, then shook her head, too.

Mother would die if she saw this place.

Still, she found herself grinning as she fluffed her sweaty bangs. This was even more fun than she'd thought it would be. And what could possibly happen to her with this many people around, as long as she didn't drink more than a single beer, and stayed completely away from the drugs all the girls around her were putting into their mouths?

One beer, and no drugs. Those were the limits she and Jennifer had set for themselves when they were still two blocks from the warehouse and heard the pounding music. When they pulled into the jammed parking lot, they almost lost their nerve completely, but paid their way in, got their hands stamped, and easily exchanged a drink ticket for a beer at the bar, no questions asked. After surveying the sea of people, she knew there was no way she'd be able to spot Dean in the crowd—if they found each other, it would be pure luck. Next time they'd arrange a specific place to meet.

A place where they could at least find each other.

Within a few seconds, some guy asked Jennifer to dance, and Jen had grabbed her hand and pulled her along to the dance floor, where a teeming crowd was twisting and writhing under the strobe lights, dancing with whoever happened to be closest.

She'd danced for nearly an hour before retreating to the restroom, but even after the short break she wasn't sure how much longer she could last, since the warehouse kept getting hotter, and the music louder. Now, she freshened her lipstick and tried not to be too obvious as she watched while two girls she thought she knew from school snorted white powder up their noses.

Echoes of her mother's voice recurred to her, but she didn't need the silent warning. She might have one more beer just to quench her thirst, but that was it. No drugs.

Making her way out the restroom door into the vast warehouse, Kimberly began searching for Jennifer. The band was back onstage and picking up their instruments, and the crowd roared as a surge of people moved once again toward the dance floor. She caught sight of Jennifer then, still with the lanky guy who had first asked her to dance. They were on the dance floor, their arms wrapped around each other, gyrating slowly even though the music hadn't yet begun again.

With only a faint twinge of jealousy that Jennifer had found a boy right away while she'd utterly given up on Dean, Kimberly moved toward one of the two bars when someone—who'd had a lot more to drink than she had—slammed into her and then careened off in a different direction.

She automatically checked to make sure the tiny purse containing her money and house key was still securely in the pocket of her jeans, and rubbed at the spot on her thigh where it felt almost like she'd been burned with a cigarette.

Her money and key were still in her pocket, and the burning sensation in her leg was already fading away.

She pushed on toward the bar, but just before she got there, her stomach suddenly knotted, she tasted bile in the back of her mouth, and for a horrible moment she was certain she was about to throw up right here in the middle of the jammed warehouse. But the nausea passed as quickly as it had come on.

Kimberly took another step toward the bar, and her knees began to wobble.

"You okay?" a voice asked.

The voice sounded impossibly close and yet at the same time very far away. The words reverberated inside her head, jumbling with the music, which was so loud she could actually see it, surrounding her with brilliantly colored waves, while the drums pounded at her until her whole body felt as if it were being attacked.

Though she felt weird—almost as if she'd been snorting coke with the other girls in the restroom—she tried to nod. Apparently, even that one beer she'd drunk had been too much for her, and now she couldn't even nod her head right. She tried to speak but couldn't make her lips form words. All that came out was a garbled moan.

"Come on," the voice said. "You need some air."

Yes. Air. All I need is a little air.

She felt a strong arm come around her and guide her toward the nearest door, but by the time they got there, her legs were starting to give out. No matter how hard she tried, she couldn't seem to keep her feet underneath her and stand on her own. But it would be all right, she thought; in a few more seconds they'd be outside, and whoever was helping her would take her to Jennifer's car, where she'd lie down in the backseat and wait until the dance was over.

But when the door closed behind them, the stranger didn't stop, let alone ask her if she had a car. Instead she was half steered and half carried toward the back of the parking lot. She wanted to protest, but even as she tried to speak, the last of her strength deserted her and every muscle in her body went completely slack.

This isn't happening. How could this be happening? I was so careful.

I'm going to be raped.

Oh God, her mother had been right all along. She never should have come here—she should have listened to her mother, and to Jennifer. She should—

Don't hurt me, she begged silently, forming the words in her mind, but unable to say them aloud. *Please don't hurt me.*

Oh, Mommy, I'm sorry.

I should have listened.

I'm . . . so . . . sorry.

JENNIFER'S HEAD WAS THROBBING, but she wasn't sure if it was from the relentless pounding of the music or from the second drink she'd let Dirk, or Derek, or whatever his name was, buy her. Either way, it was time to go home. The rave hadn't turned out to be as much fun as she'd thought it would be, and for the last half hour she'd been keeping an eye out for Kimberly, but between the flashing lights and the haze of smoke hanging in the room, she wasn't sure she'd have recognized Kim if she were ten feet away. Now, as Dirk—or Derek, or whatever—tried to guide her hand through his open fly, she decided it was time to find Kim and go home. Giving the guy a couple of kisses in return for the drink was one thing, but that was as far as it would go.

Pulling her hand away from his grip, she looked at her watch and feigned shock at the time. "Jeez—my mom's going to kill me!" she yelled, her words instantly lost in the din of the music. "Gotta go!" Pulling her hand free, she spun away from the boy before he even realized what was happening and started working her way through the crowd, realizing for the first time just how big the room was and how hard it was going to be to find Kimberly.

She finally came to the bar by the front door and paused to try to get a whiff of fresh air. Once again she scanned the crowd. The bright yellow tank top Kim had been wearing shouldn't have been hard to

spot, but the lights made all the colors look different, and she couldn't
see anything that looked even faintly yellow. As she plunged back into
the mob, which was now throbbing to a pounding rhythm, she felt
hands groping her, stroking her arms, caressing her butt and even her
breasts. "C'mon, baby," someone whispered in her ear. "I got some
black beauties." Jennifer rolled her eyes, twisted her arm loose from
the guy's grip, and moved on.

Crap! They should have had a code or something. Or a signal, or
even just a set time to meet up and check in with each other.

The music and lights and smoke were starting to get to her now,
and besides the throbbing in her head, she was feeling nauseous. What
she'd told the boy was turning into the absolute truth—all she wanted
to do now was go home.

But she couldn't just leave Kimberly here.

She slapped away another anonymous hand in the crowd and
headed for the door. At least she could get a little fresh air, and if she
threw up, she'd be in the parking lot, which was a lot better than hurl-
ing in the middle of the party.

And who knew? Maybe she'd even find Kim out there.

But before she got to the door, she heard the wailing of police
sirens, and by the time she pushed her way outside, blue and red lights
were flashing in the lot.

The band stopped playing, and suddenly there was an air of panic
as people surged for the doors.

Swell! Now she was going to get busted and her parents would
have to bail her out of jail. Why had she ever let Kim talk her into this?
And where was Kim, anyway?

Then a voice rose above the noise of the crowd of teenagers who
were trying to disappear into the night as quickly as possible: "They
found a body!"

Jennifer froze, her headache instantly forgotten. A terrible certainty began to descend over her. As the mob swirled and eddied
around her, she turned her eyes toward the far end of the parking lot,

where the police cars had gathered. Slowly, and as if of their own volition, her feet began to move, carrying her toward the flashing lights
as if she were drawn by a magnet. As she drew closer, she saw one of
the officers unwinding yellow crime scene tape. Several others were
spreading out to block the crowd, and one of them was waving his
arms, saying, "Everybody back inside. Nobody can leave just yet."

Ignoring the order to return to the warehouse, Jennifer kept moving closer until she saw something that stopped her dead in her tracks.

A solitary shoe lay on the gravel, its toe scuffed and bloody.

One of the shoes Kimberly had bought when they were at the mall
that afternoon.

Only that afternoon? As her eyes remained fixed on the blue-and-
yellow-striped espadrille that had looked adorable with Kim's new
slim-line jeans and yellow tank top, the afternoon suddenly seemed a
lifetime ago, a lifetime when the shoes had seemed impossibly cute.

Now the single shoe no longer looked cute. It looked horrible.

Forlorn.

Forgotten.

And ruined: the bow on the toe had been ripped off, the blue and
yellow leather scuffed and torn.

Jennifer's gaze shifted to the area of the parking lot now cordoned
off and filled with people. She stooped to pick up the shoe, but before
she could touch it someone took her firmly by the wrist and drew her
back to her feet. "Don't touch anything," the officer said, his voice not
unkind.

Jennifer gazed at him, her wide eyes glistening with tears. "It—It
belongs to my friend," she whispered.

"What's her name?" the policeman asked.

"Kimberly," she said as she stared at that sad shoe. "Kimberly Elmont. She was here to meet . . . " Jennifer's voice trailed off. "I was
looking for her," she finally managed to say. "I wanted to go home, but
I couldn't find her and . . . " Her voice trailed off once again, and now
the policeman took her arm to steady her.

"Come with me," he said, and led her over to a police car. He opened the back door. "Why don't you sit down? I'm going to send someone over to talk to you."

"Is it Kimberly?" Jennifer asked, searching his eyes.

He didn't answer, but she knew, because even from the backseat she could see that the matching shoe to the one she'd found was on the body that lay on the asphalt.

She put her face in her hands and began crying as grief overwhelmed her.

Grief, and guilt that she had let Kimberly talk her into coming here at all.

TINA WONG DROVE slowly past the crime scene. Police cars had blocked every driveway leading to the warehouse, and a dozen uniformed officers were trying to control the crowd of kids, most of whom seemed to be either on their cell phones or complaining to the police, or both. It was clear that they could hardly wait to get away from there.

She, on the other hand, wouldn't have been anywhere else in the world right now.

Tina drove another block, then parked her SUV, grabbed her digital camera and cell phone, and headed for the area that had been cordoned off. With any luck, she'd get a clear view and at least a few seconds of video before anybody saw her.

But climbing over a low cinder-block wall wouldn't be easy in the little black cocktail dress and heels she'd worn on her date with Richard Sexton, who was probably still sitting alone in the restaurant where she'd gotten the call from the newsroom about the murder report picked up on the police scanner. Poor Richard—this was at least the fourth time it had happened to him—but this was her life, and if he couldn't deal with it, the hell with him. She just hoped this wasn't another of the gang knifings that had become so common lately they weren't even bothering to report them anymore.

Dumping her high heels in favor of the sneakers she always kept in the car for just such moments as this, Tina stepped over the wall and started across the asphalt.

Then she saw what lay in the center of the area the police had cordoned off, and knew this was no gang slaying.

A teenage girl, clad in what was left of a skimpy yellow tank top, lay sprawled on her back, flayed open like she'd been field-dressed by a drunken hunter. A tangle of intestines gleamed in the garish floodlights the police had already set up, and scraps of other tissue—some identifiable, some not—were strewn in what looked like a rough circle.

What was left of the girl lay in the center of that circle of gore.

She'd seen this before—in a Starbucks bathroom—and recognized the handiwork in an instant. It was the same sort of havoc wreaked on Caroline Fisher a year ago.

This was the body she'd been waiting for, ever since Michael Shaw had told her she'd need another body for the special she wanted to do.

Well, here it was. The killer was back in action, and if the amount of blood was any indication, he was in top form. If there'd been anyone around to take the bet, she would have put any amount of money on her certainty that when the coroner put all the carnage back together, he'd discover that part of this girl had disappeared.

Tima looked more closely, saw that the girl was facing away, covered with blood. But there was something odd about her head. She took a step closer.

Her ear was gone! All that was left on the side of her head was a mass of bloody hair and a gaping wound on the side of her head where her ear had been.

Tina fumbled opened her phone and speed-dialed the station. "Send a camera crew to the murder site in Van Nuys. And use the chopper! Now!"

"Hey!" a cop yelled as she snapped the phone closed and dropped it back in her purse. "Get out of here."

Tina nodded, smiled affably, and held up her hand. "It's okay," she said, and turned on her digital camera. "I'm supposed to be here."

By the time the cop recognized her as a television reporter, she had already snapped off a half-dozen zoom shots of the dead girl and wide angle shots of the whole area.

"No press!" the cop yelled, heading toward her with a look on his face that might have intimidated anyone else.

"Lighten up," she said, still snapping pictures. Then she turned the camera directly on the cop. "Don't you want to be on TV?" She was about to snap the shutter, and blind the cop with the flash, when she saw something else in the camera's bright screen. A few yards behind the cop a young girl was sitting in the back of a police cruiser, a blanket around her shoulders, her head in her hands.

A witness?

Turning away from the angry policeman, Tina headed back the way she'd come, feeling the cop's eyes on her until she was back at the cinder-block wall at the edge of the cordoned-off area. The officer had turned back to the crime scene by then, and she'd worked out a plan to get close to the girl in the back of the black-and-white. She knew she would never blend in with the crowd of stoned kids, so she'd just have to act like she was part of the investigative team.

She strode down the street a few yards, then reentered the parking lot, ducking under the yellow tape as if she'd done it thousands of times before—which, in truth, she had. "It's okay," she said to a cop who seemed about to question her, and turned directly toward the girl sitting in the back of the cruiser, whose teary eyes kept glancing toward the crime scene.

"Hi," Tina said, coming up to the car. "I'm Tina, and I'm so sorry." She crouched down and put a comforting hand on the girl's knee. "You knew her?" The girl bit her lip but said nothing. "It's all right," Tina soothed. "Take your time."

"We—she's my best friend," the girl said. "We came together, but I told her it was a bad idea."

Tina felt a tingle of anticipation, certain something important was coming. "Oh?" she asked as casually as she could. "Why was that?"

The girl looked up at her. "It was an Internet date. I knew she was being set up for something—I just knew it. You don't do that. You don't go out with guys you meet on the Internet. I told her." She began to cry again. "I told her."

"Did you see him?"

The girl shook her head and blew her nose.

"What's your name?" Tina asked.

"Jennifer Livingston."

"Has anyone called your mother yet, Jennifer?"

Jennifer sniffed and shook her head. "The cops want to talk to me."

"Yes, I'm sure—" Tina began, but her words were cut off by a cold voice.

"Hello, Tina."

She didn't have to turn around to know who it was. Evan Sands's voice was unmistable.

Tina offered Jennifer a reassuring smile, then stood up to face the detective and his partner, Rick McCoy.

"How do you do it, Tina?" Sands asked, easing her inexorably away from the girl, and leaving McCoy to get all the information Tina so desperately wanted. "How did you manage to get here before us?"

Tina shrugged and smiled at the detective. "Call it a special gift," she said.

"Well, here's a gift for you," Sands replied. "Scram. We're busy here."

"The public has a right to know—" she began, but Sands just nodded.

"Yeah, yeah, yeah, and you can be sure we'll have a press conference. Until then . . ." He jerked a thumb toward the other side of the yellow tape, just as the Channel 3 helicopter began to drop out of the sky.

Tina waved to the chopper and pointed to an empty parking lot across the street, then smiled at Detective Sands. "I'll look forward to that," she said, then headed toward the crew emerging from the helicopter to set up a remote link to the station.

This would be breaking news even at this hour, and tomorrow morning all of Los Angeles would wake up to it. She'd be all over the breakfast news, and morning radio wouldn't be talking about anything else.

And she'd get her special, too. Michael Shaw had committed, and even though a year had passed, he'd make good on it. She'd see to that.

For now, though, all she could do was run her fingers through her hair and check to make sure she still had lipstick on. Then the sound man handed her a microphone, and Tina opened her mouth to utter the opening line she'd been waiting a year to speak.

"Death in all its ugliness came once more to Los Angeles tonight, this time visiting a warehouse parking lot in Van Nuys."

❖   ❖   ❖

The secret door opened silently into a dark corridor. The left hand closed the door quietly but firmly, while the right hand carried the plastic bag.

The nose drew in the smell of familiar chemicals as the feet moved silently across the floor, down the dark passageway toward another door, this one with pale green light escaping from beneath it, illuminating the hallway just enough for the eyes to see.

The fingers of the hand not carrying the bag closed on a single key that jangled softly on a ring and placed it into the dead bolt on the door.

The bolt turned and the door opened.

The nose crinkled as the smell of chemicals grew stronger.

The smell was almost sickly sweet.

It smelled like success. It smelled like money.

It smelled like the future, a beautiful future.

The smell came from the tank, which was filled with a special mix of chemicals.

The chemicals formed a viscous gel that was lit gently from above by fluorescent light in the tank's lid, which emanated a cold green glow that seemed to ooze from the tank as if the light itself were a living thing.

The fingers of the right hand released their grip on the plastic bag, letting it rest on a stainless steel counter as the fingers of the left hand found the wall switch and turned on the overhead light.

One hand gloved the other; the other then gloved the first. Then both hands, protected now by surgical rubber, lifted the lid from the tank.

From a stainless steel tray, the eyes selected a hemostat, which the right hand picked up and plunged into the greenish gel. The fingers manipulated the hemostat deftly, its jaws seizing a bit of flesh and lifting it out of the tank.

The eyes appraised the decomposition rate of the severed breast.

It was maintaining its integrity exactly as planned.

The fingers lowered the hemostat—and the breast—back into the tank, turning it gently, making certain no air bubbles remained to begin the degenerative processes. Then the procedure was repeated with the other breast, the vagina, and two small scraps of skin bearing short hair.

"You don't look like much right now," the voice whispered, speaking to the scrap of skin hanging from the hemostat. "You don't look like an eyebrow, but you will. Soon, you will look exactly as you always did. Except that on the new face, you will be even more beautiful than you were before."

Everything in the tank was in excellent condition.

The fingers of both hands worked at the plastic bag for a moment, opening it. Buried deep in ice crushed as fine as snow were two ears, complete with a narrow band of selvage.

"Can you hear?" the voice whispered into the first ear. "You will again—I promise. You'll stay alive, and hear again, and serve a purpose. A great purpose."

The gloved fingers of one hand lowered the ear into the green gel, *then, with the tip of the forefinger of the other hand, it made certain that every crevice in the ear's contours were perfectly filled. Only when the ear had been completely coated did the fingers carefully push it deeply into the tank to keep company with the other body parts.*

Parts that were waiting.

Waiting.

The second ear followed, and the same careful check was made by both the fingers and the eyes to make certain no air pockets remained.

Satisfied, the plastic bag was emptied of its ice, the gloves were stripped first from one of the hands, then from the other, and sealed into the plastic bag, and the hands returned the tank lid to its place.

The eyes looked one last time at the tank thermometer, then the finger of the right hand switched the overhead lights off, the feet moved through the door, the hands closed the door, and the fingers carefully turned the dead bolt.

The feet echoed softly as they moved down the long hallway, and all that remained inside the laboratory was the tank.

The green glowing tank.

12

"Good morning, sunshine," Michael Shaw said as his tousled daughter wandered into the kitchen, still in her bathrobe, rubbing sleep from her eyes.

"Morning," she said. "What smells so good?"

"Scott's famous French toast," Michael replied, setting three glasses of orange juice on the table.

"Made to fatten up even the most beautiful maid of honor," Scott said as he expertly flipped a thick slice of egg-soaked cinnamon bread on the skillet. "So what's up for today? It's way too nice to sit around in here."

"Beach," Alison said, but before Michael could agree, the doorbell rang.

Scott shot Michael a look. "Sunday morning," he observed archly. "It's got to be the lovely Tina Wong again." He rolled his eyes at Alison. "I keep telling him that as a gay man he has *got* to understand that Sunday brunch is sacrosanct, but he just doesn't get it. He keeps letting the lovely Miss Wong barge in anytime she feels like it, which mostly seems to be right about now."

Michael ignored the jibe, particularly since he was certain Scott was right, given what she'd had to say in her report on that morning's news, during which she was careful to wear the same dress she'd had on the night before, just to prove she'd been up all night. Girding himself for what he knew was about to come, he walked through the living room and opened the front door, and there she stood, indeed wearing exactly what he'd seen on TV three hours ago. Without waiting for an invitation, Tina walked into the house and past him to the dining room, where she pushed aside the brunch plates to make room for her briefcase. "You've got to see this."

"Good morning, Tina," Scott said, leaning against the kitchen door frame and eyeing her dress. "Must have been some party last night."

"I've been at the station all night," she said, ignoring his sarcasm. "Do I smell coffee?"

Scott rolled his eyes at Alison, who covered her grin. "How do you take it?" he asked. "With arsenic, or hemlock?"

Again the sarcasm seemed completely lost on her. "Black with one sugar. Real sugar." She snapped open her briefcase, took out two files, and set them on the table in front of Michael, who was now seated in one of the chairs. "Did you see the morning news?"

He nodded, but knew he was about to hear it all again. Sure enough, Tina launched into the details.

"The dead girl's name is Kimberly Elmont, and she was butchered exactly the same way Caroline Fisher was last year in Encino. And I use the word 'butchered' advisedly. Do you remember what happened in that coffee shop bathroom?"

"How could I forget?"

"Dead girls at breakfast?" Scott asked, setting a cup of coffee in front of Tina. "Delightful."

Tina, as always, ignored him. "Look at these, Michael," she said, opening the first folder and spreading a dozen eight-by-ten photos of Caroline Fisher's bloody corpse across the table.

"Tina!" Michael barked, shooting her a warning look and tipping his head toward Alison, whose eyes were riveted on the photos, the sugar for Tina's coffee forgotten in her hands.

"Now look at these." Tina opened the other file and laid out the grainy photos she'd taken last night of Kimberly Elmont's bloody body in the parking lot.

A strangled sound emerged from Alison's throat, and Michael glanced up to see the horrified look on her face. Before he could say anything, Scott was already there, taking the sugar from the girl's hand and turning her toward the kitchen. "Come on," he said, scowling at Tina. "If we're going to throw up, we might as well do it on the kitchen floor. Or maybe we should just do it on Tina's dress."

Michael shot Scott a grateful look, but it was too late. The damage was done—Alison had seen it all. Still, he shoved the photos back into their folders, closed them, then looked directly at Tina. "I'd like to fire you right now, but you're too good a reporter. But hear me and hear me good. Do not ever come here on a Sunday morning—or any other time—and spread stuff like that out in front of my daughter. That belongs in the newsroom, and in the future it will stay there." He could tell by the look on Tina Wong's face that she didn't have the faintest clue as to why he was angry, and he also knew that despite his words, he wouldn't fire her even if she dragged a body in next Sunday. "All right," he sighed. "Let's get to it. What do you want?"

"My special," Tina instantly replied. "The one you committed to when Caroline Fisher was killed, on the condition that I get another body." She tapped the folder containing the pictures of Kimberly Elmont. "This is it, Michael. I get my special. I need it now. There's a lunatic out there and we need to catch him before another young girl"—she tipped her head meaningfully toward the kitchen, where Alison and Scott were talking quietly—"gets hacked to pieces."

Michael put the two files into Tina's briefcase, as certain as she was that both girls had been slain by the same man. The carnage was just too similar to have been done by a copycat, and besides, a copycat wouldn't have waited a year to copy the first murder. "You need to keep me advised of every step you take," he said.

"Not a problem," Tina replied. "The first thing I need is to get a budget authorized. Then I'll go to San Diego and San Jose and get whatever information I can to connect these murders with those killings from sixteen years ago, okay?"

Michael hesitated, but then nodded.

"I'll be taking a film crew with me."

"No way."

Tina leaned in, fixing her eyes on him. "Interviews, Michael, for the special. Family members, police, coroner. These are unsolved murders, and we may find enough clues to solve them."

He hesitated.

"*We* may have the clues to solve them, Michael. We. Not the police, but Channel 3 News."

Michael thought for a moment. "Have your budget on my desk tomorrow—"

Tina pulled another sheet of paper from her briefcase. "Here it is— I worked it up two hours ago. Sign off on it, and I'll be ready to air in two weeks."

Michael scanned the budget items. "You be careful what you air. We're not a Fox affiliate, you know. I want to vet all footage before it's added."

"No problem," she said. "But Sunday night ratings haven't been much lately, so we can push the envelope a little."

Michael glanced over the budget a second time. It was far more reasonable and well-thought-out than he'd expected, especially considering that Tina Wong had put it together. Her pattern was always to ask for the moon, then settle for what she could get. But not this time. Clearly, she wanted this special, and hadn't taken the chance of blowing it by asking for too much.

Still, he drew a line through her request for a sound tech on her two trips—she'd have to make do with just a cameraman—and initialed it.

Tina put the page back into her briefcase and snapped the locks. "I'll be on the police this afternoon for preliminary information, and probably go to San Jose tomorrow."

Michael walked her to the door, saw her out, then went back to the dining room, where Alison was straightening the place settings and Scott was serving the French toast.

"What was that all about?" Alison asked. "What's going on?"

"Just Tina Wong," Scott said sourly. "Ruining yet another brunch."

"It's not ruined," Michael said. "Nothing could ruin your French toast."

Scott smiled. "Not even Tina Wong?"

"Not even Tina Wong."

Alison picked up Tina's untouched coffee, took it to the bar, and poured it down the sink. She wished the memory of the two mutilated bodies in Tina's photographs would disappear as quickly as the coffee vanished down the drain, but she knew they wouldn't.

Instead, she was sure, they would haunt her dreams for a very long time.

ALISON ACTUALLY DID LAUGH out loud reading Cindy's recounting of her parents' attempt to get the whole family ready to go to Mexico for spring break. It might have worked out if there'd only been two kids, but given that Cindy was the oldest of a flock of eight, things had gone from bad to worse to disastrous in a hurry, and by the time she got to the part where Cindy's youngest brother got left in a gas station in Ensenada, she was laughing so hard her eyes were blurring with tears. She was just about to type a response to Cindy's Instant Message when she heard a soft knock on her door.

"Come in."

Her father opened the door. "Hey."

Alison typed SB to Cindy, hoping the other girl wouldn't have to stand by for more than a minute or two, then turned to her dad. "Hi. C'mon in."

"Just for a minute—we're headed to bed, but I wanted to say good-night and tell you what a great day we had."

"It was fun," Alison said. "I love the beach."

"And we forget how much we enjoy it, so thanks for reminding us. Not that we'll find the time to get back to it on our own, but at least next time you won't have to talk us into it." Michael dropped onto the edge of Alison's bed. "I also want to tell you how much I love having you here, and Scott does, too."

Alison looked at her hands and willed herself not to start crying. "I like it, too," she said, letting only the slightest tremble creep into her voice. She wanted to ask him why she couldn't just stay here, and not go to Beverly Hills and Wilson Academy and everything else her mom was planning. If she lived here, she could take the bus to Santa Monica High every day, and even though the house was in the hills, it wasn't much different than what she'd been used to before—

She tried to cut off the thought, but couldn't quite do it.

—before everything that had happened a year ago. And now everything had already been decided, and there was nothing she could say to change it.

"What are you doing?" her father finally asked as the silence went on too long.

"Just chatting with Cindy," Alison replied, seizing the opportunity to talk about something better than the future that was about to begin. But as she saw the smile on her father's face fade, she realized she'd made a mistake.

"Chat?" Michael asked. "You chat online?" He stood up and came over to the computer.

"I'm just talking to Cindy," Alison said, but even she could hear the defensiveness in her voice. Here came the lecture, just like it had come to at least half her friends. . . .

"With anyone else?" Michael pressed.

Alison hesitated, but knew her father wouldn't believe that Cindy was really the only person she ever IMed with. "Sometimes. It's no big deal—everybody does it."

Michael's brows furrowed. "Where do you chat? How do you find people to chat with?"

"MySpace, usually."

"MySpace? You have a MySpace page?"

Alison's eyes rolled. "*Every*body does."

Michael crouched next to her desk chair so his eyes were level with hers. "Do you remember those photographs this morning?"

Alison shuddered. "God, how could I forget?"

"I'm sorry you saw them, but in a way I hope you never forget them. The girl who was killed last night was at that warehouse to meet a boy she met online. She met him through her MySpace page."

"That's like saying she met him at church. Or at school. Literally everyone I know has a MySpace page. It doesn't mean anything!"

"It means people you know nothing about can get in touch with you," Michael said, rising from his crouch. "I want your page down tomorrow morning."

Alison gaped at him. "You're kidding!" How could someone like her father be so backward as to demand something so ridiculous? "It took me, like, *weeks* to get everything I want up on it."

Michael's expression didn't change. "Do I look like I'm kidding? I want you to sign off with Cindy right now, go to bed, and take that page down tomorrow morning. And I don't ever want to hear about you chatting online with anyone you don't know, ever again. You and Cindy and the rest of your friends can use Windows Messenger or AOL or anything else. But not MySpace."

"Come on, Dad! You're overreacting," Alison insisted, but her father's expression remained implacable.

"You saw those pictures."

"Like I'm going to go and get myself killed," she said with all the sarcasm she could muster.

"Alison," he said, his voice low and calm, but even more obdurate than before. "I'm telling you to do this because I'm your father and I know what's important. One way or another, you're going to do this, and I hope you'll do it without complaining, because I'm telling you that what you've been doing is not good. Whether you believe me or not makes no difference—what you've been doing can be very dangerous, and it's going to stop."

Alison bit back the angry words that formed on her tongue and turned back to her monitor, where the cursor was blinking.

Cindy was still standing by.

And there was no use arguing. "Okay," she sighed. "I'll do it. I don't want to, and I think you're being ridiculous, but I'll do it."

Finally, Michael smiled. "You're more than welcome to think I'm ridiculous. In fact, I hope I *am* being ridiculous, but I appreciate you doing this for me. When you're eighteen, you can put whatever you want on MySpace and talk to whoever you want to. But you're still my little girl, and I love you, and I'm going to protect you whether you want me to or not." He kissed her on the top of the head. "And say hello to Cindy for me, okay?"

Alison ignored him and sat quietly with her hands in her lap until he'd left her room and closed the door. Then she began typing.

YOU WON'T BELIEVE WHAT MY DAD JUST SAID.

While she waited for Cindy to respond, she realized that her My-Space page would only be down for a week.

Next Sunday, she'd be moving to Beverly Hills, and her mom wouldn't care what she was doing on her computer. She'd have the page back up before going to bed next Sunday night.

She just wouldn't tell her father. . . .

13

Too BIG.

That was the problem—Conrad Dunn's house was just too big. The weird thing was, it hadn't seemed this huge when she'd been here before, but now that she was moving in, everything was just way too enormous.

The house. The garden. Her bedroom. Even the closet was so large that all her underwear vanished into a single one of the twenty-four shallow glass-fronted drawers built into the left front corner, while in the right front corner a rack big enough to hold at least a hundred pairs of shoes had swallowed up her half-dozen pairs as if they weren't even there.

And halfway back on the left, her clothes—*all* of them—filled no more than a tenth of the space the closet provided.

Alison took the last empty box, which had contained what seemed like way more underwear then she needed until she unpacked it into that single drawer, and added it to the pile in the hall, then went back into her room.

Ruffles, the little white terrier that had belonged to Conrad's first wife, watched her every move, looking as lost on the enormous bed as she felt in the room itself.

As she came close, his little nub of a tail began wagging furiously, and when she picked him up to stroke his soft fur, he wiggled around until he could lick her face. "I'll never get used to it," she said. "And you're so tiny, just going downstairs is a major hike. How do you stand it?"

He licked her chin.

"You'd have loved my room at home. It wasn't even a quarter as big as this, but at least I felt like I fit into it." She gazed at the king-size bed with its vast expanse of brocade spread and the array of at least a dozen designer pillows—every one of them perfectly placed—and wondered how she was going to cope with it. Even though all her stuff was now unpacked and put away, it still didn't feel anything like her room should feel.

Instead, it felt like a hotel.

A huge, empty hotel. But it wasn't a hotel, and never had been. Rather, it had been built by some old movie star who died before her mother had even been born. She still wasn't sure how Conrad's family had come to own it, let alone why they'd even wanted it.

Alison shivered and hugged Ruffles closer, carrying him to the window seat, where together they gazed out over the formal gardens and reflecting pool, at the far end of which was the swimming pool and cabana. A gardener was just finishing his day, picking up his tools and heading for the potting shed behind the garage. She sat then, with the dog, as the lights of Los Angeles began to shine and an orange sunset spread across the sky. The window seat, at least, felt the right size for her, and she suddenly knew that this was going to be her own personal space, the one small spot in the house that would be completely hers.

Getting up, she went to the closet, found the quilt her grandmother had made for her, brought it back and spread it out so it covered the needlepoint cushion on the seat. The fact that the homey, handmade quilt didn't go at all with the decor of the rest of the room was just fine.

This nook was where she would make her home.

"Miss Alison?"

She started at the disembodied voice, then looked around for its source before remembering the intercom system her mother had told her about. She went to the small speaker on the wall by the door and pressed a white button. "Yes?"

"Dinner is served," the faintly tinny voice said.

"Okay," she replied. "Tell Mom I'll be down in a minute."

Now all she had to do was find her way to the dining room.

The empty moving boxes she had just put outside her door were already gone. She turned left and walked down the wide hallway lined with oil paintings hung on silk wallpaper, the sound of her footfalls swallowed by the Oriental runner that ran the full length of both the house's wings.

At the top of the sweeping staircase that led down to the foyer, she gazed up at the domed ceiling that reminded her of a church, then started down toward the intricately inlaid marble floor, in the center of which stood a great round table with an enormous display of fresh flowers.

She paused, realizing she actually *wasn't* sure where to find the dining room, then heard voices and the sound of silverware on china somewhere off to her left.

"There she is," Conrad said, rising from his seat at the head of the dining room table as she came in.

The table had a dozen chairs around it tonight—with a dozen more standing against the walls for nights when the table was fully extended—but only three places were set, flanking Conrad. As she slid silently into the chair opposite her mother, Alison decided she'd far rather be eating at the breakfast bar at her dad and Scott's house.

"Getting settled in?" her mother asked as Alison spread a linen napkin over her lap.

She nodded as a woman in a black uniform silently placed a small tossed salad in front of each of them.

"So tomorrow's the big day at Wilson," Conrad Dunn said.

Though he was smiling at her, his expression did nothing at all to warm the chill the house had cast over her spirits. But despite her misgivings about not only the huge house, but Wilson Academy as well, she made herself nod in response to his words. "Are you excited?" her new stepfather went on.

She shrugged, not trusting her voice to conceal the misgivings churning through her.

"What's the matter, honey?" her mother asked. "Are you all right?"

Alison nodded.

Conrad reached over and put his hand on hers. "You'll fit right in," he said. "There's nothing to worry about at all."

Alison slowly drew her hand away and put it in her lap.

He was probably right—she'd have new friends eventually, but after the wedding, she wasn't sure she even wanted to be friends with the kids at Wilson.

"You'll be fine, sweetheart," her mother reassured her, and Alison nodded again, picked up her salad fork and firmly squelched the tears suddenly threatening to spill over her lids.

Taking a deep breath, she forced a smile to her face. "I want to know all about Paris," she said. Her eyes fixed on her mother. "What was the absolutely best, best, *best* thing?"

Her first dinner in her new home began.

Somehow, she would get through it.

RISA SLIPPED into bed next to Conrad, who was reading a medical journal. "Honey?"

He looked up, smiled, took off his reading glasses and set them and the magazine on his nightstand, then held his arms open to her.

Risa snuggled into him. "What if the other kids aren't nice to Alison? You know how kids can be—especially the kind who go to Wilson. They've already got their cliques. What if they don't accept her?"

Conrad rubbed her shoulder gently. "Alison? She'll do fine—she's just like you. She can fit herself in anywhere."

Risa nodded against his chest, hoping he was right, but still not sure. Alison had been so quiet tonight, at least until they started talking about Paris.

Risa snuggled closer.

"Trust me," Conrad whispered. "She'll be just fine."

Finally content, Risa fell asleep in the warm security of her husband's arms.

ALISON WAS PROPPED in the window seat with two of the pillows from the bed, her quilt wrapped around her, Ruffles stretched out along her thigh, and her computer in her lap.

She logged on to the MySpace page she had spent the last hour reconstructing.

And Cindy Kearns still wasn't online.

She heard the tone signaling incoming e-mail and clicked on the button to open the program. There was a new e-mail titled, MYSPACE FRIEND REQUEST.

She opened it.

SETH8146 WOULD LIKE TO BE ADDED TO YOUR MYSPACE FRIENDS LIST.

She went back to her MySpace page and clicked on his profile. He was very cute, in a blond, surfer-guy kind of way, but there wasn't much information about him.

An Instant Message box appeared from Seth8146.

HI. CUTE PIX OF U.

Alison's fingers absently stroked the dog's fur as she gazed at the blinking cursor.

What should she do? This was exactly what her dad had warned her about—chatting with strangers on her computer.

But what was the big deal? It wasn't like she would make a date with him, or tell him where she lived, or anything at all. What harm could chatting do?

She looked over at the big, uninviting bed and realized that even if she shut off the computer and got into it, she'd just fret about tomorrow. She made up her mind.

HI! she typed, and then hit SEND.

TINA WONG PERCHED on the edge of the hard gray metal folding chair next to Detective Evan Sands's desk, unconsciously tapping her foot and checking her watch every few seconds.

Slowly, the squad room began to fill, but even when it seemed as if the room could hold no more people, neither Sands nor Rick McCoy had shown up. At 8:45, deciding she'd wasted enough of her time, she picked up her briefcase and rose to her feet. She had a lot more important things to do today than wait in vain for two cops who were even now probably sitting in some doughnut shop swapping lies and bad jokes.

As if on cue, Evan Sands pushed through the glass doors into the squad room and instantly spotted her. To his credit, he barely hesitated, keeping nearly all of his distaste for her out of his expression, but not enough to keep Tina from reading his animosity. Not that it mattered; as far as she was concerned, her job was to get the story and report it, and if some people—or even *all* people—found her irritating, that was just tough for them. Besides, Sands had no idea that she was bringing him a gift today, and even though the gift came with a price, she was sure that in the end he'd agree that he got the better end of the deal.

"Tina," the detective said, barely nodding to her. "I thought vampires were afraid of the daylight."

"Funny," she said without even a hint of a smile. "I want to talk with you privately." Her eyes swept the room, but only about a quarter of the detective force even pretended not to be trying to hear every word she and Sands exchanged.

"Does that include McCoy?" Sands asked.

"Not a problem," Tina said, checking her watch. "Assuming he's planning to show up at all this morning."

"He had the doughnut run this morning," Sands told her as his partner, balancing two paper cups of coffee on a big, greasy box, backed through the door and let it swing shut behind him. He shot Sands a questioning look as he recognized Tina, which Sands responded to with a helpless gesture, clearly conveying that he wasn't to be blamed for the fact that she'd trapped them both by getting into the squad room early enough to avoid being stopped.

Still, she could see that Sands seemed to understand her urgency and the importance of privacy, because he jerked his head for McCoy to follow them, then led the way through the back of the squad room into a small interrogation room, closing the door as soon as they were all inside.

"I'm not going to waste your time," Tina said without spending so much as a second on pleasantries. "I want to know one thing in particular about Kimberly Elmont's murder."

Rick McCoy scoffed as he set the box on the table. "You and about a million other reporters."

"We're not giving out any specific information to anyone," Sands said. "You know the drill. So why are you really here?"

"Because," Tina said, ignoring McCoy and looking Sands directly in the eye, "I think I know something about that murder that you don't know, and if you'll answer one question, I can help you guys get Cop of the Year or Queen for a Day or whatever award they hand out around here."

"Oooh," Sands said, "I'm so excited I think I might wet myself." Then he dropped the sarcasm. "Look, Tina—you know the rules. You give before you get. If you really know something, you have to tell us anyway, otherwise you're withholding evidence or obstructing justice or anything else the D.A. can think up. So you go first, and if we like it, we'll give you something back."

Tina hesitated. If she divulged too much without confirmation from them, she'd blow the best angle she had for her special. "I need to know you're good for this information."

"What do you want to know?" Sands asked.

"Did Kimberly Elmont lose some glands Saturday night in addition to her ears?"

The look that passed between the two detectives was almost all the confirmation Tina needed.

Almost, but not quite.

"We can neither confirm or deny—" McCoy began, but Sands interrupted him.

"We can give you the answer to that one," he said, the last trace of sarcasm vanishing from his voice. "What have you got?"

"If she was missing her thymus and adrenals, the same thing happened last year to Caroline Fisher."

She waited for a reaction from either cop but got none.

"Hello?" Tina said. "Is anybody home? Do I have to spell it out? Does the term 'serial killer' mean anything to you two?"

"There isn't any reason—" McCoy began, but now it was Tina who cut him off.

"Come on," she snapped. "Obviously you hadn't connected Caroline Fisher and Kimberly Elmont yet, so at least let me have some credit for giving you that."

Evan Sands eyed her speculatively. "Which means you've got more?"

Tina weighed her options. "I do. But unless Fisher and Elmont are connected, the rest of what I have doesn't pertain to Elmont. So make up your minds."

Sands picked up a doughnut and bit into it. "Okay," he finally said after he'd munched through half the sticky ring of pastry. "According to the coroner, those glands were gone. So you're right—unless we have a copycat—"

"Copycats don't wait a year," Tina Wong cut in. "And there are two others, fifteen years ago." As McCoy and Sands stared at her, she snapped open the locks on her briefcase and brought out two sheets of paper, laying them on the table. "One in San Diego and one in San Jose. Girls slashed open and their adrenals and thymuses taken. Same M.O., same killer, right?"

"Holy Christ," Sands breathed, picking up the summary of the San Diego case and starting to scan it as Tina Wong kept talking.

"He's a serial killer, he's back, and he's in Los Angeles now," the newswoman said. "So how much of Elmont can I report on?"

"Similarities," Sands said slowly, passing the San Diego report to McCoy in exchange for the one from San Jose. "Don't give the details about the glands—we'd just as soon not tip too much to the wackos who are going to start 'fessing up the minute they hear it's a serial." He looked up at Tina. "And you didn't hear anything from me. Take all the credit for seeing the similarities yourself."

Tina snapped her briefcase shut and picked it up from the table. "Thank you, gentlemen—a pleasure doing business with you."

"Not so fast," McCoy said, holding up the San Diego report. "What are you planning to do with this stuff?"

Tina smiled sweetly. "The public has a right to know," she said. Then she opened the door and walked out, leaving them still reading the reports.

If she hurried, she could film her noon update and still be in San Diego before lunch.

ALISON SHAW FOUND her way back to her locker after the final hour of the day, her head still spinning from the differences between Santa Monica High and the Wilson Academy. Aside from the fact that the academy was on a small campus nestled in the hills above Westwood Village, and the buildings looked more like mansions than school buildings, the classes were far smaller than any she'd been in before, and the dining hall was more like a restaurant than a cafeteria. Even the lockers were different—built carefully into the walls, each with a mahogany door with a student's name engraved on a small brass plaque. Hers was on the first floor of the Science Building, and now, as she stood staring at all her new textbooks, she wondered if she could leave any of them in her locker overnight.

"Mrs. Morgan is always the priority," someone behind her said.

Alison turned and saw Tasha Rudd and Dawn Masin, the two girls she remembered from her mother's wedding.

"Literature," Alison groaned.

"Don't you just hate it?" Tasha asked. "You have to actually read the material, and God help you if you're late with a paper."

Dawn Masin nodded. "She's the worst."

"Okay, at least I know," Alison said, and pulled the heavy literature book off the stack.

"So you made it through your first day," Tasha said as Alison added her history book to her backpack.

"Well, I survived it, anyway," she replied. "In fact, it wasn't as bad as I thought it would be."

"Then you should celebrate," Dawn said. "We're all going up to Tasha's. Come with us."

Alison hesitated—neither of the girls had been this friendly at the wedding; in fact, they hadn't spent more than five minutes with her. So why were they inviting her along now?

"You need to meet some people," Tasha said, reading the uncertainty in her expression. "Come with us. It'll be fun."

"And if you don't come, my dad will think we didn't invite you, and I'll be grounded for a week," Dawn added.

Alison gaped at her. "Your father *told* you to invite me?"

Dawn nodded. "But it's no big deal—if we didn't want you to come, we would have just lied to our folks. Plus which, Trip says you're really good in trigonometry, and Tasha and I can't do it at all, so we're going to need you to help us. Okay?"

Alison found herself laughing. "Are you always this honest?"

"You'll get used to it," Tasha said as Dawn only looked vaguely puzzled by the question. "So come on, okay?

"I need to check with my mom," she said, still uncertain whether they wanted her to come with them.

"So call her," Tasha countered. "We'll wait."

Two minutes later Alison closed her phone, added her trigonometry book to the two others already in her backpack, then closed her locker. "Let's go!"

Five minutes later Tasha beeped open her silver BMW roadster, which was parked between a Mercedes coupe and a Saab convertible.

"This is *yours?*" Alison asked, her eyes taking in the row of glittering automobiles as she pulled open the passenger door of the BMW. She knew one person at Santa Monica High who had a BMW, but it was five years old, and most of the students' cars had been at least ten. Nor were most of them Mercedes and Saabs and BMWs.

"Got it for my birthday," Tasha said. She put the car in gear and led a caravan of three other cars full of kids up Roscomare Road to Mulholland Drive, where she turned right and wound her way along the crest of the hills for a mile before turning right through a pair of electric gates and down a steep driveway to a large parking area and garage in front of her family's house overlooking Stone Canyon.

Tasha parked in the garage, the other cars parked behind her, and then almost a dozen kids piled out, streaming around the house itself and down the stairs to the pool house.

"Let's go dump our stuff in my room," Tasha said, leading Alison to the front door. "Then we'll find you a suit in the cabana.

Two boys—Alison thought they were Cooper Ames and Budge Phelps—were already splashing in the pool by the time she and Tasha arrived at the huge terrace containing not only the pool and a "cabana" that was bigger than the house in Santa Monica had been, but an outdoor kitchen around a huge barbecue.

When they went into the dressing area in the cabana, half a dozen naked girls were rummaging in the drawers full of different size swim-suits. Suddenly, she felt like she was back in gym class.

"Here," Tasha said, pulling a purple striped two-piece suit out of a drawer and handing it to her. "This should fit you."

Tasha casually stripped off her clothes and got into her own pink bikini with white piping, then adjusted it in front of the mirror.

Alison, self-conscious, hesitated, but finally took off her own clothes and pulled the bathing suit on. At least it wasn't a full bi-kini, and the bottom sort of fit—it was a bit tighter than anything she'd ever worn before, and her thighs and waist bulged a bit over the spandex.

She told herself it wasn't too bad.

But the top was way too big—the cups bagged around her small breasts.

"The bra doesn't fit," she said, staring dolefully at her reflection in the mirrored wall. "Do you have a smaller one?"

Tasha opened another drawer, pulled out a pair of foam rubber falsies, and handed them to her. "These will fill it out."

Alison stared at them, praying Tasha was kidding, but knowing by the tone of her voice that she wasn't. "I'm not sure I—" she began.

"Go on," Tasha said, cutting her off. "They're the ones I used to wear before your stepdad gave me these." She lifted her chest with two hands, exaggerating the bulge of her breasts.

Alison reddened and tried not to stare. "You mean those are im-plants? *Conrad* gave you implants?"

"Well, it didn't look like I was ever going to grow them, so first I used those." She nodded toward the two foam pads that were still in Alison's hand. "They'll push you up and fill out the top. Try it."

"They fit into a pocket in the bottom of the cups," Dawn said. "Here, take it off and I'll show you."

Reluctantly, Alison took off the bathing suit top, trying to resist the impulse to hide her breasts behind her arms since the other girls seemed to be so unconcerned about their nudity.

Dawn expertly fitted the rubber push-ups into the bikini top, then handed it back to her. "Try that."

Alison put the top back on and tried not to blush as Dawn readjusted everything.

"Take a look," Dawn said when she was finished.

Alison stared at herself in the mirror and for a moment thought she was looking at someone else. How could those little pieces of rubber make such a difference? She looked like an actual woman instead of a flat-chested adolescent child.

Her breasts were actually mounding over the top of the bathing suit's bra.

"Just like me," Tasha said, nodding in approval at the new contours. "You need implants. Ask Santa for a pair."

Alison stared at her. "Me? You've got to be kidding! I could never—"

"Never say never," Dawn Masin interrupted. "You've probably got everything you're going to get from nature. So now's the time. You want to get it all done before you go to college."

Alison turned to Dawn, whose body filled her bikini as perfectly as Tasha's. "You've had something done, too?"

Everybody laughed.

"We all have," a girl Alison hadn't met yet said.

"It's no big deal," Dawn said. "I had my boobs and lips done over Christmas, and Tasha's getting cheek implants next summer."

Alison stared at Dawn's lips. They were plump and looked perfectly natural. How was it possible she hadn't been born with them?

"Believe me," Dawn said, leaning forward so Alison could see her mouth more closely, "I had no lips before. None."

Tasha sucked in her cheeks so Alison could get an idea of what she was planning, then let them back out again. "I think the way we're born is just a suggestion."

A suggestion? Alison thought as she wrapped a beach towel around her body and followed the rest of the girls out to the pool.

What were they, crazy? Yet as she listened to the whistles from the boys in the pool, she hesitated.

Nobody had ever whistled at her like that, and they weren't right now, either. They were whistling at Tasha and Dawn and all the rest of them.

"Come on in, Alison," Budge Phelps called out. "We're losing. We need you." He held up the volleyball.

"Going in?" Alison asked Tasha.

"Later," Tasha said as she smeared lotion on her long brown legs.

"Come on, Alison!" Trip called. "We need you."

Alison dropped the towel and waited.

No whistles—none at all.

They knew her breasts were not her own.

Suddenly regretting that she hadn't just gone home, she plunged into the pool, wishing that not just her body, but she herself could disappear.

DAHLIA MOORE CLOSED the file on her desk and reached for the next on the stack. Before she opened it, she rubbed her neck, trying to relieve some of the pain in her shoulders and upper back that eight hours a day of sitting at her keyboard had made into a chronic condition. And trying to decipher the scribbled notes the doctors made on the patients' charts wasn't doing anything for her eyes, either. Sighing heavily, she flexed her fingers, took a sip of her tea, inhaled deeply, and reached for the next folder on the bottomless heap in her in-box.

She was just opening the file when the door to the Records Office opened and a woman walked in.

A woman Dahlia recognized not only from television, but because she'd been in this very office at least three times before, and not once had the newswoman ever gotten anything at all out of her.

But apparently she never learned.

"Hello, Dahlia," Tina said, her lips curling into the smile she usually used only on TV.

Dahlia wondered if Tina Wong had actually remembered her name or just read it in one of the directories in the hospital lobby. "May I help you?" she said, doing her best not to let the newswoman know she'd been recognized.

"Tina Wong?" Tina said, moving close to the counter in front of Dahlia's desk. "You remember me, don't you, Dahlia? Channel 3 News?" Barely acknowledging Dahlia's curt nod, she plunged on. "I'm doing a story on the Kimberly Elmont murder, and her mother told me that Kimberly's appendix had been removed here at Holy Cross two years ago."

Dahlia scowled. Of all people, Tina Wong should understand patient confidentiality. It wasn't as if they'd never played this game before. "So?"

"So I'm hoping you can tell me who has access to her medical records."

"Her doctors," Dahlia responded. This was way too simple a question for the famous Tina Wong, so she was after something else, but Dahlia knew her job, and wasn't about to jeopardize it for a reporter. "That's assuming she was a patient here, and you know as well as I do that I can't tell you anything about a patient."

"I told you—I'm not asking for information about the patients. All I want to know is if anyone but their doctors accessed their records."

Dahlia Moore's eyes narrowed. "What do you mean, 'patients'?" she asked, emphasizing the plural. "Kimberly Elmont was only one person, wasn't she?"

Tina pounced. "So she was a patient here!"

"You already knew that," Dahlia retorted, rolling her eyes. "Her mother told you, didn't she?"

"Can you tell me if a woman named Caroline Fisher was ever treated here?"

Dahlia frowned. "How many times do I have to explain confidentiality to you?"

"Confidentiality dies with the patient," Tina said, putting a lot more certainty into her voice than she felt. Then, as Dahlia's expression turned even stonier, she changed her tactics. "Look," she said, her voice much softer. "Both of these girls were murdered. I can't believe you didn't hear about Kimberly—I broke the story, but every other station's been on it ever since. Caroline Fisher was murdered last year, and I think the same person killed them both."

Dahlia pursed her lips but said nothing. She'd certainly heard about Kimberly Elmont—there'd been practically nothing else on TV all weekend. And she remembered Caroline Fisher, too, because Caroline had been killed only two blocks from the house Dahlia shared with her husband and daughter, and she'd made Fred put extra locks on the day after they found the Fisher girl.

"Come on, Dahlia," Tina said, sensing the records clerk's indecision. "I don't even want medical information. All I want to know is if Caroline Fisher was ever a patient here, and if she was, if there was anyone who looked at both their records."

Dahlia turned it over in her mind. Technically, Tina Wong was right—the information she wanted wouldn't break any laws. On the other hand, it would sure violate hospital policy, maybe even badly enough to get her fired. On the third hand, she and Fred hadn't spent fifteen years raising Jessica so some madman could kill her, and if all Tina Wong wanted was a simple confirmation that someone had been here—

Dahlia's fingers flew over the keyboard for a few seconds, and finally she nodded. "Okay, Caroline Fisher was a patient here, too."

"Can you tell me if the same people accessed both those girls' records?" Tina pressed. "I'm not asking for names—just whether anybody worked with both of them."

Dahlia opened a second window on her computer screen and pulled up Kimberly Elmont's records, then pulled up pop-ups in both windows that showed the names and dates of everyone who had ever accessed them.

Both lists were short, and none of the names appeared on both lists. Then, just as she was about to close the window on the Elmont record, she noticed something: the last entry on the access record showed a date, but no name. Dahlia's brows furrowed as her eyes shifted to the Fisher girl's file.

"What is it?" Tina Wong asked. "What did you find?"

"Now, that's not right," Dahlia muttered, barely even aware that she'd spoken out loud.

"What's not right, Dahlia? What did you find?"

"Kimberly Elmont's file was accessed two weeks ago, but there's no log-on information. And the same thing with the Fisher girl. A little over a year ago someone looked at her file, but there's no log-on information."

"What does that mean?" Tina pressed.

Dahlia opened her mouth, but before she could say anything she remembered to whom she was talking. If there was a hole in the hospital's security system, the last thing she needed was for Tina Wong to know about it before she told her boss. "Probably nothing," she said. "It's just a violation of policy, that's all. Now I'll have to try to run it down and write up the violations."

Tina smiled knowingly. "Someone hacked into the computer, didn't they?"

"I didn't say that," Dahlia replied. "And if you say I did, our lawyers will be contacting you." She rose to her feet, fully intending to escort the newswoman out of the Records Office so she could close the door, lock it, and then get on the phone to her boss to report her discovery. But then an image of her daughter rose in her mind, and she hesitated before saying, "You promise you won't quote me? You won't use this on the air at all?" She saw the excitement in Tina Wong's eyes as the reporter swore she'd keep whatever she was told to herself. "It's not supposed to happen," Dahlia said. "It's supposed to be impossible to access our records without logging on. It's probably just a glitch in the system, and there's nothing wrong at all."

"But you don't think so," Tina said quietly.

Dahlia looked directly into her eyes. "Please, Miss Wong, if you say anything about this on the air, I'll lose my job. But I have a daughter about the same age as Kimberly Elmont."

"I'll keep it confidential," Tina assured her. "But even if it gets out, don't worry about it—you haven't done anything wrong."

After Tina Wong was gone, Dahlia sat staring at her monitor, trying to figure out what she should do next. She pulled up a few random files, hoping the same unidentified access would show, but on every record she looked at, each access had proper log-on identifications listed.

So maybe Tina Wong was right.

Maybe these were the only two.

But what if there was another?

And what if no one found it until someone else was murdered?

She printed out the two records and headed to the hospital administrator's office, deciding that even if she'd told Tina Wong too much, her boss had to know their records were no longer secure.

14

"Dinner in five minutes, Miss Alison."

The disembodied voice coming out of the intercom didn't startle Alison half as much this evening as it had last night, partly because she'd heard it before, but mostly because now she at least knew who it was: Maria, who worked for her stepfather five days a week, coming in sometime in the afternoon and not leaving until after dinner. In fact, she might not have jumped at all if she hadn't still been staring at the clothes she'd found in her closet five minutes ago.

She'd been intending to take a minute to change her blouse before she went downstairs, but then she opened the closet and saw them. Half a dozen pairs of slacks hanging neatly on wooden hangers, covered with transparent plastic covers, as if they'd just come from the cleaners. Next to them were just as many blouses, wrapped the same way. At first she thought they must be her mother's and that Maria had just put them in the wrong closet, but she didn't recognize them as her mother's. At least, she didn't recognize the pants—they were mostly in shades practically everyone had. But the blouses were gorgeous, and if her mother had ever worn any of them, she would have remembered. She took one off its hanger.

Not quite new.

And the label was Roberto Cavalli.

It had to be expensive, and even though it was gorgeous, it wasn't the kind of thing her mother would ever have worn, let alone bought. So where had it come from?

She was still examining the clothes, all of which were from designers just as famous—and no doubt as expensive—as Cavalli when she heard Maria's voice through the intercom.

"Be right down," she replied. Grabbing one of her own blouses from the back of the closet, she quickly put it on, closed the closet door, and headed down to the dining room.

Just like last night, her mother and stepfather were looking almost lost at one end of the huge table, the seat across from her mother waiting for her.

Her mother, a goblet of white wine held halfway to her lips, paused to smile at her. "How was the first day at school?" she asked.

Suddenly wishing she'd changed her pants as well as her blouse before coming down, Alison perched uncomfortably on the edge of her chair, feeling lost in the ornate dining room. It didn't help that her hair was still wet from the pool party. At least she'd combed it back and tied it into a ponytail so it wasn't making her shoulders damp, and if she didn't lean back, it wouldn't get the velvet upholstery on the chair wet, either. "It was okay," she finally admitted. "I hear the lit teacher is tough, but it's my favorite subject, so I'm not too worried."

"See?" Risa said. "All that worrying was for nothing."

Alison's eyes avoided her mother's. "I guess."

Risa cocked her head, eyeing her daughter appraisingly. Something, obviously, was wrong. Or at least not right. "And you went swimming with some new friends?" she prompted.

Alison kept her eyes on the plate Maria set in front of her. "It seems they were told to invite me."

"Told to?" her mother echoed. "What do you mean, 'told to'?"

Alison finally looked at her mother. "Conrad called their parents and told them to be nice to the new kid."

"Oh, Lord," Risa said, slowly setting her wineglass down and turning to Conrad.

"I was just trying to help," he said before either his wife or his stepdaughter could say anything. "I thought—"

Risa laughed. "You thought what any man with no children would think. But all you did was make Alison feel like—"

"An idiot," Alison finished, supplying the word her mother had hesitated to use. "How could you do that?" she said to her stepfather. "I was so embarrassed I wanted to die! How could you even—"

"But you didn't die," Risa intervened, hoping to head off the conversation before anyone lost their temper. "Conrad was just trying to make sure you didn't spend the day with no one talking to you. It was a nice thing to do."

Alison bit her lips, but said nothing.

"And I'm really sorry if it got awkward," Conrad said. "Believe me, that was the last thing I wanted."

"And apparently it turned out all right," Risa pressed when Alison still said nothing. She waited a moment, then spoke again, her voice sharper. "Didn't it, Alison?"

"I guess," Alison finally whispered, knowing her mother wasn't going to let up until she backed down.

"I really am sorry if you were uncomfortable," Conrad said. "But my intentions were good, and I can guarantee there won't be any more surprises. From now on I'll check with your mother before I do anything. Okay?"

Alison hesitated, then nodded and picked up her fork. Before she could take a bite, though, she was sure she knew where the blouses and pants in her closet had come from. She put the fork down again and looked at Conrad. "What about the clothes?" she said.

"Clothes?" she heard her mother repeat, and Alison knew without a doubt she'd been right.

"Caught again," Conrad groaned. "I had Maria put some stuff in your closet—"

"Stuff?" Risa asked. "What kind of stuff?"

"Just some clothes of Margot's. Maria found them in the basement, and Alison's about the same size as Margot, and I thought . . . " His voice trailed off and he offered Risa a helpless shrug. "Obviously I was wrong. Again."

"What kind of clothes are they?" Risa pressed, turning back to Alison.

"Designer stuff—Roberto Cavalli."

"Roberto Cavalli?" Risa repeated, her eyes widening. She turned to Conrad. "Good God, Conrad—Cavalli costs a fortune!"

He spread his hands. "How do I know what they cost? Margot used to just buy what she wanted, and I thought maybe Alison might like to have them, that's all."

"And wear them where?" Alison asked, rolling her eyes.

"Well," Conrad said, even though it was clear Alison wasn't expecting an answer, "I can think of one place right off the bat." When neither his wife nor his stepdaughter said anything, but looked expectantly at him, he went on. "Alison's sixteenth birthday is coming up, right? I thought we should throw you a party." He smiled at her. "You can invite all your new friends."

Before Alison could utter the single curt word that came to mind, her mother spoke.

"That's a wonderful idea—a Sweet Sixteen party!"

"I thought we'd have it here at the house," Conrad said, "maybe out in the garden. We'll get a band, and have it catered—you two can put your heads together about the menu."

Alison's eyes swept the formal dining room and she tried to imagine having a party there.

Tried, and failed. This was definitely not the kind of place Cindy and the rest of her friends hung out. "I don't think so," she finally said. "Maybe next year."

"But you won't be sixteen next year," her mother protested. "This is a rite of passage."

Suddenly Alison's appetite fled and an image of her father's house popped into her mind. If she were there right now, Scott would be cooking in the kitchen while she and her father sat at the counter, all of them teasing each other. And if she were going to have a party, that's where it should be—in her father and Scott's nice, small, casual house, where her friends could hang out, and they could all be who they were and dress the way they wanted to. In fact, maybe she'd ask him. At least if it was there, and all her old friends from Santa Monica were there, it would be a good party. But if it was here—

"I'm sorry," Conrad said, reading the expression on her face. "Forget it. It was just an idea."

"And it's a great idea," Risa declared. "Come on, Alison," she went on, her eyes fixing on her daughter, reading what was going on in Alison's mind as easily as Conrad had. "What's the problem? You can invite anyone you want, and it will be warm enough to use the pool. We can have a barbecue, and keep it low-key."

Alison hesitated, remembering everything her father had told her about giving her new life a chance. But why did everything have to change at once? Still, there was no reason she couldn't have the same party here that she could have at her father's. "Can I invite all my friends from Santa Monica?"

"You can invite whoever you like," Conrad said. "It's your party."

"Anyone? All my old friends?"

"Anyone," Conrad agreed. "You can invite as many people as you want."

Still Alison hesitated, but finally nodded. "All right then, maybe. It might be fun."

"Excellent!" Conrad said.

"But you won't call anybody's parents and have them tell their kids to come?" Alison asked.

"Alison!" Risa gasped, but Conrad only laughed and raised three fingers over his heart.

"Scout's honor," he promised.

"And I don't have to try to wear any of those clothes you put in my closet?"

"Well, you could at least try them on," Conrad said. "Then, if you still don't want to, go to Neiman-Marcus. If you can't find something for a party there, you're not a teenage girl at all."

Risa reached over and squeezed Conrad's hand, and Alison watched as they smiled at each other. Then she went back to her salad, moving it around on her plate until Maria finally took it away.

❖   ❖   ❖

The fingers deftly manipulated the mouse, and the screen saver on the computer monitor dissolved to reveal a series of images that the eyes devoured almost in the instant it took for the information to appear on the screen.

In the upper left-hand corner of the monitor was an image the eyes had studied for so long that every feature was imprinted on the retina with such clarity that the eyelids were no longer even required to be open for the mind to conjure up those perfect forms. But now the lids were open, and the eyes were fastened on a single feature of that perfect face.

The lips.

Those lips were blown up in a second window, and as the eyes watched in fascination, a stream of photographs of other lips— anonymous lips—flew through yet a third window on the screen as the program the mind had devised compared and then rejected thousands—millions—of them.

And in the bottom right-hand corner a high school yearbook photograph waited.

For a moment the fingers of the right hand drummed impatiently on the desktop.

The eyes flashed to the clock on the wall.

Seconds ticked by.

And finally a fourth window flashed open:

6 MATCHES FOUND

The fingers moved to the mouse and clicked rapidly through all six photographs.

Each was dismissed.

Wrong! They were all wrong!

The fingers closed hard on the mouse, almost breaking the button as the search was aborted.

So much time wasted!

Then the mind overcame the raging emotions, and the body calmed, the fingers relaxed. Moving rapidly now, the hand manipulated the mouse, the fingers tapped quickly, and the image in the upper left corner expanded to fill the screen, then kept expanding until the lips alone dominated the monitor.

Perfect.

The upper lip curving in perfect symmetry, a cupid's bow poised above the soft, gentle swell of the lower.

The right arm lifted and the tip of the right forefinger touched the cold screen of the monitor, gently tracing the perfect contours as the eyes admired the exquisite balance of upper and lower lip.

Of course! That was the missing parameter that the computer had not searched for.

The hand dropped away from the monitor and the fingers flew expertly over the keyboard, bringing up the measuring tool for the facial-recognition software. Again the lips were measured, this time with attention paid to the relationship between upper and lower lip. The ratios had to be exact, the scale perfect if a suitable match was to be found.

Fresh parameters were copied to the search window, checked and rechecked, and finally the fingers rolled the mouse so the cursor hovered over the final command button:

EXECUTE SEARCH

The forefinger pressed on the mouse, and once again photographs began to stream through the search window as the computer scoured the Internet for a perfect match.

The eyes moved to the lower photograph, then the fingers holding the mouse clicked on the command to maximize it.

The fresh young face from the high school yearbook filled the screen.

The measuring tool went over the photograph, measuring each aspect of the face down to the last millimeter between the nose and the upper lip.

The exact gap between eyebrows.

The width of the chin.

The breadth of the nostrils.

And each measurement confirmed the master plan, and the mind's confidence grew.

It could all be done.

The computer beeped.

1 MATCH FOUND

Though the constant stream of photographs still went on, the mind had to know. If the parameters still weren't right, if they had to be corrected yet again, it had to be done right away. No more hours could be lost to the stupidity of something so simple as incorrect measurements.

With a single tap of a finger on the mouse, a photograph opened on the screen, and instantly the mind felt a tingle of excitement running through the body.

It looked good; it felt right.

The fingers trembled as they deployed the measurement tool so the mind could check all the parameters one last time.

Perfect!

A moment later the fingers had found a name: Natalie Owen.

As part of the computer's processor continued scanning through millions of pictures, another part of it began searching for data on Natalie Owen, and within a few seconds the eyes were transmitting that information to the mind: Natalie Owen was twenty-four years old and worked at Sunset Vista Continuing Care Center in Los Angeles.

The focus on Natalie Owen tightened until the mind had found a back door to the woman's medical records, and the tingling in the body increased as the eyes transmitted the data from the screen to the mind.

The blood type was right.

The medical records were closed, and a map appeared, in the center of which was Sunset Vista Continuing Care Center.

The phone number was also provided.

A plan began to take form as the fingers aborted the ongoing photo search and let the computer rest at last.

It had done its job, and done it well.

Still, the mind couldn't resist commanding the forefinger to execute one last click of the mouse before shutting down the computer for the night, and the yearbook photograph at the bottom of the screen enlarged to fill the screen.

But the eyes that scanned the face of Alison Shaw were not looking at the bright, athletic, happy young teen. Rather, they were studying only the basic facial features—the brows, the nose, the lips, the ears.

More important, the eyes studied the bone and muscle structure underlying those features.

Though the eyes were looking at Alison's face, they saw nothing of Alison at all.

15

Though Alison had made Tasha Rudd promise not to mention the birthday party to *anyone,* by second period almost everybody in the school seemed to know about it, and Dawn Masin was demanding to know what Alison was going to wear.

"I don't know," Alison moaned as she rummaged through her locker in search of her history book. "Conrad said I should go to Neiman-Marcus and buy something on his account."

"Perfect," Dawn declared. "Meet me right here." She'd pointed at the spot on the floor directly in front of Alison's locker. "Right here, before lunch."

Alison agreed, and now she was in Dawn's Mercedes along with Tasha and Crystal Akers, and instead of having lunch they were headed to Neiman-Marcus.

"What are we doing?" Alison asked. "By the time we get there, we'll have, like, fifteen minutes, or we'll never get back on time." Her stomach was growling in protest at shopping instead of eating, but she wasn't about to admit that to any of the other girls in the car, none of whom seemed to care that they weren't going to get any lunch.

"We'll have at least half an hour," Dawn shot back. "And that's plenty of time. You'll see—we're expert shoppers, and you'll love the first thing you try on."

"I just don't want to be late," Allison worried.

"We're never late," Tasha assured her. "We've got this down to a science."

"You've been to Neiman's before, right?" Crystal asked.

"A couple of times," Alison said, carefully avoiding telling them she'd never actually bought anything there.

Tasha giggled in the backseat. "We go there on lunch hour all the time."

"Shopping is *way* better than eating," Crystal added, confirming Alison's suspicions about her new friends' attitude toward lunch.

As they arrived at the big store on Wilshire Boulevard, Tasha, Dawn, and Crystal wasted no time, knowing exactly where to go, and within less than two minutes a smartly suited saleswoman was smiling at them and greeting all three of them by name.

"Hi, Mrs. Wright," Tasha said. "This is Alison Shaw, and she's looking for something to wear to her sixteenth birthday party."

Mrs. Wright appraised Alison's figure, and Alison could see the uncertainty in the woman's eyes.

"She needs to look hot," Crystal said.

"And she's putting it on Dr. Dunn's account," Tasha said over her shoulder as she began to sort through clothes, picking up dresses, quickly rejecting them, and dropping them back on the racks.

Mrs. Wright's expression cleared, and now she was beaming. "Of course," she said. "You're *that* Alison Shaw! Dr. Dunn called this morning and told me to expect you."

Dawn nudged her in the ribs. "Bingo!" she whispered.

"You're on his open account," Mrs. Wright continued, and now Crystal was grinning broadly at the puzzled look on Alison's face.

"It means there's no limit!" Crystal said. "Let's get busy!"

"This!" Tasha declared a moment later, holding up a silvery black piece of fabric on a hanger. "Try this one on, Alison."

"Mandalay," Mrs. Wright said, deftly taking the dress from Tasha. "Lovely choice. I'll open a dressing room for you."

Alison watched nervously as the other three girls tore through the racks, pulling out one dress after another, holding them up against themselves and each other, rejecting most of them but keeping a few, none of which looked close to her style. They were all much too fancy, too expensive, too . . .

Too much like Dawn and Tasha and Crystal, and not at all like her.

"Time!" Dawn called out.

Alison relaxed. If they already had to go back to school, she wasn't even going to have to try on any of the dresses, let alone choose one. But a second later Tasha dashed her hopes.

"Time to hit the dressing room," she explained, and hurried her toward Mrs. Wright, who Alison could see obviously understood how these lunch-hour shopping sprees worked a lot better than she did.

A single dress hung on the wall in the enormous dressing area Mrs. Wright ushered her into, and her three classmates crowded onto a sofa, waiting.

"Well?" Dawn said. "Let's see it on you."

Wishing she could sink through the floor, Alison stripped off her school clothes and slipped into the dress.

It clung to her body like Saran wrap, and flared out into a very short skirt.

The back was cut in a vee that went so far below her waist, she was sure the tops of her buttocks were showing.

And there was far more room in the bodice than she needed, let alone could fill.

"This is a little too dressy," Alison said, doing her best not to let her embarrassment over the cut of the dress show.

"It's *perfect*," Tasha said, ignoring her words. "Let's see. Turn around."

"And hold your hair up," Crystal added.

Deciding argument would only waste time, Alison pushed her hair onto the top of her head and turned slowly. But she got a good look at herself in one of the mirrors and shook her head. "It's too old for me."

"You could use my falsies," Tasha said, instantly homing in on the biggest problem with the dress.

Mrs. Wright tapped on the dressing room door, then stepped in, her face lighting up when she saw Alison. "That is the one dress on this whole floor that is absolutely perfect for you," she said. "It shows off what a wonderful, athletic figure you have."

"See?" Tasha said.

Alison rolled her eyes, certain Mrs. Wright would have said the same thing no matter what she was wearing, as long as it was expensive.

"And you can wear it everywhere, too," Crystal said. "From now on you'll be going to lots of parties."

Alison shook her head and started to peel the dress off.

"She'll take it," Dawn said to Mrs. Wright as she glanced at her watch.

Alison frowned.

"You can always return it if you really don't like it," Dawn reasoned. "And we don't have time for anything else right now."

Mrs. Wright quickly stepped forward to help Alison out of the dress.

"How much is it?" Alison asked as the saleswoman put the dress back on a hanger.

Mrs. Wright consulted the tag. "Only twelve fifty," she said.

Alison's eyes widened. "Twelve *hundred?*"

"It's an excellent value," Mrs. Wright replied as she adjusted the dress on its hanger. "Shall I have it sent up to Dr. Dunn's home?"

"Yes," Tasha answered for Alison. "And we have to run, or we'll be late."

Less than five minutes later Alison was back in Dawn's car, the receipt for the dress in her purse. What had she been doing, spending over a thousand dollars on a *dress*?

A beautiful dress, yes. In fact, a dress that was far too beautiful for her—she couldn't even fill its bodice!

What was going on? How had she let it happen? And why had her whole life turned into something she barely even understood, that was being run by people she barely knew?

But it was going to be all right—she'd just have to learn how to live her new life in her new world, and in the end everything would work out.

RISA SHAW KNEW by the look on Lynette Rudd's face that there was little chance of selling her the house they had entered no more than a minute earlier, but that had never stopped her yet. "The great thing about this house is that it's got good bones. You can't get construction like this anymore, no matter what you're willing to pay."

Lynette nodded noncommittally as she gazed at the living room, which was certainly large enough, even if the ceiling was far too low. "Very mid-century," she said. "Way too much updating, and I don't even want to think about what the bathrooms are going to look like."

"Dated," Marjorie Stern declared, making Risa wish once again that Lynette Rudd hadn't insisted on bringing her along. Alone, she could have worked Lynette into giving the house a chance, but with Marjorie Stern, it was two against one. "Still, Risa has a point. Most of the work's cosmetic, and the basic design isn't bad." Risa's hopes rose. "If you like mid-century," Marjorie went on, making it clear that she herself did not, and dashing Risa's newfound hope before it had even fully formed.

"And cosmetic isn't cheap," Lynette said with a smile. "As we all so very well know."

"Still, it's a buyer's market," Risa interjected in a last-ditch effort to save the possibility of a sale. "We can take ten percent off the asking price right off the bat, and I suspect there's still a lot of room for negotiation."

"Twenty-five percent off the top might get my attention," Lynette sighed, "so I don't think this is the house for me."

"At least I know what not to show you," Risa replied, deciding that next time she showed Lynette a house, Marjorie Stern would not be with them. "I'll keep my eyes open."

"So enough of this house hunting," Marjorie said. "Let's go have a drink."

Risa picked up her purse and briefcase, mentally rescheduling the time she'd set aside to show Lynette Rudd what was currently on the Bel Air housing market.

"Will you join us, Risa?" Lynette asked.

Risa hoped her surprise at the invitation didn't show. She'd shown Lynette houses twice before, but never had she suggested they get together for anything other than business. "I'd love to. Where shall I meet you?"

"The club?" Lynette suggested to Marjorie, who nodded her approval. Lynette turned to Risa. "Bel Air Country Club. Just follow us."

Ten minutes later Risa's Buick was parked behind Lynette's Bentley in front of the valet stand, and the three women walked through the club to the terrace and ordered cocktails.

"How's Alison liking the academy?" Lynette asked as the waiter disappeared.

"Very much," Risa replied. "Thanks to Tasha and her friends. They seem to have taken her under their wings."

"Tasha likes Alison. I think they'll become good friends."

Risa turned to Marjorie Stern, who looked to be about their same age. "Do you have children at the academy, too?" she asked, deciding to use the same shortening for the Wilson Academy that Lynette had just employed.

"God no!" Marjorie exclaimed. "Never married—never found anyone willing to sign a prenup." She laughed and drank half of her martini.

"Marjorie's family owns half of Culver City, and most of the oil under it," Lynette explained.

"Which I'm going to need when I have my brows lifted next week," Marjorie said, signaling the waiter for a second round of drinks only a moment after he'd delivered the first. "The price has doubled since my last one. Ten thousand for two lousy eyebrows! Can you believe it? It's not like he's giving me brand-new ones, for Christ's sake."

"Who's doing it?" Lynette asked, sipping her martini.

"Conrad, of course—who else would I trust?" She leaned toward Risa. "You must be costing him a bundle, the way he's raising his rates!" Then, as Risa felt her face flushing, Marjorie Stern raised her glass. "And more power to you!" She leaned back in her chair, drained the rest of her glass, and eyed Risa speculatively a moment before the waiter set another martini down. "So what's next for you?" she asked.

Risa stared her. What was the woman talking about? Had she missed something?

"Nips and tucks, Risa," Lynette offered, reading Risa's confusion.

"You mean surgery?" Risa asked. "I've never actually—"

"Oh, my God!" Marjorie barked. "We have a virgin! So then, let me rephrase: what's scheduled first?"

"First?" Risa echoed. "I wasn't planning on having anything done."

Lynette and Marjorie stared at her blankly.

"You're kidding, right?" Marjorie finally said into the ensuing silence.

Risa felt as if she'd said something wrong. "Why? What have you had done?"

"Me?" Lynette laughed, then held up one hand and started ticking off her fingers one by one. "Let me count. Chin implant was first—and you should consider that first, too, since it's really easy. Then my nose and eyes. Breast reduction when I turned forty, which was a true load off my back. And I had a brow lift last year."

As Risa's fingers went self-consciously to her chin, Lynette turned to Marjorie, who had just finished the second martini. "Come on, Marj—give her the list, and don't leave anything out."

"Good lord," Marjorie said. "I don't even know if I can remember everything. I've had breast implants twice, a brow lift, my nose, my eyes, my turkey wattle tightened up, liposuction . . . " She sighed and shook her head with mock ruefulness. "Jesus, it seems like it's always one damn thing or another."

"You've got to be kidding," Risa blurted without thinking. A split second later, realizing how her words must have sounded, she tried to recover. "I mean, I just never would have known—looking at both of you—"

"Oh, come on, Risa," Lynette cut in. "Look around here! Do you actually think there's a single woman in this place but you that hasn't had at least half a dozen procedures?" She nodded toward a woman with beautifully coiffed white hair who was clad in what even Risa knew had to be at least ten thousand dollars worth of elegantly casual clothes and several hundred thousand dollars worth of perfectly cut diamonds. "How old do you think she is?"

Risa tried not to stare too long at the woman, and finally shrugged uncertainly. "Fifty? I'd say in her forties, except for her hair."

"Try eighties," Lynette replied. "And not early eighties, either. You need to rethink your ideas about surgery fast, Risa." Lynette's voice dropped and took on a serious note. "If you want to stay married to Conrad for very long, you'd better learn to always look your very best, and I don't mean just your clothes and hair. You're going to be the first person people think of when they're deciding who's going to work on them. You, and Alison."

"Which means you're both going to have to be perfect," Marjorie added, just in case Risa might not have understood Lynette's words.

Risa felt herself flushing again. "Conrad's not that shallow," she said, but even as she spoke, she wasn't entirely sure she believed it.

"Then I'm afraid you're underestimating exactly how much Margot did for his practice," Marjorie said. "And how much work he did on her."

Risa stared at her drink, unwilling to look at either Lynette or Marjorie Stern.

"It's not really about being shallow," Lynette said, trying to alleviate some of the sting she could sense Risa feeling. "Making women beautiful isn't just Conrad's job—it's his passion. And both you and Alison would be making big mistakes if you didn't use his services."

Marjorie reached out and gave Risa's hand a reassuring squeeze. "Let him make you gorgeous before it's too late."

"And get Alison with the program, too," Lynette advised. "Did she tell you that she borrowed Tasha's falsies the other day?"

Risa stared at her mutely, shaking her head.

"There was no swimming suit top that would fit her without them." She leaned forward again. "You can't let Alison be Wilson Academy's first wallflower, Risa—it's just not fair to her."

Risa sat back in her chair, barely able to believe what she was hearing.

"Take a good look around here," Lynette said. "Look at everybody. Do you see a flat chest or a wrinkle anywhere?"

Risa scanned the women who filled the club. This was Conrad's world, and this was Conrad's club.

And every woman in it—even their waitresses—was perfect.

Lynette was right—there was no way either she or Alison could compete with these people, not without all the help her husband could give them. Maybe she ought to ask Conrad for a consultation and a professional appraisal, not only of Alison, but of her, too. She hadn't forgotten their honeymoon night, when Conrad had called out Margot's name as they made love, and if she was going to be honest with herself, their sex life wasn't what it should be for newlyweds.

Was Conrad already losing interest in her?

Would something as simple as a little plastic surgery fix that?

She didn't know, but she intended to find out.

ALISON GAZED dolefully at the black zippered bag emblazoned with the Neiman-Marcus logo that was already hanging on the hook on her closet door, then turned away from it, pulled the textbooks out of her backpack, and settled down at her desk to start organizing her homework for the evening.

But even with her back to the black bag hanging on her closet door, she couldn't get it—or its contents—out of her mind. Maybe she should take another look at herself in the dress before she sent it back. What if she was wrong? What if the dress really did look good on her, as Tasha and Dawn kept insisting when she told them she was going to return it? What if they were right, and it was the perfect dress for her birthday party?

Maybe she should show it to her mother. That would do it—her mother would hate the dress, and she'd be right, it was way too old for her, and nothing at all like the kind of stuff she and her friends in Santa Monica always wore. The most dressed-up they ever got was a skirt and blouse instead of their usual jeans and shirts.

Except she wasn't in Santa Monica anymore, and her new friends never wore the kind of stuff she used to wear all the time. Pushing the still unopened history book aside, she left her desk, pulled down the zipper on the bag, then shed the jeans and cotton sweater she'd been wearing that day.

The dress shimmered even in the daylight of the room—under the lights of a birthday party, it would be spectacular. She took the nearly weightless dress gently off its hanger, careful to do nothing that might render it unreturnable, and slipped it over her head. The straps dropped onto her shoulders, and she delicately adjusted the fit.

She stood on tiptoe, seeing how her legs would look if she were wearing the high heels the dress demanded. And as she looked at herself in the mirrored wall surrounding the closet door, she had to admit that Tasha and Dawn were right; the dress was absolutely spectacular, and except for the bodice, it actually looked right on her.

There was a soft knock, immediately followed by her mother's voice, muffled by the heavy wood of the bedroom door. "Honey?"

Alison hesitated, feeling like a child caught with her hand in the cookie jar, then let her heels drop back to the floor. She hadn't done anything wrong; in fact, the next thing she'd intended to do was ask her mother about the dress. "C'mon in," she called, bracing herself for what she was sure would be an instant rejection. "You better see what I bought."

The door opened, Risa stepped inside, caught sight of the dress, and stopped short, staring at her daughter in silence.

Seconds ticked by.

The silence stretched.

"You hate it," Alison finally said, her voice cracking as she realized the dress looked so bad on her that her mother couldn't even bring herself to speak.

But then her mother was smiling.

"Hate it?" Risa repeated. "How on earth could I hate it? It's absolutely gorgeous! I just never dreamed you'd choose something so dressy."

"Dawn and Tasha picked it out for me," Alison said, rising back up to her tiptoes and piling her hair up the way Crystal had told her in the store. "What do you think? Is it way too old for me?" But even before her mother answered, Alison saw the approval in her eyes.

"Given the occasion, I think it's perfect," Risa said. "Your friends have good taste. All we have to do is find you the right shoes and get your hair done, and you'll be the prettiest girl at the party, which is exactly as it should be."

A flood of relief flowed through Alison, but as she turned back to the mirror to see what her mother was visualizing, she caught sight once more of the bodice, and her relief drained away. "I don't know," she said, her fingers going to the loose top. "This doesn't seem to fit quite right." She eyed herself gloomily in the mirror. "In fact, it doesn't fit at all."

Risa pulled four tissues from the box on Alison's nightstand and tucked them into the bust of the dress. "Better?" she asked.

"Oh, that'll be great—I can hardly wait to hear what Tasha and Dawn have to say about me running around with my bra stuffed with Kleenex," Alison said. Still, if she imagined the tissues were flesh instead of paper, the profile was definitely improved.

Echoes of the conversation she'd had that afternoon with Lynette Rudd and Marjorie Stern recurred to Risa. "Suppose it wasn't Kleenex?" she said. "What if it was you?"

Alison pulled the tissues out of her bodice and sourly eyed the reflection of her flat chest. "Why do I think that's not going to happen?" she asked. "I mean, given how long it's been since I hit puberty, it's pretty clear that I'm just not going to get anything else up here."

Again Risa remembered the conversation earlier in the day. "Not naturally, perhaps," she said carefully.

Alison turned to look at her mother. "What do you mean, 'not naturally'?"

"Well, there are other ways of gaining what nature isn't supplying," Risa said, still not sure how Alison might react to what she was about to suggest. But her daughter beat her to it.

"You mean implants?" she asked, her eyes widening.

"Well, it's just a thought," Risa began. "But apparently a lot more people are doing it than I ever thought."

"Including Tasha and Crystal," Alison said. "And Dawn even had her lips done."

"Really," Risa said.

For a long moment mother and daughter simply looked at each other as if each were wondering which of them was going to be the first to step across the line that had suddenly appeared in front of them.

Finally, Risa spoke again. "I suppose it wouldn't hurt to talk to Conrad about the possibilities. I mean, he's the professional."

Alison wasn't quite sure she'd heard right. "You'd really let me get implants?"

"Well, we can certainly talk about it," Risa said. "Everything is worth at least *considering*, isn't it? Besides, talking about them doesn't mean scheduling surgery." She turned Alison around to face the mirror. "Of course, your father might not agree."

"Dad doesn't have to agree with everything," Alison said, speaking to her mother's reflection. "And he doesn't even need to know that we're talking about it, since talking doesn't mean scheduling."

"How about if I talk with Conrad later?" Risa asked. "Then he can take a look at you and give us his professional opinion."

Alison felt a shiver go through her at the thought of Conrad Dunn seeing her topless, let alone touching her. "No," she said. "I don't want Conrad looking at my breasts! That's just too weird."

Risa rolled her eyes. "For heaven's sake, Alison—he's a doctor! A professional. And he's the best there is. Who else do you think should do it?"

"I don't know," Alison said, rubbing the shiver from her arms. "It's just too creepy."

Risa sighed. "Well, at least give it some thought, all right?"

"I guess," Alison replied, but Risa could hear the doubt in her voice. She slipped off the dress and held it up. "And I'm going to keep the dress. At least for now."

"You should. You look fabulous in it."

"*Almost* fabulous," Alison amended archly. Then, as her mother left the room, she hung the dress in her closet, closed the door, and eyed herself in the mirror once again, twisting and turning to see her torso from every angle.

There was nothing wrong with her waist, or her buttocks, and when she rose to her toes, her legs took on a very nice shape.

She just didn't have anything on top to balance out everything else.

She cupped her hands under her small breasts and lifted them up into mounds.

And that, she decided, is how they should look. Or even, perhaps, maybe a touch larger.

16

FOR THREE DAYS RISA HAD TRIED TO FIND THE RIGHT WAY TO BRING up the subject of Alison's breasts with Conrad, and for three days she'd failed. She told herself that the time wasn't quite right, or that there wasn't enough time to discuss it, or used any one of a dozen other excuses not to have the conversation she knew she had to have. But when Alison came down to breakfast while she and Conrad were already at the table on the fourth morning, Risa knew she couldn't put the talk off any longer.

Alison wore her usual jeans, and a tank top that clearly showed that her bra had increased by at least one cup size. She'd watched Alison's bra look a little fuller each day, but today there was no mistaking it. Alison had bought a new bra and was filling it with something other than her breasts.

And she looked good. Even that minor change had turned her from a still flat-chested adolescent into the beginnings of what promised to soon become a curvaceous young woman.

"Lit test this morning," Alison said after bolting down her orange juice and a fistful of multivitamins. "And I need to get to the library first, because I won't have a chance later." She grabbed a piece of dry toast from the buffet and quickly ate it, perching on the edge of her chair.

"Okay, honey," Risa said. "Put a banana in your backpack for later."

Alison grabbed one from the buffet. "Got it," she said, then kissed her mother's cheek, eager to get going.

"Have a nice day," Conrad said.

"You, too," she called over her shoulder as she went through the swinging door to the kitchen to meet Maria for her ride to school.

Conrad shook his head, smiling. "Now *that* was a whirlwind breakfast."

"*That* was a typical teenager," Risa corrected.

"She sure adds a lot of energy to the house." He leaned back in his chair. "I like it."

Risa eyed him carefully, trying to decide whether he meant it. "She can be a handful," she said, offering him a chance to voice any doubts he might be harboring about having taken on a teenager at this stage of his life.

"I think I can handle it," he said. "In fact, I've been thinking about a birthday present for her. Sixteen is a special age."

Risa put down her coffee cup, recognizing the perfect moment to broach the subject that had been on her mind for days. "I have an idea," she said.

"Oh?" Conrad's brows rose with curiosity. "I was thinking a car."

"Which I'm sure she'd love, but I'm not sure I'd love her having, at least for another year. But there's something I think she would rather have but is too shy to tell you about."

Conrad frowned. "What?"

Risa saw no point trying to be delicate. "Breast implants."

"Really?" Conrad smiled. "So you, too, have noticed a curiously quick expansion in her bra size?"

"How could I miss it?" Risa countered.

"Well, it's a very easy fix," Conrad replied. "Implants are nothing anymore."

"*Nothing?*" Risa echoed doubtfully.

"Okay, not nothing," Conrad agreed. "But with Alison I'd do a transaxillary incision." When Risa only looked blank, he chuckled wryly. "That's a small incision in her armpit. Then I create a channel, go in with an endoscope, and position a bladder exactly where I want it. Once it's in place, I fill it with the amount of saline required, and that's it. A little pain of course, but only a tiny scar hidden under the arm." He glanced at the date on the morning paper folded next to his breakfast plate. "In fact, if we move reasonably quickly, she'd be pretty much healed up by the time of her party."

Risa's eyes widened in surprise. "That quickly?"

"Shouldn't be a problem," he assured her with a shrug. "Want me to put her on the schedule?"

Risa shifted uneasily in her chair. "It's sort of a touchy subject."

"What is?" Conrad frowned, then reached over to cover Risa's hand with his. "Tell me."

"Well, you're her stepfather, and she's—well, she's feeling a little shy about having you see her breasts."

Conrad chuckled.

"No, really," Risa said. "I'm not kidding. So what would you think of someone else doing the procedure?"

"I'd think that's not going to happen at all," he said flatly. "Do you really think I'd trust anyone else with Alison's surgery?" When Risa said nothing, he patted her hand reassuringly. "Don't worry about it," he told her. "Believe me, over the years, I've become as good at talking to teenage girls as I have at working on them. I'll talk to Alison— maybe even tonight."

Wondering why it had taken her three days to work up the courage to have what turned out to be a simple conversation with her husband, Risa leaned over and gave him a long, slow kiss full of what she hoped he would perceive as a promise of more to come at the end of the day.

"Maybe," he whispered, still close enough that she could feel his warm breath on her lips, "I should make Alison's breasts look just like yours."

She remembered, then, what Lynette and Marjorie had said a few days earlier. "Or maybe you ought to do a little work on mine, too."

Conrad chuckled for the second time that morning. "Work on you?" he asked. "Why? Let's just make Alison perfect, okay?"

Though Risa said nothing, his comment stung, and kept stinging for the rest of the day.

CORINNE DUNN KNOCKED softly on her brother's office door, then turned the knob and entered.

Conrad was quietly dictating surgery notes into a handheld microphone, so she sat on the brocade sofa next to his desk, a file folder on her lap, and waited for him to finish.

Eventually, he put down the microphone, clicked off the machine, and turned to smile at her. "And a very good morning to you," he said. "Sorry about that—just had to finish before I lost my train of thought."

"Like you've ever lost a thought in your life," Corinne teased. She held up the folder. "The foundation's gotten a request to fix a facial mutilation on a young woman from Bakersfield."

Conrad's brow rose skeptically. "Bakersfield? Since when did Bakersfield become a center of birth defects?"

"Okay, so it isn't as heart-tugging as a cleft palate from Honduras," she agreed, "but it's still an interesting case. The girl is only eighteen." She placed the file on his desk.

"What's the nature of the mutilation?" Conrad asked, leaving the file where Corinne had placed it.

"She was attacked while jogging. Whoever attacked her slit her throat and—if you can believe this—sliced off her eyebrows."

"Her eyebrows?" he echoed. "Now that is truly weird." He removed the before-and-after photographs of the girl from the file, set them on his desktop, and studied them. She'd been almost beautiful at one time, with shiny black hair and perfectly arched, beautifully proportioned eyebrows that he was sure had never seen so much as a tweezer, let alone any cosmetics.

"Something happened in the middle of the attack," Corinne explained. "Apparently, another jogger came along, and the attacker took off before he'd killed her. Neither the girl nor the other jogger got a good description, and they never caught the guy."

Conrad studied both pictures as she spoke. While the first was obviously a high school photo, the second one had been taken by a police photographer. It showed not only the bloody mess that had been her forehead, but the gash on her neck as well. A third photograph showed the girl with poorly done, uneven ellipses of skin grafts where her eyebrows had once been. "Good God," he muttered. "Who did this to the poor girl?"

"I told you—they never caught him."

"I meant the surgeon—if you can call him that—who tried to repair the damage? He'd have done better just to sew her up and let someone else do the real fix later."

"The name's probably in the file," Corinne replied. "The point is, can you repair the damage?" She stood and moved around behind her brother, to gaze over his shoulder at the girl's high school picture. "And there's something else—I'm not sure what it is." Leaning over, she traced the girl's brows with her forefinger. "There's something about her that looks sort of familiar, but I can't think what it is."

"Let me read what her mother wrote," Conrad said, taking the letter out of the folder and laying it over the photographs.

Corinne straightened as he began to read, and found herself looking straight into the eyes of Margot Dunn, who gazed out at her from the framed blow-up of a *Vogue* cover that still hung on Conrad's office wall.

"My God," she said. "That's it! Her eyebrows are exactly like Margot's."

"What?" Conrad said, looking up at her.

Corinne pulled the school photograph from under the mother's letter and held it up. "See? Her brows are exactly like Margot's, before her accident."

Conrad scowled. "I hardly think—"

"Look," Corinne insisted, walking over to the photograph on the wall and holding the five-by-seven school photo next to it.

Conrad shrugged. "Maybe, maybe not," he finally said. "But there are only so many variations on eyebrows."

"And these are an exact match," Corinne declared. She moved back to Conrad and set the photograph down on the open file. "What do you think?" she asked, her voice suddenly gentle. "Maybe you can do for this girl what you didn't have time to do for Margot?"

Conrad leaned back in his chair, his eyes fixed on the photograph of his former wife. "You're right," he finally said. "I can certainly help with the botched grafts." He turned his gaze away from the image of Margot and looked up at his sister. "But I can't give her back those eyebrows. I can build fairly good ones, but they won't be like Margot's. Besides, even if they were, the girl's bone structure isn't right—it's not just the shape of the features that matters, but what's under them. And those perfect bones don't come along more than once—or maybe twice—in a lifetime."

"Whatever you can do has to be better than this," Corinne said, gazing at the picture again.

She put the photos and the letter back in the file, closed it, and left her brother's office, already composing a press release in her head. Now all she had to do was put it on paper and give Jillian Oglesby and her mother the good news.

Alone in his office, Conrad Dunn gazed once more at the picture of

Margot hanging on the wall. Jillian Oglesby's brows had, indeed, resembled Margot's, but no matter what he did, he wouldn't be able to replace them. Margot, after all, had been one in a million.

On the other hand, there might still be the possibility of re-creating Margot's perfection.

Given the right bone structure.

And, of course, the right features.

TINA WONG STRODE into the Channel 3 newsroom, mentally organizing the details of the special report on the series of killings even as she spoke to everyone she passed. By the time she hit her desk, she already knew the order of the first dozen calls to make, decided who she'd recruit to help her assemble and edit the video, and made up her mind to direct the show herself. San Jose and San Diego had both been great—the mothers of both victims had shed more tears than even she would have tried to evoke, and the stepfather of the girl in San Diego had an expression on his face when he talked about his wife's daughter that she was sure would put him very high on the suspects list if the cops were smart enough to watch her show.

She dropped her briefcase on the floor next to her desk, logged on to the computer, and checked her interoffice e-mail while sipping her coffee.

She'd asked for one of the editing bays from noon on, and it had been approved until 5:00 A.M. tomorrow morning, when the station would need all the editing bays to put together the morning news.

Excellent.

She forwarded that e-mail as a text message to Pete Biner, the cameraman she'd tapped to help her put the footage together. Pete was not only great with the camera, but remembered every frame of every sequence he'd ever shot, and always knew exactly where to find whatever she wanted. But even with his expertise, they'd take up the entire time they had, and probably need even more over the next couple of nights.

Still, though the pressure was starting to build, the special had been taking shape in her mind ever since Caroline Fisher's murder, and on the way to San Jose she'd sketched out the introductory graphics, and come up with a few ideas about the music and sound effects as well. If she got it right—and she was damned sure she *would* get it right—this special would be her ticket to a correspondent gig at the network, and she'd make sure her fingerprints were on every aspect of every second of the hour.

She was about to make her first phone call when her office door slammed open and Michael Shaw stood in the doorway holding a sheet of paper. "Wait until you see this," he said. "You're not going to believe it."

Tina picked up the single sheet he'd dropped on her desk. It was some kind of press release—not the kind of thing either she or Michael Shaw ever paid much attention to. "What's so special about this one?"

"My ex-wife's new husband is going to do a little reconstructive surgery on a very interesting charity case."

Tina quickly scanned the release from the Dunn Foundation, her heart beating faster as she did.

A twenty-year-old girl from Bakersfield who had had her throat cut and her eyebrows torn off.

"Eyebrows," Tina said. "So now we have breasts, ears, and eyebrows." She looked up at Michael. "When was she attacked?"

He shook his head. "You know everything I know," he said, indicating the brief press release.

"I'm going to need a helicopter to get up to Bakersfield," Tina said, her schedule of phone calls forgotten as she grabbed her briefcase.

"No helicopter," he declared. "Bakersfield is hardly more than two hours away."

"But I'm in editing at noon," she countered.

He shook his head firmly. "Sorry."

"I don't have time to argue with you, Michael," she told him as she speed-dialed Pete Biner.

"You can take a van and Pete," Michael said. "The editing bay will be waiting when you get back."

"We're going to need it tomorrow, too."

Michael shook his head. "No."

Tina's eyes shot darts at him. "It's either the helicopter or the bay, Michael. I only have so much time, so if I have to drive to Bakersfield and back—"

"All right, all right," he said, holding up his hands to stem her flood of words. "I'll see what I can do."

But Tina was no longer even listening. She was on her phone. "Meet me in the parking lot in thirty seconds," she was saying, and he knew she was talking to Biner. "We're going to Bakersfield." She snapped her phone shut. "You know, Michael," she said, her eyes narrow, "if you're not going to help me on this, you'd better at least stay out of my way."

"Have a good trip," he said, deciding to ignore the implied threat.

But Tina Wong was already halfway down the hallway.

Not that she would have cared what he said even if she'd heard him.

17

Risa checked her watch, decided that stretching dinner with her husband and daughter even another five minutes could ruin the deal she'd been working on for the last week, and waved off the waiter who was about to refill her coffee cup. "Have to run," she announced. "If the sunset's any good at all tonight, I'll be coming home with an offer. When the clients ask to see a house at night, you know you've almost got them. And this is a tough one—it's practically a tear-down, and it's six million."

"Go get 'em," Conrad said, squeezing her hand as she passed behind him.

She kissed Alison on the forehead. "I might be late."

"I'll still be up," Alison sighed. "I've got tons of homework."

"Okay. I'll come in to say good-night."

As if Risa's departure was a signal, the waiter brought the check for Conrad to sign. "Would you mind if we stopped up at Le Chateau on the way home?" he asked Alison. "I'd like to check on a patient."

"Really?" Alison said, eyeing her stepfather uncertainly. Though she'd been to his office in Beverly Hills, she had only heard about the house he kept up in the hills so the wealthiest—or most famous—of his patients could convalesce from their surgery in complete privacy. "I thought nobody but you and the patients got in there."

"Me, my family, and the patients," Conrad replied.

Fifteen minutes later he parked in a large garage under a house high in the hills of Bel Air that was almost directly below their own house, though you had to wind through almost a mile of twisting roads to get from one to the other. The elevator that carried them up from the garage opened directly into a reception area that looked to Alison like the lobby of a very expensive hotel. The floors were thickly carpeted, the walls paneled in walnut, and comfortable-looking chairs flanked either side of a fireplace in which gas logs were burning even though the evening wasn't particularly cold. The room was softly lit, and a beautiful young woman sat at the mahogany reception desk, making notes in a file.

"Hi, Teresa," Conrad said. "I've come to look in on Mrs. Wilson." Teresa stood. "This is my stepdaughter, Alison Shaw," he went on, then turned to Alison. "This is Teresa, our evening nurse."

Teresa smiled and extended her hand to Alison.

"See if you can keep Alison occupied until I get back." A moment later Conrad disappeared back into the elevator.

"Make yourself comfortable," Teresa said. "I just need to make a couple of entries in this chart."

While Teresa went back to her file, Alison wandered over to a credenza covered with framed photographs of women. Beautiful women. "Are these some of Conrad's patients?"

"Mmm-hmm," Teresa said. She opened a drawer and brought out a photo album. "Here's some more—except these have before pictures, too. And believe me when I tell you this is one album that never leaves this room."

Alison took the album, dropped into one of the chairs by the fireplace, and began turning pages, gazing at before-and-after photographs of face-lifts, tummy tucks, breast augmentations and reductions, and dozens of other procedures she had never even heard of. Far more of the pictures were of girls who looked about her own age than she would have expected. Most had been as flat-chested as her before the surgery, but they all looked beautiful afterward. And not only did their breasts look perfect, but natural as well.

Near the end of the album she found a photo she was almost sure was of Tasha. At least, the "after" shot was of Tasha.

In the "before" picture, her friend was almost unrecognizable.

She was still gazing at the pictures of Tasha when Teresa sat down next to her. "Are you considering breast augmentation?"

"No," Alison said, a little too quickly, and felt herself flush. "Well, I—I don't know," she stammered. "Maybe."

"I had implants when I was sixteen," Teresa said. "Best thing I've ever done."

Alison stared at Teresa. How was it possible? She was tall, and lithe, and perfectly proportioned. How could it have been faked? "Really?" she blurted. "You weren't born looking like this?"

"Nobody is," Teresa said flatly. "And believe me, I had nothing. I mean nothing, nada, zero. Zippo! But not anymore. Now I have exactly the shape I always wanted—nothing too much, nothing not enough. Nothing dramatic, except to me."

"Who did them?"

Teresa rolled her eyes. "Dr. Dunn, of course—do you think he'd let someone else's patient work here? And believe me, if you're thinking about having anything done, I wouldn't go to anyone else."

"But he's my stepfather," Alison said, feeling her face redden again. "Just the thought of him looking at my . . ." Her voice trailed off in embarrassment, but Teresa only shrugged.

"I suppose that might seem . . . what? Awkward? But don't forget, he sees thousands of breasts every year. And all kinds of other things, too. But believe me again, it's not an intimate thing. He's a doctor, you know? Hasn't your regular doctor ever seen you naked?"

"Yeah, but—"

"But nothing," Teresa declared. "If you're even thinking about getting something done, don't go anywhere else. You'll have one moment of shyness, and then you'll be past it. Ask anyone—they'll all tell you the same thing."

Alison looked back down at the photographs of the girl she was almost sure was Tasha, but Teresa reached over and flipped back a few pages. "That's me," she said, tapping one of the before pictures.

Alison gazed at the photograph of a torso in bikini panties that might as well have been a picture of herself—slim-hipped, with a small, flat stomach and virtually no breasts under small nipples. Then her gaze shifted to the after photograph, and she saw exactly what Teresa—and Conrad Dunn—had accomplished. Though she thought both Tasha and Dawn had breasts that were a bit too big for their physiques, Teresa had chosen perfectly. She had small, well-formed breasts that Alison knew would fit as well on her own body as they did on Teresa's. They looked good, but were compact enough so they wouldn't be a problem even if she kept running track in college.

Looking up she gazed at Teresa with something like awe. "He made you look absolutely fantastic!"

Teresa smiled. "Best thing I ever did," she said again as the elevator door opened and Conrad stepped out.

"What's the best thing you ever did?" he asked. "Besides come to work for me."

"That was second best. Best was getting *you* to work on *me*. Which," she went on, taking Alison's hand in her own, "is what Alison is also thinking about doing."

Alison felt a rush of heat rise through her neck to her face. "Teresa! I didn't say—"

"Oh, come on," Teresa cut in. "The only way to get you past this is to just do it." She turned back to Conrad. "She was looking at my before-and-after shots, and I think they looked pretty good to her."

"Well, it sure wouldn't be hard to do," Conrad said, his gaze shifting to his stepdaughter. "What's the problem?"

"She's shy," Teresa said.

Alison wanted to fall through the floor.

"Why wouldn't she be?" Conrad countered. He sat down next to Alison. "You should have seen Teresa when she first came to see me—she could barely even speak."

"Really?"

"Really," Teresa said. "It was horrible. Even worse than the moment you just had."

"Which is now over," Conrad declared. He looked down at the open photo album on Alison's lap. "How about getting me a prosthesis in B, Teresa?"

"Give me thirty seconds." Teresa jumped up and disappeared down a hallway.

"Okay, so now that we're talking about it," Conrad said as soon as Teresa was gone, "how about if I gave you the procedure as a birthday present? I know it's not a car, but you're not old enough for one anyway."

"I—I don't know—" Alison floundered. "I mean, I don't know what my mom and dad would say."

Conrad grinned at her. "Well, I can't speak for your dad, but I know your mother thinks it's a good idea."

"She does?" Alison cocked her head and looked at Conrad quizzically as the truth began to dawn on her. "Was this all Mom's idea?" she asked. "Having you bring me up here to talk to Teresa?"

Conrad spread his hands helplessly. "Well, it wasn't all her idea. I might have had just a tiny little part in it. But how else were we going to get you to start talking to me about it?"

"You could have—" Alison began, but before she could finish, Teresa reappeared, holding a small lavender gift bag.

"Just take these," Conrad said, taking the bag from her and giving it to Alison. "It's a pair of falsies, exactly like the ones Teresa tried out a few years ago. Just try them for a couple of days and we can talk about it later. Or not—it's entirely up to you."

Alison gazed at the bag as if there might be a rattlesnake inside, but then gingerly took it and peered inside. "You're sure these are the same size as yours?" she asked Teresa.

Teresa nodded.

"Very conservative," Conrad said. "Which is very smart. The last thing you want to do is too much. And if you decide you want to do it, we can have you completely recovered before your party. Hey," he added as Alison looked at him suspiciously, "a girl should have her gift on her birthday, not a couple of weeks later."

"You're having a party?" Teresa asked.

"Sixteen," Alison said softly.

"Perfect," Teresa said, and gave her a warm smile.

Alison looked up at her stepfather and saw, for the first time, genuine affection on his face.

Was it the first time it was there, or was it the first time she'd let herself see it?

Maybe, after all, she'd been wrong about him.

"Let me think about it," she finally said.

"Great!" Conrad stood up. "Mrs. Wilson is stable and ready to be discharged tomorrow," he said to Teresa, then turned to Alison. "And it wasn't all a ruse: I really did need to look in on her. Ready to go home?"

Alison nodded. "My homework's still waiting for me."

And so was her first opportunity to see exactly what she'd look like if she could perfectly fill a size B bra.

ALISON STARED DARKLY at the gift bag on her dresser.

Who put falsies in a gift bag?

Weird. Very weird.

And why did the gift bag seem to be getting bigger and bigger, even though she knew it wasn't? The answer to that one was easy: it wasn't the gift bag she was thinking about at all, or even what was inside it.

No, the real problem was the surgery the bag and its contents represented. Even as she tried to concentrate on scratching Ruffles—who was curled up next to her on the bed with nothing more on his mind than making sure she didn't pause for even two seconds—she couldn't quite get the idea of the surgery out of her mind.

For one thing, no matter what Conrad said, surgery was a big deal. People could die in surgery, even surgery more minor than implants. And what if she went through it all and didn't like the results? Maybe she could have the implants taken out again, but she'd still have scars, wouldn't she?

So why did both her mother and Conrad think it was such a great idea? Of course, she couldn't remember ever having talked about plastic surgery with either one of her parents, so maybe she'd just always assumed they would be against it.

And no matter what her mother thought, she was pretty sure she was still right about her father. Maybe Scott would think it was a great idea—in fact, he probably would—but not her father. Her father would hate it.

Absolutely hate it.

Like he'd hated her being on MySpace.

He'd probably forbid her to have the implants, just like he'd forbidden her to stay on MySpace.

Why? What was the big deal?

It wouldn't be fair—it wouldn't be fair at all!

Realizing she'd just made the decision she'd never thought she'd make, she did what she always did next: picked up her cell phone from the nightstand and speed-dialed Cindy.

"Hey," she said when Cindy answered. "Guess what I'm getting for my sixteenth birthday? Besides a party, to which you're the first person I'm inviting."

"Great!" Cindy said. "And I know exactly what I'm going to get you for a present. It's perfect for someone who lives in Bel Air."

"What?" Alison demanded, suddenly missing Cindy more than she'd realized.

"You'll find out on your birthday," Cindy shot back. "I can't tell you before then. So what kind of a party is it going to be?"

"Like nothing we've ever even been to before," Alison said. "I think it's going to be kind of a fancy thing up here at the house. A garden party with caterers and a band."

"A band?" Cindy repeated, sounding less enthusiastic. "How much am I going to have to dress up?"

Alison hesitated, glancing toward her closet where the twelve-hundred-dollar dress hung. "Some," she admitted, knowing what Cindy's clothes budget was. "It's my parents' idea."

"Ooookay," Cindy said slowly. Then: "So I better buy some really, really nice jeans, right?"

"Just wear that dress you wore last Christmas," Alison told her. "It looks great, and none of the Wilson kids have ever seen you in it."

"And they'll know exactly how much it cost and that I didn't buy it at Neiman-Marcus," Cindy said sourly.

"Oh, who cares?" Alison replied. "Anyway, the party isn't even the big news. Guess what my stepfather is giving me for my birthday."

"What?"

"Implants." Alison waited expectantly for Cindy's gasp of envy, but instead heard only silence.

A silence that stretched on way too long.

"Cindy?" she finally said. "Did you hear me?"

"I heard you," Cindy finally replied. "I just assumed you were kidding." Now it was Cindy who waited for a reply that didn't come, and finally she spoke into the void. "You mean you're not kidding?"

"No," Alison said. "Why would I be kidding?"

"Because it's the stupidest idea I ever heard," Cindy replied. "What are those kids at Wilson doing to you? It's only been, what, two weeks? And you're already getting plastic surgery?"

"What's wrong with that?" Alison demanded. "Everybody gets—"

"Everybody does not get plastic surgery for their sixteenth birthday. And a boob job? From your stepfather? You know what, Alison? I think I've got to go. I'll talk to you later."

"Cindy, wait." But it was too late—she'd already clicked off.

Alison closed her cell phone and pulled Ruffles closer. "She could have at least listened to me, couldn't she?" she whispered to the dog, who only wriggled for an answer. "I mean, she didn't even let me tell her why I'm doing it."

Ruffles whimpered.

And then, as she went back to petting the little dog, a thought came to mind.

What if Cindy was right?

What if she was making a terrible mistake?

Her eyes fell again on the gift bag on her dresser. She jumped up, got the bag, and dumped its contents onto the bed.

Then she went into her mother's bedroom, took a black bra out of her middle lingerie drawer, and went back to her own room. She fitted the perfectly molded foam prosthetics into the cups of the bra, then put it on. It didn't feel quite right, so she pushed the fake breasts around a little until they felt comfortable, then pulled on her favorite sweater—an ice-blue cashmere her father had given her on her last birthday—and turned to the mirror.

And she looked good. In fact, she looked fantastic.

She looked like Teresa at Conrad's office, with breasts that were neither too large nor too small, and looked perfect on her lean frame.

But maybe it was only the sweater.

She took off the sweater and her jeans and went into the closet. Very carefully she took the party dress off its hanger and slipped it on.

And once again the fake breasts filled the bodice perfectly.

So Cindy was wrong.

The perfectly formed breasts made her look better—a lot better—and when the implants were in, it would all look even more natural than it did now.

Suddenly, she wanted to tell Conrad to schedule the procedure as soon as he could.

But first she'd call Cindy again and tell her that her attitude was all wrong. But what good would that do? She wasn't going to change Cindy's mind—when Cindy decided something, that was that. So this would just have to be one of those things that friends accepted in each other.

But as she turned in front of the mirror, she knew she had to tell *someone* what she was going to do. And it had to be someone who would be as excited as she suddenly was.

Tasha!

Of course! Alison took off the dress and put it back in her closet, then put on her bathrobe. Even it looked better with her new shape.

She flopped back onto the bed, picked up her phone, and speed-dialed Tasha, who would not only understand and share her excitement, but also be able to tell her exactly what to expect in the surgery. In it, and after it.

And maybe—just maybe—Conrad would have time to do it next weekend.

Suddenly, life was fabulous.

NATALIE OWEN FISHED a Diet Pepsi out of the nurses' station refrigerator and dropped into the chair behind the big reception desk in the lobby, her eyes automatically going to the computer monitor. Everything was quiet tonight. Most of the nursing home's residents were sleeping, and all but one showed no signs of not making it through the night. The single exception was Manny Smithers, whose family was sitting vigil at his bedside so he wouldn't die alone, even though he'd shown no signs of recognizing anyone for the past two years.

In fifteen minutes Steve Williams would arrive to relieve her, and since she'd finished all her paperwork half an hour ago, she decided she might as well log on to eHarmony and see if the man of her dreams had noticed her yet.

With a few strokes on the keyboard, she logged into her account and found that almost a dozen people had looked at her profile since the last time she'd checked.

But nobody had responded.

And she was pretty sure she knew why: it had to be the photograph.

Double-clicking on the image to enlarge it, she gazed dolefully at the offending picture. It had been taken by her mother after her solo performance with the church choir last Easter, when she'd sung the Lord's Prayer. In the picture, she was wearing the blue choir robe with the gold V-neck stole that made her eyes look bluer and her hair even blonder than it was, and she knew it was one of the best photographs ever taken of her.

Her entire face was blooming with the spirit of Christ. Her hair was perfect, her smile attractive and welcoming.

But even her mother—who had *taken* the picture, for heaven's sake!—had said that if she was going to attract a man, she shouldn't post a picture of herself in a choir robe. Men wanted to see what she had to offer, and would be afraid she was hiding something beneath the flowing gown. But Natalie still thought it was the right picture; after all, she didn't want to attract just any man. She wanted God to send her a good Christian who would appreciate both her and her faith.

She clicked twice more on the photo to enlarge it further.

The hint of lipstick that the choir director put on her lips just before the service actually looked good—not slutty at all. Her mother always said her lips were her best feature, even insisting that they looked just like those of some famous supermodel whose name Natalie couldn't remember.

Margot something-or-other.

She had never actually bothered to find out if her mother was right, but even if she was, it hadn't seemed to matter. It was starting to look like no matter what photo she put up on any matchmaking site, no man was ever going to want her.

She was almost thirty.

It was about time she stopped all the wishful thinking and accepted that spinsterhood was going to be her lot in life.

Steve rang the bell at the front door, waving to her as she buzzed him through, and Natalie barely managed to close the Web browser before he could see what she was doing. She briefed him on what little activity had taken place over the last eight hours, then finished her Diet Pepsi, swapped her stethoscope for her purse in her locker, and walked out into the mild Los Angeles night.

Ten minutes later she pulled her secondhand Toyota into the dark carport behind her apartment building, reminding herself for what had to be the fifth time to tell the manager about the burned-out bulb to-morrow morning, and knowing even as she reminded herself that by then she would have forgotten all about it.

Not that it mattered, really, since she'd chosen the apartment three years ago because it was in the middle of the safest neighborhood in Studio City, and still was.

She got out of the car, grabbed the tote bag full of clothing that she was gathering from deceased residents to donate to the poor, and locked the car behind her.

But as she took a step toward the doorway leading to the stairwell up to her second-story apartment, icy tendrils of fear crawled up the back of her neck.

Something was wrong.

She was not alone.

"Hello?" she called out, her voice sounding oddly hollow as it echoed off the concrete walls of the carport.

There was no answer, and she told herself to stop being an idiot by letting her imagination run away with her.

Still, the carport didn't feel right, and the goose bumps on her skin weren't going away.

Refusing to give in to her fear and glance over her shoulder, she made herself walk toward the stairwell and the safety of her little studio apartment, where tonight's scripture lesson on tape was waiting for her.

She reached out to pull open the door between her and the bright light of the stairwell, but just before her fingers closed on the doorknob, an arm snaked out of the darkness, slid around her throat, and jerked her backward.

The bag of clothing flew from her hand, and she watched it arc across the carport as if in slow motion. And then she was flailing against her assailant, but before she could escape the imprisoning arm, she lost her balance and sank to the floor.

A knee pressed down on her right arm.

"Please," Natalie gasped, her voice barely even a whisper. "Take whatever you want. Just please don't hurt me."

Then she felt the point of a knife at her throat, and knew she was about to die.

Die right here in her own carport, only a few feet from the safety of the building.

She tried to think of the peace of death and the wonder of meeting Jesus, but somehow no prayers came to her mind.

All she could do was listen to her own heart hammering inside her chest.

Then, out of the darkness and through her terror, she heard a voice.

"All I want," it said, "are your lips."

My lips, she thought. Why would someone want my—

Before she could finish the thought, the knife sliced across her throat, and as blood spurted from her aorta and she felt her life draining away, rough fingers grabbed her lips and she felt the knife sink into her flesh once more.

Finally the prayers she wanted to utter came back to her, and she tried to move her lips to form the words.

But her lips were gone, and the words were lost in the blood gushing from her neck and then—

—and then it didn't matter, for Natalie Owen could pray no more.

18

TINA WONG FINISHED CLIPPING THE LAVALIERE MICROPHONE TO THE collar of Jillian Oglesby's blouse and asked her to say a few words so Pete Biner could get a volume level, then picked up the glass of water that Jillian's mother had provided—complete with an obviously hand-crocheted doily to protect the bird's-eye maple coffee table from being stained—and went over her notes for the interview.

"I can't really tell you anything," Jillian said in a soft, apologetic voice that Tina knew would tug at the heartstrings of everyone who heard it, let alone saw the pictures of Jillian's ruined face. "I didn't see anybody. He hit me from behind, and when I woke up, I was already in the hospital."

"That's okay," Tina said, searching for a way to turn this into something more than just video footage of a girl with scars where her eyebrows had once been, and a mother who was doing little more than weeping and wringing her hands. She had already had to talk the girl into washing off the makeup she'd used in a monumentally unsuccessful attempt to hide the skin graft scars, penciling in a pair of eyebrows that were neither even nor symmetrical. Now Jillian at least looked as pathetic as she sounded, but Tina knew that the big trick was to find a way to stretch the interview out long enough for the audience to truly appreciate the carnage she was displaying for them.

"We're good, Tina," Pete said.

"Okay! Showtime!" Tina smiled brightly at Jillian. "Deep breath."

As Jillian self-consciously filled her lungs with a big breath—and her mother wiped perspiration from her own upper lip, ignoring the beads of sweat covering Jillian's face—Tina's cell phone buzzed in her pocket. She pulled it out.

Michael Shaw. She flipped the phone open. "Yes?"

"There's been another murder," Michael said, wasting no words at all. "This time he took the girl's lips."

The inventory clicked through Tina's mind like cards on a Rolodex: lips, ears, eyebrows, breasts. "What about the glands?" she asked, forcing herself not to look at either Jillian Oglesby or her mother.

"Given the carnage, it looks like he took all the usual stuff."

Tina glanced inquiringly at Pete, and when she spoke, her question was as much for the cameraman as her boss. "Can we go live right now?"

Pete nodded, having already set up a satellite link to connect the truck parked in the Oglesby driveway to the studio in Los Angeles.

"At the top of the hour," Michael agreed.

Tina checked her watch. She had seven minutes to prepare. Unclipping her own mike, she went out to the tiny front porch, where the midday sun was peeling the last of the paint from the railings, the steps, and the clapboard siding of the house itself. "This guy's some sicko," she said softly to Michael, hoping she was casting her voice low enough so the two women in the house wouldn't hear her. If she was going to get the best reaction from Jillian, she didn't want the girl to have even a minute to think about what was going on. "What's the name of the new victim, the one with the lips? And give me the details. Fast."

"Natalie Owen," Michael replied, then filled Tina in on what had happened the night before. "You're not going to have a lot of time—I'm giving you forty seconds at the top of the hour, but that's it."

"It'll be enough," Tina said. "Thanks." She folded her phone, slipped it into her pocket, then went back into the house, where she gave Jillian a reassuring smile as she clipped the mike back onto her blouse.

"A slight change in plans," she said. "We're going to do some of the interview live, and broadcast the rest on Sunday." She drank the rest of the water, checked her makeup, then patted the sweat off Jillian Oglesby's lips. She was just finishing up getting the girl posed next to her by the fireplace when Pete Biner held up five fingers, then started dropping them down, one every second.

"This is Tina Wong, reporting live from Bakersfield, where I'm interviewing Jillian Oglesby, who I believe was attacked last year by the same man who has now killed at least five women in California, the latest being Natalie Owen, a nurse murdered in the carport of her Studio City apartment last night." She turned to Jillian just as the reality of her words sank into the girl, whose face had become a mask of horror. "He took the girl's lips this time, Jillian. What do you think is going on in this man's mind?"

"I—I—what—" Jillian floundered, which was exactly what Tina had been hoping for.

She turned back to the camera. "This man, whoever he is, seems to be roaming around our state, taking parts from girls as if he's trying to build himself whatever his idea of the perfect woman is. It's as if Dr. Frankenstein has risen from his grave and is back in his laboratory. But my question is this: why have the police been unable to stop this . . ." Tina paused as if searching for the words she had in fact already planned to say, then went on. ". . . monster," she finished. "How many women must be robbed not only of their lives, but of their very features before this killer—this Frankenstein Killer—is stopped? For the latest on all these killings, tune to Channel 3 at eight P.M. on Sunday, when I'll bring you a full report on what has been going on that the police haven't been telling us about. Now, back to the studio for a traffic update. This is Tina Wong, live from Bakersfield."

As the live feed ended, Tina signaled Pete to keep taping and eased Jillian Oglseby back to the sofa. Seating herself beside Jillian, Tina took her hand. "What can you tell me, Jillian? Do you remember any of it?"

The girl nodded, her eyes glazed. "I—I was out jogging, just like I always do. And he hit me on the head from behind, and—and—" Her voice broke, then: "He slit my throat." Jillian pulled aside the collar of her blouse to show a wide scar that extended all the way around the front of her throat. "And then he cut off my eyebrows. It happened so fast I couldn't even scream, but then another jogger came by and he ran away." Her voice dropped to a faint whisper. "I almost bled to death."

"Brave girl," Tina said as Pete narrowed the camera's focus to fill the frame with Jillian's face. As Pete held the shot, Tina went on. "What are the police doing to capture this murderer and stop his rampage of terror? Not enough. Not nearly enough. This is Tina Wong, keeping you up to the minute on the Frankenstein Killer, who is still at large."

The red light went out.

"Good piece," Pete said.

Tina's phone buzzed in her pocket. Michael again. She flipped it open.

"The Frankenstein Killer?" her boss grated.

"It works," Tina responded, waving to Jillian to stay where she was so Pete could film her from other angles.

"So now you're going to need all new graphics."

"That's true," Tina said. "Would you mind getting that ball rolling? We should start running promos tonight. I'm going to be here another hour finishing this interview, so I'll see you late this afternoon."

Michael sighed.

And Tina smiled.

The Frankenstein Killer.

It had been a stroke of genius, and it would stick. And from now on Michael Shaw would have to give her anything she wanted. In fact, she wouldn't be surprised if the networks started calling even before the special aired.

"Okay, Pete," she said. "Let's get this show on the road."

MICHAEL SHAW NEEDED at least two more hands to handle everything on his desk, and four would have been even better. And almost all of it had to do with Tina Wong.

Since she was still on her way back from Bakersfield—and caught in traffic, which she'd called three times to report so far, never failing to mention that she was going to talk to "the network" about his refusal to provide her with a helicopter—he had to approve the promos for her special even before she saw them. Knowing Tina Wong, that meant she would do whatever she wanted in the way of reediting, using his preapproval as her license. But after her live remote broadcast this morning, the switchboard had been flooded with calls from people who were certain they knew who the Frankenstein Killer was and who wanted to be interviewed on air by Tina. And every other station in the area was picking up the story, though Tina possessed far more information than anyone else.

Which meant Tina had the whip hand, at least for now.

Michael buzzed his intern and asked him to bring another double latte from the coffee kiosk down the block, knowing he would be surviving on them at least until Tina's special aired, and probably for a week afterward.

He leaned back in his chair and gazed morosely at the stack of other work that was overflowing his in-box and at the pile of unanswered phone messages that was growing by the minute. He rotated his aching neck in a futile attempt to get a couple of the kinks out, stretched his back, then reached for the stack of messages and began sorting through them, discarding at least half of them as nothing more than annoyances.

When two brisk raps on his door interrupted his concentration, he looked up, to remind his secretary that he'd ordered no interruptions for the next fifteen minutes—*none!*—but when he saw two men in business suits, his annoyance turned to anger. If Tina Wong had already called "the network" to complain about him—

"Michael Shaw?" one of them asked, cutting into his thoughts before he'd begun to envision upbraiding her.

"Isn't that what it says on the door?" he snapped.

"We won't take much of your time," the second man responded. "I'm Evan Sands and this is Rick McCoy." Both men reached into the inside pockets of their suit jackets and flipped open glittering LAPD badges for his inspection. "We need to talk to you about the allegations your reporter is making on the air."

"My reporter?" Michael said, deciding to play dumb even though he of course knew who they were talking about—the very thorn that had been irritating his side for the last several months.

"Tina Wong," McCoy chimed in, in case he hadn't figured out who they were here about. "She seems to have taken it upon herself to fabricate connections between murder cases that may not be connected at all."

"Which is a huge problem for us," Sands picked up, going on with a routine Michael was sure they'd used before. "First off, every loony in town is confessing to these crimes. But that's not the worst of it. The worst of it is that your Miss Wong is creating panic in the streets. Our job is hard enough without a newscaster acting like no woman is safe anywhere in the entire area."

"Really," Michael said, leaning back in his swivel chair and folding his arms across his chest. He might not like Tina, but being annoyed was one thing, gagging her another. "And exactly how do you think I can help you with that?"

"We want a little more responsibility in reporting from this station," Sands said. "Tina Wong is out of line."

"She's reporting what she's found," Michael replied. "No more, and no less. And in case you've forgotten, the government does not control the press in this country. And certainly the LAPD doesn't. We're responsible to the public here, not to you."

"That's crap, and you know it," Sands growled. "You answer to your stockholders, just like every other corporation. We're the ones who answer to the public, and it doesn't help us or the public when some showboating reporter starts making irresponsible—"

"Irresponsible?" Michael cut in, rising to his feet and glowering at the two detectives. "I see no lack of responsibility in Tina Wong's reporting. Her sources have all been well documented, and I suspect she's talked to a lot more people about all these cases than you have. If she's been more sensational than you—or even I, for that matter— might like, it's because she believes that every possible connection needs to be investigated if this killer is going to be found. And I don't disagree with her."

"Finding this guy is *our* job," McCoy said, his own anger now showing in his face. "*Your* job is to report the news, not solve crimes and make up theories."

"Please do not try to tell me what my job is," Michael said coldly. "I've been on this job at least as long as you've been on yours. I know what my job is, and if *you* were doing *your* jobs, you would be out following up on every single thing Tina's found instead of wasting my time and yours by trying to kill the messenger instead of dealing with the message."

"I'm sorry you see it that way," Sands said, glaring at him.

"I'll tell you what I'll do," Michael said, deciding to toss them a bone, though there would be no meat on it. "I'll talk with Tina, and I'll personally review all the material she plans to air, all of which is standard procedure."

"We'll want to see that material before it airs, too," McCoy countered.

"And that is not standard procedure," Michael said, "and I can tell you it won't happen."

"We can go over your head," McCoy said.

Michael waved a hand at his desk. "Would you like to use my phone?"

Sands forced a smile. "The police and the press have always had a pretty good working relationship. We don't want anything to change that, do we?"

"None of us do," Michael assured the detective, moving toward his office door. "So you two do your jobs and let us do ours. Understood?"

McCoy looked ready to leave, but Sands didn't budge. "Look, Shaw—we're asking you nicely to check her *facts* before she airs them," he said. "Make sure they're facts."

"Believe me, I'll do exactly what the law demands," Michael replied as he opened the office door just as his intern appeared with the fresh latte. The two detectives glared at Michael, then walked out.

He closed his door and returned to his desk, suddenly feeling better about everything. The adrenaline rush of sparring with the two detectives was better than ten cups of coffee; but even better was the knowledge that Tina was genuinely onto something, and knew more about it than the police.

A newsman's dream.

He grabbed the stack of messages again and started returning calls, starting with one from Scott.

He needed to tell him that he would probably be late for dinner, maybe by as much as a week.

❖ ❖ ❖

The soft trill of the cell phone thundered in the quiet room, and adrenaline gushed through the body, flushing the face. The fingers picked up the phone and the eyes checked the caller ID.

PRIVATE CALLER

The client.

It had to be the client.

The fingers deftly flipped open the phone and brought it to the ear, but the angry tirade could already be heard, as if it had been in progress even as the phone was ringing.

"How could you have been so stupid?" the voice from the phone demanded. "Are you insane? How could you have left that girl alive? Alive! And you didn't even tell me? Goddamn you, you perverted lunatic."

The hand holding the phone trembled at the onslaught, and the mind braced itself for the rest of the tirade.

The voice from the phone dropped, but its tone became dangerous. "Now listen to me, and listen carefully. I will fix this, but it is absolutely the last thing I will ever fix for you. Ever. This is not part of the deal."

The furious voice paused as the speaker took a breath.

The hand not holding the phone wiped perspiration from the forehead and the upper lip.

"Very well," the voice on the other end of the line said. It was far calmer now. "Let's go over the rules one more time. It's very simple: I give you the orders and you fill them. That's all there is to it. Do I have to actually say that you leave nothing to chance? Do I have to stipulate that once you have what I need, you finish your job? Next time something goes wrong, you contact me immediately. Immediately!" The voice dropped even further and took on a darkly menacing tone. "But of course nothing like that will ever happen again, will it?"

There was a pause, and the hand tightened on the phone. "No," the voice whispered into the telephone.

Without even acknowledging the response, the other voice resumed, the words pouring through the phone. "I made you," the voice said. "I made you and I can destroy you. I can destroy you any time I want."

The mind shrank from the words, but the ears kept listening.

"There will be no more mistakes! None. You will simply finish this job. Finish it now! And then, at last, I will be done with you!"

The line went dead.

The fingers, trembling as if palsied, closed the phone and laid it gently on the desktop.

The accident in Bakersfield would never be repeated. Could never be repeated.

Indeed, it was almost inconceivable that it had happened at all.

Yet it had.

The right hand clenched into a resolute fist.

Not again.

Never again.

There was only one more item to be collected.

One more, and it would finally be over.

The debt would finally be discharged.

No more orders. No more demands. No more deadlines.

The fingers moved to the computer keyboard.

The eyes peered closely at the monitor, the fingers typed in a few quick keystrokes, and a few moments later pictures once again began to fly by. . . .

19

ALISON GRIPPED THE TENNIS RACKET TIGHT AND CROUCHED, BOB-bing back and forth as she awaited her father's serve. He eyed her from the far line, bounced the yellow ball a couple of times, then abruptly dropped the racket to his side.

"Tell me again why can't I come to your birthday party?" he called across the net.

She straightened up, sighed, and let her right arm relax. "I already told you—it's a party for my friends! So come on and serve."

"So now I'm not your friend?" Michael countered.

"You're just trying to distract me from match point," Alison called back, resuming her stance once again.

Her father finally served, but Alison knew the instant his racket connected with the ball that he was way off his game, and she slammed the return cross court to end the match. She held up her hands in victory, and heard a lone fan from the courtside café applauding her win. She turned to give Scott an exaggerated bow, then ran over to the net to hug her father.

"Okay, you whipped me," Michael said as they walked over to Scott, who had ordered them both iced teas in anticipation of Alison's victory. Michael eyed them dourly, noting that the ice hadn't even begun to melt. "Some faith you had in my comeback," he observed. "Was it that obvious I was running out of steam?"

"Always bet on the younger horse," Scott replied, and grinned at Alison. "Well done, missy." Then he turned back to Michael, the grin turning evil. "And you're going to have to get back to the gym. She whipped your ass, old man."

Michael shrugged. "She's been doing that pretty regularly for the last two years. I should start worrying about it now?"

"And," Scott went on as if Michael hadn't spoken at all, "since it looked like you were carrying about twenty pounds too many out there, I ordered us all chicken Caesar salad for dinner."

As if on cue, the waitress appeared with a tray of food.

Michael ignored the gibe, turning back to Alison. "About the birthday party . . ." he began again as the food was put in front of them.

Alison rolled her eyes. "How many times do I have to tell you? It's for my *friends*!"

"I'm your friend."

Scott rolled his eyes.

"If you were my *friend*," Alison said with exaggerated innocence, "I would have let you win."

Michael feigned hurt feelings.

"Would you stop worrying about that party?" Scott told him. "The three of us will do something fun for her birthday."

"Like go to the beach," Alison said around a mouthful of salad.

"Perfect," Scott decided. "We only seem to get to the beach when we're with you. Otherwise, he's spending more Sundays at work than he is at home."

"I've been busy," Michael protested. "There's a lot going on." Then his expression darkened slightly, and his voice turned serious as he faced his daughter. "And I understand there's a lot going on in your life, too."

Alison tensed, certain she knew what he was about to say. His next words confirmed it.

"Your mother tells me you're thinking about having breast implants."

Scott dropped his fork and threw up his hands in exaggerated disgust. "Oh, dear God! Not this again!"

Alison stared first at her father, then at Scott. Had they been talking about it, too?

"Listen," Scott said to Michael. "I know you're her father, and I know you don't approve of this, but she's sixteen, or at least she's about to be, and this is a decision she should be making with her mother. Boobs, as you well know, are none of our concern. Some men's, yes. But not us. So get over it, all right?"

"But—"

"But nothing!" Scott waved a dismissive hand toward Michael, and turned to Alison. "Despite what your father thinks, I think your stepfather's giving you a terrific birthday present."

"But it's *surgery*," Michael said. "*Elective* surgery. It's dangerous—"

"It's dangerous just walking across the street," Scott cut in. "And since only one parent has to sign off on it, I'm assuming it's a done deal. So instead of trying to make your daughter feel bad, why don't you just be happy for her?"

Michael sighed, but finally managed a crooked smile for Alison. "Look, I just want the best for you, that's all. So I suppose if this is what you really, really want, you should probably go ahead and have it. But that doesn't mean I'm not going to worry about it. Okay?"

"Okay," Alison agreed. "But I promise you, it's going to be no big deal."

Michael's cell phone rang. He pulled it out of his pocket, sighed as he looked at the caller ID, then accepted the call. After no more than three words were spoken, he closed the phone, put it back in his pocket, and stood up. "I've got to go to the station," he told them.

"Now?" Alison and Scott said in unison.

"I'm sorry, cupcake," he said, bending down to kiss Alison. "This Frankenstein Killer thing is keeping everybody on edge." He turned to Scott. "Can you drive her home?"

"Of course," Scott replied. "What time will you be home?"

Michael shrugged. "Until Tina's special airs, my time is no longer my own."

Scott looked at Alison and lifted an eyebrow. "Like his time is ever his own."

"Tell me," Alison said.

"Look, I'm sorry. If it was up to me—" Michael stopped as he saw them rolling their eyes, and put some bills on the table for the check. "Thanks for the game, honey. And stay safe, okay?"

"I will," Alison said, though she wasn't sure if he was talking about her implants or the serial killer who seemed to be everywhere on TV lately. " 'Bye."

"See you at home," Michael said to Scott, then headed off toward the parking lot.

"Must have been hard growing up with that," Scott said as they watched him go.

"You get used to it," Alison replied, and sipped her drink.

"Well, maybe it's just as well he left us alone," Scott said, "because I wanted to tell you about this." He pointed at his chin.

Alison cocked her head quizzically. "What?"

"This cute little cleft in my chin? I've only had it for three years."

Alison's eyes widened. "You're kidding!" The dimple in his chin was such an integral part of Scott's face that she couldn't imagine him without it.

"Not kidding at all. I always had this horrible weak chin, and I always hated it, and I finally decided to do something about it. So guess who I went to?"

"Oh, my God," Alison blurted, already knowing the answer. "My stepfather?"

"None other. If you want the best, go to the best. And your stepfather is definitely the best. I told your father all about it, and I thought we'd settled it before we met you today. But apparently I didn't quite convince him that it's just no big deal."

Alison smiled, then moved her dad's salad out of the way and changed seats so she could sit next to Scott. "Okay," she said. "Tell me what it was like. I want to know everything."

ALISON CLOSED her history book and leaned back in her desk chair. No use trying to study any more tonight; she'd already read the last paragraph at least six times, and still had no idea what it said. All she could think about was what was going to happen Friday afternoon.

The minute she'd told her mother and Conrad that her father okayed the surgery—leaving out all his arguments against it, and the fact that Scott was actually the one who had convinced him—Conrad told her that he assumed she'd convince her father and had already penciled her in for Friday, right after school.

Friday!

This Friday.

Her mother had been thrilled and, if she was going to be absolutely honest with herself, she was, too.

At least at first.

But as Conrad talked about her being back in school on Monday, and completely healed by her party, her excitement slipped away.

Friday was the day after tomorrow, and somehow it all seemed to be happening too fast.

Way too fast.

But what could she do? She'd already made up her mind—in fact, she'd been ready to argue with her father for as long as it took to get his approval, or even go ahead without it. So what had changed?

But she already knew what had changed. It was the fact that it was actually going to happen on Friday afternoon. Someone from Conrad's office was going to pick her up at Wilson and take her up to Le Chateau, and they were going to put her under anesthetics, and Conrad would operate on her.

And suddenly she was frightened. Just thinking about it made her heart beat faster and her skin feel clammy and—

Don't think about it, she told herself. *Just do your homework and go to bed and stop worrying.*

She reopened her history book and found the paragraph she'd been reading over and over again. Her paper on the Boer War wasn't actually due until Friday morning, so maybe instead of trying to work on it tonight, she should do something else.

Like try to relax.

Like that was going to happen.

Three sharp knocks on her bedroom door startled Alison out of her reverie, and she reflexively pulled the book closer, as if that would convince whoever was in the hall that she'd been studying rather than worrying. "It's not locked," she called out. "Come on in."

Conrad Dunn opened the door and held up three small bottles of pills. "Hey," he said. "In the middle of something? Can I talk to you for a minute?"

"Just trying to get through my history assignment," she replied.

"And not getting anywhere with it, right?" Conrad stepped into her room, and when he didn't close the door behind him, Alison felt a strange sense of relief, and found herself nodding in agreement with what he'd said.

"I thought so. Unless you're completely different from everyone else, you've been sitting up here thinking about Friday afternoon and wishing you could change your mind."

She stared at him. How could he have known what was going on in her mind? But before she could ask the question, he answered it.

"Happens to everyone. Until the surgery's actually scheduled, it's all just an abstraction. But then suddenly you know exactly what day and what time it's going to happen, and it all becomes real. And scary. Which is one of the reasons I came up here—couldn't let you go to bed terrified and feeling guilty about wanting to change your mind. If you want to change your mind, do it. I penciled in the appointment, remember? One word from you and it goes away." Conrad crossed the room and put the three vials on Alison's desk, and when she didn't stand up, he crouched awkwardly next to her chair. "But if you don't change your mind, I want you to start taking these. They're homeopathic medicines that do absolutely amazing things to reduce bleeding and bruising from surgery, and there are others I'll give you afterward that will speed your recovery time."

She picked up the bottles one by one to read the labels as he explained each one.

"Arnica reduces swelling and bruising, and ferrum phos is good for inflammation and any kind of fever. That last one is a combination of hormones. I want you to take two capsules three times a day," he finished as she studied the label on the third bottle. "Starting now."

"And you really think I can go back to school on Monday?" she asked with disbelief.

"Barring any complications," he said, as if he hadn't heard the doubt in her voice. He stood up, his knees cracking. "You should be off all pain meds by then, except maybe for a little Tylenol. I'll keep you on the homeopathics for a week afterward, but you won't even notice them—they have absolutely no side effects whatsoever. There will still be stitches, of course, and possibly some very minor swelling, so no gym class, no running, throwing, or anything like that at all for a month. Okay?"

"Okay," Alison said, setting the three bottles on the edge of her desk.

"Okay, then," Conrad said, touching her shoulder lightly. "And don't forget—say the word, and we cancel the whole thing."

Alison looked up at him. "Thanks," she said softly. "I'll think about it, but I think I'm gonna be okay now. Maybe all I needed was a little pep talk."

"Well, if you need another, just come find me. Good night."

"Good night."

As soon as her stepfather was gone, she logged on to the Internet to look up the medicines he'd given her. Arnica and ferrum phos—which turned out to be short for phosphoricum—were easy to find and turned out to be exactly what Conrad had told her they were: fairly common remedies for pre- and postsurgical procedures.

But there was no information on the label of the bottle containing the pink capsules. All it said was: *3x/day for 3 days before and 5 days after surgery.*

That, and the name of the manufacturer, Healing Health Laboratories, which was in Beverly Hills.

She found the HHL website, and after hunting all over the site finally figured out that the company was a subsidiary of DeLorian Cosmetics. But when she tried to find out more about the pink capsules Conrad had given her, she was confronted with a page asking for a user name and password. At the bottom of the screen was a notice to the effect that more information about Healing Health products could be obtained from any one of a short list of doctors. The fourth name on the list was "Dunn, Conrad," followed by his office address and telephone number.

After trying a couple more searches for either the pills or Healing Health products, she logged off. Though she hadn't found much, she knew DeLorian Cosmetics was one of the best—and most expensive—around. And she remembered meeting Danielle DeLorian at her mother's and Conrad's wedding.

She took a deep breath, then let it out slowly, doing her best to rid herself of the last of her misgivings. She was just nervous, that was all. But not as nervous as she'd been before Conrad had told her she could back out at any time. And, as she thought about it, she realized she didn't want to back out of it. It was scheduled, and everybody at school knew about it, and—

—and she kept seeing herself in that beautiful dress hanging in her closet, and in her mind's eye its bodice was filled not with Kleenex, or even falsies.

It was filled with her own perfect breasts.

She shook out the pink capsules from their bottles, took them into her bathroom, got a glass of water, and washed them down.

Back in her room, she put the homeopathic tablets under her tongue and let them dissolve, just like the labels instructed.

And suddenly she couldn't wait for Friday.

Or, more exactly, for Friday evening, when it would all be over.

20

TINA WONG LEANED BACK IN HER DESK CHAIR, CLOSED HER EYES, AND rubbed at her right shoulder, even though she knew the pain from hours of manipulating her computer's mouse wouldn't ease for at least three days. And the work had barely begun: her editing bay wouldn't be available until five-thirty, though at least Pete had taken the footage home to make a rough cut on his personal equipment so they could get a running start this evening. So if everything went smoothly—which, of course, it never did—they'd have a good cut by morning. Then Michael could review it, run it by any executives who needed to approve it, and they could recut it if they had to.

And they'd have time to spare before airing the special on Sunday night.

If everything went smoothly.

Which, of course, it never did.

There were too many things that could go wrong. If the police caught the killer, the whole thing would have to be redone, and all the air would go out of it. Who would care about a rehash of a solved series of killings?

On the other hand, if another murder occurred, the special would still have to be completely recut, but she'd have the run of the station and all its resources to get it done on time, and the network might want to pick it up as well. It would be the biggest thing on TV that night.

She tried not to hope that another murder would take place—and soon enough so she'd have time to include it in her special—but there was no denying that one more killing would make her career. She'd be in L.A. long enough to stay with the case for the whole network, and then it would be New York.

New York, and eventually an anchor spot on the national news.

Not, of course, that she wanted it to happen, at least not that way. Still, it didn't hurt to be prepared for any eventuality, so she righted her chair, picked up the bundle of still shots from the promos Michael had okayed, and flipped through them.

They looked good. The art department had mercifully not succumbed to its original urge to use the same drippy Frankenstein font from the old movies, which would have instantly turned her special from news into nothing more than schlocky entertainment. The promos were almost ready to run, and in five minutes she was due over in production to take a final look at them and make sure they were using the best footage of her.

And that they weren't giving too much away in the voice-over.

The Frankenstein Killer.

It had been a stroke of genius—there was no denying it.

And what if it turned out that it hadn't only been a stroke of genius, but of prophecy, too? What if this guy—whoever he was—*was* trying to make someone out of all these parts he was harvesting?

What if someone was trying to put together his idea of the perfect woman? Suddenly, she had a vision of the killer. He'd be a misfit, of course—the kind of guy who could only get a date on the Internet, where he could use a picture of anybody to sucker in the kind of girl who would never go out with him if she actually met him. He probably spent most of his time alone in some crappy one-room apartment somewhere, jerking off while he paged through magazines, looking at the girls he could never have.

Then he'd started focusing in on what attracted him about each girl.

When had he decided to make his *own* girl? To find the parts, and put them together into his twisted idea of perfection? A year ago? A decade ago?

And what did she look like, this perfect girl?

The promos suddenly forgotten, Tina began to comb through the files she'd amassed on the series of killings.

Kimberly Elmont's ears had been taken.

Natalie Owen's lips.

Caroline Fisher's breasts.

Her excitement growing, Tina pulled the best photographs she could find of Kimberly and Natalie and scanned them into Photoshop, then cut-and-pasted Kimberly's ears and Natalie's lips onto a blank file.

The lips were a little lopsided because of the angle from which Natalie's picture had been taken, and only Kimberly's right ear was clear. Tina made a mirror image of it, then slid both ears into position above the lips.

But how far apart should they be? How wide was this guy's ideal woman's head?

She went back to the files, found a photograph of Jillian Oglesby before the attack, and scanned it in. Even though Jillian's eyebrows had been ripped from her face almost a year ago, it was far more likely to be related to the group of recent attacks, and not the ones in San Jose and San Diego fifteen years ago.

Was this a copycat or was the same character still around?

A shiver went through her, and she had to rub away the goose bumps that prickled on her arms.

She maneuvered the mouse until Jillian's eyebrows were cut from her photograph and pasted into place.

Now a face—very rough, but recognizable as a human face—began to emerge on the computer screen.

And fear began to creep up her spine.

The face was missing a nose.

Which meant that there would, indeed, be at least one more killing. But when?

She looked up at the calendar pinned to her corkboard, the calendar that covered the full year since Michael had promised her the special if there was another murder, and on which she'd been marking everything that had happened and everything she'd done that related to the killings.

The killings themselves had been marked with a bloodred Sharpie.

The killings were getting closer together.

Also, the killer was nearing the completion of his project.

Suddenly, she knew exactly what he was feeling: just as with her career-making special, this guy was eager to finish his collecting and get on to the next step—the actual putting together of the parts into his twisted idea of perfection.

Tina stared at the calendar, mesmerized. The time between Kimberly's and Natalie's murders was half the time that had lapsed between Caroline Fisher's and Kimberly's.

If the time was cut in half again between Natalie's murder and the next one, that would put the next murder . . .

On Friday.

This Friday!

Tina put a big X on Sunday, when her special would air, then put the tip of her pen on Friday and drew a large question mark.

If she was right—and she knew it was a very large "if"—there would be another murder on Friday.

So exactly how big was the "if"? Should she bet her career that somewhere in Los Angeles a young woman would lose her life because a maniac wanted her nose?

And her glands, too.

What was that about?

Tina saved the rough face she'd created, attached it to an e-mail to Michael, then tore the calendar off the corkboard and headed to his office. She wasn't sure what her obligation was to the police at this point, but Michael would know, and he'd surely want to consult with the station's attorneys right now.

If they did nothing, and the murder took place when she thought it would, she could use whatever footage they got in her special. She'd just have to make two cuts, one with room for footage of the latest killing, one without it.

But it might be even better to run the rough face she'd constructed with Photoshop on the next newscast tonight at six, which would give her an opportunity to speculate on the murder she was certain was going to happen. That would at least put the whole area on alert.

Michael Shaw, of course, would insist that it was too provocative and could incite panic.

Of course, it would be best to prevent the murder from happening at all. That would make Tina Wong not only famous, but a hero as well.

But how could she make that happen?

She didn't know.

At least, she didn't know *yet*.

CONRAD DUNN RAPPED briskly on the examination room door, then opened it and walked in.

Alison, dressed in a pink hospital gown, was perched nervously on the edge of the examination table, while Risa, pale and looking even more nervous than her daughter, sat in a chair that she'd pulled close enough to the table so she could hold Alison's hand.

"Who, exactly, is clinging to whom?" he asked, winking at Alison. "Seems like your mom's a lot more frightened than you are."

"I think we're both scared," Alison said.

"I'm not scared, exactly," Risa said, the tremor in her voice belying her words. "I mean, I'm not worried, really . . . I'm just . . . " Her voice trailed of.

"Terrified?" Conrad offered. "Well, there's no reason to be. I know what I'm doing, and my team is the best in the business." He leaned over and kissed his wife on the cheek. "But I really hate it when the family starts scaring the patient."

"I'm not scaring her," Risa insisted. "I'm just—"

"Here to help," Conrad finished for her. He turned back to Alison. "Okay," he said. "Let's get to it. I know you're feeling embarrassed, but in about two minutes you're going to laugh at how stupid it all seems, especially when I start drawing lines on your chest."

"I don't think it's stupid—" Alison began, but then, apparently deciding her mother had expressed enough nervousness for both of them, bit her lip and stood up.

Risa offered her daughter what was supposed to be an encouraging smile but only turned out to be another worried look, and Alison closed her eyes and opened the front of the gown.

As Risa watched, Conrad sat down on his swivel stool, gauged the symmetry of Alison's build, then took a black felt-tip pen from the top drawer of the credenza and quickly began making the marks he needed on his stepdaughter's torso. He swiveled back and forth on his stool a few times to make certain the marks were exactly where he wanted them, and when he was completely satisfied, put the felt-tip back in the drawer.

Less than two minutes had passed.

"All done," he announced, and Alison opened her eyes in surprise. Then, realizing the gown was still open, she quickly wrapped it around herself and sat down. "Now that wasn't so bad, was it?"

Alison reddened but shook her head.

"Okay, the next thing that's going to happen is that Teresa will come in here, start your IV, and get you prepped." He turned to Risa. "Once the IV starts, Teresa will show you to the family waiting room, and I'll come get you as soon as we're finished."

Risa nodded.

"Alison? Still want to go ahead? All you have to do is say no, and then wait for the ink marks to wear off."

Alison took a deep breath and shook her head. "No way am I going to chicken out now."

"Well, if you're not going to, I'm not going to. So let's go make a little magic for you. See you in the O.R."

With a wink at his wife, Conrad left mother and daughter alone.

FIFTEEN MINUTES LATER Conrad entered the operating room to find Alison, still conscious but very groggy, draped and lying on the operating table. Teresa and Kate were both already working, the nurse double-checking the instruments and supplies, while the anesthesiologist monitored Alison's vital signs.

"Ready, Alison?" he said.

She nodded without opening her eyes.

"Okay, then." He raised his mask to cover his nose and mouth. "You're going to sleep now, and I'll see you in the recovery room."

He nodded to Kate, and moments later Alison was sleeping deeply as soft strains of Stravinsky played through the speakers.

"Bring up image fifty-six, please, Teresa," Conrad said. "That one's always inspiring." If he even saw the look that passed between Teresa and Kate, he gave no sign, and Teresa stepped over to the computer keyboard. A moment later a photograph of a woman's torso appeared on the large monitor that hung from the ceiling at the foot of the operating table. Usually, the monitor displayed the reference photographs Conrad Dunn was using for whatever reconstructive process he was performing: if a patient wanted the lips of one movie star or the cheekbones of another, or the chin of yet a third, the monitor would display the original he was using as a model. But for a routine breast enhancement he'd never used anything; for a reconstruction, yes, but all he was doing today was the simple insertion of a pair of implants.

Beyond that, both Teresa and Kate knew exactly whose breasts image number fifty-six displayed: Margot Dunn's. Indeed, every slide from thirty through 274 displayed one aspect or another of Margot's face and body.

Now, as Teresa pulled the sheet back from Alison's torso and disinfected her skin one last time, Conrad Dunn's eyes fixed on the perfect breasts the monitor displayed. While Teresa finished the sterilization process, he at last turned away from the image on the monitor and shifted his full attention to the patient on the table.

"Everybody ready?" Without waiting for a response, he held out his hand. "Scalpel, please, Teresa," he said.

"IN A WEEK or so she'll be good as new," Conrad declared as he clipped the last suture and looked at Alison's new breasts with a critical eye. "In fact, she'll be a lot better than new."

"That's why they come to you, Conrad," Kate said. "You always make them better."

Conrad acknowledged the compliment with the smallest tilt of his head. "Can you bandage?" he asked Teresa.

"Of course," the nurse replied, already picking up the first gauze square with a hemostat.

"Good job, people," Conrad said, leaving the room as he pulled off his mask and gloves. He deposited them, along with his paper gown, in a hazardous waste disposal bin in the scrub room, washed his hands again, and felt the exhaustion of a long day settle over him as he made his way to the waiting room.

"All done," he said to Risa, whose head snapped up from the magazine she'd been paging through the moment she heard the door open. "She sailed through it like the champ that she is."

Risa stood up and hugged him. "Thank God."

"God?" Conrad echoed. "How about thanking me? I don't remember God going to medical school." He led her over to the couch, where he collapsed next to her. "She's being bandaged now, and then

Teresa will take her to the recovery room. When she wakes up, I'll get her settled in her suite for the night, and then I'll be home."

"Can't I see her?"

"Not until she's out of recovery—maybe in an hour. So you can either hang around here counting the seconds, or go home and break out a bottle of champagne. Tell you what—I'll call you when she's awake and you can come back, say hello, and then we'll both go home and celebrate."

"I just feel like I should be here," Risa fretted.

"You will be," Conrad reminded her. "Just not until she's awake. Now scoot. Tell Maria we'll want dinner in, and I'll be hungry as a bear." He stood up, took Risa's hand, and drew her to her feet. "And tell Ruffles that he'll have to sleep with us tonight, but that Alison will be home tomorrow."

"Okay." She smiled, then leaned against him again. "Thanks," she whispered, wrapping her arms around him and looking up into his dark eyes. "You're so . . . good!"

Conrad looked down at his wife and saw the lines of exhaustion around her eyes.

Maybe—if he had time—he'd just tighten those eyes up in the next month or so.

"WINE CELLAR DOWN THERE," Maria said in her broken English, not looking at Risa as she pointed her spatula toward a door on the far side of the kitchen.

Risa opened it and flipped on the light, illuminating a long, steep stairway. As she gazed down into the basement, she realized that she had not only never seen the rooms under the house, but until this moment hadn't even known there *was* a basement.

She started down the stairs, and as the door at the top swung closed behind her, felt the vibration of machinery and knew it must be the air conditioners, furnaces, and water heaters that supported the huge house. The vibration turned into an audible hum as she walked down the silent, industrially carpeted hallway that ran away from the base of the stairs. The door to the pool equipment room, clearly marked, was on her right, and just beyond it was another room with a glass panel in the door. Through it she could see a digital thermometer reading 57° and soft glowing lights beneath a series of wine racks.

Inside the wine cellar—which must have been stocked with at least a thousand bottles of more varieties than she knew existed—she quickly found the champagne section, chose a bottle of Dom Perignon, then took another bottle, for good measure. With any luck at all, this could turn out to be a very romantic evening.

She turned the lights down again and left the wine to its aging, closing the door firmly behind her.

She was retracing her steps back toward the staircase when something in the air stopped her. Frowning, she sniffed. Yes, there was something there. Something sweet. Pleasant.

And totally incongruous in this purely functional area of the house.

She opened the door to the room opposite the one housing the pool equipment, and found the source of the humming that permeated this level of the mansion. It was a large equipment room, with a furnace, five air-conditioning compressors, and what looked like a powerful generator, along with half a dozen large gray metal boxes that presumably contained the electrical circuits and switches needed to keep the whole thing functioning. Risa closed the door, and seeing nothing ahead but the pool equipment room and then the stairs back up to the kitchen, turned the other way and ventured farther down the hallway, where it took a turn to the right.

An unmarked door lay at the end of the hallway, where the scent was stronger. It seemed to be emanating from behind the door.

Could something have broken open in a storeroom?

Risa approached the door and sniffed the air again. The scent was definitely stronger. She turned the knob, cracked open the door slightly, and a wave of fragrance washed over her. She set the two bottles of champagne on the hallway floor, then pushed the door the rest of the way open.

The disembodied face of Margot Dunn stared at her.

Risa gasped and took an involuntary step backward, tripping on the carpeting but catching herself just before she fell.

Heart racing, she peered into the room again and realized that what she'd actually seen was nothing more than a softly lit life-size photograph of Margot.

Her pulse starting to drop back to normal, she groped for the light switch that should be next to the door, found it, and flipped it on.

The light in the room came up, a warm glow that filled the room from invisible fixtures. Risa stepped farther inside, and saw a lighted vanity against one of the walls, the top covered with ornate, blown-glass perfume bottles, one of which was open.

Combs, brushes, and a hand mirror—along with a profusion of pots, jars, and bottles of creams, lotions, and makeup—were all carefully arranged on the vanity's spotless glass top.

She moved to the middle of the room and gazed around her. Framed, poster-sized photographs of Margot Dunn at the height of her modeling career covered the walls.

A three-way mirror stood in a corner, another in the corner opposite. Three racks built along one wall held samples of Margot's signature clothing. A mannequin, wearing a slinky black Valentino dress, stood next to a blow-up of the famous *Vogue* cover with the photo of Margot wearing that same dress.

Next to the vanity there was a three-panel changing screen with a silk robe casually thrown over it as if Margot were behind it even now, changing into something . . . what?

More comfortable?

What the hell was going on in here?

Though she knew it was impossible, Risa still found herself walking over to glance behind the screen to make certain that Margot truly wasn't there. A pair of lace-topped, thigh-high black hose was draped over a small chair behind the screen, as if Margot had just taken them off a moment ago.

Risa shivered, though the room was far from cold, and her skin began to crawl with the feeling that she was not alone.

Could Conrad be home already? She stepped out from behind the screen, but nobody was there.

Except there *was* somebody there: Margot Dunn, who had been dead for a year, but whose essence filled this room to the point where the dead woman's presence was almost palpable.

Risa opened one of the drawers in the vanity—Margot's silk lingerie, neatly folded, filled it to the brim.

She opened the large jewelry box—apparently, every piece of Margot's magnificent jewelry lay perfectly aligned, as if waiting to enhance their owner's beauty. Unlike Risa's own jumbled and tangled jewelry box, Margot's earrings were sorted in matched pairs, her necklaces neatly coiled, her rings lined up in velvet slots.

And in the bottom drawer, lying alone on the black velvet lining, there was a key.

Risa looked around for something the key might fit, but saw nothing.

She closed the jewelry box, put the stopper back in the perfume bottle, and took a step toward the door, even while wishing she'd never come into the room at all. And then, as she stood alone amid Margot's clothes and jewelry and makeup, with Margot's eyes watching her from every frame on every wall, she recalled Conrad's voice on that first night of their honeymoon in Paris.

Margot!

It had been Margot's name he'd called out, not hers.

Before their wedding, he'd cleaned all of Margot's things out of the closets, taken all the photographs off the walls, and removed everything that she might find difficult to live with, and she'd loved him for it.

But now she could see that he hadn't gotten rid of it at all, hadn't gotten rid of any of it. He'd only brought it down here to store it in the basement.

But as Risa took another look around, she knew this was no storeroom.

It was a shrine.

A shrine to a woman who was dead.

Except that to Conrad, Margot apparently wasn't dead at all.

How often did he come down here? Did he prefer Margot's perfume to her own?

She pictured Conrad prowling the room, caressing his dead wife's lingerie, stroking the glimmering fabric on that black Valentino gown.

Was he happier down here, mourning at this memorial to his dead wife, than upstairs in the company of his warm, loving, *living* wife?

A terrible aching feeling of helplessness and hopelessness came over Risa as she gazed around the room once more. How could she ever compete with Margot's beauty and grace?

Her eyes glistened with tears, tears she had no strength to fight, but just as they were about to overwhelm her, she remembered the night just over a year ago when Michael Shaw had told her their marriage was over, and why.

She had cried that night. Not so much because she'd lost Michael, but because there was no way to fight for him.

But Conrad was different.

Conrad wasn't gay.

And suddenly Risa felt her strength flooding back into her, and she gazed up at Margot again, this time seeing her in a whole new light.

"You're dead," she whispered. "You're dead and buried and no longer a part of our life. *And you will not claim my husband.*"

Margot was dead, and no matter how much time Conrad spent down here with his memories, Margot could not seduce him any longer.

Not the way she herself could.

And would.

Starting tonight.

Snatching one of Margot's peignoirs off the clothes rack, a peignoir that was far more beautiful—and expensive—than anything she would have bought for herself, Risa left the basement room, closing the door firmly behind her.

By the end of this evening, she resolved, Conrad would never want to come back here again.

21

The fingers played over the keyboard with the deftness of Van Cliburn racing through Tchaikovsky's First Piano Concerto. At the top left-hand corner of the computer screen there was a photograph of a mousy young woman named Molly Roberts—whose name was of no more interest to the mind than the names of any of its previous subjects.

The eyes gazed steadily at the screen as the facial-recognition software measured every aspect of the nose that was enlarged in the center of the screen.

Molly Roberts's nose.

A nose whose perfection the eyes had perceived at once, and which was now being confirmed by the utterly objective code running in the brain of the computer.

And then the measurements were done, and as the mind had expected, the dimensions and ratios were perfect right down to a single millimeter.

The computer had finally finished its most difficult job and was now assembling all the puzzle pieces it had been gathering over the past year.

At the top right-hand corner of the screen was a photograph of Margot Dunn.

The goal must never be forgotten.

When Molly Roberts's medical records popped up in the center of the screen, the right hand manipulated the mouse, and in only a second or two the medical records shrank to fit into the lower left-hand corner of the monitor.

The forefinger of the right hand worked the wheel on the mouse, and the pages of the medical record began to flow by the window.

The blood type was a perfect match.

An attorney's office served as next of kin.

The fingers picked up a pen and scribbled the address and phone number on a Post-it.

Google Maps pinpointed the location of Molly Roberts's apartment.

But the medical records were voluminous. Why?

And then the eyes saw it: Molly Roberts suffered from agoraphobia. She was a shut-in.

A silent curse formed on the lips, and the small dog that was sleeping in his bed next to the desk stirred, as if sensing his master's fury.

Agoraphobia.

That could make this more difficult than the mind had anticipated.

White-hot rage began to build behind the eyes as they scanned the medical records over and over again.

This was the final piece—the last payment! It should be simple. But now it wouldn't be.

The chair creaked as the eyes closed and the body leaned back. The head rotated gently on the neck to reduce tension.

The mind ordered the body to relax, and slowly the body obeyed. After all, this was but a minor inconvenience, and given that this was to be the final payment of the old debt, whatever inconvenience was involved would be worth the extra effort. Soon it would all be over.

The eyes opened as a sigh escaped the lips, and once again the fingers began to fly over the keyboard, seeking avenues of access.

The girl had no next of kin. She lived alone.

Ah, but wait! Here was something: she ran a website for other agoraphobics.

The fingers moved more rapidly, and the browser opened a fresh window filled with information on the website. The masthead showed two miniature dachshunds. A quick check on the chat section of the site showed that Molly Roberts, logged in as MollyAtHome, posted more often than anyone else, and that she was constantly talking about her two elderly dogs and the mobile vet who came to the house to care for them.

An idea began to take root, sprout, and quickly grow.

The right hand manipulated the mouse, and one by one the windows closed.

The screen went dark.

The vow came back to mind: "I will do whatever it takes."

"Come here, Mr. Bojangles. Come here, sweetheart."

The teacup schnauzer got up from his bed, stretched, then clicked his nails on the hardwood floor and jumped up into his mistress's lap.

"I have a big job for you, yes I do," she cooed to him, stroking his soft fur. After a moment, when the dog was settled, Danielle DeLorian snapped its neck and felt it die in her lap.

❖ ❖ ❖

THE LAST THING Risa expected when she walked into Alison's room at Le Chateau at eight o'clock that evening was to find her daughter sitting up in bed, the TV on and tuned to one of their favorite shows. As she came over to the bed, her daughter grinned at her.

"Can you believe it?" Alison asked. "All that stuff Conrad gave me really worked. I thought I'd be feeling terrible, but nothing hurts at all."

Risa cocked her head and gazed at Alison, barely able to believe that she'd been under anesthesia only a few hours ago; indeed, when she'd called Le Chateau an hour ago, she was told that Alison was still in recovery. But now here she was, in a room far more beautiful than any hospital room Risa had ever seen, and looking as comfortable as if she were in the hotel suite the room resembled.

Unable to stop herself, Risa laid her wrist against Alison's forehead, but felt no fever at all.

Nor did Alison look even slightly pale.

"So," she finally said, dropping into a large overstuffed chair placed so it faced Alison, "I guess I wasted a lot of time worrying for nothing, huh?"

"Not as much as I did," Alison replied. "I can't believe it—I really thought all Conrad was doing was trying to get me to stop worrying!"

"And where, exactly, *is* Conrad?" Risa asked, doing her best to keep her voice as cheerful as Alison's. For the last two hours she'd been worrying about what the strange shrine in the basement was all about. But she wasn't about to mention it to Alison.

Or anyone else.

Not, at least, until she knew the results of what she'd planned for this evening.

But something in her voice must have given Alison a hint that something wasn't right, because her smile had faded.

"Didn't he go home?" her daughter asked. "He was here half an hour ago, and said he'd see me in the morning. I thought he was done for the day."

"And so I was," Conrad himself said, coming through the doorway. He crossed over to Risa, kissed her on the cheek, then took Alison's wrist to check her pulse. "Until Teresa told me your mother was on her way over." He fell silent for a few seconds, counting the beats of Alison's heart, then dropped her wrist back onto the bed. "So I figured I'd wait around, see you one more time, and make sure your mother lets you go to sleep."

"Except I'm not sleepy," Alison challenged.

"You will be," Conrad said placidly. "Everyone always wakes up feeling great, then crashes a few hours later. But it won't be bad, and I expect you'll still be going home in the morning. But I want you to sleep in, all right? I'm giving orders that you aren't to be woken up until nine. The nurses can check on you, but they can't wake you up. Okay?"

"This place really isn't like a hospital, is it?" Risa said. "Every time I've been in one, they wake you up to give you sleeping pills."

"Obviously you've been going to the wrong hospitals," Conrad told her. "And the nine o'clock do-not-disturb applies to you, too," he added. "Think you can keep away that long?"

"Can't I even come in and sit with her?" Risa countered.

"You'd never be able to do that. You'd start poking her to make sure she was still breathing."

"I wouldn't!"

"You would, too, Mom." Alison yawned.

"Aha!" Conrad said. "See? You're about to pass out for the night. What do you say I take your mother home for dinner, and leave you to sleep?"

Alison shrugged. "Actually, you're right—I think I am starting to poop out. Don't you have any more of those miracle pills you gave me?"

"Not to keep you awake. Not tonight. Tonight, all I want you to do is sleep." He gently drew Risa to her feet. "So what do you think? Is it okay if I take your mother home?"

"Sure—I'll be fine. Besides, Dad and Scott are coming by. Dad said they'd be here at eight-thirty."

"And they'll be gone by nine," Conrad instructed. Then, at the look on Alison's face, he relented. "All right, nine-thirty. But no later, understand?"

"Okay," Alison grumbled. She tried to hold up her arms but failed. Risa bent down to kiss her gently on the cheek, careful to put no pressure on her, but Alison pulled her close. "Love you, Mom," she whispered.

"I love you, too," Risa replied. "See you in the morning."

"But not too early," Alison said before Conrad could repeat the admonition.

Risa, though, didn't need the admonition repeated.

If everything went according to her plan, neither Conrad nor she would want to be getting up early tomorrow morning.

"I'M GOING UPSTAIRS," Risa said, putting a hand on top of Conrad's and glancing at the clock. It was almost ten. "Finish your wine and then come join me?"

"Sure," he replied. "I've got a stack of journals to get caught up on. Might as well do it in comfort."

"Not tonight," Risa said, sliding her chair back from the dining room table. "I have a surprise for you."

Catching the faintly seductive note in her voice, Conrad eyed her speculatively. "Oh?" He picked up his wineglass, drained it, and started to move his own chair back.

"I need five minutes," Risa said, smiling at him. "But don't make me wait too long."

"I'm liking where this is going," Conrad said, taking her hand and kissing her fingers as she passed behind his chair.

"I'll see you in bed," she said, pulling her fingers free and disappearing through the dining room door.

As she hurried up the stairs, Risa felt much, much better. Tonight was going to be their real honeymoon night—the night she had imagined so often, the two of them alone, pleasing each other until they were exhausted, then falling asleep in each other's arms just before sunrise. That it would happen here instead of in Paris was fine. In fact, the whole day was turning out fine; much finer, indeed, than she'd expected this morning. The surgery had gone every bit as well as Conrad had promised, and though Alison had gotten a little sleepy when she visited her at Le Chateau, she clearly was doing even better than he'd expected.

And since she wasn't allowed to see Alison until nine, they could sleep in.

So she and Conrad deserved the night she was determined to give them, and though they might have had a little too much wine at dinner—Dom Perignon to begin, then a bottle of Montrachet, and a split of Chateau d'Yquem to finish—being a tiny bit tipsy never hurt when it came to making love.

Moving quickly, Risa lit all the candles she had carefully arranged in the bedroom, dimmed the lights, put a second bottle of Dom Perignon in an ice bucket, set two glasses on Conrad's nightstand, then went into her dressing room and closed the door. The peignoir she had found hanging downstairs on one of the racks in Margot's room fit her almost perfectly, and she dabbed on a touch of the perfume from Margot's vanity at all her pulse points: behind her ears, behind her knees, and at her wrists.

She was just starting to brush her hair when she heard Conrad come into the bedroom. A moment later his bathroom door closed, and then she heard water running as he brushed his teeth.

She checked her makeup, brushed her own teeth, and heard the cork pop on the champagne.

Conrad—her husband—was in bed waiting for her.

With her heart pounding like a schoolgirl's, Risa opened the door of her dressing room and made her entrance, posing seductively in front of the full-length mirror.

Then she began to move, the peignoir shimmering in the candlelight.

But instead of leaning back against the headboard to enjoy the show she was putting on, Conrad sat straight up in bed and snapped on the bedside light. "What the hell is going on?" he demanded. "Where did you get that lingerie?" He rubbed his hands over his face. "And that scent! Where did you get that perfume?"

The mood she had so carefully created shattered into a million irretrievable pieces, and she froze. Then, as Conrad gaped at her, a cold fury began to break through the veil of wine, and when she spoke, her voice was as icy as the bucket in which the champagne bottle still stood. "I thought if I wore one of Margot's peignoirs, you might make love to me the way you did to her. Obviously, I was wrong."

"Take it off," Conrad said flatly. "I won't even discuss this until you've changed into something else and washed off that perfume."

Risa stood stock-still for a moment, then turned away, refusing to let him see the tears that were blinding her. Fleeing back to the dressing room, she stripped off the offending peignoir, crushed it into a wad, and hurled it in the corner. Maria could find it in the morning and throw it away for all she cared. Her fury still raging, she stepped into the shower to soap away the perfume, and scrubbed every inch of her skin a second time as if she could scour away the memory of how Conrad had been looking at her, along with the last vestiges of Margot's scent. Stepping at last out of the shower, she dried herself, pulled on a nightgown Conrad had seen at least a dozen times before, and at last returned to the bedroom.

He had turned the light off again, and lay with his hands behind his head, staring at the ceiling.

Risa perched stiffly on the edge of the bed.

"Want to tell me what this is all about?" he asked, his eyes still fixed on the plaster overhead.

Risa stared down at the floor, her plan for a romantic evening in ruins. Once again she felt tears flooding her eyes, but this time there was no way of hiding her pain.

"Where did you get that stuff?" Conrad asked.

"You know damned well where," she barked back. "It was in that *shrine* you've built for Margot downstairs."

Conrad was silent for so long that Risa finally turned her head to make sure he'd heard her.

He was no longer looking at the ceiling.

Now he was looking at her.

And he was smiling.

Then, still smiling at her, he began to laugh. "*Shrine?* That's what you think that is?"

She stared at him. Why was he smiling? And what, exactly, did he think was even faintly funny?

"Darling," Conrad said, "that's not a shrine! It's the Margot Museum. She built it herself, *for herself.* Actually, it started out as just a place to store things—clothes she wasn't going to wear anymore, and all the pictures of herself. But then, after the accident, it started to change. She spent more and more time down there, and had that vanity built, and it all started to get strange. It's where she went to . . . I don't know . . . reflect, I guess. Remember how she was before the accident . . . or pretend the accident hadn't happened at all, I guess. The truth is, I'd practically forgotten about it—I haven't been down there since she died. Since way before she died, actually."

Risa gazed uncertainly at him. "Someone goes down there," she finally said. "There's no dust. None at all."

"Maria," Conrad said, finally sitting up and pouring the champagne into the two glasses. He handed one to her, then shook his head. "Did you really think I spend time down there?"

Risa thought about the perfectly lighted vanity for applying makeup, and all the mirrors in front of which Margot could have tried on clothes and modeled them. None of that had been designed by a man—it couldn't have been.

It had to have been the work of a woman.

A vain, self-obsessed woman.

Suddenly, she could see it perfectly in her mind's eye. See Margot, alone in that strange chamber, trying to recapture her past, trying to cover her scars with layer after layer of makeup, putting on dress after dress and gazing at herself in the dozens of mirrors, seeing herself as she used to be rather than as she'd become.

Conrad was telling her the truth.

A solitary tear leaked out of her right eye and landed on the bedspread.

"Come here, darling," Conrad said, taking the glass from her hand and drawing her down onto the bed. "Margot is gone and you don't have to compete with her memory. I should have taken that room apart a long time ago, but I'll have it done immediately. I'm just sorry you found it at all, let alone that it upset you so much."

"I just—" Risa began, but Conrad held a gentle finger to her lips.

"Shhh," he said, then gently kissed her face, his lips touching her forehead, her cheeks, her eyes, and finally her lips, each kiss easing her pain and banishing her fears.

Then they were making love, and it was even better than she had imagined it in her fantasies, and the last of her doubts fell away as Conrad took the nightgown from her body and his lips moved lower, caressing every inch of her skin, arousing intense new sensations. The night stretched before her, and the last of her tears dried away, and she began to move beneath him, loving him as she'd never loved anyone before.

The night would, after all, last forever, and they would fall asleep in each other's arms as dawn began to break.

And she would never doubt him again. . .

MOLLY ROBERTS FROWNED as the sound of a doorbell echoed in the living room of her little house in Alhambra, and paused in her knitting to gaze more intently at the television set. This was the third time today that she'd watched this episode of *The Young and the Restless*, and she didn't remember any doorbell ringing. Could she have missed something? Had some plot point slipped by her while she concentrated on her knitting pattern?

"Move over," she said to Weiner, the larger—and lazier—of her two dachshunds, who had been steadily encroaching on the lap robe that covered her knees, and who was now entangled in her yarn. She gave him a small and ineffectual shove, and was about to try to push him away entirely when the doorbell rang a second time.

Then, before the sound had completely died away, there was a heavy pounding on the door.

Both dogs leaped up and began barking at the door, but Weiner quickly tumbled over, his hind legs wrapped tightly in the skein of yarn, while Schnitzel leaped at the doorknob as if he intended to turn it himself.

"Wait, wait," Molly cried out, trying to hold onto her half-finished sweater and get up without tripping over everything to get to whatever urgency had come to her door. The sweater slipped off its needle, but she let it lie in a heap on the floor, the empty needle still in her hand.

She skirted the piles of newspapers and magazines and looked out the peephole.

A nicely dressed woman, clearly in distress, with mascara running down her cheeks as if she'd been crying, stood on the porch. As Molly watched, the woman raised her hand to pound on the door yet again. "Isn't anybody home?" she called.

"What is it?" Molly called back, not opening the door. She wasn't dressed for company—indeed, she hadn't dressed for company in years. Why would she when the only people who ever came to the house were delivery people who brought her groceries, and Dr. Hansen, who came whenever Weiner or Schnitzel were sick?

"Please," the woman on the porch sobbed. "I—I've run over a dog. . . ."

Molly gasped. Even her terrible fear of the world outside vanished as she actually felt the pain of the unfortunate animal that had been hit by the woman's car. She slid the chain off, threw back two dead bolts, and opened the door. "Where is it?" she asked, doing her best to keep her own two dogs from running out of the house.

"I don't know what happened," the woman said. "I was just driving down the street when he suddenly darted right in front of me. I couldn't stop!" Her eyes streaming with tears now, the woman held out a tiny—and unnaturally still—little schnauzer, as if offering it to Molly. "Is he yours?"

Molly's hands flew to her face and she took a step back. "Oh, no. He's not mine." Her eyes flicked to her own dogs for an instant, both of whom had fallen silent, as if they knew something terrible had happened to one of their kind. "Is he breathing?" Then, without thinking about it, Molly spoke words she rarely uttered. "You'd better come in. I can call a vet." Turning away from the door, she started toward the phone, Dr. Hansen's number already snatched out of her memory. "Is he wearing a collar? Does he have a tag?"

For the first time in months another person stepped into Molly Roberts's house, and as she heard the door close behind the woman, Molly felt the same kind of fear creeping up the back of her neck that had prevented her from leaving for the last five years.

Except it wasn't quite the same feeling.

The fear her agoraphobia brought was a sort of general panic that made her want to get back into her house.

This time, oddly, she had the strangest feeling that she wanted to get *out* of the house.

But that made no sense; her house was her safe place—it had always been her safe place. Besides, what possible danger could there be? This poor woman had run over a dog and run for help to the first place she saw a light. Molly took a deep breath and reminded herself that the woman would only be there for a few minutes and then she'd go away, and she would reknit her safe space around her as carefully as she'd rebuild the sweater she was working on.

"He's got a collar, but there's no tag," the woman said.

"We'd better call the police, too," Molly said as she reached for the cordless phone that always sat on the end table next to her favorite seat on the sofa. But before her fingers closed on the phone, she heard a soft thud, the kind of sound the tiny dog would have made if the woman had dropped it on her hardwood floor.

One of her own dogs whimpered.

The phone forgotten, Molly was about to turn around to see what had happened when an arm gripped her around the throat and jerked her backward so hard she lost her balance.

"There's a terrible odor in here," the woman whispered into her ear, "but at least you won't have to smell it anymore."

A knife glinted in the light of the television set.

Molly felt a sensation of pressure slide across her throat, then felt something pouring down the front of her robe.

Realizing what was happening, she began flailing her arms, the knitting needle in her left hand lashing backward toward her attacker. She tried to jab at the woman, and finally felt the needle make contact, but it was too late. Suddenly, the mere act of breathing became far more important than trying to protect herself. Her knees weakened as she reached for something to hold onto—but there was nothing.

She fell back onto the mound of mail that had accumulated over the years, gasping, reaching for her puppies to tell them one last time that Mommy loved them.

Too late—the woman was already standing over her, the bloody knife glimmering as she clutched it.

Molly closed her eyes and felt herself slipping away as the blade plunged through the skin of her cheek, then dug deep, as if the woman was trying to dig her nose off her face. But now the pain began to fade, and a welcome darkness gathered around her, and she whispered a last good-bye, hoping her two dogs could hear her.

Then Molly Roberts was gone, unaware that her attacker had moved on from her face and was laying her belly open, quickly cutting out the treasures that lay within.

22

Risa stopped short as she walked into Alison's suite at Le Chateau at exactly nine o'clock the next morning. Alison was sitting up eating a breakfast far larger than she herself had consumed that morning, and looking as if she was on about the fourth day of a very restful vacation, rather than less than twenty-four hours out of surgery. "Am I in the right room?" she asked.

"I feel great," Alison said as her mother kissed her cheek. "All these bandages make me feel like I can barely breathe, but I hardly hurt at all." She peeled off a piece of croissant, smeared it with butter and jam, and popped it into her mouth while Risa settled into a chair next to the bed. "The only thing I really hate is the IV."

"Which will come out as soon as you've finished your breakfast," Conrad said as he strode into the room, pausing to look at Alison's purple-jacketed medical chart.

"Hello, my darling," Risa said, rising to return his kiss as he moved on to her, then dropping back into the chair when Conrad shifted his attention to Alison.

"You're looking good," he said, still scanning the pages of her chart. As she told him she was feeling good, too, he closed the chart and put it on the table next to the bed, moved her breakfast tray aside, and began a quick examination, listening to her heart and her lungs, peering into her eyes, and finally opening the hospital gown to check the bandages over the small incisions he'd made under her armpits.

"Perfect," he pronounced. "No fever, no leakage, good appetite. My ideal patient."

For the first time, Risa was certain she saw not only respect, but a little affection as well when Alison grinned up at him. "Better late than never, right? I'm starting to wonder why I was such a wuss about this."

"You weren't a wuss at all," Conrad assured her. "You were a perfectly normal almost-sixteen-year-old girl with a very healthy fear of having anyone mucking around with your body, even when they're as good at it as I am." Deliberately ignoring the mutual rolling of his wife's and stepdaughter's eyes, he checked the level of the IV bag. "I'm going to leave the IV in until the bag is empty," he told Alison. "Maybe another half hour or so, then Peggy will come take it out. Once that's done, we'll keep an eye on you for another hour, then you can get dressed to go home."

"Home?" Alison and Risa echoed in shocked unison.

"Home," Conrad repeated. "You'll heal faster at home, but I do want you to stay in bed for the rest of the day and most of tomorrow, primarily to get over the effects of the anesthesia. Also, I want you to keep taking those homeopathics for another week."

"What about the bandages?" Alison said. "How long do they stay on?"

"I'll change them tomorrow and get them down to a reasonable size, but you'll still have something on Monday."

The door opened and a tall, perfectly made-up woman in a chic dove-gray suit came in, holding a pink box. "Alison?" she said.

Risa recognized her as Danielle DeLorian. But what would the head of the company that made the most expensive cosmetics in the world be doing visiting Alison?

"Hi, Danielle," Conrad said. "You remember Risa, my wife?"

"Of course," Danielle said, extending an elegantly manicured hand toward Risa. "And don't get up," she added as Risa started to rise from her chair. She held Risa's hand for a moment, then turned to gaze appraisingly at Alison.

"This is Alison Shaw," Conrad said, stepping back so Danielle could approach the bedside.

"It's lovely to meet you, Alison," she said, setting the box on the girl's lap and lightly taking the hand that wasn't attached to an IV. "Conrad's been going on and on about you, and tells me you've got a birthday coming up that he promised you'd be ready for." She leaned closer, dropped her voice, and winked at Alison. "Fortunately, I can actually keep the promises Conrad can only make." She nodded toward the pink box. "I've brought you a supply of a salve my company makes. As soon as your bandages are off, rub this salve on the entire area, stitches and all. It will reduce swelling and bruising, make the incision heal faster, and keep scarring to an absolute minimum." She shifted her gaze to Risa. "Most people think that's just marketing talk, but it isn't. The reason my products are expensive has nothing to do with the pink boxes—they cost a lot because they actually work." She tapped the pink box. "And the public can't even buy this one. Conrad gets all I can make."

He nodded.

"Conrad gets all of it?" Risa asked. "What on earth is in it?"

Danielle smiled. "All-natural ingredients, and I can tell you I have no intention of telling you anything specific about it—I think I have more security on this formula than Coca-Cola has on theirs. I *will* tell you that the salve contains only substances that the body produces itself, but needs in extra quantities to promote the kind of healing that we're looking for."

"What kind of substances?" Alison asked as she opened the box. There was a small jar inside. She unscrewed the top and sniffed at it. "Smells good." She handed it to her mother.

"This is so nice of you, Danielle," Risa said.

"Believe me, it's my pleasure," Danielle responded, and patted Alison's hand. "Conrad is important to me, and my formulas are important to Conrad's clients. And he tells me that Alison is his most important client, so I intend to see to it that she gets nothing but the best."

"I don't know how to thank you," Risa said. "Maybe I can at least buy you lunch sometime? I know it's not much, but at least it's something."

"And not the slightest bit necessary," Danielle said, checking her watch. "Oh lord, I'm going to be late for a brunch at the Polo Lounge—have to run."

As Danielle turned to kiss Conrad on the cheek, Risa noticed a long scratch down the woman's neck that she hadn't managed to cover with makeup. Maybe she ought to put a little of her special formula on *that,* she thought, then chided herself for being catty after the woman had come all the way over on a Saturday to bring Alison a gift.

"I have to go, too," Conrad said. "I've got other patients, so I'll see you both at home." He moved Alison's breakfast tray back to her. "Your eggs are cold," he said, putting the cover back over the plate. "Drink your juice and I'll have a fresh plate brought up." He kissed her on the cheek, then did the same to Risa, grabbed the chart, and left.

"I don't believe it," Alison breathed when she and her mother were once more alone in the room. "Danielle DeLorian was just here. Danielle DeLorian! To see me!"

"I know," Risa sighed. "But I guess we'd better start getting used to it—we seem to be part of that crowd now. I knew Conrad knows everyone in town, but I had no idea they liked him as much as Danielle obviously does."

Alison started to laugh, then winced. "Don't make me laugh," she said. "It hurts."

"Sorry," Risa said, but found herself laughing anyway. After last night with Conrad and this morning with Alison, life seemed very much worth laughing about. Conrad loved her, and Alison would be home this afternoon, and suddenly life was even better than laughter.

Life, indeed, was perfect.

❖   ❖   ❖

THE GENTLE STRAINS of Stravinsky filled the operating room with soothing music, the rhythms almost perfectly matching Jillian Oglesby's breathing, as Conrad Dunn cut a solitary hair follicle from the patch of skin he'd taken from the back of the girl's neck and lifted it with tweezers.

His hand hovered over the nearly microscopic socket he'd made for the follicle on her supraorbital ridge. The single strand of hair was perfectly aligned, but at the last moment he gave it a quarter of a turn before slipping it into its receptacle.

Teresa and Kate exchanged a look, and Kate frowned uncertainly.

"Doctor?" Teresa said.

"I know," Conrad said, his tweezers already poised to pluck the hair out again. He stepped back and took a deep breath, then looked up at the computer screen, where Jillian Oglesby's high school photo had been enlarged to show nothing more than her eyebrows a few months before she was attacked. "I wish Corinne had never mentioned it," he went on as Teresa swabbed perspiration from his forehead. "I would never have noticed if she hadn't pointed it out."

"What are you talking about, Conrad?" Kate asked, her eyes never leaving the monitors tracking Jillian's anesthesia.

"Look at them!" He gestured toward the monitor with his scalpel. "Don't you see it? They were exactly like Margot's!"

Teresa again looked over at Kate, who shrugged uncertainly.

"What right does she have to have brows as perfect as Margot's?"

"She grew them that way," Kate said. "Doesn't that give her an even better right to them than Margot had?"

"I know," Conrad sighed. "But somehow it doesn't seem right that someone like this should have brows as perfect as Margot's, especially without any help at all. And certainly not without having the rest of Margot to go with them. This seems . . . I don't know . . . sacrilegious, I guess." He tore his eyes from the monitor and focused once more on

Jillian. "I just felt like I ought to give them one tiny imperfection—just a single hair slightly out of place. Add a little . . . what? Personality, maybe?"

He glanced up at Teresa, whose eyes seemed not only perplexed, but disapproving as well, then turned to Kate.

The anesthesiologist's expression duplicated that of the nurse's.

And neither of them spoke, knowing Conrad Dunn could read their expressions at least as clearly as he would hear their words.

"You're right," he sighed, plucking out the hair and discarding it. "She should be as perfect as I can possibly make her." He chose another hair, excised it from the donor patch, and inserted it into the tiny pocket from which he'd plucked the offending strand. Working slowly and carefully, he continued to transplant the hairs, one by one, until both brows were full and arched every bit as perfectly as the ones displayed on the monitor.

"Nicely done, Conrad," Kate said nearly two hours later, when he was finally satisfied with his work.

"They're exactly as they were, and if she's careful about keeping them trimmed, very few people will ever notice they're not quite brow hairs," Conrad said. Then he smiled at his surgical team. "Not that it matters—Jillian Oglesby will never be anything like Margot, at least not like the Margot I constructed before." He squeezed a tiny dab of golden ointment from a small tube labeled HEALING HEALTH LABORA-TORIES and gently applied it not only to the brows themselves, but to the area around them, and then to the stitches at the back of Jillian's neck from which he'd taken the patch of donor skin.

"Can you finish?" he asked Teresa.

"Of course," the nurse replied.

Conrad Dunn gazed down at Jillian Oglesby's face, utterly relaxed in sleep. "They really aren't Margot's brows, if you actually study them," he said. "The shape is there—no question about it. And the color. But this girl simply doesn't have the underlying bone structure to show them off properly." His eyes finally shifted away from Jillian's face to the image of Margot on the wall monitor, a picture taken from full front, which showed her eyebrows in their full perfection. "That was the magic of Margot," he said almost to himself. "That perfect bone structure."

"Which none of us will ever see again," Kate said, deliberately disturbing his reverie. "She was one of a kind, and there won't be another."

"Actually, that's not quite true," Conrad Dunn said quietly as he pulled off his gloves. "I believe Alison Shaw has it."

Part Three

TRANSFORMATION

23

"WELL, I'M STILL NOT GOING TO TELL YOU I APPROVE," CINDY KEARNS said, but even though the words hadn't changed in the half hour Alison had just spent telling her best friend the latest details of her recovery from surgery, Cindy's tone had softened, and Alison knew that when she finally saw her new figure in person, Cindy would be as happy about it as she herself was.

"I just wish you could come over right now," Alison sighed.

"I could, if you still lived in Santa Monica," Cindy reminded her.

"I know. I wish I still lived there, too," she said, but knew that wasn't quite true anymore. She hadn't just gotten used to living in Conrad Dunn's enormous house, she'd started to feel comfortable in it. When she thought about her old room in the little house in Santa Monica, she realized she didn't want to go back to it. "It would be even better if you lived up here in Bel Air," she said.

"Like that's ever going to happen," Cindy drawled. "My dad's a fireman, remember? Anyway, I'll see you tomorrow. What should I wear?"

"We're going to start inside, and then we'll go outside for dancing. Just wear what you think you'll be comfortable in. It'll be fine." Alison flipped the phone closed to end the call a few seconds later, then swiveled around in her desk chair to look around her room, trying to see it the way the Santa Monica kids who hadn't already been up here—which was all of them but Cindy—would see it. They'd be expecting a big house—practically every house in Bel Air was large, and the newest ones were so big they looked ridiculous—but most of them hadn't ever seen a bedroom as big as hers. Still, the room had started to look like her, with her favorite posters on the walls, her stuffed animals among the throw pillows on the bed, and her track medals and trophies on the bookcase.

Not all that much different from her room in Santa Monica, she told herself, except for its size.

And the thick Oriental rugs on the gleaming hardwood floors.

And the beautiful paper covering the walls above the wainscoting.

And the private bathroom she didn't have to share with anyone.

Okay, it was a lot different from her old room, but it was hers now, and she liked it, just like anyone would. So why was she feeling guilty? Or maybe the little knot in her stomach was just hunger. She looked at the clock—her mom wouldn't be home for at least another hour. Maybe she'd go down and see if she could sneak or beg a snack from Maria.

She was just getting up when there were two raps on her bedroom door.

"Come on in," she called out.

Conrad opened the door, holding a large flat white box. "Hi," he said. "Am I disturbing you?"

Alison shook her head. "I was just talking to my friend Cindy."

"I brought a dress I thought you'd look good in tomorrow at your party," he said, and handed her the box.

Alison looked at it uncertainly. Didn't he know she already had a dress?

One he'd paid twelve hundred dollars for?

She racked her brain, trying to remember if she'd mentioned it to him. But surely she had at least *thanked* him for it, hadn't she? "I—I already have a dress—" she stammered.

Conrad thumped his forehead with the palm of his hand. "Oh, for God's sake! How could I have forgotten?" Then his voice changed and he sounded almost like a little boy. "Maybe you could save the other one for another day? I found this one, and it seemed so perfect, and—"

"I guess I could," Alison broke in. "But what if it doesn't fit?" Conrad stared blankly at her, and she had the distinct feeling that the thought had never crossed his mind. "Maybe I should try it on."

"Great!" Conrad said, his expression suddenly clearing. "And if it doesn't fit, or you don't like it, you can wear the one you already have."

Alison put the box on the corner of her bed, then raised the lid.

When she peeled back the tissue paper, she gasped. A gorgeous black V-neck dress, made of the lightest fabric she'd ever seen, lay folded inside.

She stared at Conrad in stunned amazement.

"Go ahead," he urged. "Take it out."

She lifted the dress from the box. It couldn't have weighed more than a few ounces. The back was cut low and the flared skirt, cut on the bias, had a diagonal hem dropping away from right to left.

And a very discreet Valentino label.

"Oh, Conrad," she breathed. "This is beautiful."

"Try it on," he said.

She turned to look at him. "You're sure?" she asked. "It must have cost—"

"Just try it on," he broke in, lowering himself into the wing chair by the window. "If you hate it, I'll return it. If you like it, and it fits, you can either wear it tomorrow or it can stay in your closet until you need it." His right eyebrow lifted archly. "Trust me—my first wife taught me that you can't have too many dresses."

Alison was still torn, balancing the expense of the dress against the vision she had of herself wearing it. And she could see that Conrad truly did want her to have it. "Okay," she finally said, clutching the gown to her. "I'll be right back."

She went into the dressing room between her bedroom and bathroom, closed the door behind her, and quickly shucked her shorts and tank top. She no longer needed a bra, thanks to Conrad's gift of two weeks ago, so she slipped the dress over her head, letting it drop into place.

It fit perfectly.

A glance in the mirror told her the dress demanded upswept hair, so she rummaged in the bathroom for a clip and pulled her hair up into a semblance of a French twist. Then she slipped her feet into the pair of black high heels she was planning to dance in tomorrow and opened the door. "Ta da," she said, opening her arms and slowly twirling. "It's perfect."

"It's more than perfect," Conrad said, standing up. "It's like that dress was created for you."

Alison grinned happily at him. "Why don't I think Valentino's ever even heard of me?"

"Well, if he hasn't, he will," Conrad declared. "How about I take a picture of you for the album at the office? We don't have an 'after' shot of you, and in that dress you'll sell my services to everyone who sees you."

Alison hesitated. "What about my hair? And shouldn't I be wearing makeup?"

"Not needed," Conrad declared. "Better to see you exactly the way you are."

"Can't I at least comb my hair?" she asked.

"Okay, comb your hair while I get my camera," he said. "But no makeup. I don't want anything distracting from your figure."

He left her room, and Alison returned to the dressing room, brushed her hair out, then swept it back up into a real twist, this time pinning it carefully in place. By the time she was finished and back in her bedroom, Conrad had returned, with a large digital single-lens-reflex camera.

"By the window," he said, motioning her over to a spot where sunlight was flooding into the room.

She moved close to the window and leaned against the wall as Conrad focused the camera and started taking one picture after another. Like Margot, she thought. This is just how Margot must have felt.

As the shutter kept clicking, Alison wondered if Margot Dunn had felt anywhere near as uncomfortable in front of Conrad's camera as she did right now.

In fact, the whole thing felt kind of creepy—posing for her stepfather in her own bedroom. But what could she say? Conrad had been so generous to her, done so much for her.

Besides, it would be over in a couple more minutes. What harm could there be in humoring him?

If he wanted to take her picture, who was she to say no?

24

ALISON BRUSHED A FINAL TOUCH OF GLOSS ONTO HER LIPS, THEN stood back, took a careful look at herself in the full-length mirror, and decided that Conrad's procedure had been worth it.

And that's all it had been, actually—just a simple procedure she recovered from so quickly that whatever discomfort she'd felt was already nothing more than a dim memory. Nothing like surgery at all. Surgery would have hurt a lot more, and would have taken a much longer time to heal. So why had she been such a baby about it? Especially now that she was seeing the results.

The difference the procedure had made was more than simply an augmentation of her breasts. It seemed as if her whole figure had changed from that of an adolescent into one of a young woman. All her curves seemed to have been accentuated by the procedure, and with her hair swept up, some of Danielle DeLorian's incredibly expensive makeup lightly applied, and the spectacular Mandalay dress, she looked more like a sophisticated eighteen-year-old than the barely sixteen she actually was. Even more important, she looked like the kind of girl who could play hostess to the kind of party her mother and Conrad had arranged, rather than the pizza-and-games-or-a-movie birthday parties she'd had as long as she could remember. If this was how she looked with just the one procedure—

Her mother's voice on the intercom shattered her reverie. "Alison, your guests are arriving."

"Be right down," she answered, then put away her cosmetics, and took one last look around her suite to make certain everything was neat and ready for inspection—every one of her friends from Santa Monica was going to want to see it.

She opened her bedroom door and started down the stairs, seeing her mother and stepfather waiting for her in the foyer as she came around the turn at the staircase's landing.

"Alison," Risa whispered, her eyes widening as she gazed up at her daughter. "You look beautiful—just beautiful."

As she came to the bottom of the stairs, twinkling lights in the garden caught Alison's eye. "But not as pretty as the garden," she said, smiling happily.

"Nobody's going to look at the garden once they take a look at you," Conrad said. "You look spectacular."

Alison felt the color rising in her cheeks. "Thank you, Conrad," she murmured. "Thanks for all of this."

"Happy sweet sixteen," Conrad said, and raised the wineglass he was holding.

Before Alison could respond, the doorbell rang, and Ruffles came tumbling down the stairs, barking as loud as he could.

"And that's our cue to vanish," Risa said, bending down to scoop Ruffles up before he could launch himself at whoever was at the door. "We'll be in the media room if you need us."

"Have fun," Conrad told her with a wink, then followed his wife down the hall.

Alison opened the front door to find Cindy Kearns, along with Lisa Hess, Anton Hoyer, and Tommy Kline, holding brightly wrapped presents while they watched one of the parking valets Conrad had hired move Tommy's ten-year-old Honda to a nearly invisible spot next to the garage.

"Wow!" Lisa said. "Look at you!"

Alison grinned happily and hugged Lisa and Anton, but when she turned to Cindy, the girl who had always been her best friend stiffened, and Alison knew why.

Cindy Kearns still didn't approve of what she'd had done to herself.

A little of her happiness drained away, and the lights in the garden didn't seem quite as bright as they had a moment ago.

"Where did you get that dress?" Lisa asked.

Alison hesitated a moment too long. "Neiman's," she finally admitted.

"Neiman's," Cindy echoed, her voice dripping with sarcasm.

Alison felt her face burning now as she remembered the fun she and Cindy used to make of the girls their age who bought whatever they wanted in the store. *Wait'll they have to spend their own money,* Cindy had said only a few months ago. *Then we'll see how much of this stuff they buy.* And now Cindy thought she had become one of those people.

But she wasn't, was she? This was different—this was a special occasion. *Her birthday party!* Couldn't Cindy understand that?

Doing her best not to let Cindy spoil her happiness, Alison ushered the group into the house. "Jesus," Anton Hoyer breathed as he looked around the foyer, then through to the living room and the garden beyond. "What a place."

"I want a tour!" Lisa Hess said. "Show us your room."

Another car door slammed outside.

"In a while," Alison said, "after everybody's here. Come on out back."

She led them through the house to the French doors opening onto the terrace. Spread below them were the swimming pool, which had been covered over with a dance floor, and the perfectly manicured gardens. Tommy Kline uttered a low whistle. "This isn't like any party I've ever been to," he said. "It looks more like a wedding, only not white."

Even Alison tried not to stare at the enormous bunches of colored balloons hovering over a dozen small tables, with each tablecloth matching the color of the balloons overhead, and each table displaying an elaborate bouquet of flowers in the same color. A buffet table laden with chafing dishes sat next to a bar stocked with sodas and fruit juices; a second buffet table featured an ice sculpture of a dolphin that seemed to be launching himself out of a sea of shrimp, crab, and chilled lobster.

"I knew I shouldn't have worn jeans," Lisa said ruefully, and folded her arms over her pink tank top.

Cindy shook her head. "You're *fine*," she said. "It's just a house!"

As soon as Alison appeared on the terrace, the three-piece band began to play and the fairy lights in the trees that she'd seen from inside the house began to brighten in the fading daylight. Then a stream of her new friends, led by Trip Atkinson and Cooper Ames, burst through the French doors and onto the terrace. Laden with gifts far more elaborately wrapped than those the Santa Monica group had brought, they piled the packages onto the table set out for that purpose, offered Alison greetings barely less pretentious than their gifts, then went directly to the food and the bar. Tommy Kline and Anton Hoyer followed them, wasting no time filling two plates.

Alison began to relax as she watched the party begin. Though the kids from Santa Monica had seemed overwhelmed by the house, with Tommy and Anton plunging right in, maybe it was going to be alright.

"Hi, birthday girl," Tasha Rudd called when she appeared on the terrace, Dawn Masin trailing along a half step behind. Alison could almost feel Cindy and Lisa stiffen as they watched the two Wilson girls stride confidently toward them, wearing tiny dresses that were mostly made of spandex and obviously cost several hundred dollars each. Tasha waved a tiny little gift bag at her, then added it to the table that was beginning to fill with presents. "Just something I found at Tiffany that had you written all over it," she said, kissing the air next to each of Alison's cheeks.

"That dress looks simply fa-*boo* on you," Dawn said to Alison as she repeated Tasha's air kisses. "And your new boobs are *perfect*." Alison smiled, but her smile faded as she caught the look of scorn on Cindy Kearns's face. "Be sure to have Conrad do your chin next," Dawn went on.

"And that little bump on your nose," Tasha chimed in. "He could do that at the same time."

"Actually, I've been sort of thinking about that," Alison said, remembering the perfect cleft in Scott Lawrence's chin and how he'd gotten it.

"You're kidding," Cindy said, making no attempt to conceal her disdain for the idea.

"Well, I haven't decided anything," Alison said a little too quickly.

"Why would she be kidding?" Tasha asked, turning to look directly at Cindy for the first time. "It would improve her profile hugely."

"That's stupid," Cindy said. "There's nothing wrong with Alison's profile."

Tasha eyed Cindy. "And you are . . . ?" As the question hung in the air, Tasha let her gaze wander appraisingly over Cindy's straight brown hair and casual clothes, and uttered a small but audible—and pointedly hopeless—sigh.

"I'm sorry," Alison said, too hurriedly. "These are Cindy Kearns and Lisa Hess, my friends from Santa Monica." She shifted her focus to Cindy and Lisa, pleading with them with her eyes. "This is Tasha Rudd and Dawn Masin. They go to Wilson."

The four gazed silently at each other.

"Why don't we all go get something to eat?" Alison asked, trying to steer the group toward the steps down to the lawn.

"I'm not eating," Tasha said. "It's almost swimsuit season."

Alison was about to laugh when she felt a hand close on her elbow, and as the rest of the girls started down the steps, she found Cindy Kearns holding her back.

"*Swimsuit* season?" Cindy repeated, her voice mimicking Tasha's almost perfectly. "I don't believe this, Alison. It's barely been a month, and you've already turned into—" She hesitated, then tilted her head pointedly toward Tasha and Dawn, who had paused on the steps and were now looking back up at them. "—one of *them*," Cindy finished.

"One of *us*," Dawn countered. "Well, it's certainly better than being one of you. Where on earth did you buy that outfit? Kmart?"

"I'm leaving," Cindy said, turning to Lisa Hess. "I knew we shouldn't have come." She struck a pose, again perfectly mimicking Tasha Rudd. "We're *so* not their class, darling. Let's go have a pizza."

Lisa hesitated. "Come on, Cindy, we just got here—"

Alison put a hand on Cindy's arm. "Don't go. Please?"

Cindy shook her head, her eyes suddenly glistening with tears. "I don't know who you are anymore," she said, the words choking in her constricted throat. Then she pulled herself together and drew her arm away from Alison. "You have a new life and new friends. What do you need me for? Go play with your new friends. Have a good time, and happy birthday."

"Cindy. . ."

But Cindy had already started back toward the French doors. "Stay if you want, Lisa, but I'm going." She signaled to Tommy and glanced once more at Alison. "Excuse me while I get your *valet* to bring up Tommy's Honda before it brings down property values around here." She turned on her heel and continued walking.

"I guess I better go." Lisa looked apologetically at Alison. "They're my ride."

Feeling tears in her own eyes, Alison nodded and hugged Lisa, but most of the happiness she'd felt only a few minutes ago drained out of her as she watched her oldest friend walking out of her party.

A soft hand touched her arm. "Let them go," Tasha said.

"She's right," Dawn added. "Forget them—you aren't like them anymore." She opened her purse and showed Alison a pint of tequila. "C'mon, birthday girl. Let's have some *fun!*"

Alison wanted to ignore Tasha and Dawn and go after Cindy and Lisa, but as another group of Wilson kids arrived, she knew she couldn't.

This was her party, and she was the hostess, and no matter how much she'd rather be with Cindy and Lisa right now—or even upstairs in her room, calling Cindy and trying to put their friendship back together—she knew she couldn't give in to her impulses.

Instead, she had to put on a happy face and be a good hostess, no matter how she felt. As she turned back to the garden, the band picked up the tempo and Trip came up the steps to the terrace.

"Dance with me?" Giving her no chance to refuse, he took her hand, and seconds later she was on the dance floor. As the music swelled, Cindy's words began to fade, though she could still feel the pain in her heart. Tomorrow, maybe, she would call and try to fix things. But for now she smiled as brightly as if she were still at the peak of the day's happiness, and danced amid her new friends.

25

TINA WONG SIPPED AT THE PAPER CUP OF COLD COFFEE, EVEN THOUGH caffeine had been eating a hole in her stomach for hours. Ben Kardashian, the video tech who'd been cooped up with her in the editing bay all night, looked even worse than she felt, his unshaven face dark with stubble, and eyes so bloodshot it looked as though he'd been out drinking all that time.

But even after working all night, the hour's worth of tape they'd come up with still wasn't quite right. But what was missing? Tina had finished all her camera work, completed all the voice-overs.

The interviews melded well, each one flowing smoothly into the next, building the story. Yet she didn't have the climax. Somehow, despite the grisly horror of everything the hour depicted, it still lacked that final dramatic moment that would tie the whole story together and give it a sense of overwhelming urgency.

Ben leaned back in his chair, stretched his arms and shoulders, rubbed his neck for a moment, then dropped his hands into his lap. "I gotta eat."

Tina nodded, though she'd barely heard the words. "Why don't you—" she began, her mind still searching for the missing moment.

Ben cut her off. "No. I need to get out of this room and go somewhere to eat something."

"Okay," Tina sighed, leaning back in her own chair. Though she knew food would only distract her from the job at hand, she also knew that Ben was about to get cranky, and she still needed his touch with all the high-tech equipment in the bay in order to finish the final edit of the special. She glanced at her watch: 6:28 A.M. "Why don't you take half an hour?"

Ben nodded, opened the door to the bay, and left. Outside, Tina could hear the station beginning to come alive with the weekend staff; the soundproof door swing shut, the quiet of the bay closing around her, and she went back to work. Her deadline was ten o'clock; before the special could air, Michael would have to watch it, and he'd undoubtedly want to run it by the legal team. That meant hunting down a couple of lawyers on a Sunday and getting them to come in so they could see what she'd put together in time to make any last-minute changes.

All of which meant she not only had to find her ending, but have it completed by ten.

She was just about to start running the tape for what seemed the millionth time when her cell phone buzzed, vibrating loudly on the metal desk. She found it under a mound of wadded-up sheets of notes and coffee-stained napkins, then swept the trash into a wastebasket with one hand while picking up the phone with the other and looking at the caller ID.

Michael Shaw. Swell—not even seven on Sunday morning yet, and her boss was already on her.

She flipped the phone open and tried not to let her sleepless night show in her voice. "Hello?"

He spoke with no preamble at all. "They found another body, Tina."

Even as he spoke, the answer to her problem began to form. "What did he take?" she demanded.

"The usual stuff," Michael said. "And the nose."

With that final word, the end to her special flashed through her mind as vividly as if it were already on tape. The ending would be perfect now—more than she could ever have hoped for—and Ben Kardashian would know exactly how to do what she needed. "Can I get a photo of the woman before she was mutilated?"

"I don't know," Michael replied. "I don't have much information yet—I called you as soon as I heard. I can give you the woman's name and address, but for now that's about it."

Tina scribbled the information on a napkin, promised Michael the finished special no later than ten, hit one of the speed-dial keys, and waited impatiently for her assistant to pick up her phone. When a sleepy voice finally answered, she didn't bother with pleasantries any more than Michael Shaw had a minute earlier. "I need a picture, Cheryl. The woman's name is Molly Roberts, and she lived in Alhambra. Get on the Web and find her—she'll be on MySpace or Facebook, or one of the dating services. Ben's out grabbing breakfast, and I need it by the time he gets back." There wasn't even a hint of grumbling from Cheryl, though Tina suspected she was silently cursing the day she'd taken her job. She simply took down the information and hung up.

Tina made a mental note to ask Michael to give Cheryl a raise, then dimmed the overhead lights in the editing bay, leaned back in the squeaky chair, and closed her eyes, visualizing how she wanted the handiwork of the Frankenstein Killer to look.

The face she'd constructed with Photoshop, roughly combining the facial features of the murdered women into a composite of whatever the killer was looking for, hadn't worked nearly as well in reality as in her own visualization. It looked piecemeal—fragmented—and though certainly horrific, hadn't made a good, cohesive face.

Even worse, it had a hole in its center where a nose should have been, and though she'd experimented with adding various noses, including her own, it hadn't worked. Partly, of course, it was because the final image was still far too rough; but even more important, as far as Tina was concerned, was the fact that the final image she'd built was incomplete.

With the death of Molly Roberts, though, she could finally complete the picture.

At the end of the hour, she could present to the world the exact face the killer himself was constructing.

And as soon as Ben Kardashian got back, they would go to work.

Tina opened her eyes and smiled.

When she got a photo of Molly Roberts, she'd have the last piece of the puzzle she'd been putting together with Photoshop. She'd finally have a full face, and Ben Kardashian would know exactly how to bring it to life.

And tomorrow morning, they might still not know the name of the Frankenstein Killer, but the entire broadcast world would know the name Tina Wong.

26

CONRAD DUNN OPENED THE DOOR TO THE LABORATORY THAT WAS HIS most private domain and waited a moment before turning on the overhead fluorescent lights. There was something about the laboratory when it was illuminated only by the soft green glow of the sustenance tanks, and the only sound was the equally soft throbbing of the pumps that provided those tanks with the exact level of oxygen they needed to keep their contents as fresh as the day they'd been harvested, that instilled a sense of peace in him that had been rare since the accident that ruined Margot's beauty.

And nearly nonexistent since the day she died.

Perhaps it was the gentle throbbing of the pumps, which reminded him of Margot's heartbeat when he used to press his face against her perfect breast. Or the green glow that reminded him of the glint in her eyes when she smiled at him. Or the fact that it was here that he had originally created her. So now he stood quietly inside the door for a moment, just breathing in the calm of this rarely used room.

But a moment was all he could devote to his reverie.

There was work to be done.

He snapped on the overhead lights and shifted his attention to the latest acquisition in the tank.

Opening the lid, with a pair of tongs he lifted out the newest fragment of tissue that had been added to the collection in the tank, then examined it from every angle with a practiced, critical eye.

Danielle had done a superb job, as usual. The choice of Molly Roberts as the donor was perfect: the curve of the nostrils, the straightness of the bridge, were exactly like Margot's; their perfection was utterly wasted on the bland travesty that had been the rest of the woman's face. And Danielle had done her work well: the incision was clean, with plenty of surrounding tissue, which would allow him to attach it with ease. Satisfied, he carefully lowered the small mass of skin and cartilage back into the green liquid. Next, he retrieved each of the other fragments in turn, examining them carefully for any signs of deterioration.

They were as perfect as the day Danielle DeLorian had harvested them.

As perfect individually as would be the face they would soon be collectively melded into.

He replaced the cover on the tank, and shifted his attention to the small operating room that was separated from the lab by an airlock that guaranteed nothing could compromise its sterility. Thus, though it had not been used in a very long time, it was in perfect condition for what was about to take place within its walls.

Conrad took two sterile packs of instruments from one of the cabinets and opened them, laying each gleaming metal piece on the instrument tray in the order in which they would be needed. Next he arranged a series of suture packs in the same order, until the precision of the series of scalpels, hemostats, retractors, sponges, gauzes, and sutures lined up on the tray mirrored the precision with which he would carry out the surgery to come. Only when he had made certain that each instrument was perfectly aligned did he finally adjust the tray into position so he could reach whatever he needed from the head of the table.

Closing his eyes, he turned around three times. Then, his eyes still closed, he reached out and closed his fingers around the first object he touched.

It was, of course, the first scalpel he would use to execute the first cut he would make.

Satisfied, he sterilized the scalpel with alcohol and returned it to its place.

He hung the bottle of dextrose with sodium chloride, and readied the IV tube and needle he would attach to it when the time came.

He set three vials of fentanyl on the instrument tray, which would keep his patient peacefully asleep for as long as necessary. The lack of an anesthesiologist would be a handicap, but only a minor one—when he operated, every one of his senses was heightened, and he'd be able to gauge the depth of the patient's unconsciousness merely by the sound of her breath, and adjust the drugs accordingly.

From another cabinet, he took fresh sterile sheets and draped the table. He hadn't readied an operating room like this since he was an intern; the nursing staff had done this for so many years now that he'd forgotten how relaxing the ritual could be.

Relaxing and enervating at the same time.

Or perhaps he was enervated by the extraordinary procedures he was about to perform. Not that it would be the first time he'd performed it; indeed, he'd performed it twice before, each time with results that were nothing short of perfect. There was, therefore, nothing to be worried about.

And yet the fluttering in his belly was more than the surge of anticipatory energy he felt before every surgical procedure.

Something still wasn't quite right.

He moved to the other side of the table and double-checked the dressing materials he would need.

He added a second vial to the tray; it contained the special compound Danielle DeLorian made only for him.

The operating theater was ready.

When the patient was sedated on the table, he would turn on the overhead light, adjust the volume of the strains of Stravinsky, or perhaps Vivaldi, that would flow from the speakers hidden in the walls, and begin.

For now, though, everything was fresh and ready.

Waiting.

And yet that sense of something not quite right—something left undone—some tiny imperfection—still pervaded his spirit.

Then his eyes were caught by the lavender Healing Health Laboratories label on the vial he'd just added to the tray and he knew.

It was that small scratch on Danielle's neck that he'd seen the day after she harvested Molly Roberts's single perfect feature.

Conrad felt his blood pressure begin to build as he realized what that scratch must have meant.

Danielle had made a mistake.

Another mistake.

And she'd failed to tell him about it.

She had put herself, and him, and *everything,* in jeopardy.

Almost as bad, his own subconscious had known about her mistake for days now but failed to warn him. Still, in all fairness, he'd realized what had happened in time to deal with the error.

Again he regarded the lavender label, and the answer to the problem came to him.

Returning to the laboratory, he went to the drug cabinet and quickly found what he was looking for. Filling a syringe from the vial, he carefully replaced the plastic cap on the needle and put the vial back in the cabinet.

From another cabinet, he took the small leather valise he had used in medical school, opened it, and set it on the countertop. Taking a cold pack from the freezer, he put it into the valise, then added a plastic emesis basin and a fresh scalpel.

And, finally, the loaded syringe.

He snapped the clasp on his medical bag, picked it up, and left the laboratory, turning out the lights before he closed and locked the door.

Already, the fluttering in his belly was beginning to ease.

RISA GAZED AT the last two bites of Maria's perfectly seasoned Chicken Cordon Bleu, decided she could work the calories off with an hour in the gym tomorrow, but ignored the half glass of sauvignon blanc that stood to the right of her plate. The calories from the Cordon Bleu were bad enough—washing them down with the extra ones from the wine was further than she was willing to go, no matter how expensive the bottle had been. Besides, the dining room didn't feel nearly as conducive to lingering over wine as it usually did, what with Conrad still at Le Chateau tending to patients, and Alison silently pushing lettuce around on her salad plate, leaving the chicken and saffron rice untouched.

"Honey?" she said, cocking her head worriedly. "Is something bothering you?"

Alison shrugged. "I'm just not hungry." She set her fork down and folded her arms across her chest, then unfolded them as they came into contact with her breasts.

"Are they sore?" Now Risa's brow was furrowed with worry, though both Conrad and Alison had assured her only this morning that the incisions under her arms from the operation were healing as they should and there was no sign of infection.

"No." Alison sighed. "It's not that."

Risa eased her chair back a few inches. "You've been very quiet all day. Didn't the party go well last night? It sure sounded like everyone had a good time."

Alison finally looked up, and Risa saw tears pooling in her eyes. "I had a fight with Cindy. She left early."

"You and Cindy Kearns?" Risa asked as she folded her napkin

and laid it next to her plate. "What on earth would you two fight about?"

Alison pushed her plate aside. "I don't want to talk about it."

"All right," Risa said carefully. Cindy and Alison had been friends nearly all their lives, and she couldn't remember them ever fighting before. Obviously, something serious had happened. Still, she couldn't imagine them ending their friendship. "Friends have spats, sweetheart," she finally went on. "I'm sure it will blow over."

Alison shook her head, and when she finally spoke, she didn't look at her. "She doesn't like my Wilson friends. And she doesn't like me anymore."

Risa resisted the urge to leave her chair and put her arms around her daughter. Alison remained silent, quietly wiping at a tear with her fingertip. "Well, I think Cindy will come around. You two have been friends for too long to let anything come between you now." Alison closed her eyes as if to shut the words out, and Risa stood up. "Come on, honey, let's go curl up on the sofa and watch some television and you'll feel a lot better in the morning."

Alison sighed heavily once more and opened her eyes, but still didn't look her mother in the eye. "I've got homework to do," she said, her voice dull. "I sort of let everything slide before the party."

She stood up, but Risa could tell by her posture how bad Alison was feeling about whatever had transpired between her and Cindy Kearns. Still, broken friendships were part of growing up. Risa remembered when her own best friend had begun dating her boyfriend before she'd even broken up with him, and afterward she never spoke to the girl again. Nor was there anything her mother or anyone else could have done to help her get through the pain—she'd had to take those days one at a time, and so, too, would Alison.

Nothing she could say would help. Not tonight.

"I'll come up and tuck you in later," Risa said, putting her arms around her daughter to give her a reassuring hug. "I'm going to watch Tina Wong's special—your dad called a couple of hours ago and said it's going to be quite something."

"The special, or just Tina?" A flicker of Alison's usual good humor had broken through the clouds hanging over her.

"Probably both," Risa replied. "Sure you don't want to watch with me?"

But Alison shook her head. "I hate the way she treats Dad, like he works for her instead the other way around, and I don't think she cares how many people get killed as long as she gets more time on TV." Giving her a peck on the cheek, Alison left the dining room.

Deciding it was worse to waste the last of the sauvignon blanc even if it meant an extra half hour on the treadmill, Risa picked up her wineglass and carried it into the media room, when she dropped onto the sofa and clicked on the television.

Tina Wong's face appeared, along with a montage of half a dozen other faces, all of which, Risa knew, belonged to girls and young women who had been killed by the man Tina had dubbed the Frankenstein Killer.

Was it possible that she'd figured out who that man was and what he was doing?

Risa settled back on the sofa, ready to find out.

OVER.

After twenty years, her slavery was finally over.

But even as Danielle DeLorian silently echoed the thought for at least the hundredth time in just the last twenty-four hours, it still sounded as empty as her house felt.

Yet the house wasn't empty: the living room in which she now sat was filled with hundreds of thousands of dollars worth of furniture—and millions more of art—that told everyone who entered exactly how full and successful her life was. Just the chair she sat in—one of the original Mies van der Rohe Barcelona chairs, its frame bolted together rather than welded, as in the chairs built after 1950—had cost her more than she wanted to think about even now. But it had been worth every cent, and only Conrad Dunn understood the subtle joke the chair represented. But then, no one else knew her anywhere near as intimately as Conrad Dunn.

And now, finally, her debt to him was discharged and she would be free of him. Except even that wasn't true, which was why the thought that it was all finally over rang so hollow. Conrad had promised as much before, promised that he would never demand further payment. And it had always been a lie. The debt would never be discharged, and he would go on making demands, more and more demands, bending her to his will until the day she died.

And there it was—the real thought that had been lurking in the shadows of her consciousness for so long.

The day she died.

She gazed deep into the glass in her hand, the merlot it held turning bloodred in her mind's eye. Then her eyes left the glass to rove around the room. How would her blood look if it were pooled on the white carpet, or oozing across the ivory leather that covered every piece of furniture in the room?

Suddenly the room—and the thought of it all being finally over— seemed not quite so empty.

All she needed was the courage to do it.

The wine!

Perhaps more wine would give her the strength she would need.

She rose to her feet, crossed to the bar, and was just reaching for the decanter when the doorbell rang.

Danielle's heart began to pound.

Who would come to her house at this hour? Who would have wound their way up the canyon and the hillside without calling first?

No one.

Yet her doorbell was ringing.

Just as she had rung Molly Roberts's bell.

Was someone standing on her porch cradling a dead animal in his arms, as she had stood waiting for Molly Roberts? She set the wineglass on the bar next to the decanter and walked through the arched doorway leading to the foyer, then peered at the small monitor attached to the camera outside.

Conrad Dunn!

Maybe she should simply turn away from the door and ignore the bell until he gave up and went away. Except that she already understood all too well that Conrad Dunn would never go away.

She turned back the dead bolt and opened the door. "Why are you here?" she asked. "Don't you think I know it's still not over?"

"Actually, Daniel," Conrad said, setting his valise on the foyer table, "it is."

Just the sound of her birth name sparked a surge of anger in her. "Dan*ielle*," she shot back. "My name is Dan*ielle*."

"Daniel, Danielle, what does it matter at this point?" He was moving closer to her now, and there was a menacing calm to his voice that made her step back. "Too many mistakes, Daniel," he went on. "I don't like mistakes. You know that."

Danielle took a reflexive step backward, felt her heel catch on the edge of the runner that stretched the full length of the large entry hall, and saw Conrad move even closer and reach out to her with his left arm. But instead of catching her before she fell, he spun her around, his right arm slipping around her neck as the weight of his body slammed her against the wall. A second later she felt his right forearm tighten around her neck, and though she could still breathe, she felt strangely light-headed, as if about to pass out. . . .

WHEN SHE AWOKE, Danielle was lying on the floor in her entry hall. Conrad Dunn's face was hovering over her, and as she looked at him, she saw his lips twist into a dark smile.

"Awake?" he asked. Instinctively, Danielle nodded. "Good," Conrad went on, and even as he uttered the word, Danielle felt an odd pressure in her right arm.

"What are—" she began, struggling to form the words as her mind shook off the last of the unconsciousness that had overcome her.

"Don't try to talk," he told her. "In a couple of minutes you won't be able to, anyway." He held up an empty hypodermic syringe. "Pancuronium," he said. "A wonderful drug, actually. You can't move, but you stay conscious and hear, see, and feel everything that's going on."

Danielle tried to struggle now, but it was far too late—the drug was already coursing through her veins, sapping the strength of every muscle in her body. "Whaa—" she began again, but even the single syllable she was able to form emerged as nothing more than an unintelligible moan.

"This time it really is over, Daniel," she heard Conrad say. Though she could no longer make her eyes follow his movements, she could see him standing up and moving toward the table where he'd set his medical bag. A moment later he was back, standing above her, his hands covered with surgical gloves.

In his left hand he held an enamel emesis basin, which he set on the floor beside her.

In his right hand the blade of a scalpel glimmered in the light of the chandelier that hung from the ceiling.

"I'm going to put you back the way you were, Daniel," he said as he knelt next to her. "That's going to be your punishment for the mistakes you've made." Danielle felt his fingers untying the dressing gown that was all she was wearing, and a moment later felt the chill of the air as he pulled the robe away. Then he was touching her breasts, fondling them almost like a lover. "Some of my best work," he said.

My work! Danielle wanted to scream out. *It wasn't your work at all! I was the one who found them, and I was the one who figured out how to preserve them!*

Though not so much as a hint of sound had emerged from her lips, it was as if Conrad knew exactly what she had said.

"You taught me so much, Daniel," he said. He was smiling again, and Danielle felt a sudden searing pain as the scalpel slid deep into the flesh under her left breast. "And not just about surgery, either," he went on.

He changed the angle of the scalpel now, and Danielle felt an agony worse than she could ever have imagined.

"You're a freak," Conrad said, his voice taking on a cold clinical tone that made every one of his words slash as deeply into her psyche as the scalpel did into her body. "I knew that when I first met you, you know. But I knew you'd do whatever I asked, once I gave you what you wanted." The blade sank deeper, and a silent scream rose inside Danielle, but she made no sound at all. "But you made mistakes," Conrad went on. "And now they're going to find you. And you'll talk. You won't keep my secrets the way I always kept yours." He suddenly slashed the scalpel upward to rip her breast from her chest. "Except they won't find Danielle, will they?"

He gazed down into her eyes, and Danielle knew he was looking for the pain she was feeling, wanting to savor the torture his scalpel wielded, and she silently prayed that her eyes revealed nothing of her agony, that all he saw was the same hollow emptiness that she'd been feeling only a few minutes ago.

Above her, Conrad's eyes glowed with hatred, and as she stared up at him, unable to look away even if she wanted to, she knew that the hatred had always been there, had always been simmering beneath Conrad Dunn's placid surface. *Smarter than you,* she wanted to whisper. *I always was, and I always will be.*

As if he'd heard the words, Conrad slashed at her body once again, and this time Danielle felt it tear through skin and muscle from just below her breastbone to just above her groin. Her blood was flowing freely now, and she knew that soon—but not soon enough—she would fall into the unconsciousness that would come just before death. So here, tonight, in the emptiness of her own home, Conrad was doing what she knew she would not have found the strength to do herself.

Now she felt his hands plunging into her, tearing at her, pulling at her guts, ripping at her organs.

"They won't even recognize you," Conrad was saying now, but finally his voice was fading, seeming to come from somewhere far away. And the pain, the searing, unbearable torture as he ripped at every nerve in her body, was fading, too. "All they'll find is whatever I choose to leave. Scraps, Daniel. That's all that will be left—all you ever were is what I made you, and now I'm taking it all back."

The last of the pain was dying away now, and suddenly she felt herself rising out of the body she had hated for so long, the body she had tried to mold, tried to change to fit the spirit she knew was truly hers. Oddly, the ears still seemed to work, and the eyes as well. Yet as she watched Conrad Dunn rip the glands from her body, tear out her adrenals and her thymus, and knowing exactly the purpose to which he was going to put those precious organs, she no longer felt any pain at all.

And now the sound of Conrad's voice was dying away, and so, too, was the carnage that lay on the floor below her. She was floating now, floating upward and away. Away from the body she'd always hated, from the house that had always felt empty, from the life that had never felt right.

Without knowing it, Conrad Dunn was finally giving her peace. . . .

CONRAD DUNN GAZED down into Danielle DeLorian's eyes and knew it was over. There was a blankness in them that told him she was dead, and the flow of blood that had gushed from her vessels only a moment ago had already slowed to a mere trickle.

Yet in his mind he could still hear her voice, whispering to him as if she were right behind him. *They were never your secrets, Conrad. You remember, don't you? I made the compounds that made it all possible. I taught you how to make everything perfect. Smarter than you,* Danielle's voice finally whispered. *I always was, and I always will be.*

Tearing the last scraps of useful tissue from the corpse on the floor, Conrad Dunn closed his ears to the terrible words.

Danielle was gone and would never be back, and had never been his greatest creation at all.

His greatest creation had been Margot.

And Margot, he knew, *would* be back.

27

RISA HAD PICKED UP THE REMOTE CONTROL FIVE TIMES TO SHUT OFF
Tina Wong's special on what she'd dubbed "The Frankenstein Killer,"
and five times she put it aside, and felt a small wave of shame each time
she set the remote down. Now, as grotesque images of Molly Roberts
filled the screen—some of them so blurry they were barely recognizable as having once been a human being, but others so vivid that she
had to turn her head away—she knew she wasn't going to turn the TV
off.

She was going to watch it through to the end.

Then maybe she'd call Michael and ask him why he'd agreed to
put the show on at all. Or maybe she wouldn't, since she already knew
why he'd okayed it—ratings. And the ratings, she was sure, would be
just as high as Michael expected.

The section on Molly Roberts came to an end a few moments later,
and Tina Wong, her expression a careful mask of concern for the victims that didn't quite succeed in concealing the triumphant gleam in
her eyes, was now recapping the cases one by one, giving her an oppor-

tunity to show the worst of the carnage yet one more time. Risa pulled a light silk throw over her knees to quell the chill she felt, and drank the last of her wine.

And then, in the last minutes of the show, an oval-shaped frame containing nothing inside appeared on the screen. "What, then, is the Frankenstein Killer trying to make?" Tina Wong asked. "Why is he selecting the women he's chosen? What is it they have in common? Certainly not their age or their looks. The youngest was in high school when he attacked, the oldest in her mid-thirties. Physically, they were all different, but he took certain things from all of them. The adrenal and thymus glands. All of them were mutilated, but from each he also took a facial feature. Is he is collecting parts to construct a new face? This reporter, at least, believes that that is exactly what he is doing. But what does this face look like? Who is the woman he is trying to put together? Let's see what she looks like." As Tina Wong continued to talk, naming each of the victims and identifying which of their features had been taken, each feature appeared in the oval, and a face began to emerge.

And as the face took shape, Risa found herself leaning forward, her head cocked as she gazed at the image on the screen.

"Who is she?" Tina Wong asked as the last of the features appeared and some kind of computer animation filled in eyes and melded all the features smoothly together into a face. "Or should I ask, 'Who was she?' because it is highly likely that the woman he is trying to recreate is dead. So, then, who was she? His wife? His sister? Perhaps his mother as he remembers her from his boyhood?" Hair now appeared on the face that filled the screen, framing the features, but arranged so none of them, including the ears, was obscured.

And finally the face was finished. It was recognizable as human, but there was something wrong with it—it hardly seemed a face at all. Though the features struck Risa as individually quite nice, the whole seemed oddly to be less than the sum of the parts. The face had no personality; it was the kind of face you'd never see in a crowd and would never be able to describe later. And yet, as Tina Wong began exhorting her viewers to try to identify the woman whose face had been constructed out of the features torn from other women's faces, Risa had the odd sensation that she had indeed seen the face before.

But where?

"Who is the woman that this modern-day Frankenstein is trying to create?" Tina asked as the camera cut to her sitting on a stool in front of a wall-sized rendition of the assembled face. "If you know who this woman might be—if you recognize her as someone you once knew— call the police. Maybe together we can stop this monster before he kills again. But if we don't stop him, we know he will kill again. Maybe someone in your neighborhood. Maybe someone in your family." She fell silent for a perfectly timed moment, then: "Maybe even you. I'm Tina Wong. Thank you for watching."

A computer commercial came on, and Risa finally clicked off the television, but the memory of the strange composite face stayed with her. The face had reminded her of someone, but she couldn't quite put her finger on who it might be.

Maybe an old client?

But already the image was fading from her mind. Not that it mattered, really. Those artists' renditions never wound up looking like the person anyway, and there had been nothing particularly memorable about this face to begin with.

She folded up the throw and laid it across the arm of the sofa, took her empty wineglass to the kitchen, then headed upstairs, turning most of the lights out as she went, but leaving enough on to offer Conrad a welcome when he came home.

Alison's light was still on, so she knocked softly on the bedroom door and went in.

Alison was at her desk, textbooks open in front of her, her fingers flying over her computer keyboard.

"Hi, honey. It's getting late."

"I know," Alison said. "I'm almost finished." She turned in her chair to face her mother, and Risa was relieved to see that her daughter didn't look nearly as depressed as she had at dinner. "So how was Tina's special?"

"Actually, it was even worse than I expected. The charming Ms. Wong went way overboard, but I'm sure she'll get the ratings she was looking for. I suspect your father can hardly wait for her to move on."

"So what was the worst part of it?" Alison asked.

Risa's brows arched. "Probably Tina's hypothesis that whoever's killing all these women is trying to re-create someone by using other women's body parts."

Alison's eyes widened. *"Gross!"*

"Oh, it was gross, all right. But the weird thing was, when she put up a composite of the face, I had the strangest feeling that I'd seen it before. Like it was someone I know . . . or at least once knew well enough so she looked familiar. But I can't put my finger on it."

"So what did she look like?" Alison asked.

Risa thought a moment and shrugged. "That's the other weird thing. I can't really tell you what she looked like—it was just a woman's face. Certainly not ugly, or even just homely. But not really pretty, either. Just sort of—I don't know—nondescript, I guess." She moved closer to Alison, bent over, and kissed her on the cheek. "Actually, I'm glad you didn't see the show—it would give you nightmares. Speaking of which," she added, straightening up, "don't forget it's a school night. I'm going to go to bed and read until Conrad gets home."

"Okay. 'Night."

"Don't stay up too late."

"I won't."

Alison turned back to her keyboard, and Risa went to her bedroom, undressed, and put on her nightgown. But when she finally slid into bed, picked up her book, and tried to start reading, she couldn't concentrate. Instead of taking in the words on the page, she kept thinking about the nondescript face from Tina's special, and the nagging feeling that it was somehow familiar, despite its utter forgetability.

Maybe it was the hair—maybe she'd have recognized her if the rendition had shown her with blond hair, or short hair.

Or maybe it was nothing at all, and the face had simply been so bland it reminded her of everyone and no one at the same time.

She knew if she kept thinking about it, she wasn't going to sleep at all tonight. Deciding that if it was still bothering her in the morning, she'd watch the show again on TiVo, she turned determinedly back to her book.

ALISON CLOSED the lid of her laptop. Even with the distraction of trying to figure out how to make things right with Cindy, she'd still gotten a good start on two of the papers due before the end of the week. If Cindy had replied to her e-mail or responded to the Instant Message she'd sent when she saw that her oldest friend had logged on to My-Space, she would probably have finished at least one of the papers. But Cindy logged off without even acknowledging that she was online, and Alison's hurt at the snub had been gnawing at her ever since.

She stood up and stretched, but didn't feel like going to bed—she'd only think about the fight with Cindy, and dreams with her best friend walking away, telling her to "Go play with your new friends," would haunt her again tonight.

Maybe she'd just read awhile.

But none of the books on her nightstand inspired her.

Maybe she'd watch Tina Wong's special. She might recognize the face her mom thought looked familiar. At least it would keep her mind off Cindy Kearns and her other old friends.

Alison put on her bathrobe, padded downstairs in her slippers, and closed the door to the media room. Curling up on the sofa, she clicked on the TV, found the show on the TiVo list, and snuggled in to watch.

And instantly found Tina Wong's material as disgusting as her mother had said it was. What was her dad thinking, letting this go on? Feeling faintly sick at the bloody images flashing across the screen, she fast-forwarded to the very end, where her mother had told her the face slowly came together. Clicking the TiVo back to PLAY, she watched in fascination as the blank face began to fill in.

Then, when it was complete, she paused the image.

The face *did* look familiar. The trouble was, it seemed flat, and there was no life to it. Nor did it have the normal contours of a real face; instead, it looked more like a balloon with features glued on so well they seemed to have merged with the rubber.

But it was still a balloon.

And yet, something about the features . . . she gazed at the screen for a long time, trying to recall where she'd seen this woman, and then it came to her.

But it wasn't possible.

Was it?

Goose bumps crawled over her arms and a cold chill ran through her.

She clicked off the television and hurried upstairs, grateful that the light was still on in her mother's bedroom and the door stood slightly ajar.

"Mom?" she said with a tremble in her voice as she pushed the door farther open.

Her mother looked up over the top of her reading glasses.

"I watched Tina Wong's special."

Her mother frowned, and looked at the clock. "Honey, it's almost midnight."

"I know. But I also know who that face reminds you of."

Her mother lowered her book and took off her reading glasses. "Who?"

"Margot Dunn."

Her mother's jaw dropped open. "Margot?" she said. "Sweetheart, Margot Dunn was an international supermodel—she was beyond beautiful. And the face that Tina Wong showed was . . ." Risa searched for the right word, then shrugged. ". . . pretty ordinary."

"I know. But if that face hadn't been round—if it had had the kind of angles Margot Dunn's had—" She stopped abruptly, seeing the doubt on her mother's face, and shifted gears. "Whoever's killing those women is some kind of weirdo. What if he was obsessed with Margot Dunn? What if—"

"What if you go to bed?" Risa declared. "I think you've been reading way too many supermarket tabloids." She cocked her head. "You didn't watch the whole thing, did you? It'll give you the worst kind of—"

"I fast-forwarded to the end. And if I have nightmares, I'll come crawl in bed with you like I did when I was little."

"Not with me and Conrad, you won't," her mother told her. "Now off to bed. And think good thoughts before you go to sleep, okay? I think maybe I should call your father in the morning and lodge a complaint about the lovely Tina."

"Come on—she's just doing her job," Alison said, then kissed her mother. "And no matter what you think," she added as she left the room, "I bet I'm right. I bet it is some nut who's got a thing about Margot Dunn."

WHEN ALISON WAS GONE, Risa put the reading glasses back on and picked up her book again. But Alison's words were like worms burrowing holes in her concentration, and she knew she wouldn't be able to get through another page.

Margot Dunn? The image at the end of the show hadn't looked anything like Margot.

Had it?

Of course not.

And yet . . .

Before she'd even made a conscious decision, Risa slipped out of bed, pulled on her robe, shoved her feet into her slippers, and made her way down the darkened stairs.

In the media room, she sat on the still-warm couch where Alison had curled up, turned the television on and fast-forwarded to the end of the special.

She paused it when the composite filled the screen, as Alison had not long before.

And as she gazed at the image, she realized that something about that face did, indeed, remind her of Margot.

But that was ridiculous. The woman depicted on the screen was pretty enough, but hardly beautiful. If she had a picture of Margot, she thought, the differences would be apparent. She'd see it, and so would Alison.

Except that there were no pictures of Margot in the house; the only ones she'd seen were in the weird room in the basement Conrad had called the Margot Museum.

Had he cleaned it out yet? Maria hadn't said anything about clearing anything from the basement.

Risa turned off the television, got up, and walked through the house to the kitchen, then into the stairwell that led down to the basement.

She could hear the machinery of the house humming steadily.

She switched on the solitary light that was mounted halfway down the stairs, descended into the vast area beneath the house, and started down the dim hallway to the storeroom that had held all of Margot's things.

Twenty yards away she could once again smell the sweet scent of the perfume that still pervaded the area.

She opened the door and reached in to turn on the light. The room was exactly as it had been before—though Conrad had told her he would have it dismantled, he obviously hadn't. And as she gazed around at the pictures of Margot Dunn, she realized that Alison had been right: the resemblance to the composite image Tina Wong had created was definitely there.

Risa moved slowly around the museum, looking closely at each of the old photographs of Conrad Dunn's first wife, and with each image she studied, the truth of it became clearer. It wasn't that the features stolen from each of the dead women were different from Margot's counterparts, but that Margot's face had been shaped differently, the framework of her cheekbones and jaw and upper skull all combining to support each of her features at the best angle to show them off and meld them into the perfect beauty that had made Margot famous.

She scanned the images one more time. Yes, the resemblance, at least feature by feature, was uncanny. But what did it mean?

She turned away from the last one, the huge blow-up of the *Vogue* cover that had been Margot's favorite, and her eyes fell on the mannequin that stood below it.

It had been displaying the dress Margot wore for the *Vogue* shoot, but it now stood naked, stripped of the elegant black dress.

Except she saw that it wasn't quite naked; there was something pinned to it.

A photograph.

Another photo of Margot?

Risa moved closer, reached out, and pulled the eight-by-ten loose, holding it so the light from Margot's vanity fell fully upon it.

And she froze.

The picture wasn't of Margot Dunn at all.

It was of Alison.

And the dress Alison wore in it was the black Valentino that had hung on the mannequin the last time she'd been in this room.

The room seemed to swirl around her, and she sank onto the velvet vanity stool, the photograph of her daughter clutched in her hand.

CONRAD OPENED the closet door in the dressing room adjoining his private office and found a clean shirt, fresh from the laundry. The clean one would betray no evidence of his visit to Danielle, and the one he was wearing would soon be burned in the furnace below his house.

He shook the clean shirt out and unbuttoned the collar, but before he could change into it, the cell phone buzzed in his pocket. Frowning, he glanced at the caller ID.

The silent alarm in the room where all of Margot's things were gathered had been set off by the motion detector.

Damn.

Abandoning the clean shirt, he left his office and took the private elevator to the underground garage of Le Chateau. But instead of getting in his car and driving through the twisting streets that would get him up to his home, he unlocked a nondescript door that appeared to hide nothing more than a storage closet and turned on the lights.

Behind a sliding door at the back of the closet, a series of recessed lights illuminated a steep stairway that led directly up through a tunnel from Le Chateau to the private lab connected to the basement of his house.

The lab that only he and Danielle DeLorian had ever used.

Taking the stairs two at a time, he unlocked the laboratory door, switched on the lights, and looked quickly around.

Everything was as it should be. The tanks were undisturbed, the organs he'd harvested from Danielle floating in the gel exactly as he'd left them before he'd gone back to his office to change his shirt.

He moved through the laboratory and paused at the door that opened directly into the room where Margot's treasures were on display.

He could see a line of light beneath that door.

Sighing tiredly, knowing what he would have to do, he opened the door.

RISA'S HEAD SNAPPED UP when she heard the sound of a door opening from behind the dressing screen in the back corner.

"Hello, Risa," Conrad said softly as he stepped into the room.

She rose from the vanity stool, instinctively trying to hide the photograph of Alison behind her back, her mind racing. *What was Conrad doing here? Where had he come from?*

"Are you looking for something?" Conrad asked as he approached, then stopped and frowned. "What's that behind your back?"

"N-Nothing," Risa stammered, staring at the spatters of blood on his shirt.

Conrad's gaze flicked to the mannequin, and a slight smile came over his lips. "Ah! The picture of Alison. Doesn't she look lovely in that dress?"

He stepped closer, reaching out as if to take the picture from her, and Risa took a step back.

Conrad's smile faded. "She's going to be beautiful," he said. "Did you know that her face has the exact same bone structure as Margot's?"

And in an instant the truth—the unimaginable truth—exploded in Risa's mind.

She had to get Alison out of the house!

She turned toward the door, but it was too late. In two strides Conrad was next to her, his right arm curling around her neck. "I'm going to show you something, Risa," he whispered in her ear. "Something wonderful."

The pressure on her neck grew, and though she could still breathe, she felt herself starting to black out.

"But you have to behave," Conrad whispered. "Do you understand?"

As her vision began to fail her, Risa managed a slight nod.

The pressure on her neck eased slightly, and Conrad began to move her toward the dressing screen.

Even if she could scream, she knew no one would hear her. The house was empty, except for Alison, who was two floors away.

Without a struggle, Risa let him walk her through the door that lay behind the screen.

28

THE PRESSURE ON RISA'S NECK EASED JUST ENOUGH THAT SHE DIDN'T black out, and Conrad's grip on her arm kept her from falling even though her knees were buckling.

Stay calm, she told herself. *Stay calm and save Alison.*

Having moved her through the door behind Margot's changing screen, he slammed it shut behind him.

Looking around, it seemed she'd sunk into a nightmare.

Everywhere she looked there were tanks filled with a greenish fluid, and objects floating in them.

Grisly objects.

Objects that looked as if they had been cut away from human corpses.

Or living human beings.

"My laboratory," she heard Conrad say. "This is where I do all the truly *important* work." His stress on the penultimate word sent a chill through her. "Interesting, aren't they?" he said as his eyes followed her gaze to the objects in the tanks. "They don't look like much at the moment, but wait until tomorrow."

Risa, repeating the two words—*Keep calm*—over and over in her mind, tore her eyes away from the tanks. "T-Tomorrow?" she rasped, her throat raw from the pressure of Conrad's arm.

"Alison's surgery," he said, still moving her through the laboratory and into the operating room, where motion-sensitive switches turned on blindingly bright overhead lights.

Risa blinked in the sudden glare, saw the operating table, an IV stand, monitors, instrument trays already laid out—everything a surgeon would need.

All of it there.

All of it ready.

She struggled to comprehend what she thought she'd heard him say.

Alison's surgery?

What was he talking about?

Then her mind flashed back to the photograph of Alison in Margot's dress.

Then further back, to the television special she'd watched that evening.

"No," she whispered, barely able to hear her own choking voice.

Instead of answering her, he strong-armed her into a metal chair, then bound her arms and legs to it with surgical tape. She saw him step out into the laboratory and tap at a computer keyboard. A moment later one of the large wall-mounted monitors on the wall of the surgery room came to life.

As Conrad returned from the laboratory, Alison's face, at least three times larger than life, appeared on the monitor.

Risa gazed at the image of her beautiful daughter.

"It's her features," he said. "That's the problem—nature was not as kind to her as it should have been."

Risa felt her blood run cold.

"Now you'll see how God intended Alison to look." He flicked some kind of remote control toward the computer in the laboratory and the image on the monitor began to change.

As Risa watched in growing terror, Alison's face slowly morphed into a perfect replication of Margot Dunn.

"You see?" Conrad said, his glistening eyes fixed on the monitor. "That is what God intended, and that is what I am going to do."

Risa's belly churned, and for a moment she thought she might throw up.

"It's going to be quite simple," he went on. He pressed the remote again, and Alison's face reappeared, this time with black ink marks around her eyes, her nose, and her lips. "And her ears, of course," he said. "All the soft tissue. That's the wonderful thing about Alison—her underlying bone structure is perfect. The moment I met her, I knew. It was as if I could see right through her flesh to the perfection of her bones."

Risa struggled against the surgical tape that bound her to the chair. "No," she whispered, her voice hoarse. "Not Alison. I'm not going to let you—"

"*Let* me?" Conrad cut in, wheeling around to face her, his eyes glittering as they bored into her. "You should be thanking me!"

Risa gazed up at him, no longer recognizing the man she'd married. It was as if Conrad had become someone else, someone gripped in an obsession she'd assumed was only a fading memory.

Margot.

He was consumed with her, and she was dead, and now he was going to re-create her.

And make Alison—her daughter—disappear.

Risa scanned the room, looking for a weapon.

If she could knock him out—if she could get out of the surgery and the lab and call the police—

"You'll thank me," Conrad said. "And so will Alison."

"No," Risa said again, struggling harder against her bonds. "I won't—"

"You won't do anything," Conrad said, as if instructing a child. "It's too late for that now. It's not up to you. It's up to me."

Now all the doubts she'd ever felt about Conrad flooded back.

The night in Paris, when he'd called her Margot.

The shrine in the basement that no woman would ever have built to herself.

His careful seduction of Alison, until she actually wanted him to cut into her body, to make it different.

To make it *beautiful*.

And she'd let it happen. *She*—not Alison—had let it happen. She never should have married Conrad, never should have moved into his house, never should have let him so much as look at her daughter, let alone touch her.

Cut her.

Change her.

"No!" she screamed now, her guilt coalescing into pure fury. With a sudden lunge, she tore free from her bindings, her rage lending her more strength than she could have imagined. She hurled herself toward the tray of surgical instruments, reaching for a scalpel or a pair of scissors or anything else that came to hand.

Cut him!

That's what she had to do.

Cut him, as he was going to cut Alison.

Cut him, *before* he could cut Alison.

Cut him, and kill him, and—

The chair, still bound to her right leg, caught on the corner of one of the cabinets, and she lost her balance. She felt herself plunging forward and threw out her arms to break her fall, and—

—Conrad's arm was once again around her neck, and he was squeezing. Once more the blackness gathered around her, and once more she tried to force herself to stay calm, to do whatever she had to do to save Alison.

Too late.

The blackness closed in, and she felt herself slipping away.

"Alison," she whispered. "I'm so sorry . . . so very sorry. . . ."

◈ ◈ ◈

CONRAD SWITCHED OUT the last of the lights in the laboratory. It had been a long, complicated day, and he could feel the exhaustion in his bones.

He needed sleep.

A good night's sleep, given the surgery he would perform tomorrow.

A few minutes later he gently opened Alison's bedroom door and peered inside.

A pink nightlight softly illuminated the girl's young, elastic skin. Her breathing was slow and regular, and he knew that her strong young body would easily withstand the many grueling hours of surgery ahead.

It would be worth it.

Worth it for her, and worth it for him.

Alison Shaw would be more beautiful than she had ever imagined she could be.

And finally, Margot would once again be his.

"Tomorrow, then, my love," he whispered.

Closing the door, Conrad Dunn went to bed.

29

ALISON FELT THE DIFFERENCE THE MOMENT SHE ENTERED THE DINING room the next morning. Somehow, it seemed larger and emptier than usual. Conrad sat at the head of the long table, and the morning sun was bright on the garden outside the French doors. But there was no sign of her mother, nor did Maria appear with her orange juice as she always had. Then, as she slipped into the chair at her usual place, she noticed that her mother's place wasn't set for breakfast.

"Conrad?" Her stepfather's eyes shifted from the morning paper folded neatly in front of him. "Where's Mom?"

"I think she must have had an early appointment. She was already gone when I came down."

As his eyes returned to the newspaper, Alison glanced toward the kitchen. "Is Maria here?"

"She's not coming in today—something about her mother having to go to Immigration, I think."

Alison cocked her head. "She usually takes me to school if Mom has to work early."

"Not a problem," Conrad said. "I can take you."

Alison went to the sideboard, where a pot of coffee was sitting, then went to the kitchen, found a bowl and cereal, added milk to it, and returned to the table.

Conrad pushed his newspaper aside. "Just the two of us," he said. "Kind of nice, isn't it?" Before she could answer, Conrad spoke again, only now he was looking at her the way he had when she was at Le Chateau, recovering from her surgery. "How are you feeling? No fever? Pain?"

"I'm fine," she said. But instead of going back to his paper, Conrad continued to look at her, and suddenly she wanted to be out of the house.

Something, she was certain, wasn't right.

She glanced at her watch.

"Oh, my God! I'm going to be late," she said, though she still had almost thirty minutes before either her mother or Maria usually drove her down to school. She dug into her bowl of cereal, eating as fast as she could.

"Relax," Conrad told her. "We have all the time in the world."

Alison cast around in her mind for something—anything—she could use as an excuse to go to school early. "I have to go to cheerleader sign-ups this morning," she said. "Maybe I'd better call Tasha and have her pick me up."

"I'll drive you," Conrad replied. He reached for his coffee cup, then pulled his hand away. "Better not have any more of that," he went on, his eyes fixing on Alison. "Big surgery today."

"I'll get my books," she said, finishing the last of her own coffee. "Be back in a minute. Want me to meet you in the garage?"

Conrad hesitated, then smiled. "Perfect."

Alison ran upstairs and threw her books into her backpack. She grabbed her cell phone and clipped it on, then looked in her closet for the green vest she always wore with her jeans and yellow silk tank top.

Not there.

Had Maria taken it to the cleaners?

No—her mom had borrowed it the other day when she went to lunch with Alexis.

Grabbing her backpack, she hurried down the hall to the master suite, went directly to her mother's dressing room and began pulling open drawers until she found the vest. Pulling it on, she was about to turn off the light and head back downstairs when she saw her mother's big Louis Vuitton bag sitting on the dresser next to the vanity.

The bag that her mother never left behind if she was working.

Never left behind, and never forgot.

Suddenly, the house seemed even emptier than when she'd gone into the dining room. A knot of fear began to tighten in her belly.

Where was her mother?

Maybe she'd just forgotten her bag.

But then when she opened the bag and looked inside, she found her mother's cell phone, her appointment book, and her keys.

Without her keys, how had she gone? Could someone have picked her up? Alexis, maybe?

But her mother hadn't said anything last night about an early appointment, and even if she'd had one, she would have come in this morning and said good-bye.

Wouldn't she?

What was going on?

What had happened?

Something had happened—she was sure of it now.

Suddenly, every dark thought she'd ever had about Conrad came flooding back.

And she remembered the way he'd been looking at her.

And what he'd said:

Just the two of us. . . . We have all the time in the world.

What was happening? What was he up to?

Out!

She had to get out of the house and get away from Conrad, and she had to do it now.

But where could she go?

Her dad! All she had to do was call her dad and tell him to come and get her.

She turned away from the dressing room and started toward the bedroom door, fishing in her backpack. She was almost at the door when she found the phone, opened it, and speed-dialed her dad's cell phone.

But before it even began to ring, Conrad Dunn was looming in the doorway, blocking her way.

"This isn't the way I wanted this to go," he said softly.

"Where's Mom?" Alison demanded, her voice low. He moved toward her, and she backed away. *"What did you do?"* she yelled. *"What did you do to my mother?"*

Reacting to her shouts as if jolted by electricity, Conrad's right arm shot out and his fingers closed on her wrist. He jerked her around, and the phone flew from her hand, hitting the wall four feet away and falling to the floor.

"I'll show you," he whispered, his voice so low and cold, the words filled her with a new terror.

"No!" she cried out, trying to jerk her arm loose from his grip. *"Get away from me!"*

But instead of letting go, Conrad's arms enfolded her in a bear hug that felt as if it would squeeze the breath from her lungs, and no matter how hard she struggled, she couldn't get even one of her hands loose to hit him or scratch him.

He pushed her against the wall, and one of his arms moved up around her neck and she felt the pressure of it.

"You need to go to sleep for a little while," Conrad whispered in her ear. "And when you wake up, you're going to be calm again, and I'm going to show you what's going to happen, and you're going to be beautiful. So beautiful . . ."

His words echoing in her mind, darkness swirled around the periphery of Alison's vision, and with her terror becoming panic, she willingly gave herself over to the dark swirl.

◈   ◈   ◈

MICHAEL SHAW WALKED OUT of the boardroom with his ears ringing, which told him his blood pressure was far past the point his doctor would call "critical." Still, he wasn't dead, nor was he about to take a fall for the legal team that had signed off on Tina's special without anticipating the reaction from the TV audience. The reactions ranged from the threat of a lawsuit from a distant relative of one of the victims, who was claiming "severe trauma" due to her third cousin's corpse being shown on television, to the threat of an injunction from the LAPD itself.

By the time the station's owners had gathered in the boardroom, the finger-pointing had begun and the legal team, being lawyers, were already claiming they hadn't signed off on exactly the show that had aired.

They claimed there had been changes made.

Michael finally called a ten-minute break, if for no other reason than to let his blood pressure settle down a little. He needed fresh air, fresh coffee—the hell with his blood pressure—and a fresh shot at getting Tina Wong herself into the boardroom. Maybe between them they could convince the suits that the ratings would be worth the trouble, and the increased advertising rates would more than make up for the cost of defending against the third cousin, whoever she was.

"Coffee, please, Jane," he said as he passed his assistant's desk on the way to his office.

"Scott is on line one for you."

"Got it. And find Tina Wong and tell her to be here in ten minutes. *Ten,* not eleven. And I'm telling her, not asking her."

He collapsed into the squeaky old chair that should have collapsed years ago but wouldn't quite give up the ghost, took a deep breath, and picked up the phone. "Hi," he said.

"How's it going?"

He took another deep breath. "Don't ask—it's a nightmare around here. What's up?"

"Risa was supposed to show a house to a couple of my friends this morning, and she stood them up."

Michael frowned. "*Risa* stood them up? Impossible."

"That's what I told them, but they say she didn't show. And she's not answering her cell phone, either. Any idea what might be going on?"

"Risa's never missed an appointment in her life. And she doesn't get sick, so they must have gotten the time or the place wrong."

"She confirmed with them yesterday afternoon," Scott said.

"And she's not answering her phone? That's not good." He sipped at the coffee. "Let me check into it."

"Okay. Sorry to add more to your load this morning."

"It's okay. I'll call you back."

Michael hung up and immediately dialed Risa's cell, but it rang through to her voice mail. "Risa, it's Michael. It's eight-forty on Monday morning. Please call me as soon as you can."

Jane brought in a fresh cup of coffee, and he tried to get his mind back to the problem in the boardroom. Somewhere on his desk there was a sign-off from the lawyer who had seen the final edit of the show, and he intended to find it. He began searching through the clutter, hoping he hadn't given it to someone to file. If he had, they'd never find it.

He picked up his cell phone to flip through the pile of papers underneath it and noticed that he'd missed a call.

Risa?

No. It was from Alison's phone, and she hadn't left a message. And that was as strange as Risa missing an appointment, because Alison always left messages—it had become a game with them over the years, and they often had long, involved, convoluted—and generally very funny—conversations back and forth via voice mail.

There was no way Alison would call him and not leave a message, even if it was only some kind of fake gibberish he wouldn't be able to understand but would spend hours trying to decipher. He speed-dialed her phone, knowing she'd be in class and most likely had turned it off.

Sure enough, her voice mail came on. "It's me, cupcake," he said.

"Call me at the office as soon as you can, okay? Call me between classes. It's important." He hung up, but the ringing in his ears told him his blood pressure was not better, and it was now accompanied by a nervous feeling in the pit of his stomach.

He spotted the sign-off from the lawyer pinned to the cork board on the wall next to his desk and pulled it down. But now his mind was no longer on the meeting in the boardroom.

Alison had called but left no message.

Risa failed to show up for an appointment.

Something was wrong.

He hit the intercom button. "Jane, get me the Wilson Academy."

A moment later Jane's voice came over the intercom. "It's ringing on line two."

"Good morning, Wilson Academy," an efficient female voice answered on the third ring.

"Hello—this is Michael Shaw, Alison Shaw's father. I have an urgent situation and need to speak with her as soon as possible."

"Just a moment," the voice said. "Let me see where she is right now." There was a long pause, then the voice came back on the line: "Mr. Shaw? Alison isn't here today. Nor have we received a notice of an excused absence." Michael read the careful phrasing very clearly: they thought Alison was cutting school.

Another thing she simply wouldn't do.

"All right, thank you," he said, and hung up. Now the meeting in the boardroom was forgotten. He grabbed his cell phone and the memo, handing the memo to Jane on his way out. "I've got a family emergency," he said. "Give that to Tina and tell her to take it into the boardroom. That should let the lawyers know the ball's in their court. I'll call you when I can."

Jane looked at him in shock. "You're leaving? Just like that? They're all in there waiting for you!"

Michael shook his head, already heading toward the elevator. "Something's going on with Alison—I've gotta go."

As soon as he pulled out of the parking lot and into traffic, he called Scott. "Something's haywire—I can't find Risa, and now I can't find Alison, either. I'm on my way up to Risa and Conrad's place."

"What do you mean, you can't find Alison? Isn't she at school?"

"Not as far as they know," Michael said. "I'll call you when I get there."

"Be careful."

"I will," Michael said.

Closing his phone, he stepped on the accelerator.

COLD.

Freezing cold.

Alison's teeth chattered as she struggled to reach the blanket at the end of her bed, but she couldn't get to it.

Indeed, she couldn't move her arms at all.

What was wrong?

The blackness that had surrounded her only a moment ago began to recede, and as her mind rose through the layers of unconsciousness toward the gathering light, she felt a terrible tiredness overwhelm her.

If she could just sink back down into her bed and retreat into the soft, warm escape of sleep . . .

But she was too cold.

And there were noises in her room.

Noises she'd never heard before.

Strange, gurgling noises.

Alison opened her eyes and found herself staring straight up into an enormous overhead light. She reflexively closed her eyes against the painful glare, then turned her head and opened her eyes again, more slowly this time.

This wasn't her bedroom, this was. . .

A dream?

It had to be. She was dreaming that she was back in Conrad's operating room at Le Chateau.

But this time she didn't want the surgery.

Didn't want it at all.

A wave of panic rising inside her, she tried to sit up, but couldn't move either her hands or her feet.

She was strapped to the operating table and there was an IV needle in her arm!

She caught a movement in the corner of her eye and turned her head the other way. A figure was looming by the operating table, and though the surgical mask covered all of the face but the eyes, she instantly recognized Conrad Dunn.

"L-Let me up," she stammered, struggling once more against the surgical tubing that had been tied around her wrists and ankles.

"I'm afraid I can't," Conrad said, his voice calm and reasonable. "You see, we're about to get started, and with no one to assist me, I can't run the risk of you accidentally moving."

Started? Her mind honed in on that single word. She still felt confused, foggy. What were they about to start?

Another operation?

But that was impossible—after what had happened with Cindy Kearns, she was already wishing she hadn't let him do the implants. So what was he talking about?

"Just relax," Conrad said. "It'll only be a few more minutes before everything is ready."

As he turned away again, she struggled to clear her mind, to banish the strange fog that made this feel like a nightmare. But it wasn't a nightmare—she was sure of it.

She was awake, and what was happening was real, and she had to remember what had happened.

How she had gotten here.

Breakfast.

Conrad had lied about her mother having gone to an early appointment.

"Where's my mother?" she asked, but without the force she'd intended to put into her words. Instead of sounding commanding, her voice seemed tiny and almost inaudible in the cold, cavernous room.

Conrad turned and looked down at her, his dark eyes ominous over the top of the surgical mask. "She didn't approve of our project."

There was a note almost like sadness in his voice, and it sent a terrible chill of certainty through Alison.

Her mother was dead.

And she was alone.

She wanted to cry out, wanted to give in to the terrible grief rising inside her, but she knew she couldn't. Her mother was dead, and she was alone, and if anyone was going to save her from whatever Conrad was planning, it would have to be her.

"P-Project?" she said, cursing herself for the stammer and determining not to let it happen again.

Conrad laid a cold gloved hand on her arm, sending shivers all the way up to the back of her head. "I am going to do for you what no one else on earth could do."

Alison searched for the right words—the words that would stop him from what he was about to do, or at least slow him down long enough for her to find some way to escape the bindings that held her to the table. She said, "I—I don't understand. What are you going to do?"

He reached out as if to touch her, and she instinctively turned her head away.

And saw the green tank that stood next to the table to which she was bound.

The tank that had to be the source of the gurgling sounds that seemed so loud when she was first waking up, but now was no more than a murmur in the background.

She focused on the contents of the tank, and suddenly found herself back in the grip of the nightmare.

An ear.

Lips.

It wasn't possible—in a second she would wake up and be back in her bed and the dream would be over and—

And she remembered the woman in the composite who had looked like Margot.

Margot Dunn.

The cords in her neck strained as she struggled yet again to sit up, to get loose, to get away.

And once more she failed and fell back, gasping for breath.

"Let me show you," Conrad said. "What we're going to do is very exciting—absolutely revolutionary, in fact."

Alison lay still, trying desperately to take a deep breath. She needed her strength—needed to keep her wits.

Conrad stepped over to a computer keyboard.

An enormous flat-screen monitor came to life, and she saw an image of herself, wearing the black dress he'd brought to her to try on. The screen zoomed in on her face, then split in two.

Next to her face there appeared a photograph of Molly Roberts—the same photograph from Tina Wong's special.

The special on the Frankenstein Killer.

And now she knew who that killer was.

Conrad Dunn.

Unable to tear her eyes away from the screen, she watched in mute fascination as Molly's face faded away, except for her nose, which moved—almost by magic, it seemed—over to her own face, replacing her nose.

And she understood with terrible clarity exactly why she was here.

"No," she whispered. "Oh God—please, Conrad."

She twisted her head again, and saw the flesh that had been Molly Roberts's nose suspended in green gel.

"That's just the beginning," Conrad said.

Unable to bring herself to look away, Alison stared at the monitor as his fingers manipulated the keyboard with as much skill as they could manipulate a scalpel. She watched in growing horror as her face slowly morphed, piece by piece, element by element, into the face of Margot Dunn.

"This will be our end result," Conrad whispered when the transformation was complete. His voice was rapt now, as if he were caught up in religious fervor and beholding the Madonna herself. "I will make you into the most perfect woman in the world."

"No," Alison breathed. Everything that she was, he was going take away from her. He was going to make her into someone else, and the person she was—the person she had always been—would be gone.

Alison Shaw would no longer exist.

And Margot Dunn would live again.

Tears welled in her eyes and ran down her cheeks as a great sob racked her chest and throat.

"You'll thank me when it's over," Conrad assured her. He moved around the end of the table to the tank. "I hated putting those implants under your breasts," he went on, dipping his gloved hand into the tank and pulling out what at first looked like nothing more than some kind of misshapen mass. But as Conrad cradled it in his hands, turning it so Alison could see it from every angle, she realized what it was.

She felt her gorge rise, and struggled against the wave of nausea that gripped her.

"We should have done this graft the first time," he went on, his tone still utterly clinical, as if he were discussing nothing more than a minor adjustment that would amount to practically nothing. "But the timing wasn't right. After today, though, your breasts will be perfect. As perfect as Margot's. And with nothing false in them—no silicone, no fatty tissue stolen from your thighs or buttocks."

As his voice droned on, Alison realized that there would be no escape, that she didn't have the strength to free herself from her bonds.

There was, though, one weapon he hadn't taken from her.

Conrad had a whole staff of nurses and aides at Le Chateau twenty-four hours a day, and if she could just make them hear her—just make even *one* of them hear her—

With all the strength she could muster, Alison filled her lungs with air and let out a scream.

A scream that built, growing louder and louder, echoing in the operating room, its force straining every fiber in her.

She screamed again, then repeated it until even her own ears were ringing with the sound.

Her eyes shut, praying that someone—anyone—would hear her, she screamed out her terror and her rage and her grief. Even as a burning that felt like liquid fire began to course through the vein in her arm, she kept screaming.

Yet no matter how loud she screamed, the fire consumed her and the darkness began to close around her once more, and when the last iota of her strength had been drained away, she dropped back down into the void, praying that she might never wake up again.

30

MICHAEL KNEW CONRAD DUNN'S HOUSE WAS EMPTY AS SOON AS HE entered through the unlocked French door after walking around to the terrace at the back of the mansion. The air itself felt vacant, abandoned. Though he had yet to look anywhere but in the library in which he now stood, he knew that no hearts but his beat in this house.

Still, he couldn't keep calling out for his daughter and ex-wife. "Alison! Risa! Hello?" He moved from the library into the living room, calling out again in the irrational hope that someone—maybe a housekeeper—would respond, but his certainty that the house was empty was reinforced by the echo of his voice coming back to him, bouncing off the cavernous ceilings.

He took the stairs to the second floor two at a time, heading straight for where Alison had told him her room was.

Empty—not only of Alison, but her backpack as well! Hope suddenly flared within him. Maybe she was all right after all. Maybe she'd merely cut school today and didn't want to answer her phone.

But what about Risa?

He moved on, coming to the master bedroom, where his brief flash of hope faded as quickly as it had come: Alison's pink cell phone lay cracked on the carpet next to the wall. Just the sight of it—abandoned, vulnerable, broken—brought a silent prayer for her safety to his lips. He bent to pick it up, then stopped.

Better not to touch anything.

Not yet.

He straightened up, struggling against the panic rising inside him.

A panic that intensified when he saw her backpack open on the floor near the bed, books spilling out.

The phone, broken.

The backpack, open and spilling out its contents.

So Alison hadn't gone anywhere without at least some kind of fight.

Michael forced his panic down—if she hadn't given up without a fight, neither would he. The last of his panic dissolving into cold resolve, he backed away from the bedroom door, opening his own cell phone to speed-dial Scott.

"I'm at Conrad Dunn's house," he said when Scott answered. "Something's happened—call the police."

"What do you mean, something's happened?" Scott asked.

"I don't know, and I don't have time to explain. I'm looking for Alison, and I can't do that and answer the questions 911 will ask— I don't even know the address up here. So just call them for me and tell them to get up here right now." Before Scott could say anything else, Michael folded his phone and dropped it back in his pocket.

In Risa's closet he found the Vuitton bag, complete with cell phone and wallet.

Now he moved quickly from room to room, calling out Alison's name, throwing open every bedroom door, but knowing in his heart she wasn't up here.

Nor was Risa.

Back downstairs, he took in the remains of breakfast on the dining room table with a single glance, and when he looked into the garage from the kitchen, he saw Conrad's Bentley and Risa's Buick.

With a growing sense that he was missing something—that he was wasting time—he went through the rest of the house.

Empty.

Every room, empty.

It was as if three people—four, if he counted the housekeeper—had suddenly vanished from the face of the earth.

He went back to the kitchen, trying to decide what to do next, when his eyes fell on an unobtrusive door just off the kitchen that he'd been in too much of a hurry to notice the first time around.

He threw it open and stared down a flight of stairs leading into the basement. Without a second's hesitation, he ran down the stairs into darkness below, shouting once more.

"Alison? Risa!"

One room after another opened off the corridor that seemed to run the full length of the house: wine cellar, pool equipment room, furnace room.

All empty.

None of them with places to hide, let alone doors to the outside.

Then he caught a whiff of something sweet, and followed the fragrance around the corner to one more door.

A door that stood ajar, with a soft light emanating from the opening.

His heart suddenly beating faster, Michael pushed the door wide, and found himself looking at some kind of dressing room.

But why would there be a dressing room in a basement?

Then he saw the photographs that covered the walls.

Photographs of Margot Dunn.

CONRAD DUNN'S CELL PHONE BUZZED in his pocket.

"For God's sake," he muttered. "Always when I'm sterile." He tried to ignore the interruption, but the phone continued to buzz, and at last he peeled off a glove, pulled the surgical gown aside and reached into his pants pocket.

The silent alarm in Margot's room!

But who could be in there?

He'd sent Maria home.

Someone looking for Alison?

Or even Risa?

Damn!

Still, he'd locked the door behind the screen, and even if whoever was in the house found the laboratory, the operating room was impenetrable.

And it was far too late to stop the surgery—Alison was already unconscious, and he couldn't leave her alone on the table while he went to see what was happening in the house. If Alison died on the table, he'd never find anyone else with her bone structure.

He threw the two dead bolts on the airlock door that kept the lab and the operating room from contaminating each other, turned off his cell phone, and stepped over to the basin to begin scrubbing his hands all over again.

MICHAEL GAZED around the room once more. Was it possible that Margot Dunn had built a dressing room in the *basement*? It made no sense—it was two floors away from the master suite, and there were enormous closets and dressing rooms up there—he'd just seen them.

So if it wasn't a dressing room, what—

The answer came to him before he completed it in his own mind, for as he scanned the walls once again—walls covered nearly completely with life-size photographs of Margot Dunn—it was suddenly obvious.

A shrine.

A shrine that Conrad Dunn had built to his first wife, hiding it away in the basement so no one—especially his *second* wife—would know it was there.

Rage gripped him as he realized that once again Risa had married the wrong man. He, at least, had loved her, even though it wasn't in a way that could satisfy her.

Clearly, Conrad Dunn hadn't loved her at all—he'd still been in love with Margot.

So why had he married Risa?

He looked around again, certain that the answer to that question was somewhere in this room.

He saw the magazines stacked on the vanity, and quickly went through them, then the drawers of the vanity itself. Then he spotted a crumpled piece of paper on the floor near the screen in the corner.

He picked it up, smoothing it.

It was a photograph of Alison.

Alison, in a dress that was far too old for her.

But a dress that looked somehow familiar.

He looked up, trying to think, and found the answer hanging on the wall directly above the vanity.

It was a blow-up of a Vogue cover depicting Margot Dunn wearing the same dress Alison wore in the photograph.

The image his eyes beheld was suddenly replaced by a whole series of images that rose in his memory—images he'd seen over and over again in the past few days, images hundreds of thousands of people had seen last night as they watched Tina Wong's special.

And the last image—of the face the killer was building—suddenly came clear.

It was Margot Dunn's face, and he knew that Conrad Dunn was going to build it on his daughter.

He was going to turn Alison into his dead wife.

A howl of fury and frustration rose in his throat. Without thinking, he seized the dressing screen, lifted it from the floor and hurled it at the image of Margot. As it shattered both the glass over the picture and the vanity mirror below, he saw what the screen had hidden.

A door.

He tried the knob.

Locked.

With both fists, he pounded on the door and howled his daughter's name.

The door held, solid.

He looked around for something he could use to break it down, to burst through it, to smash it.

But there was nothing. Nothing but a flimsy floor lamp and an equally fragile clothes rack.

Then he remembered something.

Something he'd noticed but hadn't thought about while searching in the vanity. He went back to the vanity, opened Margot Dunn's jewelry box and began pulling out its drawers.

And there, in the bottom one, he found it.

A key.

A perfectly nondescript, ordinary key.

Could it really be this simple?

He picked it up, the spent adrenaline in his system making his hand tremble.

His heart racing, his breath ragged, he tried to slip the key into the lock.

It fit.

Not breathing at all now, he tried to twist the key.

It turned.

Suddenly wary, Michael paused to take a deep breath, then opened the door.

A dark vestibule lay before him, with another door beyond.

The second door was not locked.

A moment later he stood in Conrad Dunn's laboratory, gazing through a glass wall at the masked figure of Conrad himself.

He was leaning over Alison, and he held a scalpel in his hand.

◈ ◈ ◈

"I DON'T KNOW the exact address!" Scott Lawrence said, taking the cell phone from his ear just long enough to glare at it. "It's up on Stradella Road, way up near the top, near Roscomare."

"And what exactly is your relationship to Dr. Dunn?" the impersonal voice of the 911 operator asked.

Scott swore under his breath as the stream of traffic ahead of him on the San Diego Freeway slowed to a near stop. He was still two miles from the Skirball Center exit and now he was going to have to waste time trying to explain—

He swore out loud as a black Mercedes cut in front of him, then decided that breaking two laws wasn't any worse than breaking one, and dropped over to the shoulder of the freeway. "Can't you just send someone up there?" he pleaded with the operator as he drove on the shoulder. "Surely there's got to be some way for you to get Conrad Dunn's home address!"

"This is an emergency line, sir," the operator explained with a patience that was starting to grate on him. "If you can't give us any specifics at all, I can't see how—"

"Fine!" Scott barked into the phone. "I'll call you when I get there and know exactly what's going on." Snapping the phone shut and dropping it on the passenger seat, he pressed down on the accelerator and in less than a minute was pulling off the freeway.

And not a cop in sight, which he wasn't sure was a blessing. At least an actual officer might have been willing to follow him up to Dunn's place. Barely glancing to the left as Skirball Center Drive merged into Mulholland, he passed half a dozen cars before abruptly cutting back into the right lane to turn on Roscomare. Minutes later he pulled into the Dunn driveway and parked behind Michael's car.

Though nothing looked terribly wrong, a chill still ran up his spine.

He retrieved his cell phone from the passenger seat, got out, and approached the front door.

He rang the bell a couple of times, then circled the house, searching for a way in.

On the back terrace, one of the French doors stood half open. He pushed it wide. "Michael?" he called out.

No answer. And the sound of his own voice had that oddly hollow note peculiar to empty houses.

"Anybody home?" he called out, stepping into the library. "Michael?"

Scott's fingers tightened on the cell phone, and he opened it as he moved farther into the house.

"Michael! Risa! Alison!"

No answer.

He dialed 911 for the second time in less than fifteen minutes, and when the operator answered, knew he still couldn't tell her exactly what the emergency was. But now at least he had an exact address, and a door that had been standing open at an apparently empty house.

A house Michael had been in fifteen minutes ago, and in front of which his car was still parked.

"Something is terribly wrong at the residence of Conrad Dunn," he said, then gave the operator the exact address.

"What do you mean, 'terribly wrong'?"

"I mean I got a call saying something was wrong and to call the police. Nobody would do anything because I didn't have the address. Now I'm here and my friend is missing. His car is here, but he's not. Nobody's here. A door was left standing open and there's no one here."

"All right, sir," the operator said calmly. "I'm sending a car right away. I don't want you to do anything at all. Do not go into the house or anywhere else until the officers arrive, unless you are in immediate danger. Do you understand?"

"I understand," Scott said, but even as he folded his phone and dropped it into his pocket, he knew he wasn't about to follow the woman's orders. Michael was in trouble, and if there was anything he could do to help, he would do it.

And there was no telling when the cops would arrive.

Doing his best to make no sound whatsoever, Scott Lawrence made his way through the house.

Somewhere—somewhere not far away—Michael needed him.

Needed him right now.

He could feel it.

31

Michael Shaw gazed about him in stunned confusion. Wherever he'd thought the door behind the screen might lead, he'd never imagined the bizarre scene spread before him.

He was in a huge windowless room that was obviously underground.

It was some kind of laboratory, with stainless steel counters and sinks, all of it lit by the shadowless glare of the fluorescents that filled the entire ceiling. But even in the white brilliance of the lights, a large tank glowed a poisonous shade of green, as if it were filled with some kind of algae.

A pump was running steadily, and he could see some kind of gas being slowly forced through the green substance in the tank.

To the right, taking up nearly half the space in the laboratory, was what looked like an operating room, entirely enclosed by glass walls, with what looked like an airlock sealing off its interior from the rest of the laboratory.

Every wall of the operating room held a large flat-panel

monitor, and both the monitors he could see displayed the same image.

His daughter's face.

Her face, marked with heavy black lines.

But it wasn't possible—none of it was possible!

Yet even as he tried to reject the reality of the scene, he found himself charging toward the glassed-in enclosure and pounding on it with both fists. "Alison!" he howled. *"Alison!"*

He moved around to the outer door of the airlock and wrenched at its handle, but it was locked. Swearing, and bellowing his daughter's name again, he scanned the area for something to smash the glass with. On one of the stainless steel counters there was a metal stand holding some kind of beaker. Michael seized the stand, knocking the beaker to the floor, and ignored the shards of the shattered object as he swung the stand at the glass.

Nothing—not even a chip, let alone a crack.

THE SCALPEL IN CONRAD DUNN'S RIGHT HAND STOPPED in midair, barely a millimeter above the cut line he'd so carefully drawn on Alison's face. The noise that had penetrated the strains of Vivaldi filling the operating room had come from behind him, and now he turned and looked for its source.

The ex-husband.

How had he gotten in here?

Not that it mattered. The surgery had already begun, and there was no point in stopping now. Even if the ex-husband were to call someone, he would be far enough along by the time they arrived that no one would dare stop him.

If they did, they would not only destroy Alison Shaw's beauty, but might easily kill her as well. And when he was finished, and everyone saw what he had accomplished—saw that he had once again created perfection—that would be the end of it.

Taking a deep breath to recover the total concentration he needed to finish the surgery, Conrad turned back to his patient.

He gazed at the monitors for several long seconds, rehearsing each careful incision in his mind.

Using the remote control to turn the Vivaldi up enough to cover any further commotion from outside, he used the fingers of his left hand to pull the skin taut around Alison's upper lip.

Once again he readied the scalpel.

MICHAEL SEARCHED for something else, and spotted a chair almost hidden by a large bundle wrapped in a plastic sheet. In two steps he crossed to the chair and yanked it off the floor. The bundle tipped over and the plastic sheet fell away, and he was staring into Risa's face, ashen in the pallor of death, her empty eyes staring up at him.

It froze him for a moment, and he was seized again by the certainty that none of this could be real, that it was all a terrible dream from which he would awaken and find himself home in bed, with Scott sleeping peacefully next to him.

He took an involuntary step back, his heel catching in the plastic sheet and pulling it all the way off Risa's body, and now he saw her ruined torso, slashed open from just above the pubis all the way up to her chest.

Her ribs had been cut open, and what had once been her internal organs lay in a bloody heap on her thighs. Michael's gorge rose and a wave of towering fury came over him. Turning away from Risa's body, he crashed the chair against the wall of the operating room, but instead of the glass shattering, the chair's frame broke.

The figure on the other side of the glass turned, and Michael found himself staring into Conrad Dunn's darkly hooded eyes. The surgeon held up the scalpel in his right hand as if it was explanation enough, then shifted back to his unconscious patient.

Michael dropped the broken chair, already searching for something else to use against the barrier between him and his daughter.

The computer stand! It was big, looked heavy, and had enough sharp angles on it that—

He swept the computer off the stand and sent it crashing to the floor.

Every monitor on every wall in both the laboratory and the operating room instantly went dark.

Now Conrad Dunn whirled around to glower furiously at him, his eyes dark and menacing above the white surgical mask.

"I'm coming for you, you bastard," Michael whispered, and seizing the heavy computer stand in both hands, lifted it up. Using every bit of strength he could muster, he swung the stand against the glass wall. A searing pain shot up Michael's arms as the shock of the blow knocked the stand out of his hands and sent it crashing into the racks of test tubes on the countertop behind him. Though Michael was knocked almost to his knees, the heavy tempered glass held.

Taking a deep breath, and wiping the sweat from his palms, he pulled the stand from the countertop, gripped it even tighter than he had a moment ago, and swung it again.

The stand hit the glass and bounced back, but this time Michael let it go and ducked out of the way.

A small crack appeared in the lower right-hand corner of the glass panel.

Michael took a deep breath, heaved the computer stand up for a third time, and swung it once more into the glass.

CONRAD DUNN STARED at the crack in the glass panel with unbelieving eyes. The glass was supposed to be unbreakable—bulletproof!

And now Alison's father had broken it.

Broken it!

Suddenly everything he'd been working on for so long—every careful plan he'd laid, every perfect feature he'd collected, *every sacrifice he'd made,* was in jeopardy.

Everything—*everything!*—could be ruined.

All the work he had done could be ruined right here, right now.

But that wouldn't happen—he wouldn't let it happen.

Not now, not in the final moments, not when he was on the verge of creating perfection.

So he would deal with it.

He would deal with—what was his name? Michael!—yes, he would deal with Michael Shaw just as he had dealt with Daniel DeLorian.

The way he had dealt with his wife.

Nothing—nobody—would stand in his way. Not now, not when he was so close.

Not when everything could be so easily ruined.

Conrad Dunn took a fresh grip on the scalpel just as the computer stand crashed through the wall, showering shattered glass everywhere.

Over him.

Over his instrument tray.

And—worst of all—over his patient's unfinished face.

MICHAEL LEAPED into the operating room, but his pant leg caught on a thick shard of glass still jammed in the window frame. He tripped, his pant leg tore loose, and he skidded over the thousands of pieces the single pane of glass had exploded into.

Trying desperately to hold his balance, he slammed into the operating table, sending it crashing against a glass-sided tank filled with the same greenish substance he'd seen in the lab. The tank shattered and the green stuff spilled out onto the floor.

But the green slime wasn't all the tank had contained.

Against his own will, Michael's eyes closed against the gruesome sight of the fragments of human flesh that were now mixed in with the broken glass on the floor.

❖ ❖ ❖

A ROAR OF PURE FURY FORMED in Conrad Dunn's throat as he watched years of work spew across the floor. But even before he gave vent to his rage, he'd already repressed it.

Not now!

This was not the time to indulge himself in mere anger.

It wasn't ruined yet—not all of it. If he worked quickly—

A new sound now rose over the blaring strains of Vivaldi.

Sirens.

Conrad snaked his arm around Michael's neck, knocking his feet from under him and squeezing off his carotid artery.

Michael thrashed wildly on the floor, trying desperately to get his feet back beneath him but succeeding only in slashing dozens of cuts into the palms of his hands as he tried to grab hold of something that might help him escape from the choking arm around his neck. But Conrad only increased the pressure on his neck, and then Michael could no longer breathe.

He clawed at the arm around his neck. He wouldn't die—not here, not now, not as long as Alison needed him. But even as he tried to find new strength, he felt his body weakening.

And with the weakening, a strange blackness began to gather around him.

The blackness of death . . .

I'm sorry, he silently cried out to Alison and to Risa. *I'm sorry. I'm so sorry.*

Just as the blackness was enveloping him, Michael reached over his head and tried to grab Conrad by the back of the neck to pull him down to the floor with him.

Then his muscles went slack and he slid into the blackness.

CONRAD BARELY NOTICED a new shadow in the room before he felt fingers close on his hair and jerk his head backward. The attack came so quickly that he lost his grip on Michael Shaw and let his body drop away from him. Then he was twisted around and forced down as well.

Michael rolled over onto his back and lay still. Then, as his lungs took a deep, convulsive breath, the darkness began to clear from his vision.

He saw Conrad Dunn squirming on the floor next to him, and heard a scream of agony as an oddly familiar tan shoe ground the fingers of Conrad's right hand into the broken glass.

As the music of Vivaldi that still filled the air faded to a quiet passage, Michael could hear the crunching of glass beneath the heavy shoe—or maybe it was the sound of the surgeon's fingers being crushed.

Next to the shoe lay the scalpel that Conrad Dunn had clutched only a moment ago, and without hesitation, Michael picked it up.

With a quick glance up at Scott Lawrence, who still gripped Conrad's hair in both his hands, Michael's rage suddenly came into tight focus.

His eyes fixed on the wide expanse of Conrad Dunn's throat.

Without making any conscious decision at all—without even thinking—he slashed the blade upward, its razor-sharp blade cutting deep into Conrad Dunn's exposed flesh.

A gush of blood spurted from the artery the scalpel opened, pouring down Conrad's surgical gown to mix with the green gel that covered the operating room floor.

"Are you okay?" he heard Scott ask.

He nodded quickly, then: "What about Alison? Did he cut her?"

The ensuing silence seemed to go on for an eternity, then he heard his partner say, "He was just beginning. I think she's fine."

As the sirens in the background abruptly fell silent and he heard voices shouting in the distance, Michael took a deep breath, chasing away the last dark cobwebs of unconsciousness.

The voices came closer, growing louder.

He heard the squawk of a radio.

At last he stood up, battling the weakness in his legs and the wrenching pain in his back. With Scott's hand steadying him, he moved through the shattered glass wall into the laboratory.

He limped over to Risa's still form and knelt next to her, then gently pulled the sheet away from her face. Laying a gentle hand on her cheek, he felt a terrible wave of grief wash away the last of his energy.

"She's safe," he whispered to Risa, gathering her body into his arms. "Our little girl is safe."

One Year Later

ALISON DUG HER TOES INTO THE WARM SAND AND LAY BACK ON HER beach towel. It was the kind of perfect day in Santa Monica that had always made her love living there; not too hot, but far from cool, with the breeze off the ocean keeping the smog well back from the coast.

Not like Bel Air at all, or at least not like she remembered it. In fact, she was already forgetting a lot about those weeks when she'd lived up in the hills above Westwood Village and gone to Wilson Academy and lost not only her mother, but even herself and all her real friends as well.

The memory of her mother's death still caused her a pain that was almost physical, and thinking about what had happened up in Conrad Dunn's house seemed to make the sunlight dim, as if a cloud had drifted over it. But when she looked up into the sky, it was as clear as it had been a few minutes ago.

So much of it was like a bad dream, and sometimes when she woke up in the middle of the night, she still had the awful feeling that she was back up there in the hills in Conrad Dunn's mansion instead of in her bedroom in the house her father and Scott had bought—and insisted on moving into even before they'd sold Scott's house above Hollywood. The new house was perfect—an easy walk to Santa Monica High, and an even shorter one to Cindy Kearns's house.

On an identical towel next to her own, Cindy rolled over, propped herself up on an elbow and looked at Alison, her expression serious. "I have to tell you something."

Alison reached into the cooler for a bottle of water while she tried to decide what Cindy's look meant. With Cindy, of course, it could mean almost anything, since Cindy not only liked to surprise her, but was a good enough actress that she could almost always do it.

And her expression now didn't give anything away.

Still, she looked serious enough that it might be bad news. Maybe boyfriend problems? "You're going to break up with Justin Rhodes?"

Cindy rolled her eyes. "Not until the end of summer—guess again."

Alison cocked her head quizzically. "You already tell me everything as soon as it happens. So what is there I don't already know?" She handed Cindy the bottle, then grabbed two more and handed them to her dad and Scott, who were sprawled out next to them in their canvas beach chairs, both of them buried in books.

"I got my letter."

My letter. In the spring of their senior year, that could only mean one thing: college. They'd both applied to half a dozen schools, and Alison's acceptance at Stanford—her first choice—had arrived two weeks ago. Now she tried to analyze Cindy's expression—and her tone—one more time. Cindy wasn't even looking at her anymore, and Alison thought she saw a tear glistening in the corner of her eye.

But it wasn't fair—it seemed like it had only been a few weeks since they'd put their friendship back together again, and—

"I got in!" Cindy shouted. "I got into Stanford!"

"Shut *up!*" Alison looked squarely at her friend. Was she kidding? She had to be kidding. But if she was, Cindy was an even better actress than she thought.

Cindy shook her head. "Don't have to shut up—it's true!"

"No way. Really?" Alison sat up. "I didn't even know you applied."

"I didn't think I had a chance, so I didn't want to tell you, but I went ahead and applied anyway. And I got in!"

"We'll be roommates!" Alison shrieked, grabbing Cindy in a bear hug.

"Hey, watch those boobs," Cindy said. "Those ought to be registered as lethal weapons."

Alison's grin faded and she adjusted her bikini top.

"Oh, God, I'm sorry," Cindy said, her eyes tearing. "How could I say something that stupid?"

"It's okay," Alison sighed. "I'm just still not over it all." She took a quick glance at her dad, and was almost certain he was pretending he hadn't heard. Scott, however, made no such pretense.

"It's just going to take time—after *my* mother died, I was a wreck for *two* years." Scott said.

"But you're a big sissy," Michael said, finally putting down his book. "And you were five years older than Alison, too, which is really pathetic."

"It wasn't pathetic," Scott began. "It was very tragic. Alison has a right—"

Alison suddenly found herself laughing. "Will you two stop it? Yes, I really miss Mom, but I'm okay. But let's be honest," she added, looking down at her breasts. "Cindy's not that far wrong. If I had it to do over again, I wouldn't, but at least Conrad gave me good ones. So let's talk about something else, okay? Like Stanford."

"Well, I didn't get a scholarship like you did," Cindy said, "so I'll have to find a job."

Alison brightened. "Oooh, I'll get one, too, and then we can live off campus."

"Slow down, amigos," Michael said. "I think you can both live in the dorm, at least for the first year."

"I say we celebrate with a frozen yogurt," Scott said. "Ladies? What's your pleasure?"

"Vanilla," Alison said, lying back down on her towel as Cindy ordered chocolate. Typical—best friends and total opposites.

With Cindy on one side and her two fathers on the other, and with the warm Santa Monica sun shining down on her from above, Alison felt some of the weight of her grief for her mother lift.

Scott was right—it was going to take time. But she had time, and for the first time in a year, she was starting to see that in spite of everything that had happened, she still had the future stretched out ahead of her.

If only her mother could be here to be part of it . . .

"Hey, Mom," she whispered. "Did you hear that? Cindy and I are going to be roommates at Stanford." Then, realizing she'd actually spoken the words out loud, she opened her eyes and found her father smiling at her. "I'm going to make Mom proud of me," she said. "I really am."

"She already is, cupcake," Michael said. "She always was."

ABOUT THE AUTHOR

Faces of Fear is JOHN SAUL's thirty-fifth novel. His first novel, *Suffer the Children*, published in 1977, was an immediate million-copy bestseller. His other bestselling suspense novels include *In the Dark of the Night, Perfect Nightmare, Black Creek Crossing, Midnight Voices, The Manhattan Hunt Club, Nightshade, The Right Hand of Evil, The Presence, Black Lightning, The Homing,* and *Guardian.* He is also the author of the *New York Times* bestselling serial thriller *The Blackstone Chronicles,* initially published in six installments but now available in one complete volume. Saul divides his time between Seattle, Washington, and Hawaii.